MAIL

MAIL

MAMEVE MEDWED

WARNER BOOKS

A Time Warner Company

A chapter of this book was first published as a short story in *The Missouri Review.*

Warner Books, Inc., 1271 Avenue of the Americas, New York, NY 10020

 A Time Warner Company

Printed in the United States of America
First Printing: May 1997
10 9 8 7 6 5 4 3 2 1

Library of Congress Cataloging-in-Publication Data

Medwed, Mameve.
    Mail / Mameve Medwed.
      p. cm.
    ISBN 0-446-52088-8
    I. Title.
PS3563.E275M35   1997
813'.54—dc21   97-1
                                           CIP

Book design and composition by L&G McRee

For Howard
For our sons, Daniel and Jonathan
and
To Mimi G.

ACKNOWLEDGMENTS

Elinor Lipman has squeezed time out from her own novels to act as my fairy godmother and this book's midwife. Her criticism is gentle but right on the mark, her enthusiasm boundless, her generosity astounding, and her friendship a gift. My debt to Ellie is huge; my thanks, immeasurable.

Sarah Rossiter and Lilla Waltch, two writers, and two dearest of friends, have provided years of laughter, love, and discerning readership.

I had the good fortune to move next door to Eliza McCormack the summer her novel was coming out. Eliza signed me up for her first writing workshop. She needed warm bodies to pad the enrollment, she told me, I didn't have to show up. I showed up. All beginners should have such beginner's luck.

I am grateful to Mary Nash's uncanny eye for every detail. And to Sally Brady, Ruth Daniloff, Marjorie Forté, Carol Magun, Ellen Wilbur, Delsa Winer, and Marjory Wunsch who also read and commented on the manuscript. Additional thanks to Susan Goodman for hand-holding and the zippiest ad copy in town. And to Elena Castedo's porch-table literary salon.

My mother Mimi Stern is a natural at book promotion. My sister Robie Rogge, whose alliterative name is a welcome counter-balance to my own, gave advice and support. My sons, Daniel and Jono, are every mother's dream. Bedia Ahmad, Judi Levin, Jayne Merkel, Mike Otten, Evelyne Otten, Rosie Purcell, Patrizia Smith Leoni, Patricia Welbourn, and Barbara Wheaton have been steadfast companions on the long march. My gratitude also to the Sterns and Goldens whose hearts, if not all their feet, reside in Maine.

Jamie Raab, my editor, is as good with authors as she is with their books. For her guidance, intelligence, humor, and grace I would like to express my deepest appreciation.

As for agents, no one is warmer or funnier or smarter than Lisa Bankoff. Thanks. Thanks. Thanks.

And finally, Howard, whom I met in nursery school, who thinks writing is noble work, and who never once, in all our years together, said go get a job. This is for you, kid.

MAIL

My mother calls me from Old Town, Maine, at eight in the morning, an hour into my writing time. "You sound grumpy, Katinka," she says. "Did I interrupt something?"

"Just my work."

"As long as it's *just* your work," she says.

It's her social-whirl voice, her social-work voice. Send this girl to the prom. I sigh. It's my own fault for answering the phone. But what if a publisher should want to ring me up? I turn off my computer. Somedays it hums, a companionable sound. Other times it chugs like *The Little Engine That Could,* an accusatory gasping that seems to imply that all the effort is coming from it, not from me. This morning it's full of complaints. "Can't you write a little faster," it seems to say. "Can't you write at all?"

"Any news?" my mother asks.

Meaning men. "Since I talked to you two days ago?"

"You never know."

I keep silent. What can I tell her, that I think I'm falling in love with the mailman, that the thud of his mailbag in the vestibule makes the earth move to nine point five on my personal Richter scale.

She clears her throat. "You haven't asked about me."

Meaning men. I gird myself. "So?"

"So, I met someone. At the taping books for the blind place. A retired manufacturer. Princeton class of '49."

"Great," I say. I can't help but smile. I'm always amazed at how my mother, who's sixty-three, still defines people by where they went to school. My father, dead for thirteen years, was Harvard '48. My mother still sends in his class dues. Her sister-in-law is Mount Holyoke '42. My mother is a graduate of the University of Maine. My grandfather, School of Hard Knocks 1900, didn't have the money to send her to Vassar, whose unaccepted acceptance sits framed on her dressing table beside her wedding picture and me in my graduation robes.

I should have gone to the University of Maine with all my friends from Old Town High. I hated Radcliffe (called Harvard by the time I went, but my mother clung to the R-word: "More cachet," she explained. "My daughter the Cliffie," she'd exult.). Whatever the name, I hold it responsible for both my thirteen-month marriage to my Joyce professor, Yale '60, Oxford D. Litt '63, and my Crimson-bred arrogance to think I can be a writer. I'd be happier teaching second grade and canning blueberries like my girl-friends from the U of M.

Now my mother and I discuss what she'll wear on her date with the Princeton man.

"Orange and black," I say.

"Oh, Katinka." She laughs and I hear her bracelets clang.

We decide on the navy dress from Neiman Marcus that we bought in Filene's Basement when she visited me last year. And the burgundy shoes. "With the Cuban heels," my mother adds. I look at my sneakers. They are polka-dotted with holes.

2

"I'll give you a report," my mother says now.

"Go tiger go," I say and hang up.

I turn on the computer. It chugs. I switch it off. I check my watch. The mail comes at eleven. I'm not kidding about the mailman.

When I wed Seamus, my Joyce professor, I looked upon it as the marriage of true minds, granted that one brain had twenty-five more years of seasoning. Besides, he didn't care about my clothes since he was always pulling them off me. We had seven good days, not including our wedding night when Seamus threw his back out lifting my suitcase onto the luggage rack. After that week, what I had imagined as evenings of blank verse before a blazing fire became in reality arguments about underdone meatloaf in front of the stove. What I had imagined as nights of lovemaking before the same blazing fire turned into calisthenics in his orthopedic bed. His back was delicate. His sinuses were unreliable. He piled Ian Fleming paperbacks behind the toilet seat. His sour breath did nothing to fill my heart with poetry. Soon enough I discovered he preferred choruses to Molly Bloom soliloquies. He left me for Melissa and Melinda, sophomores with nothing between them and their Calvins but a little baby fat.

"Imagine, and such an educated man," moaned my mother at the time, "with that Oxford degree."

Unlike my mother, my friends were not surprised. "What do you expect marrying a father figure?" sighed they who'd all taken Intro to Psychology. I'd nodded, summoning up a picture of my father, Harvard '48, who'd died when I was nineteen, found keeled over an actuarial report at his insurance firm with the same lack of fuss with which he'd lived his life.

Like my father, these days I'm pining for a life with little fuss. My time with Seamus, our marriage and his flight from it, left me feeling colorized. In spite of its lofty academic ideals, Harvard has a *National Enquirer* soul. My fifteen minutes of fame was tabloid stuff. People snickered about Seamus and his M&M's.

Next week it will be nine years since my divorce. I see Seamus sometimes in the Coop or in Sage's buying wine. He married first Melissa and then Melinda, or was it the other way around? Now he squires a TA in biology named Georgette. She wears leather miniskirts and earrings from whose wires dangle silver skeletons of fish. I bumped into them the other day at a revival of *Women on the Verge of a Nervous Breakdown* at the Brattle. I was going in, they were coming out. Seamus didn't seem to recognize me. I don't really think it was a snub. He prides himself on his tolerance for past relationships. He's nearly sixty with a matted Moses beard and glasses faceted like prisms. He has the wild slightly exaggerated look of a bad actor playing a poet in residence. He wears sandals over argyle socks. What did I ever see in him? What does Georgette see in him? The movie was pretty good, though I must admit my capacity for the fey (Is Seamus fey?) is fast diminishing. Georgette, of course, loved it. I heard her telling Seamus it was awesome. Her language, I was pleased to note, wasn't Joycean. She herself is attractive enough if flamboyant.

I, on the other hand, am back to my black and white life. I pass a hermit's days and nights writing, reading, going out for an occasional movie or a dinner with old friends. I'm thirty-one now and ready to make my literary mark. I want to be a writer. My mother thinks it time once more for me to be a wife.

But I've sworn off marriage. I've quit my library job at Widener. My apartment on the first floor of a Harvard-owned building two down from the Fogg Museum was part of my divorce settlement. The money I've saved and my father's bequest helps pay the rent and keeps me in macaroni casseroles. Up to now, things have been going well. I've placed two stories in literary quarterlies whose names you've never heard of. I've received several rejection slips that say *Sorry, but please send more.* These are signed by real people whose initials I spit on to test whether they blur. Still, if biology is destiny, then hormones at thirty-one (and seventy) seem determined to waylay the best-laid plans. Which takes me to the mailman.

4

For starters let me explain why I got to know him in the first place. My building's tenants are professors, teaching assistants, grad students, administrators, librarians, and their spouses. In the logic of somebody like my mother, it would follow that because they're Harvard, they're movers and shakers. And it just so happens that by nine in the morning they're all out moving and shaking in their offices and lecture halls. All, that is, except me, who's moving the mouse around my Macintosh, and the super, who's shaking up his rum and cokes in his basement hideaway.

And who's available to accept packages and sign for registered letters? To keep the *New York Reviews* from being swiped, to protect paychecks and credit cards, to pile up toothpaste samples and upscale marketing questionnaires? Me, of course, whose apartment door is directly across from the wall of letterboxes in the vestibule.

I admit I planned it that way, picked an apartment to be mail-accessible. For a writer, mail is not just a collection of bills and letters and offers to subscribe to *Sports Illustrated*. It's an umbilical cord, a connection to the outside world, the giver of pleasure and pain. It shapes the day, is the moment, inexorable as the tide, toward which all the hours rise and fall. If to the madras-clad clubman the day crests when the sun has passed over the yardarm to signify the cocktail hour, to the writer the arrival of the mail charts the peak on any graph. It's like sex, the slow building of anticipation, the delivery itself (good news, bad, no news), and the postcoital glow or gloom. And except for Sundays, there's always the Scarlett O'Hara tomorrow bit.

So, within days of quitting my library job, I was out in the vestibule stalking the U.S. Post. I guess I couldn't disguise the mail-hungry look on my face because people coming and leaving the building began to ask me if I'd accept their UPS and FedEx deliveries. I was all too happy. There was life out there in the front hall, grist for the mill. The exterminator confided who had the most cockroaches, who was the biggest slob. The diaper service man for the newborn on the fifth floor flexed his expanding biceps. The cleaner for 3E was hoping to go to community college in the spring. Mr. Sullivan, our former mailman, was having trouble with his bunions and showed me his can of mace, which in twenty years he only had to use once on a German shepherd north of Broadway.

Besides being able to indulge fully in my obsession (and doing good for others at the same time), I was also able to check out the men in my building. Given Mr. Sullivan's erratic delivery schedule, I was eventually able to observe the arrivals and departures of most of them. Frankly, the men didn't amount to much. Distracted scientists with terrible hours, brisk business school types who looked you in the eye and addressed you by name three times in every sentence, the others too old, too young, too married. For a while I had my hopes pinned on an art historian, but he, Mr. Sullivan whispered, lived with Gregory the Florist, who always wore camel hair.

Then Mr. Sullivan's bunions really got bad. Gregory took up a collection, and on a Saturday the building gave him a poinsettia plant and fourteen tulip bulbs as a farewell.

The next Monday was Louie's first day on our route. It was November, a cold morning, and my story about a UPS woman and diaper man wasn't going well. I decided to run around the corner for coffee since even the instant was all used up. I stuffed myself into my down parka. I looked like a sausage. My hair was a mess. "Hi," he said, bounding up the three front steps. "I'm your new mailman, Louis Cappetti." He pronounced it Louie. He thrust out his hand.

I took it. He was tall with a gleam of patent leather hair under his earflaps and a big smile which made his eyes widen not narrow the way most people's do. He was about my age. Maybe a little younger. He had that buttery-olive skin that doesn't wrinkle. "How ya doing?" he asked. The buttons on his blue uniform shone. My stomach did a little jig. I love a man in a uniform my mother would announce, meaning West Point or Annapolis. No matter, he was the best thing I'd seen all year.

Was I holding the mailman's hand too long? I gave a quick squeeze, then let go. "Katinka O'Toole," I said.

"Hey, that's an unusual name."

"The O'Toole's my ex's. Katinka comes from some writer in *The New Yorker* during the fifties. I hope it's prophetic. My mother had literary illusions," I confided.

He looked puzzled.

I blushed. I was a damn fool. Insular and arrogant. Literary illusion, literary allusion . . . The lingua franca of Cambridge is the literary allusion. Seamus prided himself on his common touch, which was apocryphal. Like most in our set he was the master of the inside aside.

"I mean," I translated, "since I'm a writer I hope having a writer's name will bring me luck."

"Right . . ." he said. "Wow," he added. "I don't think I've ever met a writer before. What do you write?"

"Stories, mostly."

"About what?"

I lowered my eyes modestly. "Life."

He nodded. Then gave a kind of *c'est la vie* shrug. "Have you published them?"

The inevitable question, in all languages, across all class lines. "Two," I said. Sometimes I lie and say "a few" or "a couple," which I suppose isn't *technically* a lie.

"How about that. Where can I read them?"

"In magazines you've never heard of." I caught myself. "I mean, *nobody's* ever heard of."

"Except me. After all every single magazine passes through the hands of the U.S. Mail."

"I hadn't even thought of that."

"Besides," he added, "wouldn't the library have them?"

My heart lifted. A library-goer! "Probably not. But I'll give you Xeroxes if you're really interested."

"You bet."

And that, Louie, as Humphrey Bogart said to Claude Rains, was the beginning of a beautiful relationship.

Now it's the beginning of December and my relationship with Louie is, if not something beautiful, the sun passing over the yardarm of my days. At ten-thirty every morning I put on lipstick and brush my hair. I spray my pulse points with Arpège. I remember when I was at Radcliffe and how I used to sign up for conferences with Seamus on the sheet pinned to the English department bulletin board. Inside his office he'd lock the door and pull a shade over the square of rippled glass. For the allotted thirty minutes we'd clutch at various parts of each other's bodies. Time up, he'd shake my hand and say "I do quite enjoy our little chats, Miss Graham."

"I sure do enjoy talking to you, Katinka," Louie tells me now. I am leaning against a row of brass letterboxes. He is bent over his mail bag. As he pulls out a sheaf of magazines, I can smell just the faintest scent of his shampoo. I wonder what it would be like to have one of Seamus' little chats with Louie. I stare at a lank of thigh under its U.S.-issue cover of postal blue. I wonder what he'd look like in civilian clothes. A pair of snappy boxer shorts. I realize that I am going round the bend. I force my eyes from his knee to the hand that is now passing me some envelopes. I take the manila envelopes from him and recognize my punishment for all these dirty thoughts. My SASEs, my rejected stories coming back to me, the stamps licked by my own tongue, the envelope addressed in my own hand.

Louie points to my mail. He has long graceful fingers, the tips slightly spatulate, the skin a golden sheath. "Can I ask you a question?"

"Shoot."

"These envelopes. I mean you get so many. All with the same writing. But from different places . . ."

I explain.

His eyes ooze sympathy. They have black irises wreathed in the softest brown flecked with little yellow suns. Ah, life they say.

"That's life," I say now. "Some I sell, some are sent right back." What I don't tell him is that for the two I "sold," the payment for one was a year's subscription to the quarterly. The other, three published copies of my own work.

"Geez," he says, "and I'm the guy's got to deliver the bad news."

"Next time maybe you can bring me a big fat check."

"Right," he says, "I'm gonna get to work on that." He pauses. "Mind if I ask you how you pay the rent?"

"I've got money saved. And a small inheritance."

"That's a relief," he says, "after all those stories about starving artists."

I smile. That he's concerned about the bareness of my cupboard touches me.

We discuss the weather, the job the city's doing salting the streets. "Hey," he says, "about those stories, you know, those Xeroxes . . ."

"Hang on a sec." I run across the hall to my apartment where they are sitting on the table just inside the door. I have kept them there for several weeks hoping he'll remember them.

Carefully he folds them into his bag after first asking my permission to crease their smooth surfaces. "Great," he says. "I can't wait." And as he turns to go, he touches one of those golden fingers to my sleeve.

Seamus calls me just as the diaper man is about to ask the UPS woman out. *I'm not sure . . .* I start to type when the phone rings. My hello must be grumpier than usual because Seamus says, "You sound so mad, Katinka, as if you knew I was on the other end."

"What do you want, Seamus?" I ask.

"To wish you a happy Christmas, my dear."

"Cut the crap, Seamus."

"To find out how your writing is progressing. You know I always took, indeed still take, an interest in your literary development."

I can't resist showing off. For some reason that perhaps only a full course of analysis might reveal, I need Seamus to see I'm succeeding without him. Even after all of this time. I clear my throat. "Actually, I'm doing well. Have published quite a few stories."

"Where?"

"You know, the usual. Literary quarterlies. Small but respectable."

"Soon *The New Yorker,* I trust. Have you got Xeroxes?"

"Actually not. I'm much more interested in what I'm working on now. For me those stories are already in the past."

Seamus seems to chew this over with a long intensifying hum which hurts my ear. "Speaking of the past," he finally says.

"Why did you call?" I ask.

"You've got my *Portrait of the Artist* . . . and I've got yours."

"What difference could that possibly make?"

"*Mine's* a first edition."

"And it's taken nine years for you to discover that?"

"Georgette's talked me into contact lenses. Now I see everything with a new and startling clarity."

Seamus says he'll be over in half an hour. I emphasize that I'm working and can only take a minute to exchange books through my door. "No more time," I joke, "than it took us to pass divorce papers." Seamus chuckles. He understands, he says. He, of all people, knows the vagaries of the muse.

I go to the bookcase and find *Portrait.* Sure enough it's his, *Seamus O'Toole* scrawled possessively on a card tucked next to the frontispiece. I sit in a chair and start to read. Two hours later I am in a slough of despair. I think of my story. It is garbage. More trivial than this flyspeck on the bottom of this page. I should move back to Old Town and become something more suitable to my abilities: a dental hygienist, a grammar school crossing guard. I look at my watch and realize it's after eleven. As usual Seamus is late. And so sunk have I been in Joyce's language, I didn't even hear Louie arrive. I have missed the one bright moment in my day. I get carried away and tell myself I have missed the Joycean revelation in the story of my life. I am just about to squeeze out a perfect tear, when there's a knock.

I open the door the width of the book.

"Wait a minute," Seamus says. "I've got your mail."

Seamus pushes through the door. Without his glasses his eyes look funny, like windows missing their shutters. He blinks rapidly. He hands me my book on top of my mail, which contains, I notice, manila envelopes.

I give him his book. He points at my mail and blinks some more. "Had a little chat with your mailman," he says. "Quite the sympathetic sort. Feels terrible that your stories keep coming back like this. Maybe he's afraid you'll shoot the messenger."

"If there's any messenger I'll shoot, it will be you."

"And a happy Christmas!" Seamus declares after I have shut the door.

My mother has come to spend Christmas with me. Neither of us has the Christmas spirit. "We have seasonal blues," I explain. "It's some kind of affective disorder having to do with the lack of sunlight at this time of year."

"Nonsense," my mother says. "It's all to do with men."

She sighs. I sigh. We tack some holly to a shelf and swoon back onto the sofa. We've done enough Christmas decorating, we both agree. Things have not worked out well for my mother and the Princeton man. He turned out to have a wife, Smith '51. "Dowdy," my mother says, "Lily Pulitzer and one of those lightship basket pocketbooks. But well educated," she adds.

I nod. I know exactly how far well educated gets you. These days not even into my front hall. Since my mother's been here, I've missed my talks with Louie. By eleven every morning we're out the door and stalking markdowns. I'm avoiding Louie, I tell myself, because now that my mother and I are a temporary twosome, he's not something I want to share. Am I afraid her X-ray eyes will detect the light in mine when I raise mine to his? Or shudder at an insignia embroidered U.S. Postal, not U.S. Naval, Academy?

After a while my mother and I force ourselves from the sofa and into my kitchen where we are making a batch of gingerbread men. Tonight the art historian and his roommate Gregory the Florist are throwing a Christmas party for the whole building. This isn't such a crowd as you might imagine since the building is now nearly half empty, so many academics having gone away during the long break. My mother and I ice extra-cheerful smiles onto the faces of our gingerbread men. Under one's raisin eye I place another raisin vertically. "See," I say. "He's smiling through his tears."

My mother smiles through her own tears. "How about that Princeton man," she groans.

We layer the gingerbread men into a cookie tin and put doilies between the layers. My mother presses the cover shut, and I attach a red satin bow. There'll be an auction at the party tonight, and we have all been asked to bring a contribution. The proceeds will go to a shelter for the homeless. We have no right to have a seasonal affective disorder, my mother and I tell each other, when there are people with no homes. We decide to wear our discount Diors. We are determined to have a good time.

The apartment of the art historian, who is named Derek, and Gregory the Florist is furnished in *le style Rothschild*, which I gather means lots of red brocade, gold tassels, and fringe on everything. My mother is immediately swept off to meet Gregory's mother, who herself seems to be swathed in *le style Rothschild*. She is wearing a tent of gold Lurex. At least she is not in Lily Pulitzer. My mother, animated, seems to be enjoying their conversation. Perhaps they are talking about men.

Young men in black are passing trays of hors d'oeuvres. One stops in front of me and extends his platter. "These are fabulous," he says.

I look. The hors d'oeuvres are arranged in concentric circles like the monoliths at Stonehenge. Each round and square mound is topped with a flower. I take one. I touch a petal of a pansy. It is not candied but feels velvety as if just seconds ago it was thrusting up from damp soil.

I shudder. I turn my head to look at the other people in the room. They are all drinking champagne and eating flowers. All the trays that the young men hold seem to have flowers on them. All the guests are eating flowers. "I don't eat flowers," I confess.

The young man raises an eyebrow.

"You know that book, *Please Don't Eat the Daisies*? I've taken it to heart."

The young man shakes his head. He is not amused.

I pick up an hors d'oeuvre. I eat it. Salmon mousse with pansy. I live. I take another. A mushroom with nasturtium. It sticks a little in my throat, but I get it down. I do not require the Heimlich maneuver. When it finally dawns on me that here I am, Katinka O'Toole, eating flowers and still standing, I decide that nothing will surprise me. Thus when I see a familiar face across the crowded room I am not surprised, only puzzled. Who is this person I seem to know?

He's a tall man with dark hair, nicely dressed, not in *le style Rothschild*, but in jacket and tie. Then he sees me and waves. Even from this distance I recognize the spatulate fingertips. Louie, in mufti, and looking fine. My heart turns over.

He makes his way toward me. "Katinka," he says. "Isn't this a great party?"

"It's improving." I point at a passing tray. "Did you eat the flowers?" I ask.

"No way. I'm a meat-and-potatoes guy. There's a bowl of peanuts over there on the piano. Shall I get you some?"

I grab a pansy-topped asparagus tip and tilt it into my mouth. "Actually I'm developing a real taste for plant life," I say.

"Right." He laughs. "Bring on the Pepto. You look real nice," he adds.

I don't tell him how nice he looks. I indicate my dress. "Filene's Basement," I say.

He points to his lapel. "Filene's Basement, too," he says. We laugh. It warms me to realize our clothes have been folded into identical cardboard boxes, have been marked down with identical rubber stamps.

We talk a bit about the apartment's decor and whether the rumors of the super's giant binge are true. He is too polite to mention the hordes of my stories that lately seem to be coming home to roost. I'm too polite to ask whether he's read my Xeroxed offerings yet. I notice my mother standing by a window watching us. Some fringe from the red velvet drapery trails over her shoulder like an epaulet. She telegraphs her delight and is about to make her way toward us when Gregory announces it is time for the auction. Louie and I jam ourselves into a loveseat that already has a person sitting on it. Louie's hip pushes into mine, our knees bang. My shoulder-duster earring gets caught in the tweed of his jacket. And his arm, as he untangles it, brushes against my breast.

It's hard to concentrate on the auction.

The gingerbread men my mother and I have baked are bought for seven dollars by a professor emeritus of philosophy. The dean of the Business School wins an anniversary flower arrangement. Louie and I are sitting so close together that as we applaud the successful bidders, our shoulders knock intimately. For a moment I allow myself to wonder what it would be like to bump against those shoulders in bed.

"Now we have something really unusual," Gregory the Florist, who is acting as auctioneer, announces. He holds up a folder with papers inside. "These are donated by Louie Cappetti. Two stories by our writer in residence, Katinka O'Toole, from the first floor."

I, of course, want to disappear, but there is no space in which to disappear. "I hope you don't mind, Katinka," Louie whispers. His breath in my ear takes my breath away.

My mother bids one dollar. Gregory's mother raises it to two-fifty. A man I don't know says he thinks he could use the folder and bids two-seventy-five. Somebody asks whether Gregory will throw in his camel hair smoking jacket. Louie jumps to ten dollars and claims the prize to much applause. "Those are the best stories I ever read," he tells me. "No way would I give them up."

After the auction, everybody mills about eating more flowers. I have another pansy and two more nasturtiums and start to feel sick. I head toward the piano and the bowl of peanuts. Louie is already there. The top of the piano is up, and it makes a kind of screen we stand behind. Louie holds the folder with my stories in one hand. With the other hand he points to the ceiling. A spray of mistletoe is tacked to the molding. Louie bends over me. I smell peanuts. Louie's lips touch mine.

The next morning, it's after ten when I wake up. I have a headache. My stomach hurts. I spent a restless night twisting on a bed of pansies turned by spatulate fingertips, jabbed against shoulders, and nearly smothered by a blanket of manila envelopes. I put on an old robe and stagger into the kitchen. I have a sense of being off balance, the way I always feel when I have to make a decision and either choice could mean a big mistake. But you don't have to decide anything, I tell myself, it's just a hangover, the seasonal affective disorder. My diagnosis is verified when I look out the window to a world of gray clouds and sleet.

My mother, on the other hand, is bouncing around my kitchen in a red dress. Her Cuban heels dance on the linoleum tiles. The professor emeritus of philosophy has invited her to a concert this afternoon. For her the sun shines at least metaphorically.

I slump into a chair and fill my coffee mug.

My mother pulls out the chair across from mine. "About your young man. The one who bought your stories . . ."

"What about him?"

"Where did he go to school?"

"Harvard, Yale, and Princeton."

"All three?"

"Oxford and Cambridge, Trinity, the Sorbonne . . ."

"Now, Katinka," she begins. Fortunately her cross-examination is interrupted by the thud of the mailbag in our vestibule. We both rise from our chairs at the same time. "I'll get it," she says. "You can't go into the hall like that." She points at my robe.

I pull it closer around me. It is missing its tie. I study my bare feet. I have ugly feet, pale and knobby. The toes are crooked and of illogical lengths. The big toe is in fact shorter than the designated little one. Seamus used to tease me about my toes. *This little piggy that nobody but me would take to market,* he would chant. I wipe a mustache of coffee from my upper lip and trace the shape of my mouth. I can still feel the imprint of Louie's kiss last night. I can taste its warmth. Louie's feet, I am sure, are beautiful. His toes are sorted like pearls into a perfectly graduated row. And the thought strikes me that I might never get to see Louie's beautiful, bare toes.

This is confirmed by my mother, who skips back into the apartment carrying a pile of bills. She has an expression on her face that Archimedes must have had when he sprang from the tub yelling *Eureka!* "Katinka," she yells now, "your young man is the *mailman!* I never forget a face."

I consider putting up a defense, the usual democracy, classless society bit. I consider going out into the hall. Saying to Louie, "About last night . . ." Saying to him, "Maybe sometime we can have a drink . . ." But I don't move. My mother's astonishment pins me to my place. And I am so heavy with sadness I don't think I could

16

lift a knee if I tried. Will I ever make it to spring? I wonder. To summer, even. But the very word summer eases my woe. I think of sand, of waves. Of sunburned shoulders. Of letters limp with humidity. Of long tanned fingers. Of sandals wrapped around bare and beautiful toes.

2

My mother goes home the day after Christmas. She is ecstatic. She thinks she's in love. The professor emeritus of philosophy who bought our gingerbread men seems to be courting her. Arthur Haven, Harvard BA, MA, Ph.D., is seventy, wears tweed, and has aristocratic cheekbones. He has a dead wife (Wellesley '47) and a living live-wire daughter (Wellesley '85, Harvard Ph.D. '90). The daughter's name is Zenobia. She in turn has a husband, son, cat and dog, and tenure at Simmons College where she teaches art history and has already published a book on the field colorists and has more in the works. My mother adores many things about Arthur, but two things, in addition to his tail of degrees, especially delight her. That he has a daughter my age and that he lives in my building. I'm not sure about the daughter. I reminded my mother how in Old Town all the children of her dearest friends hated each other. "I loathed Shirley Mercer all through school," I told her.

"How childish of you, Katinka. Shirley turned out fine. She has

19

three well-behaved daughters and is president of the Old Town/Orono Garden Club."

"My very point."

My mother ignored this. "You know," she said, "your father and I always hoped to give you a sister."

"I've had thirty-one years to adjust."

"A little sibling rivalry couldn't hurt."

Which remark hurt me enough to dislike Zenobia Haven (she keeps her maiden name) on principle.

But what I really dislike is the fact that Arthur Haven lives on the fourth floor.

Now that he and my mother are dating (is that the appropriate word for sexa- and septuagenarians?), I seem to run into him everywhere. In front of the elevator, around the corridor, at the dry cleaners. "Ah, Katinka," he'll wink, as if we have a special bond. Yesterday, there he was again in the express checkout line at the grocery store. He was buying a single carton of yogurt and a Hershey bar. I had a couple items over the allotted eight, that is, if you insist that two apples aren't one pair. Professor Haven obviously did. I saw him cast a cold eye on my basket. Still, his voice was warm. "Katinka, my dear," he smiled, "I had the most enchanting chat with your lovely mother last night on the phone."

I couldn't help it. All I could imagine was one of Seamus' little chats on the English department floor.

Professor Haven must have read part of my mind because then he went on—"And the most amazing coincidence. I'm teaching one night a week at the Harvard extension, just to keep these old fingers in. And guess who's running a fiction-writing workshop in the next room?"

I shook my head. I hadn't any clue.

"Seamus O'Toole!" he exclaimed.

Oh God, I thought. "How interesting," I said. Obviously Professor Haven was one of those who assumed that any spouse, even an ex, was a cherished extension of oneself. "But Seamus is a *Joyce* scholar," I protested.

"Precisely my sentiment. But he'd always been interested in young writers, he explained, and had written a bit himself as a youth."

His interest in young writers was certainly true, I was able to attest to that. But as far as Seamus' own writing . . . I was pretty sure Seamus' fiction was a fiction. But what could I say? Professor Haven was beaming at me. "Now we are connected on both sides, as it were," he said.

I thought of that song—I knew a guy who had danced with a girl who had danced with the Prince of Wales. Guilt by association. And all too cozy for words.

No, cozy isn't the word, I think now. More like smothering. It's quarter of eleven and I'm out in the front hall waiting for Louie. Yes, I'm back stalking Louie. After all, I'm thirty one years old, a grown daughter and an ex-wife. Why should my mother pick out my boyfriends the way she chose my barrettes when I was eight? Besides, she approved of Seamus, and look what happened to that. So, the morning after my mother leaves, I am leaning wantonly against the letterbox of 2B wafting Arpège without an ounce of shame. It's certainly easier to go after an unsuitable man when the person who finds him unsuitable is two hundred fifty miles away.

Louie arrives at five of eleven. First the door rattles. I get a glimpse of his earflaps through the smudged glass and know by the fact that he's wearing them it's below thirty-two. Perhaps I can offer him coffee. Cocoa. Warm those fingertips between my own.

The door opens. My knees go weak. He slaps his mailbag down against the entry tiles. A sound which causes my shoulders to give a little jerk. He looks up at me from the bottom step. I feel like Juliet on her balcony. I smooth my hair. "Hey Katinka," Louie says, "haven't seen you in a while." He gives me one of those wide-eyed grins that make heat rise in my body like a slowly filling glass.

I manage what I hope is an enigmatic Mona Lisa smile.

"In fact in another week I would've started to think you'd been avoiding me."

"Oh, no," I protest in a rush. "My mother just left. We were out every minute shopping up a storm."

Louie nods. His earflaps flap. For one treacherous moment I see him through my mother's eyes. If only he weren't a mailman, if only he had a degree or at least the mitigating presidency of some garden club . . . I hold my breath. I am turning into my mother. "You know mothers," I say with a vehemence that startles me.

"Mothers," he says.

I nod, and a look passes between us which passeth all understanding.

Or so I think until he says, "Your mother is a stunning woman."

Which astonishes me. I suppose she's cute with her cap of tinted curls and the rhinestones that glitter in the corners of her designer eyeglasses. She has tiny feet. "Size five, the sample size," she boasts. She flaunts her shapely calves. When miniskirts went out, she was in despair—"a woman's legs are the last to go." But despite her ageless legs, she's sixty-three and my mother, neither a sibling rival nor some rival cheerleader chasing the captain of the team.

Perhaps Louie notices my confusion because he adds, "You take after her."

"Thank you," I say, figuring, given the context, this is flattery. I decide it's time to change the subject. Shall I suggest the coffee? Compliment him on his way with a kiss? Any more where that came from, I want to ask. Instead, I lead with a scintillating, "So, it's pretty cold out there."

"You bet." Louie rubs his hands together and blows on them, his lips puckered adorably.

"I can always tell the temperature by whether you wear your earflaps down."

"No kidding," he says as if I have made a brilliant observation. "I guess I'm a kind of human barometer."

Thermometer you mean. But I don't say anything. Who am I to correct anyone's English? To this day I still remember the moment in ninth grade when I spoke before the whole school and pronounced the word gesture with a hard *g*. But I learned. So can Louie. Only a little teaching's needed to narrow the gap in syntax.

Now Louie reaches into his mailbag and starts to pull out some magazines. The letters themselves are separated into bunches and wrapped in rubber bands. But the magazines are loose. There are the expected *New Yorkers*, *New Yorks*, *New York Reviews*, *Atlantics*, *Smithsonians*, *National Geographics*, and the esoteric, scientific journals, volumes on linguistics, deconstructionism, astrophysics, a journal of parisitology. Louie fans them out like a deck of cards. I scooch next to him. I smell soap, mint. "No *Playboys*," I joke. "I suppose not in this crowd."

Louie's face turns serious. "I wouldn't know," he says. "Postal personnel aren't supposed to check the content of the mail."

"Really? In Maine our mailman used to stand blatantly under the maple and read our *Time* magazines. 'How about that Man of the Year,' he'd say to me."

Louie smiles. "But I can't help looking through yours, Katinka, just in case one of those places has sent you that big fat check."

I think of Seamus' messenger. No matter what the news, *this* messenger I'll kiss. But once again the very thought of Seamus seems to release some powerful telegenic rays because Louie frowns and says, "You know that guy, with a gray beard and sandals. He visited you once, brought you your mail . . ."

I shiver. "Seamus . . ."

"He's on my route. I knew the name, of course, but never met him till the other day. I put two and two together. So did he. He's pretty sharp. Figured out who I was. Said he never forgot a face."

It wasn't the *face* that Seamus always remembered. "What a coincidence," I say.

"I think you told me," he goes on, "that O'Toole's your ex-husband's name. But this guy . . ." He shrugs. "Is he your uncle? Some kind of relative?"

"Husband once. Now ex. Thank God," I add.

"Wow." Louie's mouth forms an O, an open kiss in which I can make out the tip of a glistening tongue. "I mean isn't he kind of—"

"Old?" I finish. "Exactly. It was my father-figure stage."

Louie looks puzzled.

"Which I'm out of. Now I'm looking for someone more my age." This I say pointedly. I can't tell Louie's reaction, though, because he's bent over the magazines and his face is turned from me. He picks up a *Daedalus* and rolls it into Professor Haven's box. All at once I am warmed with joy. Not only have I been given a reprieve from further dissections of my Seamus complex but I have been handed the opening I've been waiting for. I point to the white rectangle on which "Professor Arthur T. Haven" has been carefully lettered in black. "This guy's got a crush on my mother."

"Whattya know," he says, then adds, "I'm not surprised."

"He's the one who bid on our gingerbread men. At Derek and Gregory's party."

"How about that."

"They met at that party."

"Gee."

"That was the start."

"It was a great party," Louie says.

"I had a great time."

"Me, too." Louie rubs his hand along his chin. His top button, I notice, dangles from a nest of loosened thread.

"There's no reason that there shouldn't be more get-togethers," I begin. "Maybe sometime you and I—"

But I am interrupted by an "Oh, Katinka, my dear," as Arthur Haven, my ubiquitous building mate, appears bundled up in tweed and sporting one of those fur hats that Russian politicians wear. We mill about the hall discussing the weather, the new traffic light at the end of Linnaean Street, the best way to carry a mailbag to save your back. Louie tells Professor Haven about the coincidence of Seamus being on his route. They discuss the stunning qualities of my stunning mother. They discuss my writing. Professor Haven says I must have learned a lot from Seamus. He thinks my mother would make a splendid heroine. I tell Louie he needs to have his button attended to. Louie tells me if I go outside to wear a hat, that the largest percentage of body heat escapes from the head. I am pretty sure that his body heat escapes from somewhere else, a place where I don't dare to look. I keep my eyes on his loose button, my thoughts to myself. We are a cozy group, the three of us plus my mother's ghost and Seamus', and God knows who else's. Then we all smile warmly and say good-bye.

Later that afternoon my mother calls. "I've just had the loveliest conversation with Arthur," she announces without even a preliminary hello.

"Arthur?" I ask.

"Professor Haven."

"Of course." There is a tattoo of coffee rings on my desktop which looks like the interlocking circles from the Olympics. I place the telephone over it and notice I have uncovered a matching set of rings. I try to move the phone in such a way to camouflage both marks. This doesn't work. As if to emphasize the inadequacy of this solution, the receiver erupts in a burst of static.

"Are you still there, dear?" my mother asks. "This connection isn't good."

"Sorry. You were saying . . . ?"

"Well, Arthur invited me for New Year's Eve. I plan to come back to Cambridge on the thirtieth . . ."

My head swirls with disconnected thoughts: My mother has a date for New Year's Eve. Will Louie lose his button? Will I ever know if he has lost it or if he sews it on? I need to put the garbage out. Did I enclose a SASE with the story I posted Saturday? I look across my desk to the sofabed. A corner of a Laura Ashley sheet peeks out from its tweed upholstery like an untucked shirttail. "Fine. I won't even have to change the sheets."

"Actually, Arthur," my mother pauses, clears her throat, "invited me to stay with him."

I scratch at the desktop with my letter opener, which is a head of Shakespeare on a silver blade. I notice I have put stems on the Olympic rings, turning them into bunches of balloons. Before I can process my mother's startling announcement or vandalize any more of my furniture, she counters with a parry and a thrust. "Now, Katinka dear," she asks, "what are *your* plans for New Year's Eve?"

A low blow. In Old Town, Maine, possessing a date for New Year's Eve and being a cheerleader are the Oscar and Nobel of social life. My mother knows this, having held my hand through the will-he-or-won't-he-call seventh- to twelfth-grade phase. In college she wrote me pep letters and enclosed clippings from *Vogue* of the perfect little black dress. And when Seamus and I eloped, she sent me a telegram which read *Congratulations! No more worries about a date for you know when.* A year after the marriage I didn't have the heart to tell her I watched the ball drop over Times Square with my friend Jenny and her cat Tigger on their black and white portable.

"I'm not sure what my plans are yet," I say. This is not entirely a lie, for I haven't decided with what fellow wallflower I'll lift a Diet Pepsi to toast another socially unfruitful year.

"Good," my mother says, surprising me, "because Arthur wanted to have a little dinner party. With his daughter and her family. So we can all get to know each other."

"How cozy."

"Isn't it? Of course afterward, Arthur and I will go to something at the Faculty Club. And Zenobia has plans . . ."

"Me, too. I mean I have a bunch of invitations. I just have to pick one."

"Well, that's perfect, dear," my mother practically trills. I picture her eyes twinkling behind their twinkly rhinestone frames. I can hear the twinkling of her delight. She is happy about Arthur, his Harvard Ph.D., his little dinner party, and her daughter, who seems to be—oh glorious word—popular. "To think," she says, "that you and I are both so popular."

We discuss what we will wear to the dinner party and the subsequent sites of our various invitations. I garnish this mixture with the names of a few deluxe hotels. My mother mentions Harvard three times in two sentences.

The minute we hang up, something happens that if I wrote it in a story would seem too contrived. But at this very moment, someone slides an envelope under my door. It's a small pink square which, when I bend to pick it up, I notice smells like the perfumed inserts in fashion magazines. Tuberoses, maybe, or those huge pink lilies that look like they belong to movie stars.

It's an invitation, surrounded by a border of painted violets and written in mauve ink. Gregory and Derek request my presence from ten o'clock on to ring in the New Year. And if I'd like, I may bring a friend.

I know just the friend.

For the rest of the afternoon I write in a heat. It's a literal heat. By dinnertime the path from my desk to coffee machine is strewn with discarded layers of my clothes. A sweater. Kneesocks. A ribbed turtleneck. I finish the first draft of my story though I can barely tell if it is any good. When I read it through, every line the diaper man speaks to the UPS girl vibrates with innuendo, even on the first page when they've just met. The baby has a come-hither look. His mother might as well be wearing a black garter belt.

I put my story in the file of things that need work. I warm up a bowl of chili and eat it in front of the TV. I watch television straight until eleven. I watch sitcoms and quiz shows. A variety hour. The last program I watch is a rerun of a sitcom about a group of friends. The plot seems to hinge on previous episodes I've never seen. I usually allot my TV time to the news and programs that are good for you on PBS. I think I'm trying to atone for all those years in Old Town watching reruns of *Father Knows Best* and wanting desperately to be the kind of daughter my own father would call Kitten or Princess. On this one everybody seems to be jumping in and out of bed. One character's T-shirt says "Princeton." Another's says "Penn." This is a program for my mother, I decide. But maybe she's already a fan. I am more than pleased, though, when one character in Yale sweats kisses the guy painting her kitchen wall.

In bed I fall asleep immediately but wake after half an hour. I feel confused. There is something I have missed. Something I have overlooked. Is it a problem with my story? Have I left the oven on? I lie back against the pillows. I pull the blankets up under my chin. My nose itches. I rub it with a corner of the sheet. I remember.

My mother will be staying upstairs with Arthur T. Haven, Harvard Ph.D., professor emeritus of philosophy. My freshman year I took a course in logic in the Philosophy department. We studied the Greeks, Plato's dialogues, syllogisms, and hypotheses. I was hoping to develop a rational form of mind. As I've grown older, my mind has become less rational, and I've forgotten most of the logic I've learned. I do have a vague sense, however, of how to set up a syllogism. (A) Humans are sexual beings; (B) my mother is a human; (C) if my mother is staying with Arthur Haven, it will come to follow that she'll be staying in Arthur Haven's bed. I feel the first stirrings of panic. I sit up. My knowledge of logic is illogical, I comfort myself. I have probably structured the proof wrong.

I picture the family in *Father Knows Best.* I picture the parents' bedroom. I see the narrow virginal twin beds bisected by the night table with its little coolie-hat shaded lamp. Here, in their pressed, buttoned-up pajamas and their lilting good-humored voices, the parents discussed the children. How to surprise Kitten. What about Bud's grades. I read somewhere that the children in real life turned out bad. Kitten was a druggie. Princess married in multiples. Bud, I think, pumped gas.

I picture my own parents' bedroom in Old Town. Similar twin beds. A night table on rickety mahogany legs. A hooked rug of red flowers. My mother wore flannel nightgowns edged in rickrack. My father's pajamas were blue and white stripes. Nevertheless, somebody crossed that flowered rug to create me.

Now I picture Arthur Haven's bed which, though I don't know this, I assume is queen-sized if not king. The sheets are a swirl of twists and knots. Across them lies my mother, brazen in backless satin mules and strapless black lace. I sigh. At sixty-three my mother is having a nineties sex life while I am having none at all. Maybe there's a reason sixty-year-olds are called sexagenarians.

I stop. There is, after all, something wrong with this picture. It's not so black and white. Once, as a child, rummaging in my mother's bureau drawers, I found a round rubber disk in a pink plastic case. And, at the back of the closet, a book, printed in Sweden, called *The ABC's of Love*. Near the end of that alphabet, there were drawings that might make even the guys from the Kama Sutra blush. A big bed does not necessarily a sex life make, I tell myself. I think of Seamus' office in the English department. Of the tiny strip of floor between the bookcase and the desk. The floor was cold. The desk was metal and sharp-edged. No matter. The dust motes that danced in the light could have been stars. The planked boards could have been a mattress of eiderdown.

I am in such a state that it's after three by the time I get back to sleep. I only manage this by forcing myself to think of pleasant things: waves, beaches, bylines, Louie's kisses at the strike of twelve. But I sleep late and my schedule is skewed. I don't have breakfast till ten. It's ten-thirty by the time I make it to my desk. It takes me so long to get into my story that when I check my watch I realize I've missed my chance to waft Derek and Gregory's invitation under Louie's nose.

For the first time it dawns on me that maybe Louie, like my mother, like most of the population of Old Town, Maine, and unlike me, has already got plans for New Year's Eve. I start to make myself even more miserable. I project girlfriend, I project Person of Opposite Sex Sharing Living Quarters, I project wife. What do I know of him? Just because he came to the Christmas party without a date, just because he kissed me once under the mistletoe—he would have kissed my mother if she'd been standing there, or Gregory himself. The mention of Gregory opens up a whole new set of possibilities that I can barely stand to contemplate. I am saved by the knock at the door.

"Who is it?" I call. Since the outside buzzer hasn't rung, I figure it's someone from the building. Probably Arthur Haven coming to inquire whether my mother prefers satin sheets or Egyptian percale.

"Louie. Louie Cappetti. Your mailman," he adds as if I didn't know.

I do a quick damage-control check. I've got my writing clothes on. Sweatpants and a velour shirt. My socks have holes. But gold hoops shine from my ears and lipstick glistens from my mouth. Louie's seen me worse.

His eyes shine at me when I open the door. His hair gleams. His button's sewn back in place. He holds a thick white envelope. "I really shouldn't be doing this," he begins, "but I got a feeling maybe it's good news."

I grab the envelope. My name and address are typed—professionally. *Playgirl* magazine is printed in the top left hand corner. What looks like a leopard or a panther straddles the P and the L. I rip open the envelope. I pull out a letter whose first sentence tells me the editors of *Playgirl* have accepted my story "Mismatch" for the February issue. There is a check enclosed for seven hundred dollars with the same leopard or panther stamped on it. I let out a shriek. I jump. I fling my arms around Louie's neck.

Louie lifts me into the air. He twirls me around. I feel like a feather. Like a prima ballerina spun by Baryshnikov. I point my toes. I arch my back. Then I bend my head forward and kiss Louie full on the lips. I hear the swoosh of Louie's intake of breath. A soft moan as he exhales. I smell peppermint toothpaste. Our mouths open. Our tongues touch. They circle. They explore. If I weren't a writer I might hazard a cliché: the earth moves, for instance.

Louie is the first to pull away. His mouth is slashed with my lipstick. He's having trouble looking me in the eye. But he says, "Wow," while staring at my socks. "If I knew that was gonna be my reward I'd bring you more letters." This he addresses to my ugly big toe in its frame of frayed wool.

I'm having difficulty looking at him myself. I'm a little embarrassed. I didn't plan this assault on the object of my desires. I got carried away by animal instinct. My animal instinct. After all, if (A) all humans are animals, and (B) I am human, then (C) I am an animal.

Louie rubs his Revloned lips across his sleeve. He's the sleekest kind of animal. Shapelier than the logo on the *Playgirl* stationery. "Guess I got to be going," he says.

I grab his hand. "Come have a glass of champagne to celebrate," I pause, "my *story*."

"I wish I could. But I haven't even done Professor O'Toole's block yet."

Seamus' name triggers its predictable response. "If you see him, tell him I sold a story and that they're paying me scads." Even in the midst of passion, I'm not above a little self-promotion.

He laughs. "Well," he says, "maybe I could take a raincheck." He turns to go.

"Wait a minute." I run to my desk and come back waving the invitation. My front hall starts to smell like the cosmetics counter at Bloomingdale's. "Gregory and Derek are having a party on New Year's Eve. Will you come?"

He shifts his bag. "You're asking me?"

I nod.

"To be your date?"

I nod.

"On New Year's *Eve?*" He shakes his head, incredulous. From where Louie comes from (where does he come from anyway?) a date for New Year's Eve must carry the same cachet it does in Old Town, Maine.

"That's right, on New Year's Eve."

"Wow," he says.

"It's not till ten."

"Well . . ." He sounds, I am chagrined to acknowledge, rather tentative. "I guess so," he adds, then gaining steam says, "Yes."

"Great. Come cash in your raincheck first."

He looks puzzled.

I explain. "You know, the champagne. We'll have a drink before we go upstairs."

After he leaves, I am in heaven, on cloud nine, the earth moves, I am in ecstasy. I'm not sure what pleases me more, that I have sold a story or that I have a date. I touch my lips. I touch my envelope. I caress my check. I flop onto the sofa where I read the rest of the letter from *Playgirl* magazine. The fiction editor's name is Betty Jean Williamson. She suggests I telephone her to iron out the details. The area code is in California. She tells me to call collect.

I call collect. I'm not sure what the time is in California, but here it's before five, before the lower rates. I feel daring, rich, as if I've just bought something upstairs at Filene's.

The call goes through right away. The receptionist, the secretary, even the operator seem to recognize my name. "Katinka!" Betty Jean Williamson exclaims as if she has known me all her life. That's California's instant intimacy, I think. Maybe I should move there if things don't work out.

Betty Jean Williamson tells me my story is "awesome," that it's "outtasight." I want to ask her if she's got a sister in Cambridge name of Georgette. Then she becomes more businesslike. She explains the terms of the contract, the procedure of sending the galley proofs. She tells me I will join a long line of noble *Playgirl* authors that includes Alice Adams and Joyce Carol Oates. My ego swells, my head grows fat. "And let me reassure you . . ." she begins.

The hairs along my arm stand up.

"That you'll be a separate insert, on good quality paper, no ads."

"Oh . . ."

She must detect some puzzlement in my voice, for then she asks, "Are you familiar with our magazine?"

"Actually not," I confess, "I got your name from the fiction market book."

She gives a little giggle. "Not to worry" is what she says.

The minute she hangs up, I worry. I chew my nails. I twist my hair. I think of my story "Mismatch" about an artist who marries a computer nerd. It's a funny story with no graphic sex but much eating of grapes. The ending is happy, if ambiguous. I have sent it out for two years, it having taken that long to go from A to P on the fiction market list. I'm not Groucho Marx who'd refuse to join a club that would have him as a member. I'm not the kind of writer who wouldn't want to be in a magazine that would publish her stuff. Still, I'd better take a look at *Playgirl.* I zip on my coat.

The magazine rack at the Prescott Pharmacy is right inside the front door. I check through the magazines once, then twice. There are *Penthouses* and *Playboys, Car and Drivers* and *Modern Brides.* There is no *Playgirl.* This is not an equal-opportunity drugstore. I can hear the pharmacist, Barney Souza, typing behind his high wall which is a fortress turreted with apothecary jars and Cambridge Rindge and Latin High School mugs. A lower counter displaying cold-sore remedies and heating pads serves as the moat. "Say, Barney," I begin as I approach.

Barney doesn't answer me until he's finished typing, which, from the sound of it, is of the painstaking two-finger variety. Then he peers out at me between two milky-white jars. Barney is younger than I am. His hair is as feathery as down. But he wears a wedding ring and has old eyes.

Which doesn't surprise me considering the troubles he's seen. I think of what he knows of me, my birth control pills and when I stopped using them, the urinary infection I had last year. The yeast problem that keeps coming back. Not to mention Seamus' high blood pressure medication, the possible side effect of which is you-know-what. But Barney makes no judgments. His voice is uninflected, his face inscrutable. Condoms, Kotex—Barney can smooth a rite of passage so you hardly know you passed. "What can I do for you, Katinka?" he asks me now.

"I'm looking for *Playgirl* magazine."

This he takes in the same stride as he would someone's confession of a virulent venereal disease or minor sore throat. He makes some rustling sounds and then hands me a package already prewrapped in its plain brown paper bag. "We keep them behind the counter," he explains. "You know, the kids."

I refrain from asking about the effects of *Penthouse* and *Oui* on unformed little libidos. I refrain from making a case for women's rights. I refrain from a diatribe about censorship. But my instinct for self-protection, for self-justification is too strong. "They have really great fiction writing in this magazine," I confide, then hate myself.

Barney nods. Nothing human is alien to him. His eyes are wise. Barney knows.

Back home I sit at the kitchen table with my contraband. Should I pull the shades? The cover comforts me. It's of a well-known actor fully clothed. An actor, even, who received rave reviews for an astounding Macbeth. Who studied drama at Yale. I remember the *Playboys* my high school classmates used to stick inside their geometry books. There were ads for Cadillacs and Chivas Regal, socially redeeming articles on politics, how to care for fine wool. Not that these snickering teens were interested in anything other than the centerfold. I open the magazine at random. My heart sinks. If *Playboy* is cashmere, *Playgirl* is a polyester blend. I see ads for Frederick's of Hollywood, for dildoes. I check the table of contents for the short story. I am stopped by an article entitled "Mailmen of L.A. in a Sizzling Pictorial." I turn to page 51. All thought of fiction leaps from my head.

Later I find the story. It is an insert, on nicer paper, free of ads for sensual aids. The story itself is free of sensual aids. It's a decent story by a writer whose name I've seen in literary quarterlies. I try to make myself feel better. This is after all a national magazine. With a large circulation. And I have been paid, in comparison to my usual recompense, an astounding amount. I am certain, however, that no one buys this magazine for its fiction. In fact, a half hour later, I can't remember a word of the story I just read. But I don't forget the sizzling pictorials of the Mailmen of L.A. I take it as a sign. I am filled with hope for the new year as I study the mailmen—their hats, their bags, their ensignia, their pectorals, their abdominals, their buttocks, the dazzling variety of their penises.

I wake up early on the thirty-first even though I haven't set my alarm. I planned on getting my beauty sleep. Two hours more beauty than the usual eight would give me what?—a dewier cheek, a smoother brow? Some of that beauty will now have to be artificially induced. Not that I'm complaining. At five-four, I prefer to be taller. But I've got good bones, wide green eyes, and, thanks to braces, a barely discernible overbite. By eighth grade, though, I reached my prime. I was princess of the Old Town junior high prom. I was also crowned queen of a school for juvenile delinquent boys in the Berkshires. A second cousin, now doing time for felonious assault, submitted my photograph. You should have seen the letters I got from some of those boys.

What am I going to wear tonight? This might not be a question you'd expect from a Radcliffe graduate, a writer, living in Cambridge without serious furniture. I confess I don't fit the classic image of intellectual or bohemian (a point Seamus was all too fond of making during our all too many fights). I have tried. One half of my closet attests to that. There the tattered jeans, black tights, stretched-out sweaters, ethnic cottons heavy with Third World embroidery; T-shirts that save the forest, save the whales pronounce me politically, socially, materialistically correct. But that other half—padded shoulders, Italian linen, French labels, SoHo avant garde (bought, in my defense, *always* on sale, often *drastically* reduced)—reveals my secret guilty soul. Let me blame a childhood in which college catalogues alternated with *Seventeen* and *Mademoiselle.* A childhood in which my friends and I knew both that hard work meant good grades and that the right shade of lipstick might summon a cute guy. A childhood in which, after my father died, my mother would announce, "We need a little lift." Then we'd drive five hours south to Filene's Basement, shop for five hours, drive five hours back. From such a background springs a predictable dichotomy—Old Town and Cambridge, *Ulysses* and *People,* *The Atlantic* and *Playgirl,* Seamus and Louie, denim and lace. I choose black gabardine for dinner. For later, red silk.

I try to stay in bed longer. There's so much I need to do. I sit up. My pillowcase is blotted with the oils and creams I slathered all over my face and neck last night. Three days ago, after slathering all over *Playgirl*'s mailmen of L.A., I flipped to an article about the need to moisturize. The age of twenty is not a minute too late, the author warned. Since I am aeons too late, I tripled the amount suggested on the label. Now I slither out of bed, my knees, my elbows, my heels overlubricated, leaving a trail of grease. This doesn't bother me. I have already planned to change the sheets.

I stand in front of the linen shelf and contemplate the choices: flowers, stripes, plain blue, Donald Duck, hemstitched white. At the back lie a pair of red satin sheets that a student (male) of Seamus' gave us for a wedding present. We used them once. They didn't work, Seamus complained, because he kept slipping *fro* when he wanted to slip *to.* Though younger flesh might find this a challenge,

I decide against them. Perhaps another time. If there is another time. I pick a set of gray and white stripes in conservative good taste. I shake them out. They smell of lavender from the sachets I have tucked around them.

I make the bed. I form perfect hospital corners. I pull the sheets so taut you can't even see where they were folded. I fluff the pillows. I fold the quilt. Underneath the bed I vacuum up dust kitties the size of tumbleweed. I find a shoe I have been missing since 1986. I stand back to admire my handiwork.

I check the ceiling over the bed. There is a tracery of cracks in the plaster as fine as lace. A patch of damp. Nothing you'd notice in the dark. Nothing you'd notice if you were otherwise engaged. A Radcliffe dean lives directly over me. She tiptoes around on her little cat feet. I never hear her. The summer I moved in she went to India with her sister, a Wellesley dean, and sublet to newlyweds. Seamus had flown off to his M&M's by then and what I'd lacked in a sex life had been overcompensated for upstairs. All day, all night, the bed would rock and roll, the springs would sigh and moan until, frantic, I moved my mattress into the living room. That didn't work. They did it everywhere, even in the tub. To see them in the hall would make *me* blush.

As to what's going on three floors above in Professor Arthur T. Haven's bed, I prefer not to know. Though we share brick and mortar and a mailman, my ceiling, thank God, is not their floor. My mother arrived yesterday morning, but I've seen her only once. She popped in for coffee while Arthur went to rent a video. I didn't ask her what sort of video. I hoped something intellectual, foreign, with subtitles and lots of Nordic beating of breast, not baring of it. My mother looked dressed to kill. Her smile implied secrets. She gulped her coffee with satisfied smacks. "Do you detect a certain glow?" she asked.

"It's hot in here," I said. There are some things between mothers and daughters that shouldn't be shared. I thought of my poor father, a kind and measured man. On Main Street he would parcel out an elbow to each of us. Perhaps my mother did go through *The ABC's of Love* with him, and is now dancing down the rest of the alphabet with Arthur Haven. Perhaps Seamus was my dry run for another, better-lubricated race.

All these thoughts of sex and moisturizer reminded me. I told my mother about my story.

She clapped her hands. She couldn't be more pleased, she said, even though I'm pretty sure since my acceptance at Radcliffe she views all my other achievements as a slide downhill. What really surprised me was she didn't bat an eyelash at the name of the magazine. Didn't regret it wasn't one of the seven sisters in the publishing Ivy League. Didn't bemoan the harsh reality of the marketplace. This from a woman who, when I was a child, used to ink in fig leaves on *National Geographic* photographs. Perhaps centering her life on Arthur T. Haven allows her more tolerance for the centerfold.

"I'm so proud of you," my mother said. She finished her coffee. Caressed the handle of the mug. "Arthur has the most delicate ankles," she sighed. "I think we were related in another life."

"You sound like Shirley MacLaine. In a minute you'll be telling me about the healing power of crystals."

My mother laughed. "They're cheaper than diamonds, anyway."

Was she thinking about diamonds, I wondered. I checked her third finger, left hand. The wedding ring was still there, its platinum worn thin as a wire. I remember when Shirley Mercer's mother was widowed. Within a week she'd discarded her rings and had excised her husband's name from their joint listing in the telephone book. What do I have from my own father? His pointed chin, his double-jointed thumb, some money, five letters he wrote me at summer camp, a string of seed pearls. Some days I can hardly summon up his face. I was glad, then relieved, to see this proof against his vanishing.

My mother looked moon-eyed into her coffee cup until Arthur

40

returned with *Dial M for Murder* and *Vertigo*. I was a little surprised, however, that neither made the pretense of inviting me to watch the movies with them.

I fluff the pillows once more so that their indentations match. I probably won't see my mother today. She's got a hair appointment. Then she will be busy getting ready for the dinner party tonight. She hasn't met Zenobia Haven. She's a little nervous. "You know daughters and their fathers," she said.

"She's not your daughter yet," I reminded her.

I guess I sounded irritated because she said, "Of course not, dear," in her most irritating mother/shrink voice. Then added, "One daughter is quite enough."

I straighten the quilt at the end of the bed. I hope that one woman is quite enough for Louie. I hope that that one woman is me. I am not looking forward to the dinner party. Only to dessert. Gâteau Louie. Louie à la mode. I hope that Gregory and Derek have hung mistletoe everywhere. I wonder if there will be more flowers to eat. I wonder if Louie might prefer the flowered sheets. I think I am losing my mind. Be sensible, I warn myself. There is after all the possibility that Louie will not see my sheets, flowers, stripes, or Donald Duck.

The phone rings.

"It's Seamus," says the voice.

"How extraordinary. Twice in one week."

"Don't be poisonous, Katinka. I call bearing good will."

"Oh, yeah . . ." I say.

"I've heard splendid news about you. From our mutual friend."

This stumps me on two counts. What news? Who is our mutual friend?

"Louie Cappetti," Seamus goes on, "the mailman we share."

I am disturbed by this image, implying, as it does, a kind of joint custody.

"So?"

"A fine chap. A diamond in the rough."

41

There's nothing rough about Louie, I think, picturing the smooth angle of his cheek, the sleek glide of his hair. He's a diamond, a crystal, some higher form from another life. "Get to the point, Seamus."

"I'm quite taken with him. We have these little chats . . ."

I keep my mouth shut.

"He's rather literate. Unschooled of course but intelligent."

These words give me more pleasure than I like to admit. My freshman year when Seamus had addressed them to me in his Sermon on the Mount voice, I was thrilled. Now hearing them applied to Louie, I'm still thrilled. Even though Seamus O'Toole is no longer quite the God of Intellect I once worshipped, his pronouncement is a corroboration. I am starting to feel almost tender toward him.

"At any rate," Seamus says now, "Louie told me you sold a story to *Playgirl* for big bucks. My heartiest congratulations."

"Thank you."

"How much?"

"A lot."

"I'm not surprised. Remember that article I wrote on Molly Bloom for *Playboy.* Ten years ago and still an incredible sum."

It's the usual one-upsmanship that Seamus with all his tenure, talent, women, prizes, accumulated years has not outgrown. Some things never change. My heart hardens. "Well, thanks for calling," I say.

"Of course, Georgette says only gay men and teenyboppers read the magazine."

I refrain from asking into what category Georgette fits. Or how she knows. "A story is a story, Seamus," I say with a finely tuned world-weariness.

"You're telling *me?* I'm on your side, Katinka. Georgette has the impossibly idealistic standards of the very young."

Implying I have the sellout mentality of the very old. I say nothing.

Seamus laughs. "Remember you owe it all to me."

I rise to the bait. "What do you mean?"

"I taught you how to write."

"You taught me *Joyce*, Seamus."

"Much the same thing." He chuckles. "I'm running a fiction workshop this semester. Maybe you'll enroll."

"Not on your life."

"Ah, now that you've moved from the high two figures, you don't need me anymore."

"I never did."

"Bull-twoddy," he says. Then he wishes me a happy New Year. I wish him one. He asks what I'm doing. I tell him I have a date. Wow, he exclaims, a date *and* a story. I tell him to stuff it. He laughs. He and Georgette are spending a quiet evening at home because he's hurt his back. How? I ask. The usual way, he replies. I tell him I'll pray for his back to get better. Like hell, he says, he's sure I am hoping it will get worse.

I hang up hoping Seamus' back will get worse. Maybe it will get so bad he won't be able to get up to have one of his patronizing chats with Louie. I look at my watch. It's after eleven. While I've been on the phone with Seamus, Louie must have made his last delivery of the year. That's okay. I hadn't planned to see him anyway before our rendezvous tonight. I'm like a bride hiding from her groom until the actual event. I'm not quite sure what the actual event with Louie will be. But I've got my hopes. All's left is to get through the dinner party. The trial before the verdict. The dark before the light.

I climb the three flights to Arthur Haven's apartment carrying a bottle of California champagne and a box of chocolate truffles which Barney Souza assures me Harvard professors are mad about and which the Prescott Pharmacy can hardly keep in stock. I am sweaty and out of breath when I arrive at the door, which is opened by my mother as if it has been her life's work. "Darling," she exclaims. She is not wearing her glasses. From the way that she squints at me, however enchantingly, I wonder if I am recognized. No doubt she deduces who I am by the process of elimination because she adds, "Everybody else is here."

As we walk to the living room I notice that Arthur Haven's apartment has the same layout as mine. But while mine is furnished in graduate student transience—bricks and boards, bamboo shades, posters, Conran's sofabed—Arthur's exudes English gentleman's permanence—leather, mahogany, oriental rugs, portraits of ancestors framed in gold leaf, Blake etchings, old books.

"Katinka," Arthur comes toward me and pecks my cheek. He is wearing a red velvet smoking jacket. He has a certain glow. Or is he just flushed from the fire blazing in the fireplace? My fireplace downstairs doesn't work. I use it to store my running shoes.

Two people pop up as I am guided over the living room threshold by my mother and Arthur as if I am a bride they are about to give away. "Hello, I'm Zenobia Haven," says the woman who takes my hand. Her hand is cool and firm. She herself looks cool and firm, stately. She's tall, handsome, in a charcoal wool dress fastened at the neck by a cameo. She has straight eyebrows and small flat ears. Although I know she's my age, she seems older somehow. Older than my mother even. Perhaps it's because she exudes such competence. A quality for which my mother and I possess the defective gene. I find her intimidating.

Her husband, Harriman Slade, isn't quite so intimidating in spite of the fact that he nearly wrenches my hand off in its firmer-than-firm clasp and fixes me in the eye with such a masterful gaze I feel nearly mesmerized. Is it because he's a man and thus a different species? Certainly he's fine-looking. About Zenobia's height with a sculpted face and light brown hair combed back. He is wearing an impeccable dinner jacket, a pleated white shirt, and plaid bow tie matched to its cummerbund. If Zenobia's quality is competence, then her husband's is cleanliness. His skin gleams, his eyebrows seem combed, his fingernails and teeth are whiter than white. He's scrubbed, soaped, sandblasted with not, I'm sure, one excess body hair. I picture Harriman Slade in seersucker and wingtips, the centerfold in a Brooks Brothers catalogue.

"And that's Max," Harriman Slade says, pointing to the bay window. "Max, come meet Grandpa's guest."

On the other side of the room, a child of about eight is sitting in a rocker cradling what looks like a sack. His hair stands up in cowlicks and his ears stick out. Still, I see the line of his mother's nose, the shape of his father's mouth. But his eyes are crossed; freckles spatter his cheeks.

Max climbs out of the rocking chair and places his bundle carefully on the seat. He takes a step toward me, then turns back. He removes the package and puts it on the rug. He grabs some pillows from the sofa and rings his package with these. He pats and adjusts. Then he moves toward me once more. He's pigeon-toed. His shoelaces are untied. "Hello," he says. He holds out his hand. His voice is gravelly. His hand is sticky. His mouth is filled with Chicklet teeth. I fall in love.

This is the first time, I think, that I have fallen in love with a child. Aside from having been one, I haven't much experience with them. I have no brothers or sisters, my mother having had three miscarriages before she'd managed to produce me. On both sides our families are small. There was only a second cousin who lived a five hours' drive away in Aroostook County and who had been "somewhat of a problem" from the age of two. As a teen, I baby-sat—an activity that had consisted mostly of putting my charges to bed or in front of the television while I spent hours gabbing on assorted Princess phones and eating my way through the contents of unfamiliar refrigerators. I was happy to leave that career for a job taking inventory for a manufacturer of auto parts. I preferred spark plugs and cables to diapers and strained apricots.

Still, I always thought I'd have a kid someday. The trouble was Seamus didn't want one. He'd cite how badly Joyce's children turned out, the one insane, the other floundering. And though I'd say you're not Joyce (which, though it was meant as solace, seemed to bother him), I couldn't quite see Seamus as a father. In fact, as I was all too soon realizing, he wasn't much of a father figure either. When I pictured Seamus' child, I imagined a kid with a big brain and a gray beard. A kid who cried a lot. I concluded I was lacking in maternal instinct. After all, the baby in our building—the one with the diaper service twice a week—is right out of central casting. Golden curls, button blue eyes, dimpled and pink. The yuppies drop their briefcases and cootchy coo. They play googly eyes. Not me. Not till now.

But perhaps I am suffering from a perverted form of sibling rivalry. I want Arthur's apartment. I want Zenobia's child. I want the neighborhood's mailman for my own. Still, I wouldn't mind playing googly eyes with Max. He's probably too old for such a game. But anyway he's back in the rocking chair caressing his bundle, his eyes on his lap. Maybe I prefer older kids, and funny-looking ones. Is there something kinky about me? A person who is turned off by someone's cleanliness, who is unmoved by dimpled baby flesh? Is there something kinky about Max? Even though I don't know much about children, I can't help but notice a certain peculiarity about Max's bundle. Is it an imaginary friend? A security blanket? Should I comment on it. Ignore it. Pretend it's normal. Is it normal? I am stumped. I move closer to Max and see that he is holding a ten-pound bag of flour. *Native Brand* is lettered across its side. He hums to it in a croaky voice. Our eyes meet. He holds a stubby finger to his lips. "Daniella is sleeping," whispers Max.

My mother pulls me back into the circle of grown-ups. She bustles in and out of the kitchen waving away all offers of help. Arthur makes me a drink. He passes a bowl of salted almonds. Zenobia talks about women in the arts. Harriman talks about reverse triangular mergers. It has something to do with taxes, I gather. He's a lawyer in a Boston firm. He has a harbor view. I admire anyone, I tell him, who can read a tax return. I realize I have made a faux pas when he tells me, I don't do tax returns, I structure *deals*. I plead ignorance and ask him leading questions whose answers I don't listen to. He mellows somewhat and gives me a sanitary smile. My mother bustles around refilling glasses, spreading cheese. Zenobia discusses male domination in the art department. I long for male domination in the postal department. My mother pats Arthur's shoulder. He puts an arm around her waist. Harriman touches Zenobia's elbow. She brushes a nonexistent crumb from his lapel. I wish I had something to touch other than the stem of a glass and a cracker daubed with Brie. Just wait, I console myself. I look toward Max.

Max gets up from the rocking chair. He places his sack of flour back inside its buttress of pillows. He walks down the hall toward the bathroom. This I know because our bathrooms are in the same place. When we hear the bathroom door shut, his parents give a collective sigh. "I loathe Daniella," Harriman says with a startling ferocity.

Zenobia turns to him. "Your own grandchild," she teases.

Harriman is not amused. "This has gone on long enough."

"Darling, just one more night."

"I'd like to pour Daniella's insides out. Toss her in the garbage. Bake her into bread . . ."

"Now darling, Max has learned a lot."

Arthur and my mother nod as if they both know what Zenobia and Harriman are talking about. Though Harriman's vehemence is making me uncomfortable, they don't look the slightest bit alarmed.

Zenobia bends toward me and lowers her voice to a little-pitchers-have-big-ears level. "It's Max's school," she explains, "they're so concerned about teenage pregnancy."

That Max is not a teenager and thus incapable of pregnancy seems a moot point. I nod.

She goes on. "They've assigned each child, boy and girl, a baby. A ten-pound sack of flour. For two weeks the designated parent has to take it everywhere. To class, gym, meals, home. If not, he has to find a baby-sitter. It's quite marvelous. After all there are so many children out there having children for all the wrong reasons."

"Especially in Max's upper-middle-class country day school," Harriman snorts.

Zenobia ignores him. "Children bearing children to seem grown-up, to have someone to love them. Now Max is learning what responsibility for a child is like."

"I think it's a lovely idea," my mother says. "And terribly important."

"You'd be surprised the number of schools that remain unenlightened even in these times," Zenobia confides. "Harriman and I visited dozens."

"All so I'd be asked to give up a tennis date to baby-sit a sack of flour." Harriman shakes his head, incredulous.

"Max has had a valuable learning experience," Zenobia says. She takes a sip of her drink. "His school refuses to do anything by halves. For instance, there was originally a photograph of Daniella stapled to his bag. It caught in the zipper of his jacket and ripped. Poor Max was investigated for child abuse. It was touch-and-go whether Daniella would be taken away from him."

"If only," Harriman sighs.

Max comes back. With one hand he picks up Daniella. With the other he tucks in his shirt. Then with both arms he cradles his illegitimate sack of flour, nestling it lovingly against his single parent's child-sized breast.

We go into dinner. Damask swathes the table. A yard of silverware surrounds each plate. The china is rimmed with gold. The glasses are fluted, their stems as thin as my mother's wedding ring. Candlesticks of Ionic columns colonnade the centerpiece of holly crowning a lusterware bowl. "How lovely," I exclaim.

"My mother's things," Zenobia says.

I can't read her face. Do I detect a hint of possessiveness across her calm and competent exterior? Does she see my mother, who seats herself across from Arthur, as a usurper? Does she begrudge her mother's napkin on my mother's lap? I look at Arthur beaming at the head of the table. I like him. I'm glad for my mother. I wish only that he didn't live so close. Given that my subconscious may be churning blackly, my feelings for Arthur don't seem complicated. Zenobia, however, is a person whose feelings are harder to know.

Max, on the other hand, has feelings that are as plentiful and apparent as the silverware. Paternal protection and concern knit his brows. Affection shapes his mouth. He sits next to me. On his other side a place has been set for Daniella, though abbreviated, fitting her lowly flour status. Daniella gets no salad fork, no wineglass, no equal opportunity to make a social gaffe, to use the cream soup spoon for the consommé. It's been a long time since I've had to worry about etiquette.

For a while in Old Town, teas were held for us ladies-in-waiting. We wore white gloves and ruffled ankle socks. The local newspaper would report who poured, who passed the plates of crustless sandwiches. Years later, those teas came back to haunt me when Seamus and I would be seated apart at banquet-sized Brattle Street dining rooms dispensing chatter from side to side like the queen parceling out waves to her colonials. These days it's Lean Cuisine from its own carton or a chicken leg gnawed à la Henry the Eighth while talking on the telephone. I suppose it's what you'd expect from a writer for *Playgirl.* You'd need chafing dishes to have a *Vanity Fair* life.

Max is now settling Daniella in her chair, which is not that easy given how the bag flops and slides. Daniella is one child you wouldn't dare to admonish to sit up straight. He manages finally to prop her just so, even to tuck a napkin onto her bottom half. He sighs with relief, then climbs into his own chair. He flattens his cowlick, which pops right back up. He spreads his own napkin across his corduroyed knees. He turns to me. "Where do French fries come from?" he asks.

This is a test. I ponder my answer. Do I say France? Do I say potatoes? Sometimes at night I wake up in a sweat with the classic student's panic about a test for which I haven't studied. Or the test is algebra and it turns out I've been memorizing Latin verbs. Now some of this same anxiety assails me. If I pick A, then Max won't admire me. If I pick D, then Louie won't kiss me. If I pick X, then *Playgirl* will take its acceptance back. "Where do French fries come from?" I scratch my scalp. I shake my head. "I give up."

Max giggles. He covers his mouth. "Greece," he announces from behind his fanned-out fingers.

"Aha!"

"Get it?"

"I think so."

He's not taking any chances. "It's really grease," he explains, "because French fries are so greasy."

"That's good."

"I know," he says.

Our dinner is not from Greece, or grease. There are no French fries. There's a roasted leg of lamb with white beans, and artichoke hearts. Consommé in translucent bowls to start. I check what spoon Max picks and follow his lead.

He sips the soup silently, tipping his spoon toward the outside rim of the bowl. His school's curriculum must range from the lower depths to the upper echelon. Or else he's learning Emily Post at home. He looks up at me. A drop of consommé glistens on his upper lip. "Do you know any jokes?" he asks.

I rack my brain. I know the standard priest, minister, and rabbi variety. Probably not appropriate, and besides I always mangle the punch line. There are Seamus' Irish stories that go on and on and rarely have a point. The political ones that are already passé. A Girl Scout cookie joke that is really gross. I have a sudden inspiration. "Why did the moron throw his watch off the Empire State Building?" I ask.

Max wriggles with glee. "To see time fly."

"Why did the moron tiptoe past the medicine cabinet?"

"Not to wake the sleeping pills!"

We are off and running. We trade moron jokes. Elephant jokes. Knock-knocks. We poke each other's ribs. We whoop. We groan. Max is neglecting Daniella. I am neglecting my hosts. Our etiquette is lousy but what can you expect from a single parent and a divorced writer of near pornography.

Arthur taps the side of his glass with his spoon. Max and I fold our hands in our laps. Lower our eyes. I am afraid I'm being admonished. I'm afraid I've let my mother down. But both she and Arthur are smiling benevolently. Arthur wants to make a toast.

Arthur stands up. He hoists a bottle of champagne from its silver bucket. He wraps a napkin around its neck. Expertly he pulls the cork. We applaud the resounding pop. He walks around the table and fills our glasses. He pours an inch into Max's glass. "You and Daniella can share," he tells his grandson. He returns to his seat. He clears his throat. He lifts his glass. "As Aristotle once said . . ."

His family groans. An in-joke.

"Just kidding." He winks. "Seriously," he begins, "on the cusp of this new year we have many things to toast. Not least among them," he bends to my mother, "the enchanting Janet Graham."

We raise our glasses. "Hear, hear," we say. I sneak a look at Zenobia. She is smiling noncommittally. Perhaps she likes my mother, sees her not as a usurper but as an ally. Have I got a deal for you, I address her silently. I'll share my mother if you'll share your child. I put my hand across Max's shoulder. The bones are knobby, the hair at the back of his neck is as wispy as cornsilk. I stroke it. He shifts and settles against my arm.

My mother touches Arthur's velvet sleeve. When she takes her hand away there is a dark mark on the nap. Harriman straightens his already straight tie. "Go on, Dad," Zenobia says.

Arthur goes on, "Now as Plato once . . ."

Hisses all around.

". . . said I have the best grandson any man could have. Not to mention Daniella, who is, at the very least, unique. And a fine son-

51

in-law, a master of the corporate art." He pauses. "But in this publish-or-perish world, my congratulations go to two outstanding ladies. Zenobia Haven, whose just-completed manuscript on twentieth-century women in the arts has been accepted by Oxford University Press, and Katinka O'Toole, whose story has been bought by *Playboy* magazine."

My mother touches Arthur's sleeve again. "Play*girl* magazine," she corrects.

"*Playgirl,*" Arthur says.

"Hear, hear." We raise our glasses. They sip. I gulp. I think of the Oxford University Press. I think of *Playgirl* magazine. Arthur is gracious, treating them as if they are siblings equally loved. But they're not even apples and oranges. More like a child and its flour-filled sack. That's life, one's small steps always overtaken by somebody else's giant ones. I feel bad for my mother, a loser in the daughter sweepstakes. It's not good enough to have gone to a good school. You need to be published by one. It never ends. But if I feel bad for my mother, she doesn't look as if she's feeling bad for herself. To her credit she looks pleased as punch. Zenobia, too. Harriman is studying me, his eyebrow raised.

"What's a playgirl?" Max asks.

"Never mind," his father says.

"What do *you* think?" his mother asks.

Max considers. He tilts his head. "A girl who plays!" He deduces triumphantly. Then adds, "Like Katinka, who knows good jokes!"

Everybody laughs. I blush. Out of the mouths of babes, but I am flattered to know good jokes. Harriman leans toward me. "I say," he says as if my new Playgirl status sets off a cartoon lightbulb, "are you seeing somebody?"

"Yes," I say. I look at my mother. "Maybe. No."

"I've got a guy for you. A lawyer in my office. Recently divorced. He may be just your type."

Which is what? A playboy for a playgirl? A lawyer husband for a lawful wife? A mailman for the mail-obsessed? "I doubt it," I say. "Not that I'm not grateful," I add.

"His name's Jake. I'll tell him to give you a call."

We have salad. We have dessert. A chestnut mousse with curls of bittersweet chocolate on the top. Arthur passes my truffles, which my mother has arranged on a Canton plate. There are mints frosted in pale pink. Zenobia talks about her book for the Oxford University Press. The bibliography itself consumes a chapter's length. Max talks about the dancing class he has just started to attend. He hates it, he complains. The girls are too tall, and besides they're the kind of girls who, when boys bump into them, are the ones to apologize. Zenobia asks me about my story for which I try not to apologize. We discuss it as if it were something out of *Dubliners.* Arthur asks about theme, about metaphor. I am diminished by earnestness. I think of my characters: computer nerds, diaper men, UPS women. Zenobia's characters are real women struggling to make it in a man's world. Creative geniuses. My women are struggling simply to make a man. Even lumpy Daniella seems more real than anything I have written on the page. I am wrapped in the familiar folds of discouragement. Only thoughts of Louie sustain me from sinking my head into the chestnut mousse.

We have espresso in front of the fire. Then it's nine-thirty and time to disperse. My mother and Arthur are going to a party at the faculty club. Zenobia and Harriman are going to a senior partner's house in Dedham. Max is included. There will be a children's party in the playroom. "As long as there's no dancing," says Max. He puts on his jacket and snuggles Daniella under his arm.

"No way are we taking that sack to Dedham," Harriman says.

"I have to," Max says.

"You'll leave it here with your grandfather," Harriman says.

"But Grandpa's going out."

"No one will ever know. No one will ever tell."

"That's not the point," Zenobia says. She grabs Harriman's arm.

Harriman pulls away. "I'll be damned if I'm going to explain this ridiculous project to Laurence Adams and his guests. And I certainly don't want Max to feel like a fool."

"I won't feel like a fool, Daddy," Max implores. "I just can't leave Daniella."

"Daniella!" Harriman spits out the word like a mouthful of ground glass.

"Now, Harriman." Zenobia's voice is placating. She sounds rehearsed, as if she has made this speech many times.

"I'll take Daniella," I say. "I'd love to baby-sit."

Everybody stares at me. Max grins. Zenobia looks grateful. Harriman relieved. Arthur beams. I feel empowered with the wisdom of Solomon.

"But, Katinka," my mother says, "you have your own plans."

I need the wisdom of Solomon both to save the day and not to let her down. "A party in the building. It's no trouble to bring Daniella," I explain.

"It is just for one night," Zenobia adds.

"But you have a date," my mother persists.

"My date won't mind."

My mother raises an eyebrow.

"He'll be *honored*."

"Well, then," she says. Arthur helps her into her coat. She pulls on her gloves. "Is it somebody special?" she asks me.

If we were alone, she'd be unrelenting in her third degree. She wouldn't rest until she'd elicited name, college, age, place of birth, Social Security number. But she's never the Grand Inquisitor in public. I am grateful for the haven of the Havens. "Yes, it's somebody special" is all I say.

Max hands me Daniella as if he is passing me the Olympic torch. I accept with delicacy. With humility. We, he and I, have a sacred trust. By nine-thirty I am in my own living room. I curl up on my sofa. I take Daniella on my lap. I stroke her lumpy seams. I touch the bump of a staple which once attached her photograph. I am amazed by the feelings of tenderness that rise in me. I tear off her price tag. I finger her bar code. Holding her, I wait for Louie.

Louie arrives fashionably late at twenty seconds after ten. I tuck Daniella into a corner of the sofa and rush to the door. "Wow," he says, "you look beautiful."

"You, too," I say though I am not exactly telling the truth. Louie is wearing a tuxedo with lapels wide enough to bridge Arnold Schwarzenegger's chest. Ruffles edged in black braid cascade down the front of his shirt. Under the hall light, the fabric seems to iridesce. My heart sinks.

Which if our two hearts beat as one, his heart must sense since he says, "Pretty bad, huh?" He hands me a sheaf of carnations.

The carnations are pink and surrounded by unnaturally bright green ferns. They're the kind of flowers you give blue-haired ladies on Mother's Day. My heart falls to my toes. "Not at all," I say.

"I knew it was a mistake. I checked with Derek and Gregory, who said the party's black tie. My mother bought my brother and me these monkey suits for my sister's wedding. She even took my picture before I left tonight." Louie examines his reflection in the mirror that hangs over my hall table. This he has to do at an angle since the mirror's too low for him. He limbos toward it from both sides. He groans. "I look awful."

"You could never look awful," I say, this time telling the truth. Clichés burst from me like sneezes: "You'd shine in a barrel. Besides, clothes don't make the man. It's what's underneath that counts." This last of course is intended to refer to the soul when what I, crass nonspiritual Katinka O'Toole, mean is the body, Louie's body—Louie's flesh, muscle, bone. I smooth my own clothes-make-the-man red dress. There have been times in my life—mostly in the past with occasional present-tense relapses—when wearing the wrong clothes was right up there with getting a story rejected. I take Louie's polyester elbow. "Come on into the living room," I say.

I point Louie toward the sofa and go find a vase for the carnations. These I arrange and put on the mantel next to my framed postcard of Virginia Woolf and a rusty horseshoe I dug up in my backyard when I was nine.

"And the flowers are all wrong, too," Louie says, shaking his head. "I should have brought roses or—"

"They're fine. Perfect. Just right. Couldn't be better . . ." I am prepared to go on and on, but Louie stops me.

"I've got something else." He reaches into his pocket and brings out a small package which is wrapped in plain white paper with a little silver bow. Immediately I worry. The package is the size of a ring box, and since I spent every Saturday morning of my childhood at the movies, the scenario is all too familiar.

Thus I am relieved when I pull off the wrapping paper to discover a plastic stamp holder containing a roll of twenty-five-cent James Fenimore Cooper stamps. And I am extremely touched. "Louie," I exclaim. "I am touched."

Louie smiles. "I figured you could always use stamps."

"That's so thoughtful."

"Having to send out all those manuscripts."

"Not to mention the SASEs to make sure I get them back." I pause. "Which I usually do," I add.

Louie frowns. "Don't put yourself down, Katinka. *Playgirl* didn't send your story back."

"Keep reminding me."

"Besides, I plan to bring you a lot more checks."

"I hope so." I pat James Fenimore Cooper's lithographed brow. "Maybe these will be my lucky stamps."

"I wanted to get you ones with a writer on them," he points to my postcard on the mantel, "but they didn't have any Virginia Woolf."

That he recognizes Virginia Woolf thrills me. I put my hand on his arm. The man-made fiber of his sleeve is no barrier to the warmth of his God-given flesh. "It's the perfect gift."

He covers my hand with his. His fingers stroke mine. "There wasn't much choice. No thirty-two-cents writers," he says. "They were out of the Dorothy Parkers. James Fenimore Cooper was the only one in stock."

"Hmm," I say. His fingers are like velvet. He tickles my wrist where under its knot of veins my pulse throbs wildly. My thoughts run wild. I wonder if Louie can get stamps at a discount since he works for the post office. I wonder what Zenobia Haven's pulse does when Harriman touches her wrist. I wonder if Harriman touches her wrist. I wonder if Louie and I will go to bed.

"We read *The Last of the Mohicans* in high school," Louie says. "It wasn't bad."

"We did, too, that and *Silas Marner*."

"Same here." With his free hand, Louie gives his thigh a how-about-that slap. "Hey, maybe we went to the same school."

"Impossible. I could never have overlooked *you*." He smiles. I smile. We grin and bob like circus clowns. "Do you read a lot?" I finally ask.

Louie nods. He's spinning circles on my wrist, dots and dashes, a hieroglyph.

"Who's your favorite writer, Louie?" I ask.

"That's easy." He bends his head toward mine. His breath drifts against my cheek like the brush of the thinnest airmail envelope.

"Who?"

"My favorite writer is Katinka O'Toole." He kisses me. There is no mistletoe to placate, no good mail to celebrate. Louie kisses me of his own free will. His tongue finds mine. His fingers find the top of my Victoria's Secret camisole. He leans back on the sofa. He pulls me on top of him. Abruptly he sits up. He tugs at the sack of flour. "What's this?" he asks.

I laugh. I picture another movie scenario: the baby's cries just as the parents start to make love. "Daniella," I say. I explain about Daniella, about Max, about single parenthood.

Louie listens. His face is earnest. He doesn't laugh. He looks so sad. And when he places Daniella on the coffee table, it's with a gesture of paternal tenderness that reminds me of Max. "I think it's a good idea," he says, "this bag of flour."

I bring out the champagne. Louie opens it. We toast the new year. We toast James Fenimore Cooper. We toast publication. We toast the mail. We toast Daniella. Louie puts his arm around my shoulder. We sit back. We look into my fireplace, its sneakers piled like kindling. Louie nuzzles my ear. "All that's missing is a fire," he says.

I tell him about the other apartments, about working fireplaces that receive deliveries of logs as regularly as the mail.

"Let's do something about that." Louie kneels at the hearth. He scoops away the sneakers. He squeezes into the opening and pokes his head into the flue.

"You'll get filthy," I warn him, having once fiddled around in there and ended up blackened with ash.

"I'll take off my shirt." Louie unbuttons his jacket. He unbuttons his shirt.

His skin is golden. The shoulders wide, the waist narrow. His chest is thatched with black curls so fine they could be spun of silk.

These taper to a thin line which points like an arrow to the still-buried treasure underneath his sister's wedding pants. I exhale. I slip to the floor. I put a hand against the sharp edge of his shoulder blade. "Forget fixing the fire," I say, "these sneakers are plenty hot."

He laughs. "Oh, Katinka," he whispers. My earring jiggles. He undoes my dress. There's no fumbled zipper, no stubborn strap. Louie is a virtuoso. It's as if he has been doing this forever. The minute I think this, I am aghast. *Has* he been doing this forever? For the length of time it takes Louie to unroll my pantyhose, I hypothesize his sexual history. What, why, where, with whom? When I get to know him better, *if* I get to know him better, we'll trade secrets the way lovers do. But now comes the inevitable realization that I am no longer groping in the back of somebody's father's Chevy in Old Town, Maine, with a kid I finger-painted with. I am carrying on with a stranger in Cambridge in the era of sexually transmitted diseases, in the era of AIDS. What is the etiquette, what is the right spoon, what are the right words? I try to remember those public interest ads on TV, the ones in which video stars wink knowingly while saying something sassy yet apropos. I'm stuck. It's the midterm I haven't studied for. Lately, except for a few clinically correct interludes, my sex life has been about as quiet as the bed upstairs since the Radcliffe dean came back from India. "Louie . . ." I begin.

"Don't worry, Katinka, I've come prepared."

I sigh with relief. I sigh with pleasure. I lean wantonly back and enjoy the remarkable things Louie's fingers are doing to my breasts. Louie's tongue dances in my ear. Louie and I lie down on my oak-planked living room floor. The floor is cold. The wood is hard. "This may be romantic," he whispers, "but actually I prefer the bed."

I am relieved. I've had my share of floors with Seamus and look how that turned out. As for other places, well, my friend Milly tells me that when her kids are at summer camp she and her husband do it on their kitchen table. I know her table—peeling Formica and a ragged edge—having stirred Seamus' shortcomings into many coffee mugs there—and am skeptical. Sometimes originality can be overdone.

In the bedroom there is no time to admire the sheets let alone to look at them. Louie makes some safe-sex adjustments. We fall together. We cleave. We clasp. The earth erupts with the force of a thousand mailbags in a thousand vestibules.

We start again. Our bodies, a marvel of angles and curves, shift into new patterns like the bits and pieces in a kaleidoscope. Our legs entwine; our fingers lock. Our lips tap out masterpieces on each other's flesh. I kiss the back of Louie's neck, the hollow in his throat. Louie cups my breast.

Then, smack in the middle of this earth moving, I have a Joycean epiphany—that Louie makes love the way good writers write, gracefully, effortlessly, never blotting a line. There is not a wasted stroke. No writer's block. He is poetry in motion, language in action. He is a sonnet. He is an epic. He is a haiku. I get carried away with analogy. I turn his arms into adjectives, his penis into a verb. "Don't stop, don't stop," I cry out.

We stop at midnight when my clock radio blasts "Auld Lang Syne." "Happy New Year," I tell Louie.

"Happy New Year," Louie says. "It's sure off to an incredible start."

We bring champagne into this bed of damp sheets and musky smells. I sit between Louie's knees and lean against his chest. He wraps his legs and arms around me, and I am contained inside him like a nested Russian doll. "Wow," Louie says.

"Wow," I say. It's the only word I have to describe something that deserves a Molly Bloom soliloquy.

For a long while we sit there. We finish the bottle of champagne. I run my hand along the length of his leg. I comb my fingers through his toes. I play this little piggy goes to market. I play a Bach fugue. "Your toes, your toes," I sing.

"My toes?"

"I am into your toes."

Louie laughs. "Are you one of those—what do they call them—foot . . . ?"

"Fetishists?"

"Whatever. Are you?"

"Only as far as a certain set of toes," I say.

Louie moves alongside me and reaches for my feet. I try to pull away. "Oh, no," I exclaim, "mine are the world's ugliest."

"Nothing about you is ugly," he says. He takes my toes into his mouth.

I swoon back onto the bed, gasping. Louie is the Columbus, the Vasco da Gama, the Admiral Perry of erogenous zones. He has discovered dark continents of delight hitherto undocumented. "Stop. Please stop. Don't stop," I moan.

Louie doesn't stop.

"Seamus hated my toes," I pant.

"What does he know?"

"Quite a bit, if measured by all his degrees."

Louie takes my toes from his mouth and pats them dry with a corner of the sheet. He turns around and moves back up to lie beside me. He holds my chin in his hand. He pulls my face to his. His eyebrows arc into commas over his eyes. His eyes are sad. "Does it bother you," he asks, "that I have no degrees?"

I smile at him. "Right now I can honestly say it's the farthest thing from my mind."

"Right now," he says. "But in the future? I don't want this to be just one roll in the hay."

Technically this hasn't been just one roll, but I don't point this out. Anyway, I have a fondness for collective nouns. For multiples. I forget about degrees. I can only focus on what Louie says about the future, a future in which there will be more in-body experiences, more tingling toes.

"I mean," Louie goes on, "it is weird. A mailman and a writer. A writer for *Playgirl* magazine."

"Not that weird," I say. I climb out of bed. I slide on my erogenous toes to the bureau. I tug at the middle drawer where under its shield of half-slips lies *Playgirl* magazine.

"See," I say to Louie, back in bed. I open to the Dazzling Pictorial of the Mailmen of L.A. "We are connected in ways you'd never dream of."

"Wow," Louie says. He turns the pages. He shakes his head. "Look at that!"

I study the picture of a man leaning against a tree. His backlit buttocks gleam. Another man sits on a windowsill, letters fanned out just underneath his testicles. "Isn't that something?" I whistle through my teeth. I eye them more closely. "Their faces aren't so hot, though. Not that you'd notice."

Louie gives me a sharp look. "A brain like you. You go for this stuff?"

"Number one, Louie, I'm not a brain. I only got into Radcliffe because of geographical distribution. In fifty years, no one ever applied to Harvard from Old Town, Maine. Number two, the major proportion of me is not above the neck."

"Still, a girl of your class . . ."

"This is America. We're supposed to have a classless society."

Louie thumbs through a few more pages. He shakes his head. "When my sister turned thirty, we sent her a male stripper. He wore this G-string. She and her girlfriends tucked dollar bills into it. The way they screamed and carried on . . ." He pauses. "But I'd never think that you . . ."

I slide my hand along Louie's hip. Goosebumps rise against my fingers. Look, Ma, I can raise goosebumps. I can make grown men swoon. "I've got my own male stripper anyway."

"I wouldn't do *that*, Katinka."

"Just kidding. A figure of speech."

"Nevertheless," says Louie, not quite convinced. "This magazine, does it turn you on?"

"The *writing's* excellent."

He grins.

"You turn me on."

He grins again, so wide a silver filling glints. "I do?"

I nod. I pinch a bit of luscious flesh.

He points at a photograph of a man splayed across the grass wearing only his postal deliverer's cap. "This guy's unbelievable."

I look down at Louie. At the slender line of hips, at his sweetly nestled genitals. "You're miles above the lot of them."

He considers the photograph as if it were a test. "I don't know," he says. "Some of these guys are really big."

"That's not only what I mean," I pause, "not *just* the body."

"You're talking about the *soul?*"

"Of course. Besides, these magazines use all kinds of tricks. Ever hear of photo enlargement?"

"You know, you may be right." He reaches for me.

Later Louie and I go into the kitchen. Louie wraps himself in a bath towel. I tell him he looks like Tarzan in a loincloth. I put on his tuxedo jacket, which falls to my knees. Louie tells me I look better in it than he does. I bet your mother wouldn't agree I say, remembering he told me how she took his photograph before he went out tonight. "Mothers," he says.

"Mothers," I sigh, another plot of common ground. We discuss our mothers. Louie's is of the old school. She makes enormous meals, waxes her kitchen floor to a mirror shine, wants her children to produce steady paychecks and healthy grandchildren and to live within spaghetti length of her Sunday dinner table. Louie asks about my stunning mother and is astonished to learn she's nearly the same age as his own. I tell him about her romance, which is probably flowering even as we speak. I tell him that she's a snob but a superficial one and that she'll come round.

"Come round to what?" Louie asks.

"Whatever," I say, ambiguous.

Louie and I tango between the sink and the refrigerator. From the stove to the overhanging cabinets. We make peanut butter and jelly sandwiches, we heat up a can of soup. We find a jar of pickles, a brick of Monterey Jack.

"Do you live with your mother?" I ask him.

He shakes his head. He lives in a triple-decker in Somerville, he explains, his sister and her family on the bottom, his father and mother on top.

"Something else we have in common," I say. I lift a finger to indicate the ceiling. "I, too, have a mother on top."

We are amazed by coincidence, incredulous over such bonds. "Here I am living alone, paying my rent, doing my own laundry, having been married and divorced not to mention having passed the big three-O, and I still haven't managed to get out from under my mother—quite literally."

"I hear you," Louie says, "though from my point of view, it's not all bad."

I don't ask him what his point of view is. I am less interested in picking his brain than in plucking at other body parts. We put our food on a tray and carry it into the living room. We place the tray on the coffee table. We snuggle into a corner of the sofa, clutching each other like teenagers. At our feet is slung the flour sack.

Louie points. "Poor Daniella," he sighs.

I bolster her against the sofa leg to give support. "We've rather neglected her," I agree. "I'm afraid I'm one of those baby-sitters who run off with her boyfriend the minute the kid's parents are out the door."

"I won't tell," Louie says.

Louie and I dip two spoons into one bowl of soup. We bite off opposite ends of one sandwich half. "I don't even have a high school diploma," Louie says.

I am trying to unscroll a sheet of peanut butter from the roof of my mouth, so I don't say anything. I'm not sure what to say anyway. I'm about to announce that if I were principal I'd award Louie a summa cum laude diploma in making love, but the look on Louie's face stops me. It's a familiar look, parental, one I've seen before.

Louie finishes his triangle of sandwich. He puts his spoon on the tray. He leans over for Daniella. He picks her up. He cradles her in his arms. My heart turns over. He's the image of Max. "You see," he says, "I thought I had to go to work."

I touch his shoulder. "That's nothing to be ashamed of. My grandfather quit school in the sixth grade. He had a widowed mother and six younger sisters to support. He was the world's smartest man. He went to New York to make his fortune. Every Monday he took seven books out of the Forty-second Street Library. The following Monday he returned them practically memorized and took out seven more. He was a millionaire at twenty-one." What I don't tell Louie is that my grandfather went bankrupt at twenty-two, the land he bought in Florida turning out to be a swamp.

Louie covers my hand with his own. He places Daniella in his lap. "That's some story," he says, "but not mine." He pats Daniella. "If I had had one of these, maybe it would've turned out differently." He leans his head back on the sofa. He shuts his eyes.

"What do you mean?" I ask.

"The usual. The same old story." Louie's voice takes on a mechanical tone, as if the story's so old it's memorized. "I was seventeen. Carried a pack of Trojans around in my wallet with my driver's license. Cheryl Corelli was sixteen. Cute with these whopper breasts. What did I know? Sex and love, it was the same thing. We only did it twice. I dropped out of school. Thought I'd get a job. We'd get married. Her parents wouldn't have it. My dad's a barber. Works in my Uncle Vincent's shop. Cheryl's father owned a store. He wanted something better for his daughter. I know it was silly, but I figured I'd keep the baby, that it might be a kid who looked like me and was good at basketball. I thought maybe my mother could take care of it while I was at work."

I stroke Louie's hair. His voice is hushed, his face a mask of dramatic suffering.

He hesitates like a comic waiting to deliver the punch line, though not, in this case, expecting laughs. "Then she went and had an abortion without letting me know."

"Oh, Louie," I say. I pause. "Though maybe it was the best decision—under the circumstances."

"I agree. It was probably all for the good. But somehow, after that I didn't know what to do. Didn't go back to school. Didn't really work. I drank beer and watched TV with the blinds pulled shut. I wasn't even against the idea of abortion like so many Catholics are. Everything just seemed kind of empty. I was pretty messed up."

"We've all felt like that."

He nods. "I know this now. That everyone has tough times. But then . . . Of course Cheryl had no idea what she was doing, she was so confused. She says this still."

I sit up. "You see her still?"

"Sometimes." He shifts, rubs at his cheek. "It's funny, we had nothing in common before, but after. Well, it's been a kind of bond."

"I can understand that," I say. "You made a child. You had a loss." I pause. With the introduction of Cheryl, my role as Lady Chatterley seems about to switch into a character closer to *An American Tragedy*. "What happened to Cheryl?" I ask with more desperation than I intend. "Did she marry? Have kids?"

"Nope. She lives at home. She works as a nurse's aide in Children's Hospital. Sort of, you know, to compensate."

Louie strokes the sack of flour in his lap. I stroke Louie. I have a thousand questions I want to ask. They bobble to the surface like so many bubbles rising in our champagne flutes. What does Cheryl look like, what do they talk about, does she still have whopper breasts and how does he know, what does she wear when she's not in her nurse's uniform—black leather, pastel polyester, bikini underpants? I think of Louie's story. If I read it in a magazine at the doctor's office, saw it on TV, it would be the stuff of soap opera. That's the difference between life and fiction. What's trite in fiction is real in life. Right here, on this sofa, is Louie's life.

I take Louie in my arms. He pulls me against him. There is

nothing between us but a towel, a tuxedo jacket, and Daniella. We get rid of Daniella. Then the towel, then the jacket. We go to bed.

Sometime in the middle of the night I wake up. I check my clock, which clicks quarter to three. Louie's arm is flung across my breasts, his knee wrapped around my thigh. There is noise in the outside hall, and that and my shifting weight awaken him. "Are you up, Katinka?" he whispers.

I twist around to face him. His hair is tousled over his forehead. I smooth it back. His breath smells of peanut butter, of pickles, of cheese. His cheek is creased from the pillowcase and his eyes are crusty with sleep. He rubs his eyes. I think of what he must have been like at seventeen, his startled eyes. I'm not surprised that Cheryl of the whopper breasts fell for him. What surprises me is that she didn't stay fallen. How could she resist? Did she? Has she? Does she still?

In the vestibule, footsteps stomp. Voices rise. There is laughter. The outside door bangs shut. "What's that?" Louie asks. He rises on one elbow.

"Somebody must be having a party." We hear the bleat of a paper horn.

"Oh my God," Louie says.

"Derek . . ."

". . . and Gregory's party," Louie finishes.

We have entirely forgotten. "We missed the party," I groan.

"We didn't miss anything," says Louie. He locks his arms behind my back.

"Ah," I say.

Gently he pushes me against the pillow. He moves on top of me.

It's after noon when we get up. I put on a bathrobe. Louie puts on his tuxedo, which, to me now blinded by a night of love, could be what the Duke of Windsor might have worn. I make coffee. I scramble eggs. We eat jammed together at one end of the table. And then Louie has to leave. He has to go home, take a shower and change his clothes, climb the stairs to his mother's Sunday manicotti in marinara sauce.

At the door, I can barely let him go. We kiss. We hug. I wipe egg from the corner of his jaw. "When can I see you again?" I ask.

"Tomorrow."

"Tomorrow?"

"Tomorrow, when I deliver you your mail."

5

It's mid-morning on February second, and I am taking a break from the story I'm writing about the terrible suffering of an unwed father. I pour myself a cup of coffee and bring it to the kitchen table. I glance at the front page of the *Globe*. It's Groundhog Day, and one of the *Globe*'s star reporters has been put on watch. There's a photo of him, wrapped in sheepskins and ponchos like some Arctic explorer poised over a mound of frozen earth. In mittened hands the size of boxing gloves, he holds a camcorder and steno pad. The weather has been gray all week. Sleet slides across the window. If I were a groundhog I wouldn't leave my hole.

I stir another spoonful of sugar into my coffee and gulp it down. I've been getting enough exercise these days—or nights—so that for the first time in a while I don't have to watch my weight. I look over an article about business in the downtown department stores. Christmas sales were one of the best in a long time, the director of Macy's proclaims. Just yesterday, the first, I was in the Prescott

71

Pharmacy refilling my birth control pills. I prided myself on chatting so casually to Barney Souza I could have been stocking up on aspirin rather than obsessing about whether he had noticed the long hiatus followed by recent heavy market activity on the fertility front. "Christmas was pretty good," Barney admitted, "but January has been out of sight."

"I know what you mean," I agreed, smug about my own contribution to the clanging of his cash registers.

Louie has been spending a couple of nights a week in my bed, enough so that he's gotten to see all of my sheets through several rotations. Most times he comes for dinner, though between the first course and the entrée there can be astounding delays.

So far we've been pretty discreet. Louie comes late. After work he goes home, has coffee with his sister downstairs, a grappa with his parents upstairs, protesting all the while the huge meal he shared earlier with his fellow mail deliverers. He naps, he showers, then comes to me. We eat, we fool around, we eat some more. He rarely runs into any of the people in the building. And if he does they don't recognize him out of uniform. Once, he said, Arthur T. Haven held the door for him and wished him a good night as you would a stranger you tip your hat to on the street.

He leaves at five in the morning. He has to be at the central post office to sort the mail at six. Then it's still dark and even the most intrepid jogger isn't out yet. Though I've offered to get up with him, to make coffee, toast English muffins, scramble eggs, he wouldn't think of it. "Have a nice day, beautiful," he says, then kisses me and leaves me curled up in my warm and musky-smelling bed.

"It won't last," says my friend Milly of the Formica kitchen table. "Sex like that never does."

I remind her of her own acrobatics when the kids are off to summer camp.

"We feel obliged. It's real work." She sighs. "We've been married fifteen years and I think we're both ready to call this teenage stuff quits. But who's going to admit it first?"

Perhaps what's going on between me and Louie is teenage stuff. But it doesn't feel like it. Not like the groping in the back seats of cars in Old Town with bodies smelling of Noxzema and Clearasil. Not even like the rolling around on Seamus' office floor. Louie and I talk over our sorry reheated dinners. We share past secrets the way lovers do. I tell him about Seamus, how he picks his toenails, how he reads trashy novels on the toilet seat. "Somehow I can't figure Seamus reading so much as the sports page." Louie shakes his head. "I bet Albert Einstein never did."

"Geniuses go to the bathroom. Besides Seamus isn't a genius."

Louie shakes his head again. His hair ripples. He and Seamus have talks sometimes when he delivers Seamus' mail. Heavy talks. "He knows so much," Louie says, "he's all brain."

"That's *all* he is," I say.

Later, Louie asks me about my old job at Widener, about the students who haunted the stacks. As I talk, Louie listens with his head cocked. His body seems primed to catch the words before they're half-formed. When it's his turn, he describes his own job: he likes it, the people he meets, the outdoors, the fact that he doesn't have to own a bunch of gray flannel suits. The pay is pretty good. Especially, he adds, for someone who lives rent-free. Though he's not sure it's something he wants to do all his life. He talks about his parents, about Cheryl. "What does she look like?" I ask every time he brings her up. I can't help myself.

"Not half so gorgeous as you," he says this time. Last week he called her ordinary.

"Then she's semi-gorgeous," I persist.

"Semi-semi."

"That much?"

"Actually, not a bit."

"You're just saying that."

"It's the truth."

The truth is that I worry about Cheryl. More than I have a right to. It's not that I have any claim on Louie. I'm not sure that I'd even

73

want one. Sometimes I see Louie through my mother's eyes. A good-looking mailman whose collar is glaringly blue. What would my friends think? My neighbors back in Old Town? This is no longer the sixties, after all, when Harvard doctoral candidates went to work on assembly lines and shipyards and an invitation to hoist a few in a workingman's bar was more prized than a tap for Skull and Bones. But the minute I start seeing Louie through my mother's eyes, shame and fury slam them shut. Then another image of Louie appears, rising like a male version of Botticelli's Venus, all pink and creamy and lit by an otherworldly light. That's when I start obsessing about Cheryl.

Cheryl. Cheryl of the whopper breasts. I remember reading in *Vogue* that those women who cannot tuck a pencil underneath their breast look best in clothes. That I am a better candidate for the little black dress is small consolation for the thought of Cheryl, legions of Mongol No. 2s nestled under her giant mammaries.

Louie sees Cheryl once a week, usually on Wednesday nights. She makes him dinner in the Pullman kitchen of her apartment over in Jamaica Plain. Usually Shake 'n Bake, he has volunteered. I asked him once what size bed Cheryl had.

"Small," he said. "It's a small apartment."

This doesn't make me feel much better.

And why does he keep seeing her, I have to wonder, over a period of time that must add up to at least a decade. There's no child after all, not even a Daniella to share. Just the memory of one who was never even born. "What do you talk about?" I asked Louie then.

"Nothing much. The Sox, her work, my work, our kid."

"Kid?"

He coughed, then cleared his throat. "You know, the one we lost. He'd be eleven now, just getting ready for junior high. Maybe heading off to Harvard eventually." He paused. "When you tell me about Widener Library I can just about picture him there," and a look of such pride shone on his face I had to turn my head away.

Although today is Wednesday, I don't have to worry about Cheryl. Louie's off in Florida for the week visiting his aunt and uncle. His mother's brother married his father's sister. There are seven cousins. "We call them the seven dwarfs," Louie said, "though the oldest's only twelve and taller than me."

"Are you sure Cheryl isn't going, too?" I asked. "A close family can always make room for one more."

"Come on, Katinka."

"She could be the eighth dwarf."

"Very funny."

"You told me your family likes her."

"They'll like you, too, when they meet you."

I changed this subject right away. This family stuff is getting to me. How can I justify meeting Louie's family when I spend all my time keeping Louie away from my own family and potential family to be. I feel like one of those characters in a Feydeau farce where doors slam shut and characters disappear around corners leaving behind a faint odor of cologne or a dropped handkerchief. This all has to be managed without Louie noticing the extremes to which I'm going to keep them apart. Not that Louie is particularly anxious to get to know my mother and Arthur in any other way but in the mailman sense. He is after all perfectly intelligent and socially aware. "I bet your mother will be really shocked that you're dating the mailman," he once said.

"Of course not!" I had protested a little too much.

"Sure."

"No more than your mother would be, then, at the thought of her precious Louie carrying on with a divorced woman with no bra who isn't even Italian."

"You've got a point."

"You mean she wouldn't like me?" I'd rushed to ask.

"How could she help but," Louie grinned.

My mother couldn't help but either, I think now. Once she got beyond the lack of ivy. It's been hard having her upstairs so much of the last month, but I'm getting pretty good at compartmental-izing my life. "So what's new?" she asked last week over a lunch of salade Niçoise on Arthur Haven's wife's Spode ironstone. "Has that young lawyer Harriman wants to fix you up with called yet?"

"Oh, Mom."

"Not that I'm meddling. But you've got that certain glow." My mother removed an olive pit from between her teeth and dropped it onto her plate with a ping. "We'll see," she said.

I didn't ask what she meant by that. No sense in encouraging her.

I turn the paper to Confidential Chat, but there are no helpful hints on impossible mothers of thirty-one-year-olds. There's a letter on how to recycle egg cartons, one on toilet-training twins. Another on planning vacations for senior citizens. The senior citizens in my life are already on vacation. My mother and Arthur have rented a condo in Jamaica for two weeks. I took them to the airport on Sunday night and must have been so enthusiastic about hurrying them through the ticket line and the security check that my mother accused me of wanting to get rid of them. "I'm just anxious for you to have the time of your lives," I'd said.

"We've been having that already, my dear," Arthur had replied. Arthur looked stately dressed for the Colonies in a straw boater and navy blazer buttoned with brass. I smiled trying to picture him in the bikini bathing suit my mother had bought for him, blue with Greek capitals. If (A) Arthur loves my mother and (B) thus loves anything she gives him, it will follow that (C) he will love the bikini. "Of course he'll never wear it to the *beach*," she'd confided when she sneaked it down to show me.

"Where will he wear it?" I asked.

Did she blush? "In the privacy of our boudoir," she replied, "nat-urally . . ."

Naturally, I tell myself, now picturing dignified Arthur as a cen-terfold. "Professors Emeriti in Their Teeny Bikinis. Senior Citizens in the Buff" would be the *Playgirl* headline for the sizzling pictorial. I am still chuckling when the phone rings.

76

"What's so funny?" accuses Seamus, the other senior citizen in and out of my life.

"You, of course."

"Indeed. If you knew from where I am calling and my circumstance you would never make such light of it."

"Okay, where are you calling from and what's wrong?"

"From where. Remember Winston Churchill's 'up with this I will not put.' And you a writer . . ."

"Seamus!"

"The hospital. I am at death's door."

For a moment my heart lurches. We do, however incompatibly, share a past. But then I realize that if Seamus were indeed at death's door he would not be barking so vigorously over the threshold of my phone.

"What hospital?"

"Mt. Auburn. I need disk surgery."

"How awful for you."

"Awful doesn't begin to describe it. The thing is pressing on a nerve. I am in excruciating pain."

"Poor Seamus," I say.

But not with enough conviction obviously because Seamus groans theatrically. "The surgeon is amazed I've stood it so long."

"You're one tough old goat," I say.

This he lets pass with a few more token grunts. "Then after the surgery I'll be flat on my back for two months."

"In the hospital?"

"At home. Georgette will tend to me."

Poor Georgette, I think, for the first time. Somehow a vision of her in miniskirt and dangling fish earrings hovering like an angel of mercy at Seamus' bed elicits in me a wave of sympathy. "That's very kind of her," I say.

"Some people rise to the occasion," Seamus sneers.

"Meaning?"

"Meaning, my dear, that some people take things in stride. Make allowances for the artistic temperament, the bohemian soul."

Meaning of course that running off with Melissa and Melinda was the equivalent of sneaking an egg salad sandwich on a diet of low cholesterol. "The only reason that Georgette takes things in stride, Seamus, is that you're too old to rise to the occasion anymore."

"How cruel, Katinka, and quite uncalled for. Not that you'll ever know."

"Thank God for that. And thanks, Seamus, for telling me. I truly wish your surgery goes well. I'll send you a card. Maybe I'll even make those brownies you like."

"That will be much appreciated. Georgette's idea of cooking is heating up Chinese food cartons in the microwave."

"Well, good luck."

"Don't hang up, Katinka. Forever grateful as I am for your good wishes, that is not the reason I called."

Suddenly I am on the alert. I stiffen, all suspicions primed, adrenaline readying its fight-or-flight response. With Seamus there's always a hitch.

Which turns out to be a complete surprise. "I want you to take over my course," Seamus says.

"Your course?" I ask.

"My creative writing course. At the Harvard Extension School. It starts second semester. In a couple of weeks."

"You want *me*, Seamus?"

"I asked you, didn't I?"

"But Seamus I don't know if I'm qualified."

"Of course you are. You were my student after all. You've had enough publications to impress the great unpublished. They'll love *Playgirl*—it'll give you a certain raffish quality."

I am stunned by Seamus' vote of confidence, what I suddenly decide must be his secret admiration of my writing all along. "Seamus, I am absolutely amazed. Flattered that you'd think of me."

"And rightly so, my dear. Still, don't be *that* flattered. In all honesty, you weren't my first choice. Three people already turned me down."

This, as Seamus must have known, stops me cold. I don't say anything.

"You still there, Katinka?" Seamus finally asks.

"I'm afraid so," I say. For a moment I think that I don't want to be in any club that Seamus would invite me to join either; I want to align myself with the three refuseniks. But common sense takes over. Teaching one course in writing will still keep me in the writing mode, pay for computer paper, get me out of the house, provide me with colleagues, fellow sufferers, and give me something to tell people at cocktail parties when they ask what I do. To be able to answer "teaching at Harvard" is worth sacrificing the privilege of turning Seamus down.

"I'd love to take over your class, Seamus."

"It's all set, then, I'll have Georgette Xerox my notes and send over the particulars."

"I can't thank you enough—" I begin.

"Don't even try—here's Nurse Ratchet now about to bring me my pill."

As soon as I get off the phone with Seamus, I pull out my mixing bowl from under the sink and rinse away its ring of rust. I sift flour and sugar together, beat in eggs, melt chocolate. I fill two square baking pans and slide them into the oven. Within ten minutes wonderful smells are wafting through my apartment. I sit back, feeling domestic and professional, two sides of the equation perfectly balanced. The woman who has it all. But as soon as I think I'm the woman who has it all, I think of all the things I don't have, all the things I want—a novel on the "Recommended" shelf at Barnes & Noble, a child like Max, breasts like Cheryl's, Louie but a Louie with the kind of trimmings even my mother could love, a class of my own, not Seamus' hand-me-down . . .

I make myself stop. I am going to be happy with what I've got, not turn it into something inferior. If my mother were here I'd call her. "Guess what, I'm going to be teaching at Harvard," I'd exclaim, awarding her this jewel in her crown. If Louie were here I'd call him.

"I'll be teaching at Harvard next term. No big deal," I'd let drop. I could telephone Milly, tell Barney Souza or any number of people I went to school with or passed books to at Widener Library. I could even write this up for the Old Town High School Alumni notes. But I decide to hold off a bit just in case it doesn't work out. Knowing Seamus, after one of Nurse Ratchet's ministrations, he could be right now leaping from his bed demanding his job back.

Which is the correct decision, for immediately the phone rings, and I pick it up waiting for Seamus to say he's changed his mind.

"Is this Katinka O'Toole?" a man's voice asks.

"Speaking."

"I work with Harriman Slade. He suggested I call you. I'm Jake. Jake Barnes."

"You're kidding,"

"Not at all. Harriman said you—"

"I mean the name. Jake Barnes."

"It's a perfectly ordinary name. Much more ordinary, dare I point out, than Katinka . . ."

"Don't you know whose it is?"

"Mine of course. Jake, aka Jacob, Barnes. Yours truly."

"In literature, I mean."

"I was an economics major myself. Prelaw."

I must already be preparing for my Harvard class, for my voice has clicked into a schoolteacher mode. And though I sound pompously pedagogical even to myself, I am bent on enlightenment. "In *The Sun Also Rises.* Ernest Hemingway. Jake Barnes is the narrator."

"How about that," he says. "Is he the hero, too?"

"In a way."

"Then we probably have a lot in common." His voice is confident, happy. Even as an economics major, he no doubt knows enough about Hemingway to picture himself battling fascists or shooting elephants.

I hesitate. Socially speaking I know it's not in the best of taste to tell a stranger, a potential date, about Jake Barnes' problem. As a writer and soon-to-be-teacher, however, I have a certain loyalty to the text. Besides, to tell him the truth might save him future embarrassment. "I'm afraid I'd better give you the real scoop right off the bat: he's impotent."

This he greets with silence, and for a moment I regret my rush to educate. When I first read *The Sun Also Rises*, I explain to him, I had no idea what Jake Barnes' affliction was. When I asked my mother she replied I was much too young for Hemingway.

Now the real as opposed to fictional Jake Barnes clears his throat. When he speaks his voice sounds amused. "Let me assure you from the outset that I'm not."

I say nothing.

"Impotent, that is."

"I never meant—"

He cuts me off. Chuckles. "We're talking rather intimately for two people yet to meet."

"I suppose so," I agree.

"Shall we rectify that?" Before I can reply he adds, "Harriman has nice things to say about you."

I am absurdly pleased. That somebody so polished, sophisticated, so *clean*, somebody who fathered the world's most adorable child would have nice things to say about me. It is all I can do to keep from asking him to repeat Harriman's exact words. I remind myself I am a published author. That I'll be teaching at Harvard. That I have nice eyes if ugly feet.

"Harriman says you have nice eyes," Jake Barnes says. "I'm an eye man myself."

He asks me to have dinner tonight at Biba. "That is, if you can on such short notice," he adds so apologetically that I feel no need to pretend to be busy. I accept. What good timing. For a fleeting moment, I'm relieved that Louie is away. But it's Wednesday anyway, I realize, Cheryl's night. I pull my shirt tight against my breasts. I feel defiant. I've never been to Biba and hope they won't have flowered canapés. Jake Barnes says he'll meet me there at eight. He'll go straight from his office downtown. "You take a cab," he says to me.

When I get off the phone, my brownies are burning. I pull them from the oven in a cloud of smoke. They can be resuscitated, I decide, with a little judicious CPR. I scrape off their blackened bottoms, then plump them up like pillows, which gives them, nevertheless, the lopsided look of children's Play-Doh cakes. "Good enough for Seamus," I say. Immediately I feel guilty. Poor Seamus from his bed of pain making an extreme act of generosity in offering me my job. I fold the brownies carefully into an envelope of tinfoil and add a red satin ribbon from a stash of recycled Christmas wrappings in my bottom kitchen drawer. These I drive to Mt. Auburn Hospital where I leave them with the lady at the reception desk. She gives me a card on which I write get well soon and sign my name beneath three X's and three O's. "Is something burning?" a kid standing next to me asks his mother. "These smell good," the receptionist says diplomatically.

I take the T to Biba. Cabs are for lawyers and investment bankers. Not writers whose discretionary income is earmarked for extra postage stamps. I am dressed in black and have smudged an outline of smoky colored crayon around my nice eyes. I must look good, for a teenager with a giant radio stares at me. "Your sneakers are untied," I point out to him in a breathing space between raps.

He turns up the volume, but not loud enough to mask "You ugly bitch."

"Kids," the woman next to me sighs. She carries a large red pocketbook which jabs my ribs. "Honey, there's lipstick on your teeth."

I change at Park Street and ride the T to Arlington Station. I keep my eyes down and my elbows tucked tight against my side. I roll my tongue back and forth across my teeth.

Jake Barnes is waiting for me right inside the door to Biba's bar. He doesn't resemble his namesake, or how I've pictured his namesake, one bit. He looks more like Wally Shawn. A little taller perhaps. But not much. He has a skimpy fringe of red hair and chip-munk cheeks nestled into a scarf of ubiquitous Burberry plaid. He's wearing a thick tweed coat that can't quite hide his narrow shoulders and the belly of a gnome. His eyes, not the melting limpid dark pools of passion that smolder from Louie, are more like little blue dots, off-center but intelligent. His looks aren't important, I tell myself. Having the beauty (Louie), I can accommodate the beast. "Katinka?" he asks.

I nod.

He puts a hand on my back and steers me to a corner table near the lady checking coats. She is wearing black, and behind her hang a wedge of fur coats. In Cambridge we don't wear fur coats. Except for the odd battered shearling or recycled muskrat that once kept a flapper warm. I look around. One sweep of the room is enough to make me readjust my long-held view of a Cambridge/Boston fault line of dowdiness: those intellectuals in faded corduroys and defeated misbuttoned cardigans, those preppies safe at home plate in Talbots or J. Crew. *These* people could be from New York. The women in short black dresses tight as leotards, the men in Italian-looking nubby suits, their shirt collars open and settled softly about their necks like draped silk.

Jake Barnes gives our coats to the chicly bored coat checker. Jake is wearing a Brooks Brothers gray suit, blue Oxford cloth button-down, and an old Harrovian tie. I know them all—Eton, Windsor, Charterhouse. Seamus taught me, buttonholing astonished students and demanding they doff what they had no right to don. Yearly he writes a protest letter to the Harvard Coop equating the selling of these ties to the awarding of a Harvard diploma to anyone with twenty dollars and ninety-eight cents. This, all the while celebrating his working-class origins. His Irish poet, man of the people, Dylan Thomas, Brendan Behan bullshit. He is in fact embarrassingly bourgeois, his grandfather having made a pile in enameled toilet seats.

But I give Jake Barnes the benefit of the doubt. He is just unpre-possessing enough that I'm sure he chose that tie for its colored stripes oblivious to the connotation of privilege and old-boy net-working. Though when he orders a martini I'm not sure, so metic-ulous is he in instructing the waiter about the degree of coldness, the virtues and deficiencies of the olive versus the lemon peel that I can only think of James Bond's shaken but not stirred and how I'd much prefer Sean Connery. He smiles sweetly, however, when his martini and my kir arrive, and I think that he is probably nice but pompous in the way of short insecure men. We all have our hang-ups, I decide, though at that moment I can name only a dozen of mine and none of Louie's.

"So," Jake Barnes says with a smack of his lips.

"So," I say with a click of my tongue.

"So, I had a cancellation this afternoon and sent my secretary to B. Dalton for *The Sun Also Rises.* I finished it right before I left to come here."

"You must be a fast reader."

"Sure am. I took a speed reading course. I can cover two hundred pages in under two hours."

"I'm impressed." Actually I am. How bad could someone be who in the middle of a busy day rushes out to do homework for a blind date. Harriman must have been extremely flattering about my eyes.

Jake Barnes leans closer toward me. "You do have exceptional eyes," he says now, his own eyes squeezed into a squint. He looks like those cartoons of Mr. Magoo I used to watch in Old Town before the regular Saturday matinees.

I feel heat rise to my cheeks. At the next table a couple are toasting each other, elbows interlocked. The woman's champagne glass is ringed with lipstick kisses at the top. "Well, they work fine. I mean I can see perfectly well. Did you like the book?"

"I did. I thought Lady Brett was a good character. And given my namesake it was hard not to identify with his plight. Maybe a little dated. All that drinking and lost generation stuff. Not that I read a lot of fiction. Mostly history, biography, an occasional John le Carré."

"I like John le Carré," I say, "especially the George Smiley ones." Most of which, I do not admit, I haven't read but have watched on *Masterpiece Theatre* or was it *Mystery?*

Jake Barnes grins. I settle back relaxed. Things are not going badly, considering. We talk of books, writers, favorite teachers although both of us have been a long time out of school.

"Funny," Jake Barnes says now, "but nobody has ever pointed out this business of my name before. And I'm nearly forty."

"It is strange. It's not like you live in a backwater."

"You know my mother went to Smith. I'm sure they were reading Hemingway. I wonder if she knew."

"It's hard to believe she'd name her son after, you know, someone who was impotent."

"In spite of her education, she wasn't exactly up-to-date. She even hid away a book of Rubens nudes in case I'd become 'over-stimulated.' "

I laugh.

He laughs. His laugh is high-pitched, slightly hiccupped but seems genuine. "Maybe she just didn't get it, like when you first read Hemingway, and never figured out exactly what his war wound was."

"Probably," I agree. I look at his hands, which are walled around the base of his martini glass. They're small, the nails like a baby's cut straight across. Red hair sworls his knuckles and the bottom finger joint. I think of Louie's hands, his fingertips, the poetry they tap out against my bare goosebumped flesh.

We eat upstairs in front of a window where all of the Public Garden lies beneath us looped and braided with light. Jake Barnes studies the wine list as if he's about to take a test on it. I study my menu, frightened suddenly that I'll pick out the wrong answer among the multiple choice and, worse than failure, will miss out on something truly ethereal. Who knows but this might be my only chance at Biba. I don't picture myself coming here with a friend. Or horning in on one of my mother's dates. What's between me and

Louie has nothing to do with food. Louie wouldn't like this place, I suppose, looking around at the satellites of beautiful people, of the obsessively stylish or the conspicuously rich. Or would he? What would he think of the wine list, the offerings of sweetbreads or truffled pâtés? Perhaps a person who has tasted pansies or merely contemplated a plateful of them would be beyond surprise.

"Have you decided, Katinka? I need to figure out whether we want a white or a red?"

"I'm paralyzed. Afraid I'll make a mistake."

Jake Barnes shakes his head. "Whatever the choice, you'll make no mistake."

Too bad that isn't true of life, I think and make my choice.

When our appetizers arrive, Jake Barnes, in Boston and in Paris, is eclipsed. Unlike my time with Louie, here all of my attention turns to the food. I stuff myself with bread, pâté, dumplings with three different sauces, lamb of a color so delicate, a texture so velvety I nearly weep, Brussels sprouts such to redeem all Brussels sprouts for eternity. The wine arrives. Jake Barnes swirls it, sniffs it, holds it to the light, examines the cork, the label. He takes a little sip. He grins. His chipmunk cheeks puff up as though they're stuffed with nuts. His wisps of hair weave a little red corona around his head. "What a wine," he says. "A Brunello di Montalcino, 1985."

I smile. "The year I graduated." I frown. "The year I wed."

"Marriage," he says.

"Marriage," I say.

"You don't approve of marriage?" he asks, his voice taking on an edge.

"I do," I say. "At least in the abstract. I have friends happily married. My own parents were right out of *Father Knows Best*." And my mother, I tell myself, with not even beginner's luck, will probably be just as happy the second time around.

"Zenobia and Harriman seem to have a fine marriage. What do you think?"

"I've only met them once." I picture Zenobia's high intelligent forehead, Harriman's impeccable white cuff. "But they appear well matched." I picture Max, his sack of flour, his wise and funny face.

"Perhaps we can go out with them sometime."

"Like on a double date?" I laugh. "I don't think I've used that term since I was a freshman at Old Town High."

Jake Barnes laughs. "It is ridiculous. For dinner, then, the four of us."

So there'll be another "date." I'm not happy, but I'm not displeased either, I discover, taking my emotional pulse. Jake is nice enough. The dinner is sublime.

"I'd like to marry again," he says now. "To have a child."

"Me, too. Someday. I'm speaking generically, of course," I feel obliged to point out. "I mean I don't have anyone in mind."

"I'm glad to hear that."

Which bothers me—does that mean he's glad to hear I'm not checking him out as a future father of my child or that he's glad there's not another potential future father in my life which means what—that he's in the running? that he's not?—my brain feels addled by food and wine and its own inadequacies. Perhaps I need one of Arthur Haven's syllogisms to figure it out. I am just starting to set this up—if (A) . . .—when Jake moves on to Seamus, who was already a legend at Harvard, it turns out, when he was at the Law School.

I don't say too much. Maybe because Seamus is flat on his back. Or maybe because Seamus gave me his job. But it feels disloyal to be telling this small un-Hemingway stranger stories about Seamus' matted hair and Ian Fleming paperbacks. "We weren't compatible" is what I say.

"Understandable, given the vast difference in age."

"And that wasn't even our biggest difference," I announce though I'm at a loss to name our biggest difference.

Fortunately Jake Barnes doesn't ask but offers up the sad tale of his wife, Laura, whose progression from feminist to radical feminist to man-hating feminist covered the eight years of their own incompatible marriage. She kept putting off having a baby because it would interfere with her postdoctoral work in molecular biology. She sacrificed molecular biology for her biological clock when she met Harriet, who owns a women's health club where Laura climbed the ladder to head masseuse. "And now she's *pregnant*," Jake exclaims. "Artificially inseminated. She and Harriet are both going to be *mommies*—*that's* how they announce it to the world. It'll be Harriet's turn next year. Turkey baster babies!"

He looks so miserable in spite of the wine and the wonderful food that I switch the topic to his work, what any young lady well brought up in the art of gentle conversation with the opposite sex knows how to do. He's a real estate lawyer and, like Harriman Slade with his taxes and reverse triangular mergers, is off and running. What is it about lawyers, I conclude from my scientific sample of two, and the way they love to talk? And what a language they use, mortgages and liens and mergers and syndications, easements and quitclaims, theretofores and heretofores and it is my understanding that . . . Jake Barnes' little eyes crackle and beam and his red-haired hands shape skyscrapers and bungalows, shopping centers and condominium complexes in the scented air above our plates.

And because he, too, is well brought up in the art of gentle conversation with the opposite sex he asks me about my writing. He doesn't raise an eyebrow when I tell him about my stories in back issues of *Running Bull* and *Gypsy Moth Review*, of my commercial breakthrough with *Playgirl* magazine. He doesn't look unduly impressed when I tell him I'll be teaching at Harvard next term. He's the kind of man who expects to be surrounded by published writers and dwellers in the ivory towers of academe. And to his credit, he doesn't say "I'd write, too, if I had the time."

We order a sampling of all the desserts and a brewed decaffeinated coffee each. A chocolate orgy, I decide, is almost but not quite as good as sex. When we are finished, I'm so full I nearly have to walk sideways down the stairs. He drives me home in a fancy car with buttery leather seats, German I think; I am not up on cars. There are no parking spaces within two blocks of my apartment building so he double-parks next to the super's pickup truck. He turns on the hazard signals, which remind me of those neon lights in movies which flicker the letters *bar* or *café* through the windows of cheap hotel rooms where lovers spend illicit nights.

"Please let me pay your cab fare to the restaurant," Jake Barnes says.

"Absolutely not," I state indignantly and leave it at that. What would he think if I told him I took the T. Would he offer to reimburse my eighty-five cents? Pay extra for the pain and suffering of my being called an ugly bitch? Would he admire my thrift? Would he despise it?

"Then would you be insulted if I walked you to the door? Laura, my ex-wife, would have thrown a feminist manifesto at me."

"I'd be delighted," I say. I am feeling gracious, relieved. Because of the double parking, I don't have to ask him in. This is a real first date, I think, with all those rules, those Old Town rules, attendant upon it. There is security in the predictable.

He comes around to my side to open my door. Which isn't easy because the super's truck with its peeling paint and rust spots, its dented fender and splayed bumper and its tangled chrome like barbed wire makes quite an obstacle course. We sidle out of the car careful to keep our coats away from rust stains and sharp protuberances. On the stairs to the front door, he shakes my hand, then leans over and kisses my cheek. His lips are cold, slightly chapped. "I've had a good time," he says.

"Thank you for a wonderful dinner," I say.

"I'd like to read your stuff," he says.

"I'll send you some stories."

"No need for that," he says. "Give them to me when I see you next. And I'll bring along a copy of my article on tenancy by the entirety from the *Journal of Boston Real Estate*. Good bedtime reading. Better than a nightcap. Guaranteed to put you to sleep."

"I doubt that," I lie politely.

"You're just being polite." He laughs. "As soon as I work out this dinner with Harriman and Zenobia, I'll get back to you." He gives a little wave and trips just slightly on the bottom step.

6

Thursday. Tonight's my first writing class, and it feels worse than the first day of school in seventh grade. Will they like me? Will they hate me? Will I make a fool of myself? Will yesterday's slang fall from my lips and brand me forever as a nerd? Do they still use the term nerd? Am I wearing the right thing? What is the right thing? And isn't there something funny about my hair? I have laid out five different outfits five different times. What combination of wool and plaid will make me look intellectual but not arrogant, mature but with-it, pretty but not cute, interesting but not intimidating.

Finally I play it safe and pick various layers of black. These I wrap around me. I check the mirror and have more than a moment's hesitation. I look either like a Sicilian widow mourning three sons lost in internecine warfare or like a college girl of the fifties inhabiting coffeehouses and trying to be bohemian. What do real writers look like anyway? The backs of book jackets flash before me: Edna O'Brien in Chanel, Ann Beattie in Levi's, Muriel Spark in no-

nonsense tweed, Joyce Carol Oates, silk dripping from her bird-boned wrists. Even if, in an Arthur T. Haven syllogism, I can look like a writer and *ergo* be one, I'm still not sure which model comes with the guarantee. I unwind my widow's weeds and choose dark green corduroy.

For the umpteenth time I sit at my desk and go over, for want of a better phrase, my lesson plan. Faithful Georgette has mailed me a copy of Seamus' so-called syllabus, which seems to consist mostly of illegible scrawlings about voice, point of view, and something called narrative integrity. I have no idea what narrative integrity means except the term appears as a leitmotif in Seamus' notes. *Narr. Integ. Re. Dubliners,* Seamus has scrawled. Georgette has written her own note to me on the top. Her handwriting is small and cramped. The O's are flattened. Not the round bold ones I learned through the Palmer method and Miss Drinkwater's ruler cracked across my knuckles in Hannibal Hamlin Grammar School. "Dear Katinka," Georgette writes, "you are a Lifesaver. Love from Seamus and Georgette." I spent a while trying to decide if I was a Cryst-o-Mint or Bit-o-Clove. Then I moved on to the meaning of Georgette's "Love." Was that a word with narrative integrity? If that note were mine, I'd close with "Sincerely" or at the least a "Very truly yours." But I give Georgette credit for a greater generosity of spirit than my own. Besides we're not exactly the strangers that "Sincerely" suggests, both having had intimate congress with the possessor of the damaged disk.

I shuffle Seamus' papers around. Maybe he wrote this syllabus when he was in pain. I take a deep breath. I am in pain. It's only first-day-of-school stage fright I remind myself again. If I can move beyond my terror the course doesn't seem that bad. I'll have eight students. They'll submit their own stories, which they'll read aloud and we'll discuss. If we don't have enough material I'll fill in with John Updike or Alice Munro. We'll have conferences; they'll rewrite. I'll re-read. I'll talk about writing—voice, point of view, narrative integrity. I'll be brilliant, is what I tell myself.

I'll be terrible is what I feel. Fortunately, I've had the sense not to blurt out the news of my first class. Except for the generic "I'll be teaching at Harvard next semester" that I dropped casually before Jake Barnes and the man at the photo developing place who demanded my work number, I haven't told a soul. I have this death wish mentality I need to fight against, a tendency to reject myself before others can reject me. I once sent an agent half a novel and a few stories that, I explained, I wasn't sure about. "If the author doesn't love her work," the agent wrote back, "why should an agent even want to look at it?" These days I try either to express confidence or keep my mouth shut.

"What's new?" my mother asked on one of her Sunday night regular-as-clockwork calls from poolside.

"Not a thing," I said, my mouth a prison warden to my words. I didn't tell her about Harvard. I didn't tell her about Jake Barnes. It was too early. Harvard could fire me; Jake Barnes could dump me, and then I'd be eating crow instead of one of Biba's specialties. "How's Arthur's bikini bathing suit?" I asked—oh clever conversational ploy.

"Too small," she confessed. "I'll have to buy a larger size when we get home. Speaking of which," she added, "we decided to extend our stay another week."

"Good idea," I said. "Prolong the honeymoon."

"It's not a honeymoon. Not technically."

"I'll never tell."

"Katinka, dear, you always make a joke." She sighed. "Sometimes I wonder what your father would have thought of me, the president of the Old Town branch of the American Association of University Women, living in sin. And in Jamaica yet!"

"You mean if it were Skowhegan or Bangor, it would've been okay."

"Very funny."

"He'd have thought it great. He'd want you to be happy."

"Perhaps you're right." She paused, considering this.

And what would my father have wanted for me, his only daughter? I wondered. A quiet settled life in Old Town, Maine. Not this sitcom–slash–soap opera I was now in the middle of.

Which, on the other hand, intrigued my mother, who didn't know the half of it. "So, nothing new?" she asked again, her hope an eternal flame under the studied casualness.

"Not a thing."

She sighed again. Then her voice became more animated. "Arthur talked to Zenobia. Her monograph's won a prize. They're flying her and Harriman to Amsterdam."

"How great for her," I said. Shit, I thought. Here I was again the loser in the daughter sweepstakes. Unless of course—and this was a sudden and not entirely welcome flash—my mother looked upon Zenobia as the second daughter she never had and thus, along with her, adopted her accomplishments. Gain a daughter; gain something to brag about. It took the burden off me while casting me as underdog. Either way I was an also-ran.

When I was young I mourned my mother's miscarriages, mourned the brother and sister I wouldn't have. At the same time I was elated to be the single apple of my parents' eye, center stage in all our family theatricals. If, in our Freudian times, I was heir to the general Oedipal struggles and the assorted complexes that we human beings share, I was spared specific sibling rivalry. Until now.

Oblivious to my archetypal suffering, my mother continued, "Arthur is so proud. As am I. They'll leave in a couple of weeks. They need to make arrangements for Max."

"I'll take Max," I said. The phrase, unbidden, bubbled up as naturally as water from a spring, surprising me.

And surprising my mother, who finally sputtered, "That's out of the question, dear. You know nothing about children."

"I've been one," I began. "I've had the authentic experience."

"Besides," my mother went on, "they'll want to hire a *professional*."

"No dispute there." I sent along my congratulations to Arthur and asked about West Indian cuisine. We discussed flora and fauna and Jamaican rum. I remained pleasantly noncommittal until she announced she had to go, cocktails were being served.

I hung up, congratulating myself that I had revealed none of my secrets however provoked. Given Zenobia's triumphs, I was even more tempted to fill my mother's plate with my own delicious morsel. In spite of sibling rivalry, I refused to compete. Usually in my excitement I bare all—the editor considering my story, that agent who asked to see my work—then, ultimately rejected, I end up having to share that, too. Once at a neighborhood meeting to fight the granting of a liquor license to a pizza joint down the street, I told a roomful of near strangers that I'd entered a writing contest. Naturally the next day I heard I'd lost. The next week, at the market or the drugstore, I'd bumped into nearly every one of them. "What about that contest?" each would brightly ask. If I fail tonight at my first class, if the students hoot me out, at least it won't be reported on the six o'clock news.

My mother was harder than Louie. Maybe withholding the truth comes more easily with practice. Certainly it was easy enough not to tell Louie about my Harvard course or the Biba dinner with Jake Barnes when he called last night. He'd just come back from Florida, he said, and after hours of quoting each of the seven dwarfs' out-of-the-mouths-of-babes to his parents, he was about to collapse into bed. I didn't inquire whether he was collapsing into bed with Cheryl, even though I thought of it, it being a Wednesday night. How could I ask him to tell me stuff when I had my own stuff I wasn't telling him? "I miss your feet," I said to him.

"I miss *all* of you."

He had an appointment, he apologized, and couldn't see me tonight till after dinner. "I may be as late as ten."

"That's fine," I said. I didn't ask about his appointment either, didn't even ask if he was seeing Cheryl two nights in a row so relieved was I not to have to explain about what I had convinced myself would be my one-night stand on academic row.

Now I go over Seamus' notes, my own notes. I pack them into

my briefcase with four sharpened Mongol No. 2 pencils which I am not even tempted to tuck underneath my breast, paper clips, *Best American Short Stories* in case none of my students brings anything to read, and a pack of Life Savers—Cryst-o-Mint—for my breath though I hope my students won't be close enough for me to fear being close. I jump into my second shower of the day—worrying brings on a sweat—and button on my dress of dark green corduroy.

Sever Hall is just inside Harvard Yard through the Quincy Street gate. Snow crackles underfoot, and though the walkways have been sanded, there are patches of lethal-looking ice. I have not worn my sensible L.L. Bean Antarctic lace-ups with the crenellated rubber soles that all the students wear. Instead, now that I am on the other side, black leather with a stacked heel. I picture myself slipping on the ice, slipping a disk, and being tucked into a bed near Seamus on the orthopedic ward, the consequence of which is my slipping round the bend. Worse than the pain of a slip, even a metaphorical one, however, would be losing the job before I even get a chance to deserve losing it.

Which I shouldn't have accepted in the first place I tell myself, inching toward the terrifying destiny which waits behind the heavy doors of Sever Hall.

My class is held in a small corner room suitable for seminars and not, mercifully, in one of those huge banked lecture halls where over two hundred students used to scribble notes in introductory survey courses, their green bookbags piled like cairns up and down the aisles. A few students mill outside the open door and barely glance at me as I thread through them excusing myself. Inside I turn on the light, arrange four chairs along each side of the battered rectangular table and one at its head. I erase the blackboard on which is diagrammed what look like galaxies of stars. I bang two erasers together and raise a cloud of chalk dust. This was my job in second grade, to stand on the school steps and clean the erasers. How far

I've come, I marvel, almost thirty years later to be raising the same clouds of dust at Harvard University.

I sit myself at the head of the table and open my briefcase. I string a line of short story anthologies, notebooks, pencils from edge to edge. Dead center I place Seamus' syllabus.

Five minutes later I am convinced that nobody will show up. Maybe nobody has enrolled. Or worse—that word has spread of the substitution of a cubic zirconia for the diamond in Harvard's faculty. I brush some chalk dust off my dress and feel sorry for myself. All this suffering for nothing. All this preparation for nothing. I am relieved and disappointed. Only slightly heavier on the disappointment. But just before I'm about to sink my head onto Seamus' syllabus, perhaps even to turn his notes into Rorschach blots with my tears, the students arrive and take their seats.

At first they're a blur of color, a chorus of clatter. Then I begin to sort them out. There's a tall, large-boned, middle-aged woman who dangles chandelier earrings and is purple-shawled and maroon-caped and silver-ornamented like those swaddled and cluttered grand pianos one sees in photographs of Victorian drawing rooms. Her hair, too, is the glossy ebony of a Steinway.

Next to her slumps an ethereal-looking young woman in a white turtleneck whose face and lips and eyes are so pale that the only contrast in tone lies in the smattering of freckles over her nose and the light brown lashes on her rapidly blinking lids. It's as if her resplendent table mate has leached all color by sheer proximity. Together, they're the positive and negative in a photographic print.

Separated from the others by a chair on either side—like a trench-coated patron of an X-rated movie—sits an earnest thirty-something man. He wears a plaid flannel shirt whose collar is open on the stretched-out neck band of his Hanes undershirt. A row of ballpoint pens and mechanical pencils marches across his pocket flap like medals arrayed on a four-star general's chest. He has the large two front teeth of an eager beaver and in fact is already taking notes, which his neighbor one space over is straining to read.

This man's in his forties, barrel-chested, his forearms ornamented with tattoos. But his eyes look gentle.

As do those of a young black student with a round sweet face and the air of an undergraduate. He's talking to two women, probably fellow undergraduates. One looks like a California Valley Girl with the species' curtain of blond hair halfway down her back. Her companion's more like a small red fireplug. She has a short squat body wrapped in army surplus and a head of red curls so badly shorn they form a peak at the top. The St. Joan haircut reminds me of Pollyanne Mulligan, who lived two houses behind me in Old Town and went to St. Joseph's Academy where the Mother Superior insisted that the Huns had short squat bodies and pointy heads. In every room of Pollyanne's house hung a crucifix and a picture of a suffering Christ. This student has the look of one of the Mother Superior's Huns. Her mouth is pursed as if she's just swallowed something sour.

Though there are only seven students out of the promised eight, it's already ten minutes past the hour the class is supposed to start. People are making impatient noises, pushing papers around and clearing their throats. "I think it's time to start," I say.

"But the teacher's not here," says the voice of reason, the man with the pens.

"I'm the teacher," I explain and nearly apologize.

"Are *you* Professor Seamus O'Toole?" he asks.

I hesitate. Now's the time for one of Arthur T. Haven's syllogisms. If the teacher's Professor O'Toole and I'm the teacher, ergo I'm Professor O'Toole I'm tempted to reply—*Quod erat demonstrandum.* "Actually," I begin.

But before I can say another word, the red-haired fireplug shakes her head. "Of course she isn't! I know Seamus O'Toole and she's no Seamus O'Toole!"

Haven't I heard this before? I wonder. But now's not the time to start a riff on originality. "Let me explain," I say. I grip the edge of the tabletop to steel myself against what I see as seven pairs of hostile eyes fixing me in their masterful communal gaze. "Professor O'Toole is laid up in the hospital with a bad back. A *very* bad back," I add.

"That's too bad," the sweet-faced black student says sweetly.

"Then who are you, my dear?" asks the woman draped like the Steinway.

"I'm Katinka O'Toole," I begin. I know the minute I say this I've made a mistake.

So does Fireplug. "I knew it!" she shouts. "Just like a man to send his *wife!*" This last word she spits out as if wife were even lower on the evolutionary scale than rat.

"I'm not his wife," I say, indignant.

"That's Harvard for you. Sexism *and* nepotism."

"Ri-i-ght," agrees Valley Girl, extending the one syllable into three.

"I'm not related," I insist. Though I'm not really telling a lie, what would this crusader think if she knew the truth, that I was one of those women so gravely lacking in feminist genes to take a husband's name in the first place and then, compounding the crime, to keep it after divorce. "The name is mere coincidence."

"How about that," says the black student.

"In fact," I go on, seizing the pedagogical opportunity, "this is after all a writing class. If you were to use such a coincidence in your fiction it would sound contrived. What's real in real life doesn't often seem real in fiction." I am pleased to hear the scratch of ink on paper as the man with the ballpoints commits this profundity to his notebook.

"Like nothing personal," says Valley Girl as she stands and sweeps her coat and books into one aerobicized arm, "but I'm outta here. I need *Professor* O'Toole on my résumé. You know how it is if you go to the theater to see, like, Mel Gibson, and he's sick and an understudy goes on. Well, like you've got an option to leave and get your money back." She's halfway across the room now. Her jeans are pressed and the word *Cindi*, with an *i*, is stitched in rhinestones across her belt.

"Anyone else?" I ask. "Anyone else who wants to leave?"

"I think we should give you a chance, my dear. *Harvard* wouldn't hire a teacher who wasn't good," says Steinway.

And because I am turned toward my savior to bestow upon her my most blindingly grateful smile, I miss what happens next. I hear a commotion, the fall of books, Cindi's irritated "Oh, shi-it." When I look up I realize my eighth student has arrived and collided with the departing Valley Girl. For a second the doorway is a tumble of arms and boots and overcoats. Then Cindi leaves and the splayed and vaguely familiar figure moves.

I stare. "Louie!" I exclaim.

"Katinka!"

"Oh, goody," my savior claps and turns to me. "I just knew you were experienced. Here's someone who's had you before!"

For a minute no one moves. We're all actors freeze-framed into a movie still. My hands hover above the table like a medium's. But no spirits appear to shake and rattle it. It's my mind that rattles. Races. *What's he doing here. What does it mean? Maybe it's a mistake. If only it were a mistake. How ridiculous. Help! Why my class? Why me? Why not me?*

Then Louie bends over to pick up his books, and my mind empties into my heart. I look at him. His face is bronzed, the backs of his beautiful hands are brown, their palms delicately white. I'd never thought of this before, but now I'm struck by how those hands resemble the stylized ones steepled in prayer over the chests of Pollyanne Mulligan's many Jesuses. And at the same time I'm beatifying him, I'm sticking him in the pages of *Playgirl*, posing him in the sand on a Florida beach, a knee angled so, an arm raised. I think of tonight, of how I'll trace the pale outline of his bathing suit against his darkened skin. I shudder. I'm a mess of complexes, a Freudian test case: sibling rivalry, performance anxiety, father figure difficulties with both Seamus and Arthur T. Haven, not to mention the castration connotation of dating someone named Jake Barnes. What is Louie Cappetti doing in my class? And what am I going to do with him?

Louie, to his credit, looks as panicked and shocked as I. But he recovers quickly and takes the seat to my right. It is all I can do not to press my leather-tipped toe against his calf. He's close enough for me to smell him—his familiar Louie smell mixed with coconut oil and the briny tang of the Florida sea. I try to take him in with the same abstraction I have exercised on the blackboard or on the man with the ballpoint pens. He's wearing jeans and a Shetland sweater. It pleases me that he looks like junior faculty.

"I was expecting Professor O'Toole," Louie apologizes, avoiding my eye.

"You and everyone else," says Fireplug.

"He suggested I sign up for his class."

"Does that mean you'll want to leave?" asks Ballpoint.

"Leave?" Louie's startled eyes widen.

"That dame you bumped into—" the man with the tattoos begins.

"Woman," Fireplug corrects.

"Woman. She was on her way out. Wouldn't accept a substitute."

"*Miz* O'Toole's no substitute," Louie says. "She's—hey," he grins, "she's better than the original."

"See," says Steinway triumphantly.

"You mean you know her work?" Ballpoint has one of his pens poised as if to copy down my résumé.

"She's an incredible writer," Louie says, "a real professional."

Fireplug addresses me. "Is this another relative?"

What do I answer? He's my mailman. My lover. I even hesitate at friend. "He's from the neighborhood" is what I say. Then worry that Louie thinks I'm hiding something, that I'm ashamed.

Steinway clanks some bracelets in Louie's direction. "What has she published?" she asks as if I'm a deaf-and-mute child for whom he's interpreter.

"Lots," Louie says. "In really good places. She's just had a story accepted by *Playgirl* magazine."

Which falls like a stone into a well. There's a long pause. If the question had been addressed to me, I might have omitted this last fact.

"Whattya know," says the man with the tattoos. He leans forward with lecherous eyes fixed on my breasts.

Fireplug's face turns nearly as red as her hair. "I knew it," she exclaims. "Harvard's stuck us with a writer of porn. In a magazine notorious for the exploitation of women."

"That's Play*boy*, not Play*girl*," admonishes Louie.

"No matter, they're all the same."

"*Playgirl* publishes some good writers," I protest. "Alice Adams, Joyce Carol . . ."

But no one's interested in my literary test case. Even the ballpoint pen has stopped its scratching.

"I'd sure like to read *your* story," the man with the tattoos grins.

"Well, I think it's hunky-dory," says Steinway, who is turning into the mother I always wished I had.

"Look," I say, "I have perfectly acceptable literary qualifications which I will be glad to discuss with each and every one of you outside of class. But right now, right here we have work to do."

Which seems to have been the right tone to strike since they quiet down. A couple even look interested.

I know enough not to let a second lapse and launch right into a discussion of voice and point of view. I'm on a sinking ship that only words can keep afloat. In an emergency, I can come through. The words keep tumbling out as if Seamus' Irish gift of them has been bestowed upon my tongue. To my own ears I'm producing lyrical gobbledygook, but I must be making some sense since Louie and Ballpoint are scribbling away. Louie's notebook is a Harvard one, crowned by a silver *veritas*. Steinway is nodding furiously. With the exception of Louie she's the dearest shepherd in my flock.

By the time I get to third-person omniscient-impersonal I'm out of breath. "Why don't we go around the table and have you introduce yourselves," I suggest. "Tell us a little about what you've written and what you hope to do."

"I'll start," says Steinway, whose name is Muriel Kingsworthy. She's raised four children, outlived three husbands, was a social director on a cruise ship where she met the late Captain Kingsworthy—"the best of the three" and wrote a newsletter that everybody's just loved and is now in charge of social activities at an old people's home. She's had a Ripley's believe-it-or-not life, she confides, which she wants to put into a novel with a lot of lust. At this last word she pulls out a fan from her carpetbag of a pocketbook, unpleats it, and waves it against her chin. She bats her eyelashes, like a middle-aged Madame Butterfly, over the top of the fan, which is pale pink with a border of twirling parasols. "Would one of you kind gentlemen mind opening the window the teeniest bit?"

The man with the tattoos is the first up. His biceps bulge alarmingly while he struggles to raise a window that has probably been varnished shut since 1888. After a few grunts he gets it open. A cold gust of air blasts in and lifts Seamus' syllabus, blowing it around like a paper airplane tossed from a movie house balcony. The man makes a tackle and a dive, intercepts it and brings it back to me. "Well done," I say and tuck it under a corner of the *Best American Short Stories* anthology.

"Edward Horgan, friends call me Eddie," he says. "I drive a cab. Gives me time to make up stories in my head. Hope to get some down on paper."

"I'm India Germaine," says the ethereal creature in the turtleneck, "and I'm freezing." She's hugging herself. Her lips are turning blue.

There follows a lengthy meteorological discussion with a lot of raising and lowering of the window and the measuring of various apertures. Finally a consensus is reached at about a crack and a half.

India Germaine puts on her coat. "I'm really susceptible to colds," she explains. "I've had mono. And pneumonia twice." That's how she came to writing, she confides, being laid up in bed. She's a junior at Harvard majoring in psychology. She used to write poems as a child. She hopes to put what she's learned about people into "the fictional mode."

"I'm a junior here, too," admits the sweet-faced black student. "I need another English credit, and this class fits my schedule perfectly. My name's Jonathan Marshall, and I wouldn't be all that adverse to seeing it in print. So far my writing has mostly consisted of term papers and letters to my girlfriend back home. Term papers about C plus, letters rated X."

"Very funny, Jonathan," says Fireplug with a withering look. "Some of us are serious about writing. I'm a senior here, Rebecca Luscombe. Gloria Steinem sends me personal rejections. 'Dear Rebecca,' she writes. I feel I'm getting somewhere since the earlier ones were addressed to *Ms.* Luscombe. I've published two essays in the feminist press. Last summer I quit my waitress job—they made us wear these demeaning skirts and push-up bras—and peddled my writing in Harvard Square. Some times I cleared fifty-sixty bucks a week!"

Immediately I tuck this tidbit in a corner of my head in its already crowded something-to-fall-back-on-if-all-else-fails category.

"Well, I have not published anything yet," admits the owner of the ballpoints. He speaks slowly with pauses between words. "My name is Russell MacQuillen, Junior. I work in a computer company along 128. There's a lot that happens there—you know, between management and personnel. Stuff that would really be revealing. Unbelievable." He gulps and his Adam's apple jiggles above his undershirt. He has wide bulging eyes that don't seem to blink.

"This certainly seems like a good group, a real diversity," I say. "Let's get to work."

"Wait," says India Germaine, "there's one more." She points to Louie.

"How could I forget Louie," I say. If only I could forget Louie, I think. "Why don't you introduce yourself."

"Louie Cappetti. I'm a mailman. I spend so much time reading the covers of magazines I figure maybe I can get inside. I've started writing a bit."

"You have?" I ask, stunned. I who know your toes, your mother's name, your penis in living color and 3-D, don't know this.

"You are?" asks Rebecca Luscombe. "Are you the teacher's mailman?" she says, though from her tone it sounds as if what she means is teacher's pet.

"Professor O'Toole's."

"Which one? A woman can be professor, too, of course."

"Seamus," he says, and I'm relieved.

"Now that that's settled, let's get to work," I say. "Has anybody brought something in to read in class."

"I didn't know we were supposed to," says India, already anxious over being unprepared.

"It was in the catalogue, dear—please bring a story or novel chapter to the first class," Muriel instructs. "I personally don't have anything that's half ready to show."

"I haven't written a word," admits Eddie.

"My stuff's too rough yet," Jonathan explains.

"I wanted to see what the class was like first," Rebecca says, "so I could select the appropriate piece of my work."

"No matter." I grab one of the story collections and open it randomly. "I'll read you Andre Dubus."

"I've brought something," Louie whispers.

His voice is so low that if I wanted I could ignore him, start reading "The Fat Girl" as if all I've heard is the hiss of the radiator. I'm tempted. That Louie is a mailman, that Louie is my lover, I've accepted. I don't want to know what kind of writer Louie is. Even if he's been doing it on the side since the age of two. Practice doesn't make perfect. Hallmark card writers don't become Nabokov after ten years. I figure Louie's not a good writer. If he were, he wouldn't be a mailman.

But it's only my mother's snobby voice rattling round in my head. After all, Conrad went to sea. Wallace Stevens worked in an insurance company. Other writers have scaled fish and polished rich people's gold-plated bathroom taps though their names escape me at this moment. Wouldn't it be amazing if Louie turned out to be a great writer?

I look at Louie. Terror maps his face. His eyes are expectant as if it's only seconds to a *Psycho* stabbing scene. I empathize. Even we published writers have felt those knives. "That's money in the bank," I say to Louie. "Shall I read it now?" I check my watch dramatically. "Or I could rush through Andre Dubus and hold you over till when we'd have more time next week."

Louie's relief is that of a drowning man swept ashore. "Next week."

Later I lie in bed after Louie has fallen asleep. After class we had taken separate icy paths to outside the Harvard gate and had come together with an urgency that obliterated all memory of the writing group. Now I slip out of bed and take Louie's story out of the briefcase I've dumped on the hall table. I bring it into the bathroom and read it, shivering slightly on the cold toilet seat:

High School Dropout

Michael Leone was seventeen and pretty cool. He was a part of a close Italian family in the North End. He went to mass on Sunday. He played in his church's basketball league. He was great-looking. Tall with a great body and great hair which his father tried to trim too short in his barber shop.

The girls in the girls' part of the parochial school—Saint Anthony's was the boys, Saint Margaret's was the girls—really liked him. They figured he was as cool as he was trying to act. Especially Brenda Morelli who was the prettiest in her class. She had curly blond hair and whopper breasts and legs that wouldn't stop.

Michael was pretty smart. His teachers said if he really applied himself he might have a chance at BC. His mother thought it would be a step up for the family to have a son at BC. His father thought college was a way to keep a boy from growing up and to fill him with fancy ideas that he was better than anyone else, like his father for example.

But Michael had ambition. He wanted a car and nice clothes and a classy girl-friend like some of the women who came from the colleges around Boston to have coffee in the North End with scarves draped around their shoulders and voices that sounded almost like the ones in English movies he had seen.

106

But Brenda had these whopper breasts. And Michael had these Trojans he's carried around in his wallet from day one even though some of the older kids warned him it was like taking a shower with a raincoat on. They only did it twice, two times and there went his future.

"I'm pregnant, Michael," she said with tears in her eyes.

"I'll marry you," he said with tears in his own eyes.

"My father wants something better for me," she whispered, "than the son of a Sicilian who works in a barber shop."

"That's okay," he said because Brenda wasn't looking that good, her hair kinda flat and her eyes all red from crying and all and he kept thinking about those cool-looking women, college kids, in the Cafe Paradisio.

But then he decided he'd keep the baby, that it would be a kid that looked like him and would be good at basketball. "Have the baby," he said, wiping his tears. "I'll get a job and my mother can take care of it while I'm at work."

"Michael, you're a real good person," Brenda sobbed.

Then she went and had an abortion without telling him.

I skim the rest. There's more about how his life fell apart, how he drank beer and watched TV. Not absolutely terrible, I think. A familiar story not just in its generic sense. But of course Louie has already told me this story. Write what you know is standard advice. Though what you know doesn't have to sound like something you've memorized. When I was ten I was pronounced artistic and was given a series of expensive art lessons. Over and over again I used to draw ballerinas at their barre. My teachers would heap praise. Then a real artist visited who had taught children's classes at the Museum of Modern Art in New York. When I held up my ballerina, this teacher shook her head. "I can tell you've done this hundreds of times," she said. "Let's try something fresh."

What did I expect, I think now, as I get back into bed. If I looked at my own earliest scribblings I'd probably throw up. I fit my body to Louie's. Along the march to improvement, there are compensations.

7

The following Thursday I'm sitting at my desk filling in my social calendar. It's the *Women's Writers* desk calendar which I buy each year thinking it will cheer me or inspire me. It doesn't do either. The women writers, even the ones of a certain age, look so young and happy—and why not since they're successful enough to have their photographs sell a calendar—that I can only find myself wanting.

Still, things are looking up. This February's page compared to last year's is practically an illuminated manuscript. Last year's was so blank—week after week of white space like a deadly metaphor for writer's block—that I took to filling up the pages with my grocery list. Mushrooms, one pint of yogurt, bananas crowded out the lone Tom, Dick, or Harry.

But now my weekends, and weekdays, are chockablock with not only items from the fruit family, but also individuals from the family of man. Louie's name snakes all over the calendar—Friday, Sunday, Thursday, Tuesday, like a set of embroidered underpants.

Then come my students, whom I need to schedule for individual conferences. And then there is Jake Barnes. I'm having dinner with him, Zenobia, and Harriman in Harvard Square tomorrow night. When Jake invited me, my first instinct was to say no. I've moved so quickly from famine to feast that I feel as glutted as a Strasbourg goose. And confused. When you think of it, there I was this fall empty of calendar, pounding out one rejected story after another, the light hardly ever blinking on my answering machine, the high-point of the day a chat with the super or a trip to the store. Now I'm orchestrating two men (though Jake Barnes's more the variation on a theme in a minor key), a mother no longer safely stashed in Old Town, a tableful of students, a story accepted for publication, a potential sibling, a potential surrogate child, an improved menu, real dates, and reasons to buy new shoes and a dress.

"I'd love to," I told Jake with my mother in mind. Keep your options open, I heard her whispering in my ear. I can't help but agree. If Cheryl is Louie's option, mine will be Jake. Mad money for the piggy bank. I also don't want to risk turning down Zenobia in case one day she and I will be breaking bread at my mother's on her mother's Spode ironstone plates.

"Maybe next time, you'll let me cook for you," Jake added.

If I can fit you in, I think now as I write down my mother and Arthur and Russell MacQuillen, Junior, who needs an appointment to discuss his state of crisis over page five.

I'm in a state of crisis over my life. Arthur and my mother come home Sunday. I'm picking them up at the airport since, according to my mother, "Zenobia and Harriman have too much work." Perhaps I should tote along this calendar—exhibit A—the proof there's more than one busy daughter here. Then when Arthur and my mother are back and overhead, what do I do with Louie? Keep him hidden or bring him out as exhibit B, to account for some of my newfound busyness. I could produce him in his Shetland sweater and preppy corduroys. I could tell my mother he's a Harvard student—how could she complain?—that he's writing the great

110

American novel while delivering mail on the side like those waiters and waitresses in New York who ladle out soup between auditions for Broadway.

Now I put my calendar aside and pick up the syllabus for my writing class. I've scribbled so many notes on top of Seamus' and Georgette's that the syllabus is starting to look like one of those paintings in which the artist, probably stuck in a garret with no money for canvas, paints over somebody else's work. It's time I make up my own syllabus since I've already taught one class and haven't yet been fired. Perhaps I will start to like my class, to feel almost comfortable. I imagine myself smiling at Rebecca Luscombe's fiery feminism, ready to raise a fist for sisterhood. Or getting to count on the steady breeze from Muriel Kingsworthy's fan.

The spanner in the works is Louie. I keep wishing he were Seamus' student instead of mine. Why aren't I proud he's taking a class? That he has intellectual aspirations. That his writing, with work, could show promise. That he and I are ending up having more in common than I ever thought? I have no answers, only that his being in my class makes me uncomfortable, that I dread discussing his story. In class the balance between us shifts. How to account for it—that it's simply the student-teacher relationship, that I'm pushed into the role of dominatrix? In bed, we're equals. In Sever Hall, though, I know he's uncomfortable, too. It's not something he and I have talked about.

But we should talk about it. Before class tonight, maybe Louie and I can clear the air. I check my watch. It's not yet eleven. Time enough to corner him in the vestibule, to communicate among the letters and the magazines. In the terminology of self-help books, "to work on our relationship." I shudder at the impoverishment of language which, by reducing complicated actions to catch phrases, trivializes them. In writing, how you get there is as important as where you end. In relationships maybe it's only how you end that counts.

I run a comb through my hair. Outside it looks as if all

Cambridge should be hunkering down in the nearest groundhog hole. Snow powders the windowpane. Ice frosts the corners. On the street in front of our building cars spin their wheels. My keyboard rattles as the big DPW trucks roll by with their heavy loads of salt and sand. When the weather's bad like this, Louie is usually late. Everything takes longer, he explains, the mail, the traffic, his route. When I was married to Seamus, the gentlest April shower would cancel our mail let alone a smattering of snow. Back then I wasn't so obsessed by mail or its deliverer. Later, bitten by the writing bug, made into a mail junkie as its side effect, I would call the Central Square post office to rant and rave when an occasional storm turned our street into the Donner Pass and thus prevented even a solicitation for life insurance from getting through. "Whattya expect, lady, an Eskimo?" the postal clerk would sigh.

Louie, however, could be the model for "neither rain nor sleet nor snow . . ." He is dauntless. He's a hero. He's my deliverer. I open the door to the hall a crack so I don't miss the heroic sound of his dauntless delivery.

I've done a lot of revision of the syllabus by the time I realize Louie's really late. My watch says after twelve. I look out the window where the sidewalk has turned into a skating rink. A toddler layered like an onion in a yellow snowsuit slides along his bottom. The first prickles of worry start to form. Then I hear him. A creak of the front door. A heavy shoe.

I run out into the vestibule.

But it's not Louie, trim of hip and sleek of head. It's an interloper in a gray beard and a hefty-sized uniform hoisting his bag like a blue-clad Santa Claus. One not about to burst into a "Ho, Ho, Ho" I sense when I look at his face. "Damn, Damn, Damn," he grunts. He's just dropped a stack of letters, which lie fanned out at his feet.

"Pardon my French," he apologizes when he catches sight of me.

"Where's Louie?" I ask.

"Who's Louie?"

"The regular mailman."

"Slipped on the ice. Been took off to emergency." He smiles.

I gasp. "My God!"

"Damn right, miss." He nods. "Ten mailmen's off to emergency already. It's treacherous out there. Called me up on my day off. Should be getting hazard pay." He pats his Santa's belly. " 'Course some of these young guys is so skinny a little snow would knock 'em off the curb."

I lean against a row of mailboxes. I hold on to the narrow shelf piled with menus from the neighborhood Chinese take-out. "Where is he?"

"I just told you, miss."

"I mean, what hospital?"

With a grunt he picks up an envelope from the floor. "Cambridge City or Mt. Auburn's the likeliest. I'll need you to move, miss, I got a letter for 20B."

I rush back into my apartment and pick up the phone. I dial Cambridge City. They have three mailmen, the receptionist explains, but Louie Cappetti's not among them. Fate, the gods, the weather are all conspiring against me, I moan. A malevolent power is refusing to allow me to keep the pieces of my life separate. Some hostile takeover in the sky has installed my mother in my building, Louie in my class, and no doubt my mailman/lover in the extra bed in Seamus' hospital room.

I call Mt. Auburn and am told that, yes, Louie Cappetti is among the newly admitted. I am enormously relieved to discover his room number bears no relation to Professor O'Toole's. "What's wrong with him?" I ask.

The voice is firm. "I'm sorry, but we are not allowed to discuss the nature of a patient's personal injury."

The nature of a patient's personal injury . . . The words trigger panic. I think immediately of Jake Barnes. Hemingway's. My throat tightens. Katinka, be sensible, I tell myself. People don't slip on the ice and break their penises. Logic doesn't comfort. Logic has played

113

no part in my life these last few weeks. Besides, I am guilty of favoritism, holding some areas of Louie's anatomy more dear than others. If I were truly good, I would protest a damaged pinkie or a broken elbow as loudly as something more personally significant— like the Jains in India who value an ant as much as an aunt. Maybe this bad-mother flaw in my character is due its just deserts. Poor Louie. For a moment I can only think that whatever's wrong with him is my fault. No tears, I order, until I know what to cry about. I pull on my boots. All that's left is for me to get to the hospital.

But how? I wonder when I'm finally outside. The streets are glazed. Ice coats the front stoop like the crust on a crème brûlée. In Old Town we had chains on our car. The snow removal crew was as fiercely trained as the Green Berets. Here I don't dare to drive. I plan to enter Mt. Auburn Hospital only through the doors marked visitor.

On the walk in front of me a student slides along sideways as if he's on a skateboard. He must be made of rubber, the way he bends into a curve. As for me, I'm suddenly all too aware of my fragile skeleton. I remember reading that the foot alone has almost thirty bones. Still I have no choice but to propel my thirty bones times two over this solid sheet of ice. Even if I decide to take a bus, I'll need to walk to the Square to catch it. What's important here is to get to Louie.

I make it to the end of my street by holding on to the fences, hedges, a child's swing set, a *No Parking* notice on a green metal rod. Crossing Mass Ave at the top of the Square is a free-for-all. A woman has fallen, and two people tumble themselves as they help her up. I stretch my arms out as if I'm crossing a high wire with no safety net. "Quite a feat," we few brave and hearty pedestrians say to each other with a conspiratorial smile. There's a sense of cama-raderie, people pulling together the way they did in the London blitz.

Through the center of the Square it's not so bad. The merchants are out in front of their stores scraping and sanding. The shops are empty. It's not a day to pick up a copy of *The Sorrows of Young Werther.*

114

Turning from Brattle onto Mt. Auburn Street, I decide against the bus. I'm on a roll. My technique is to hug the buildings and hobble like the wooden-sandaled geishas in period films about the Orient. I feel as if I've mastered a complicated dancing step. If only Louie could see me now, see how well I do, see what I will do to get to him.

A Cambridge street person comes lurching toward me. He's holding a tattered pizza box straight out in front of him. From the way he slips and slides, he looks exactly like a carhop on roller skates with a big tray. I hope he realizes it's not the kind of weather in which to stop to negotiate spare change. He stops anyway. He shakes his head at me. His beard is tangled. Under his open jacket his sweatshirt says "Harvard" with one of the R's torn out. "Those bozos in Washington have really screwed up this time," he explains. "What losers."

I steady myself against a stone wall. I pull a five dollar bill from my purse and stick it under a corner of his pizza box. "Save the planet," he says, and skates off.

By the time I get to the post office I am out of breath. Considering the object of my mission, this seems the metaphorically appropriate place to take a rest. Inside it's nearly empty, none of the usual lines snaking through the maze of ropes. At the overnight mail window two postal employees are shooting the breeze. "You're my main man," one says to the other and slaps him five. Once Louie and I were buying toothpaste at the Prescott Pharmacy. The door opened. "Where's my main man?" a customer yelled to Barney Souza half-hidden behind his apothecary jars.

I turned to Louie. "You're my main man," I said.

"I'm your *mail* man," was his reply.

"Can I help you, ma'am?" a postal clerk asks now.

"Not really," I say. "I've just dropped in to get warm."

"Lucky for me I work indoors. A dozen carriers have fallen in the line of duty and had to be hospitalized."

• • •

115

When I finally climb the hill to the visitor's entrance at Mt. Auburn Hospital, I feel as if I have conquered Everest. I stop at the receptionist's desk to ask directions to Louie's room. The woman looks up at me. "No brownies today?" she asks.

"Brownies?"

"You brought them once. They smelled so good."

"I remember. For Seamus, Professor O'Toole."

She nods.

"They turned out to be burnt. Barely edible," I have the need to say.

"It's the thought that counts, isn't it?" She pauses. "Of course, today's weather's too bad for carrying anything." She flashes me a sympathetic smile.

But I don't feel excused. Here I am visiting somebody in the hospital and I haven't brought anything. I think of my mother. She never went anywhere without a box of mints, a package of cocktail napkins, a tissue-wrapped trio of lace-edged handkerchiefs. I turn my hands palm up, stunned by their emptiness.

"There's a gift shop at the end of the hall."

Inside the gift shop I pick out a chocolate heart. I am considering the stuffed animals—there's a cuddly teddy with a saucy grin—when I remember I gave away my last five dollars to the bum. I have nothing but loose change, not enough for the three ninety-nine chocolate heart. I buy a Peanut Butter Cup and a Milky Way. I try not to sound too sheepish when I ask for them to be gift-wrapped. The salesperson sighs but wraps them anyway in paper printed the egalitarian pink and blue meant for newborns. "I suppose you want a ribbon, too?" she asks, her voice a sullen grunt of disapproval.

I nod. "Sorry, but yes."

Louie's room turns out to be on the same floor as Seamus' but on the opposite end of the corridor divided in two by the nurses' station. A nurse's back is turned to me as she talks on the phone. On a shelf directly above her perky cap stands a row of African violets in terra-cotta pots. The leaves are yellow, the flowers droop, the stems are flaccid. Perhaps the nurses spend so much time nurturing their patients there's none left over for their plants.

Still I am incredibly relieved when the nurse hangs up the phone and tells me Louie broke his leg in three places and has already had surgery.

"Thank God," I sigh.

She gives me a look. "It's no picnic. He's got a metal plate in there. He's in traction. A terrible fracture. He's got several screws." She shakes her head. Her hat is attached with bobby pins. "In fact, you can't see him now. He's just up from recovery. Unless, of course . . ." Her voice is challenging, accusatory. ". . . you're his *wife*."

"No."

"Then come back later this afternoon."

The prospect of renegotiating the icy streets makes me decide to stay put. I consider the cafeteria but realize I don't have enough money for even a Diet Coke. Asking the nurse for a handout will only confirm her negative impression of me. I take the elevator down to the lobby where, given the weather, the people watching is skimpy but the *People* magazines plentiful. I become so absorbed with the marriages and divorces of celebrities that the hours fly by. My hunger is slaked by a three-page spread on Julia Child. When I go back upstairs this time, I notice a blond woman exiting the door of Louie's room. It's Cheryl I know immediately. Her coat is open on a pink sweater through which the outlines of two distinct nipples are clearly visible. I must begrudge her a certain prettiness. She has feathered blond hair and a tilted nose. Traces of old acne scars, though, pit her cheeks. Unlike me, she did not spend her puberty slouching in chairs in the waiting rooms of dermatologists.

"I see Mr. Cappetti's already having visitors," I complain like a ten-year-old protesting favoritism. Reluctantly, Cerberus lets me through.

I open Louie's door a crack and peek in. Three people are

standing around Louie's bed. Above them suspended in a network of pulleys and wires hangs Louie's plaster-wrapped leg like a crane towering over a construction site. Beyond Louie's bed lies another, this one almost completely curtained off. Is somebody in it, I wonder, trying to sleep? Clearly I should come back at another time. I am just about to close the door when an elbow shifts giving Louie a keyhole view. "Katinka!" he croaks.

The room falls silent. So sudden is the quiet it could be the aftermath of an explosion in which a whole population has been wiped out.

"Katinka, you came," Louie says. His words are slightly slurred, their rhythm slowed. His face is the pale, suffering face of a Renaissance saint. "Come meet my family."

Three faces turn toward me. Still, if there are only three faces, I can't help but notice that there are more than a dozen brightly wrapped and beribboned gifts piled on the table next to Louie's bed. I add my own pathetic offering to the pile and extend my hand.

Which in turn is shaken by Louie's mother, Rosalie, his father, Sal, and his sister, Diane. Rosalie is short and plump with Louie's eyes. Diane is a slightly taller slightly thinner version of her mother. Sal is Louie's height and dapper. His hair's slicked back like a matinee idol from an earlier time.

Finished with the amenities, I hang outside the family circle not sure what to do. "Where are your manners?" Rosalie admonishes. "Give Louie's visitor some room."

I squeeze between Rosalie and Diane to reach Louie. I have the sense not to bend to kiss him. He's wearing a hospital johnny. Against its vee neck his chest hairs curl adorably.

"Are you in pain?" I ask. I reach for his hand.

"Not really. Not now."

Louie's father is tinkering with the adjustments on his bed. He cranks Louie's head up another ten degrees. "Any better?" he asks, and without waiting for an answer, cranks it down again. Louie's mother seems to be concentrating on my hand. I pull it away.

118

"Katinka's my writing teacher," Louie explains.

"That's nice, dear," Rosalie says.

"She's a friend, too," Louie says.

"The teachers always loved Louie," Rosalie says. She fusses with his pillows, smoothes his sheets.

"It was the nuns," explains Diane. "Louie looked like such a little saint."

"He didn't act like one," Sal chuckles.

What does Sal mean by this? I wonder. Did Louie develop his sexual technique in parochial school? Perhaps it's a natural talent, I comfort myself, like being a good dancer or having a special color sense.

Sal cranks up the head of Louie's bed another ten degrees. "Better?" he asks.

"Fine, Dad."

"Hey, Chris," Sal yells, addressing the draped bed over by the window. "Want me to adjust your headboard? I've just figured out how this gizmo works."

An ashen face peers out from behind the curtain like the ghost in the window of a haunted house. "No thanks, Sal. But if you wouldn't mind helping me to the john . . . I can call for the nurse."

"Don't you bother. I need a rest from all these girls." Sal waves a hand toward us as if he's introducing a chorus line. Then skips around to the other bed from which, after grunts and groans and rustling of sheets, he produces the pajamaed and bathrobed apparition. "This here's Chris," he says. "And this here's one of Louie's friends." He points to me.

"Katinka O'Toole," I introduce myself.

"Chris Smith," he says with more a grimace than a smile.

How young he is, not even thirty I think, but he walks like the thousand-year-old man. No, I look again, more like a cowboy who's been glued to his horse. I remember the gross-out jokes book of my childhood: *The Yellow Stream* by I.P. Freely. *Twenty Years in the Saddle* by Major Assburn. I make a note to remember to tell them to Max.

119

"Eeee," Chris winces. From the look of him, Chris Smith's passed Major Assburn's twenty-year mark. He walks bowlegged, rolling on the sides of his feet.

"Still hurts something terrible," consoles Diane.

"I'm a bit better today," says Chris. His knuckles, where he is holding Sal's shoulder, are ridged white knobs.

We watch as he and Sal take their tortoise steps across the room and into the hall. When the door shuts, we all exhale.

Rosalie is the first to speak. "That poor child," she sighs.

"He brought it upon himself," Diane says.

"What some people will do for love without any thought for the consequences." Rosalie shakes her head.

"What's wrong with him?" I ask.

"He's marrying a Jewish girl," Rosalie begins, then stops.

Louie takes over. "And her family insisted he get circumcised."

"At his age?" I am astonished. A few years ago I was invited to the circumcision of Milly's son. He was eight days old, and it was a party held in her living room. There was food and drink. High spirits. Everyone gathered round. I couldn't watch. "Come on, Katinka," Milly had laughed. "At this age, it doesn't even hurt."

At Chris' age, however, it looks like some advanced form of torture. I think of *The Sun Also Rises.* Of Louie under the fig leaf of his sheet. How much do people do for love? How much am I prepared to do for love? And damn the consequences. What are the consequences? Do I love Louie? If I love Louie, would I, if I were appropriately equipped, be circumcised for him? Would I declare him my main man and give up all minor ones? Would I forsake all other dinner dates to reheat the chicken Divan? Could I love him enough to tell my mother about him? To kiss him in front of his mother? To take him to the reunion of my Radcliffe class? To enjoy him in my writing class? What is the correct answer to this multiple choice test? "What some people will do for love," Diane says again as if she's read my thoughts.

"We know what some people will do, then live to suffer for their sins," cautions Rosalie.

Sal comes back into the room and touches her arm. "Not that again. Not after all this time and when our boy's just had surgery."

"Enough, Ma," Louie says.

"Well, this circumcision—I think it's a sign," Diane says.

"A sign?" I ask.

"Yeah, like some people shouldn't be together."

"That's right," Rosalie adds. "Some people need to know their place."

I hold my breath, then exhale. I think of crossed stars, uncomplementary signs. Are they trying to tell me something? What is the message here? But their faces seem open, pleasant. No judgments cloud their dark eyes, their generous mouths. Once in England, Seamus and I were waiting at the Cambridge train station to go back to London after a lecture he'd given at the university. We shared a bench with a couple who were visiting their daughter who'd just won a scholarship there. "How wonderful," I'd exclaimed.

The father knit his brows. He pulled his ear. "We're working-class," he'd confided in a cockney Professor Henry Higgins would have loved. "No good'll come of it."

His wife had agreed. "Some people need to know their place."

Meaning me, I think now. Or meaning Cheryl? I look at Louie.

Louie looks at the table next to his bed. "How about I open some of these presents?" he asks with the diversionary tactic of a talk show host.

"Here?" My heart sinks.

His lovely spatulate fingertips unwind ribbon, rip off paper. He receives a box of chocolates, lotion for dry skin, slippers, a Walkman, a sports almanac, a tortoiseshell comb, and—my heart plummets to my toes—the saucy-grinned teddy bear. "From Cheryl," announces Diane, who reads the accompanying card.

"Now whose is this?" Louie asks as he holds up my pink and blue wrapped package which seems the size of a postage stamp. At this moment Sal and Chris come through the door, just in time to stand as two more witnesses.

Louie tears off the wrapping on one Peanut Butter Cup, one Milky Way. Immediately I notice just how much candy bars have shrunk since I was a kid. But they must look big enough to Louie. "What I love!" he exclaims. He sounds genuinely touched though I can't help suspecting the false enthusiasm of a kindergarten teacher who has just been handed a mud pie.

"How nice," says Diane in a voice which says cheapskate.

"How thoughtful," says Rosalie in a voice which says poor teachers make even less than postal clerks.

I start to explain, then hold my tongue. Never explain, never complain was a motto my mother once told me was embroidered on a pillow on the Duchess of Windsor's bed. I never admired the Duchess of Windsor though I envied her rumored arcane knowledge of oriental lovemaking techniques. Besides I'm not sure how the assembled will take my giving my last dollars to a person bad-mouthing our government. Somehow Louie and I haven't yet got around to discussing politics.

"Thanks again, Katinka," Louie says now.

"It's nothing," I announce with Duchess-like dignity.

Sal points to his watch. "Better get going, girls. We've all taken enough time from work. And Louie needs his rest."

We say our good-byes. Rosalie squeezes my hand. "It was nice meeting you, Corinna," she says. "When Louie gets out of the hospital, maybe you can come and have supper with us sometime. Sal and I, well, we always like to get to know Louie's friends."

"That would be lovely," I say.

The minute they are gone he pulls me toward him. I see a red blot of lipstick at the corner of his mouth. I kiss his lips. I smell what I'm pretty sure is Cheryl's scent, her musky perfume, the hint of vanilla coming off her lipstick print. But when Louie's tongue finds mine, I manage to forget about her.

"I brought you a really chintzy gift," I whisper.

"Oh, Katinka, you brought me something wonderful."

We share a Milky Way. Louie tells me about the accident, how he slipped on the patch of ice at the very start of his route, how the mail spilled all over the walk ruining a *Highlights for Children* and a *Bon Appétit*, how his leg swelled up so fast they had to cut the pants leg off his uniform, how when he looked at his leg stuck out in such a funny way he didn't think it was his, how nice the neighbors were, how one brought a blanket, how another sprinkled kitty litter so the ambulance could climb the hill, how all he thought about was me, about what I would think when he wasn't there to deliver me my mail. "At the hospital, they asked me who to notify," Louie explains. "I wanted it to be you. 'Miss Katinka O'Toole,' I wanted to say. But in the end, I figured it had better be my folks."

"You did the right thing," I say. "They don't like me," I add.

"Who?"

"Your folks. I'm sure they think I'm terrible."

"They think you're wonderful. They certainly will when they get to know you."

"What about Cheryl? Funny how she managed to get in to visit you. They must know her pretty well. They must like her."

This Louie doesn't deny. "Cheryl's okay," he says.

"You must be all pretty close. For her to come ahead of your own family on the first day of your surgery."

"You know hospitals. If they're busy at the nurses' station, visitors can sneak through."

"That's not what I mean. That's not the point."

"The point is—*you* came, Katinka."

"And she brought you this teddy bear." I pick it up.

"An awful silly present for a grown man. That's the problem with us, we still think of each other as sixteen. I much prefer the Milky Way."

I am inordinately pleased. I point to the box of chocolates on the table next to his bed. "Somebody brought you these fancy ones."

"Cheryl. That just goes to show you."

"Show you what?"

"How much she knows me. They're the kind filled with cherries. I've always hated them."

I laugh. "Me, too. They're Seamus' favorites, though." I pause. "You know," I say, "he's on this very corridor. In the opposite wing."

"Professor O'Toole?"

I nod.

"No kidding. I knew he had back surgery, but right here? Maybe I'll go visit him when they let me out of bed."

All at once I feel nervous. "He'll probably be gone," I say. I hope. The possibility of Seamus and Louie meeting in the hospital corridor brings out my teenage fears of people talking behind my back, junior and senior prom dates comparing notes. Not that I was any happier about Seamus' being on Louie's route, but how much time did they have to get beyond small talk? In a hospital, though, afternoons slow to the pace of one of Chris Smith's tortured steps. Time enough for Seamus to find out the particular nature of Louie's and my relationship. Time enough for Seamus to switch from a treatise on James Joyce to a treatise on Katinka O'Toole. I can just imagine Seamus' version of *A Portrait of the Artist as a Not So Young Man*. He won't bother to mention Melissa and Melinda, only Katinka's inadequacies as a brilliant professor's wife.

Now I wind my fingers around Louie's hand. I hold tight. "I'd just as soon you wouldn't talk to Seamus," I begin to plead. "I prefer to separate the pieces of my life."

Louie's voice is soft, his grip is hard. "Sometimes that's impossible. Secrets aren't all that easy to keep. Some, anyway," he amends.

"Do you have secrets, Louie?"

His brows arch. His face wears the mask of innocence donned by naughty boys who've been dipping fingers into the forbidden cookie jar. "Of course not, Katinka," he vows, making an effort to meet my eye.

I pull my hand away. "Then what are you saying? That we should tell everyone? Tell everyone about us?"

"Not until you want to. I'm a mailman. You, you're . . . well, educated, a teacher, a writer. You're a different class."

He's said it: class. In America, class is the thing "that daren't speak its name." What we both feel, fear, have felt, have feared has now been given words. It hovers in the air between us, up near the pulleys and the wires and the intravenous drip, the invisible bacteria to invade the healthiest romance. If these are the words of communication, they're ones I don't want to hear. "Shit," I say. "It doesn't matter."

"It does. Though the truth is I've always wanted a classy girl, a classy college girl."

"You sound like my mother," I say. But what he really sounds like is a character from *An American Tragedy*, a book that lately seems to have been hovering around the edge of my consciousness. I composed an essay on Dreiser once for an American lit course criticizing the way he wrote. The professor gave me a B minus for being more concerned with Dreiser's style than with what he said about the poisonous distinctions of class. Louie could be Clyde. Cheryl, Roberta the pregnant factory worker. Me the society girl for whom Clyde drowned Roberta in the lake. Never mind that I am hardly a society girl, that Cheryl's hold on Louie doesn't seem to bother him—in fact he may even welcome it. You can still make the analogy. Of course that's the power of fiction, I rationalize, its universality. Any character can be tailored to a real-life counterpart. Any story adjusted to a modern time. Since the sixties, the boundaries between people are more flexible.

"Anyway, whatever happens with us it's been all worthwhile," he says.

It depends on what happens with us, I think, picturing Roberta's drowning, Clyde's death in the electric chair. I shudder. I blame the weather, the hospital, seeing Cheryl for giving me these morbid thoughts.

"Besides," Louie grins. He pokes my ribs. "I'd never talk to Seamus about you."

"Then what would you talk to him about?"

"Men talk. The Sox. The Celts. Books. Sometimes he gives me lists to read."

I touch his cast. "You'll have a lot of time for that."

"But not for your class, Katinka. I won't be walking for months. I'll have to drop out. The story of my life."

For a moment I'm relieved. My wish come true. But then I realize that Louie's absence from my class means Louie's absence from my bed, means Louie's absence from my vestibule. May all your wishes come true, I remember, is an oriental curse.

Louie points to his leg. "It's going to be tough. I won't be able to work. I won't be able to drive. I'll be laid up at home in bed for quite a while."

"I'll have to make conjugal visits."

"With my parents upstairs! If only! My mother never leaves the house. She starts cooking dinner the minute the breakfast dishes are done. Every ten minutes she'll bring me a snack. It's a three-decker. With Sheetrock walls thinner than cardboard."

"You are a grown man, Louie," I say, "with only yourself to support. Why do you live at home anyway?"

Louie frowns. He plucks at his hospital gown. "It's convenient. Cheap."

Cheap maybe, I think, but certainly not convenient. At least, not for love affairs. I have a thousand questions, but it seems hard-hearted to interrogate someone who's just had surgery.

Louie brightens. "Hey, if you come for dinner, we can play footsie under my mother's dining room set."

"As long as I sit near your good foot," I say. "We'll work something out. All that food, you're going to need some exercise."

The nurse comes in bearing a basket of towels and soap. She needs to change Mr. Cappetti's bed, she explains. She needs to sponge him down. She has white hair pulled into a bun and is as straight and thin as the pole that holds his IV. She opens a bottle of medicinal-smelling liquid soap the color of chartreuse.

"I suppose I'd better go," I say.

Louie hands me Cheryl's box of chocolate-covered cherries. "How about taking these to Professor O'Toole?"

126

I put them back on the table on top of the tortoiseshell comb. I shake my head. "Another time. Today you're the only invalid I want to see, the only one that neither rain nor sleet nor snow could keep me from visiting."

"Katinka," Louie implores with the voice of a child, his arm out-stretched.

But the nurse is already working on his neck, pushing her wash-cloth around his golden skin. I can't even figure out where to squeeze in a kiss. Her fingers, not mine, touch the curls of his chest. I study Louie behind the stick of the nurse. I want to cry for his leg, for his beautiful eyes, for his knowledge that things may not work out, for the parts of his body that are no longer so often or so easily going to be mine. What are his secrets, I wonder. "I can't stand this," I nearly cry. "I'll miss you so much. We'll figure out a way." But at the very moment I am saying these words, at the very moment I am feeling most deprived, I am aware of a window of opportunity opening to let in Jake Barnes.

8

Jake Barnes telephones and offers to pick me up for tonight's dinner at Harvest restaurant. I demur. "The walk will do me good."

"Is this a generic objection or specific one?" he asks.

"Meaning?"

"Whether you object on principle to a person of the male persuasion fetching you."

I remember his ex-wife. "Specific," I say. "I need the exercise."

He sounds relieved. "It's still icy out there," he warns.

"I'm the original Admiral Byrd."

"Of course. I forgot you're from Maine." He laughs. If I'm determined to be hearty, he explains, he'll drive in with Zenobia and Harriman, whose house is only a mile away from his.

"You live in a house?" I ask.

"I'm the original Homo sapiens domesticus. You act surprised."

"As a born-again city person, I find it hard to picture single people with backyards and bedrooms up a flight of stairs."

"A center entrance colonial. My ex-wife loved it, but when she left me, she left the house to me. 'I hate it,' were her words. 'Living room on the right, dining room on the left, half-bath under the stairs. Boring and predictable, just like you.'"

He gives an apologetic half-laugh. His voice, turned up on the last line, implies a question.

Leaving me no choice but to reply, "Boring and predictable are not the terms for someone who reads *The Sun Also Rises* for a first date."

"I hope you can still say that when you get to know me more."

Now as I push through Harvest's heavy glass doors and hang my coat on the hook next to the public telephone, I wonder if getting to know Jake Barnes more means getting to know Louie less. Isn't there some principle of physics about displacement, some law that states two bodies can't occupy a single mass. Lately, I've got more mass to be occupied. My mornings are flat, my nights empty. Since Louie's roommate's condition has improved—the fever and infection that kept Chris Smith in the hospital has started to clear up—visiting hours with Louie leave no privacy. Chris' curtains are open. The ellipse his legs make is narrowing. He wants to chat. He's a new man. He's thinking of getting bar-mitzvahed. His fiancée's parents have come round. "With a vengeance," Chris boasted. "I'm practically the messiah."

"If that's all it takes," Louie said, "a little foreskin . . ."

"Not on your life," said I protectively. "Anything lopped off you is something that I'll miss." The truth is I miss Louie even when I'm at the hospital with him. Though I stagger my visits to avoid the Cappettis and the ubiquitous Cheryl—who Louie keeps insisting is a "family friend"—I still feel bereft. It's hard to analyze. Is it because I have to share him with nurses and orderlies and a messiah newly circumcised. Or is it just sex. Is Louie a sex object? Am I becoming one of those fast, overstimulated girls Miss Deegan my seventh-grade hygiene teacher always warned us about. Last night my bed seemed so large, my sheets so cold, I forced myself to focus on my class, grateful for its distractions. I tried to think of India Germaine's story, how to fix her point of view. But my point of view was fixed on Louie.

Now I try to find Jake Barnes. As always on Friday nights, Harvest is mobbed. People are three deep around the bar. It's happy hour. A happy hunting ground. I have two friends who met their husbands here. One ended badly; one's still going strong. As for me, I never had much luck, always being sidled up to by men with red faces who want to discuss politics. "If only Kennedy . . ." one of them starts, eyeing me. I sidestep his boat-shoed foot. Briefcases and shopping bags crowded against the railing make an obstacle course. Somebody trips, and somebody's new Caphalon wok slips out from its cardboard box. A gray-haired man in a continental suit with a nipped in waist—not made for his American hanging out body—sends a bottle of champagne to two blond girls standing at the horseshoe curve of the bar. The man looks familiar. When he salutes the girls, like Montgomery in old newsreels, I recognize him, recognize the same jaunty salute with which he serves chopped liver on a Bulkie roll from behind the deli counter in Inman Square.

I see no sign of Jake, of Zenobia and Harriman Slade. I check my watch. I am exactly on time. I could have a drink and survey the prospects even though I'm already sure the pickings are slim. Not that I'm in the market. Imagine fitting yet a third man into this jigsaw puzzle that has become my life. I yawn. You'd think with such uneventful nights I wouldn't be so tired. What I'd really like is a Leonard Woolf. "Virginia better today," Leonard would write in his diary, or "Worried about V's lack of sleep." Oh that somebody would be uxoriously worried about Katinka's lack of sleep.

The man in the boat shoes moves down to the end of the bar where the two blond girls are drinking the deli man's champagne. You're wasting your time, I want to say to him. And probably I am, too. I move away to find the maître d', who informs me that while things are being readied in the dining room, the party in question is having a drink at the corner of the long table behind the bar. It's not surprising I didn't see them since this end of the table is out of sight, tucked behind a wall, good for a discreet tête-à-tête, lousy for people watching. I never sit there myself. Being a writer I need a first-row center view of people, proximity and acoustics to hear their dialogue.

When they see me, Jake and Harriman break off their own dialogue and pop up like perfect jack-in-the-box gentlemen. This isn't easy since they are wedged behind table legs and have been sunk into a squishy Marimekko-pillowed banquette. Then ensues some complicated jostling. Both Harriman and Zenobia Slade have to step out into the main room to let me squeeze in beside Jake. "I'll just sit here," I say pointing to a bentwood chair.

"No, no," they chime.

When we are as cozy as four mismatched peas in our Marimekko pod—the handsome Slades, the short chipmunk-cheeked Jake, me in black wool and combat boots—Jake asks what I want to drink. He and the Slades have already been served. Jake holds a martini. Zenobia and Harriman are tippling goblets of wine.

"The house white," I say, indicating Zenobia's and Harriman's stemmed glasses.

"They're having Chardonnay," Jake explains.

"I like the house white. I always order it."

"Maybe it's time for a change," coaxes Jake in the gentle voice of a shrink.

My first instinct is to hold my ground. My second—how far I've come!—is to consider the possibility: perhaps it *is* time for a change.

The Chardonnay arrives with nary a pause between request and its delivery. Jake Barnes watches me sip it with such intensity I could be the *Times* restaurant reviewer on whose pronouncements depend whether he'll be slicing onions or slicing his throat. "It's fine," I say. "Marvelous, actually." The wine tastes fruity, cold velvet on the tongue, richer than what I'm used to. But I have a certain ambivalence about people who know what I want better than I know what I want. Especially when they turn out to be right. Maybe Jake's wife ran off with Harriet from the health club simply for the surprise. Or maybe she couldn't stand to be told anymore what to eat. Don't put your eggs all in one basket, I hear my mother say, don't put your mail all in one bag. Look Ma, I'm dating, I want to cry, all too aware of being jammed up against Jake Barnes' diminutive-seeming thigh.

I remember a blind date I once had with a tiny MIT student in an enormous cashmere coat. He bought me a dish of ice cream at Brigham's. "We're not leaving until you finish every bit of this," he'd commanded when I'd pleaded a curfew. Are arrogance and pomposity necessary components in the equation of insecure short men? To be honest, Jake's style is more suggestion than ultimatum. I shouldn't generalize. My father, not tall enough for even junior varsity basketball, never overcompensated by bossing my mother around or becoming a born-again gourmet. Besides, Jake isn't that short, I remind myself now. He's taller than I am even in my thick rubber soles. It's the comparison with Louie, those long and lovely and broken bones. I start to feel sorry for Jake whose wife did abandon him to a center entrance colonial. Perhaps if he had a significant other couched in his right-side living room, he might learn to love the reheated tuna noodle casserole (with the house white) served in his left-side dining room. "I don't know that much about wine," I say. "I'm afraid I'm a bit of a Philistine."

Jake Barnes smiles. "Stick with me, kid. We'll get your palate into shape."

If only it were a matter of palate. If you are what you eat, then I could be anything. I sip the delicious wine and think how easily I could get used to it. How easily I could slip beyond the house white.

Harriman brings up property values. Jake discusses real estate. Zenobia bemoans the lack of funding for the arts. I bemoan our local Chinese take-out, which is being renovated by Harvard and turned into an office for student affairs.

"As long as it's not for student-faculty affairs," says Harriman.

We all laugh, me included, though I don't think it's that funny and wonder if he's intended some reference to Seamus and me. I wouldn't put it beyond my mother to keep informing the world—particularly Arthur T. Haven and his relatives—how I snared the Harvard English department's teacher of the year. This, despite her horror at the M&M's and despite her concession that Seamus comes off better on paper than in the flesh. Look, I understand; the competition in the best-daughter sweepstakes is something fierce. In a brilliant tactical maneuver, I switch the topic to steamed dumplings. Jake Barnes waxes enthusiastic about the best Hunan scallops he has ever had until we are called into the dining room.

Our table rests on a small raised platform like a stage. Jake Barnes asks permission to pull out my chair, inviting my sympathy. This man is *burned*, I think, as I graciously accept. Trial by fire has made him question all preconceived notions and actions in male-female relationships. Unlike Seamus, he's capable of change.

And the first thing I'd change, I think, is all this endless talk about food. For me, the act of eating doesn't require foreplay. I remember a Japanese movie—a sellout at the Coolidge Corner—in which a courting couple sucked a raw egg from each other's mouth the way you tip a yoke from half shell to half shell to separate the white. Why the egg, I wondered, when simple tongues suffice. It's like embellishing a good sentence with a lot of unnecessary adjectives. "Did you ever see a movie called *Tampopo?*" I ask Jake now.

He slaps his fist against the table. "One of my all-time top ten." He leans closer. "When I'm really down in the dumps, I rent it from the video store. That egg scene never fails to cheer me up," he confides, his mouth practically within egg-sucking distance of mine.

I nod, deeming it not worth explaining that for major depressions I always choose *Singing in the Rain*. I push my hair from my face and manage to tilt my head away. I hope it's a subtle enough gesture for him not to notice he's invading my personal space. I remember reading about a study some Harvard professor did on how people in different cultures place their faces at varying distances from each other when they talk. He made precise measurements. Latins speak nose to nose, a position which makes colder-blooded species uncomfortable.

Jake's closeness makes me uncomfortable. He chews his lower lip. I think of Louie's lips, of Louie's teeth, of Louie's tongue. Sucking an egg yolk from Louie's mouth wouldn't be so terrible.

"Now that I think of it, I saw that movie, too. That scene was pretty gross," Harriman says.

We discuss the erotic qualities of food unerotically—milk baths, aphrodisiacs, a performance artist who paints herself in chocolate—the way you might suggest soaking an ankle in Epsom salts. Jake studies the menu. Moving on to the wine list he's headed for a doctorate. Tonight there's much more ado than at Biba. I suppose it's because the addition of Zenobia and Harriman multiplies everything by two, including the exponent for fussiness. I put my menu down. "Order for me. I place myself entirely in your hands."

Harriman excuses himself to wash his hands. The butter from a roll glistens on his index finger. Moisture from the wineglass anoints his thumb. "You could use a napkin, darling," Zenobia suggests, but he's already risen from his chair. From the way he's examining his hands, you'd think he was about to perform open heart surgery instead of cutting into a boeuf en daube. "Harriman is impeccable," sighs Zenobia in a tone filled either with admiration or rue. I'm not sure.

"It probably makes sense given what's going around," I console.

Jake looks up from the red-tasseled wine list. "What do you say, a Montrachet or a Meursault?"

"Either," Zenobia shrugs.

"You know, you're right. I'll order both."

Zenobia leans across the table. "My father tells me you've volunteered to pick them up at the airport. That's nice of you, Katinka."

"It's no big deal."

"For me it would be. I've got an incredible amount of work."

And I on the other hand have nothing to do but loll around in a bathrobe in backless mules, drinking wine out of half-gallon jugs, eating chocolate-covered cherries, reading Danielle Steele, watching soaps, a *New Yorker* reject, a Seamus O'Toole reject. "Well, writers' hours are more flexible," I grant.

"Not my kind of writer. I need to do research. I'm dependent on libraries, which are starting to cut back to banker's hours. And of course I teach full time."

And bake your own bread and spin straw into gold and raise a child and are building a telescope on your lunch break. "I'm teaching, too," I feel defensive enough to point out.

"You are?"

Jake Barnes beams. "Katinka's teaching at Harvard," he exclaims.

My mother couldn't have said it better. "A writing course," I admit modestly.

"Many's the time I've thought of taking up writing myself," Jake says.

"You have?" It's my turn for astonishment.

"Why not, I've lived an interesting life. It would make a good book. The story about my divorce alone . . ." His voice trails off. He looks as if dollar signs of big advances are dancing before his eyes. As if made-for-TV movies are flitting across his screen. "Maybe I should take your course."

Help, I plead. Louie's seat in Sever Hall hasn't even had a chance to gather dust. What is this with writers, turn over a rock, turn up a writer. Up from under a bucket of mail. Up from under a wine list. "I'm not sure that's a good idea," I begin.

"What do you mean?"

"To have somebody I know in my class, a friend . . ."

"I'd think it'd be a comfort."

I shake my head. "These things can get sticky." I try to think of an example and say, stupidly, the first thing that comes into my head: "I know from experience. I was a student of Seamus O'Toole."

"Some people would say that worked out fine since you married him," says Jake.

"My biggest mistake."

"Which doesn't mean all student-teacher relationships are doomed. Especially when, like us, they're more age-appropriate."

And class-appropriate, and Ivy League–appropriate, and mother-appropriate. But body-appropriate is another matter. "Have you written before?" I ask Jake.

"Only briefs. And my article, *Tenancy by the Entirety,* a copy of which," he pats his inside jacket pocket where there is something rolled up nearly the size of the Sunday *Times,* "I've brought you, Katinka. But I'm sure I could. Write, that is. Once I put my mind to something . . . I did get an A on my *Beowulf* paper my freshman year at Penn."

"Writing's hard," says Zenobia, my new best friend.

I nod. "Harder than it looks."

"Besides," Zenobia continues, "I would assume Katinka's course would be limited to undergraduates."

She's got me. "It's the Extension School," I have to confess.

"Oh, that," Zenobia says dismissively. "I taught there once before I finished my doctorate. A course on Mary Cassatt. My students were taxi drivers and hairdressers."

Impeccable Harriman arrives back to save me from submitting a defense. "You'd think in a restaurant like this," he says with a shudder, "the bathrooms would be kept up."

"Never mind, dear," Zenobia gives him a pat.

"That's Cambridge," I say. "The concession to the bohemian."

"The unsanitary, you mean," Harriman grunts.

But is cheered when the next course arrives with the accompanying stellar bottles of not-the-house wine.

Which involves another half hour of ohs and ahs and wonderful-meals-I-have-knowns. Also a comparison of the different kinds of noodles you can get in Japan—Zenobia delivered a paper there last year—versus those offered in Japanese restaurants along the Boston–Cambridge axis—a mere shadow of the real thing. During the salad course, served continental style after the entrée, Jake slips me his article "lest I forget and carry the damn thing home."

I fold it into my pocketbook. "I'll read it before bed."

"Breakfast would be better, with a lot of unadulterated caffeine." He smiles.

Harriman frowns. "Don't undercut yourself, Jake. It's first-rate stuff."

"For what it is." Jake turns to me. "Since my divorce, Zenobia and Harriman are on a mission to bolster my self-esteem. Nevertheless, *The Sun Also Rises* it ain't."

"That's a relief," I say. "Three Jake Barneses might seem a tad excessive."

He laughs. "So where's the reciprocity?" he asks.

"The what?"

"Copies of your own stories. You said you'd bring them for me."

"You're right. I forgot." Which is incredible since usually I'm as trigger-happy as a tourist just back from Alaska with his carouselful of slides. The vaguest *I'd like to see your stuff sometime* tends to bury a perfect stranger in an avalanche of my Xeroxes. Why did I forget to bring my stories to Jake Barnes?

"Never mind. I'll pop in and you can show them to me."

"The proverbial etchings," Harriman chuckles.

Very funny, I think, but don't say anything. Instead, I work on maintaining an expression of pure ingenuousness. One thing I'm sure of is that I didn't forget to bring the stories as a ploy to lead Jake Barnes down the wayward corridor into my apartment. "I can always mail them," I say.

"At the price of stamps these days?" exclaims Harriman in the same tone Seamus used to take me to task for splurging on ground round rather than chuck. "Serve the papers in person is my advice."

What is it with Harriman, I wonder, playing Miles Standish to Jake Barnes' sphinx-like John Alden. Am I witnessing male bonding, a fraternity with its own rituals? A prearranged scenario?

"Katinka and I will figure something out," says Jake.

"Darling," Zenobia says with a restraining hand on Harriman's elbow, "did you know that Katinka is teaching at the Harvard Extension School?"

"Where you taught, darling. I thought you hated it."

"I never really—"

"But you said the students were terrible."

"Now you tell me, when I was set to join the ranks," Jake says. "Before Katinka gave me the heave-ho," he adds pointedly.

This last I ignore. "They're actually fine," I say. "Many are regularly registered undergraduates."

"It's probably changed, Zenobia," Harriman says. "You taught there so long ago. You were just starting out."

I don't need to hear any more about what was for the baby Zenobia a stepping-stone and for the mature me a literary pinnacle. So I do one more exercise from Janet Graham's textbook of social graces—the flattery will get you anywhere pirouette. "Zenobia," I say, "my mother tells me you've won a wonderful prize."

Zenobia nods. Her marble cheekbones pinken.

"She certainly has," says Harriman, suddenly avuncular. "For her monograph on women painters of Dutch domestic interiors. They're flying us both out to Amsterdam."

"Is that the prize?" I ask. "The trip, I mean." I catch myself. I can't believe I'm asking that question, I who am always explaining that two copies and seeing one's story in print is payment enough. "Not that that isn't a wonderful award."

"The prize is the trip. Plus a dinner."

"Don't forget the medal," Harriman adds. "There's always a medal, or plaque, or statuette, or trophy. Like an Oscar for art history. Zenobia's got a shelfful of them."

I picture my own medals. Most improved conduct in third grade, second runner-up in the Voice of America Contest in seventh. If I had a husband like Harriman, he could describe the lamp of knowledge, slightly raised, nickel-plated on tin, that graphed the incline in my deportment. How wonderful to have someone boast of your accomplishments, allowing you to stay acceptably humble. Mothers, of course, do it all the time, but they're mothers and therefore not to be trusted. But to have a husband to blow your horn. Too many of the husbands I know are too threatened by the success of their significant others to extol their significant others' significance. Harriman is a man of more parts than just cleanliness.

And Seamus, with the soil of Ireland clotted under his nails, is a man of less. Seamus hogged the limelight, deflected any overspill onto himself. If someone dared to admire my writing, he'd explain how he taught me everything I knew. I think of Louie. Would Louie be as proud as Harriman? Who would he have to tell? Cheryl? Not likely. Chris Smith? Even in his less-incapacitated condition, one just circumcised would not be a person to whom Louie should be pointing out the merits of *Playgirl* magazine. And I'm sure Mr. and Mrs. Cappetti have no interest in the teacher from another class who taught their son's writing class. No, Louie, curtained inside his hospital bed, exiled on the middle floor of his triple-decker, cloaked in an anonymous blue uniform would find no audience for my résumé. But that's not true, I remember. I take it back. It's Louie after all who told Seamus about my story. It's Louie who's indirectly responsible for Seamus' choosing me, after three turn-downs, for the Harvard job.

By dessert, hazelnut cake and brewed espresso (Jake checks to make sure it's been decaffeinated by the Swiss water process) all around, I am full of fine feeling for my fellow man. I like how Harriman admires his wife, how Zenobia blushes at her medal shelf, how Jake Barnes has neither pressed Harriman's etching analogy to my stories or his thigh to mine. And thus when Zenobia suggests she wrap up some of the cake to take home to Max, I am given the opening I have been waiting for. "What are you doing with Max when you go to Amsterdam?" I ask.

"That's a problem," Zenobia says.

"It doesn't have to be," Harriman says.

"It's vacation week at Max's school. So the families of his friends are off to Aspen or St. Barts or Palm Beach. I've tried an agency. But

I haven't been that impressed with the care providers I've interviewed."

"Your standards are impossible, darling."

"And you, darling, have none. Max is at a vulnerable stage now. Even though the school has declared the experiment over, Max is so attached to Daniella he wants to keep her."

"Damn Daniella," Harriman exclaims, stirring his coffee so hard it splatters against the tablecloth. "It's got to stop. You coddle him, Zenobia."

Zenobia's cheeks are nearly crimson. Her eyes flash. "And you'd prefer to run your household like a boot camp."

"My father was from the old sink-or-swim school. It didn't hurt me. And even with *your* father as such a pushover, you still never had the need to lug around a sack of flour."

"I had a blanket."

"As did I. But let's face it, neither of us suffered from a Linus problem. I've never glimpsed that blanket in any of your baby pictures. And your father has shown me albumsful."

"I might have had other talismans."

"Like what?"

"I'll never tell."

"Now, now," says Jake Barnes in the measured judicial tone of one as expert at mediation as at tenancy by the entirety. "Time to resolve the problem at hand. If I may be so bold, why not start to wean Max from Daniella by using this vacation? Tell Max Daniella's taking a vacation, too."

"And leave Max without both his parents *and* Daniella? I'm surprised at you, Jake. You have no understanding at all."

"That's not fair, Zenobia. Just because I don't have children myself. Let me point out, I was a child." As is all too clear since Jake's voice is starting to sound like a six-year-old at the supermarket counter who's being denied a Hershey Bar.

Harriman turns to Zenobia. "Let me remind you that I, too, was a child."

Which is harder to believe since he looks as if he's stuffed his snowy white shirt forever.

"No kidding," Zenobia says.

"Darling . . ."

"Men," Zenobia declares with a dismissive wave.

"Men," I sigh, joined with Zenobia in sisterhood. I pause. "I know this isn't any of my business," I begin, "but why shouldn't Max keep Daniella for as long he needs her? I had a friend in college who arrived as a freshman wearing a locket that contained a pink postage-stamp-sized square of all that was left of her baby blanket. She was still wearing it when she finished medical school."

"That's the damnedest—"

"Harriman . . ." warns Zenobia. She turns to me. "I think that's a wonderful story."

"Which is all," I continue, "by way of my offering to take Max. *And* Daniella while you're both away. Provided, of course, that Max would like to stay with me."

"Why, Katinka," Zenobia exclaims.

"That's not such a bad idea," Harriman considers. "Your father would be right upstairs."

"You've just complained about Daddy's incompetence with children."

"Janet will be there, too."

This Zenobia chooses to ignore—whether out of loyalty to the late Mrs. Arthur T. Haven who brought her up so well or dislike of her usurper, I'm not sure. Then again, she could have a little sibling rivalry of her own or simply find the mention of Janet Graham irrelevant.

I press my case. "I'm completely smitten with Max. And since I work at home, it's no problem. The one night I teach, well, Max could go upstairs, or my mother could come down."

"Or I could come over and baby-sit," Jake Barnes offers. "I'd love to help."

"Whatever," I say.

Zenobia cocks her head, puts a finger to her chin like Aristotle contemplating the bust of Homer. "You know, this may work out."

"Of course it will," I sum up triumphantly.

Zenobia pauses, then begins to speak, choosing her words with the kind of delicacy people use when they're about to introduce the topics of money or sex, ". . . now I know that writing fiction is not remunerative, so this would be only under condition that you let me pay you . . ."

"Absolutely not," I insist, enjoying the privilege of being indignant. "Besides, lately my writing has been bringing in something larger than the usual modest check."

Is there new respect in her eyes, a dawning sense that the goodies have been parceled out more equally between potential siblings after all.

Between the time the check is brought and paid—Jake the real estate lawyer thinks the tip should be figured with tax included, Harriman the tax lawyer insists the tax should be subtracted; they compromise—the arrangements with Max have been settled. In a few days I am to have him for four days. "With Daniella," I say.

"With Daniella," Zenobia agrees.

We put on our coats and go outside. The air is clear, cold, but there's no wind. The ice is melting. The sidewalks are sludgy with puddles and hardened ridges of old snow. A crowd is letting out from the Loeb a block away. People are walking gingerly trying to avoid the murkiest pools. A Robert Wilson version of an Ibsen play has been running for two weeks and some of the theatergoers look as if they've been sprung from life imprisonment. "Everyone could hear you snoring," a woman complains to her companion.

Farther along Brattle Street, a musician twangs Bob Dylan from the doorway of Cardullo's shop. Near Church Street a parade of teenagers in studded leather and streaked hair are heading to the Harvard Square Theater for the midnight *Rocky Horror Picture Show.*

Zenobia and Harriman go to fetch their car from the lot under the Charles Hotel. Jake Barnes and I stand in companionable silence eavesdropping on Ibsen's bad reviews. When the last of the stragglers go by, I turn to him. "I really could walk home," I say, "it's a fine night."

"Not alone."

"I do it all the time. It's perfectly safe."

"I'll walk with you."

"That's ridiculous. How will you get to Lexington?"

"I'll take a cab."

"To Lexington?" I ask, sounding like Seamus O'Toole in one of his tightwad fits of incredulity.

"Then I'll take the T to Alewife, and find a cab from there." He pauses. "Or . . ." he says, eyebrows quizzical as question marks.

"Or?" I ask.

"Or I could spend the night." He's avoiding my face, concentrating on a puddle forming a skim of ice near the corner of my boot. But he must have eyes in the back of his head to register my astonishment because he adds quickly, "On the couch or in a sleeping bag."

I shake my head.

He looks sheepish. "Do you think I'm the kind of guy who expects to take a girl, woman—sorry—to bed on the second date?" Implying that I'm not the kind of girl—woman—to go to bed with a man on a second date. I should be flattered. I'm not. Instead, I think of Louie, of our first date, which we technically missed since we were so fully occupied in bed. I'm afraid I've turned into a slut, albeit a selective one.

And it's not that I don't like Jake Barnes either. He's sweet, the way he's breaking up pieces of ice with the toe of his shoe. The way he smiles so shyly at me. The way he tries to find a balance between Emily Post and Betty Friedan.

"Besides, you look tired, Katinka," he says now with Leonard Woolf solicitousness. "Warm milk, my article, and a good eight hours is what Dr. Barnes prescribes." He pauses. "Can I ask you one thing?"

"Go ahead."

"Is there someone else?"

"It's complicated," I say. "I mean there's someone, but I'm not sure how serious . . ."

He holds up his hand like a traffic cop. "You don't need to say anything more. So long as I'm a contender." He lowers his hand. It brushes against mine, then hangs there as if his glove and my mitten are clothespinned to overlap slightly on a line. I'm just about to ask him *contender for what?* when Harriman's car pulls up.

Not surprisingly, it's a silver gray Volvo the inside of which is as shiny and sanitary as Harriman's ideal restaurant bathroom ought to be. This is in contrast to every car I, through family membership or marriage, ever carried insurance for. These were always litter bins on wheels, filled with Coop receipts, grocery ticker tapes, candy bar wrappers, twigs, leaves, old Life Savers, old gum. If I ever needed spare change I'd only have to run my hand along the ripped and matted rug underneath the front seat to come up with a piggy bank's worth. Though Harriman's car lacks the coziness of bad housekeeping, it is a relief to know the back of your coat isn't going to have something embarrassing stuck to it when you step out to the curb.

Harriman pulls into Prescott Street and double-parks. I thank Zenobia and Harriman. They thank me. Zenobia says she'll call me about Max. That we'll all get together as soon as Arthur and Janet are home. Jake Barnes says he'll walk me to my door. Harriman says for us to take our time, he wants to warm up the heater, put on a tape, and besides the baby-sitter isn't expecting them for another hour.

"Jake will just be a minute," I say. "He'll just see me inside the door."

And just inside the door, I shake his hand. "Thank you for a wonderful dinner."

"I'm glad you enjoyed it."

"I did, especially the Chardonnay."

He laughs. "What about your stories?"

"Harriman's waiting. I'll mail them to you."

He takes out his business card on which he's already added his Lexington address. "I can hardly wait."

"Well," I say, "good night."

"Can we do this again?"

"Sure."

"I'm in Chicago next week. On business. Some meatpackers I represent. But I'll call you when I get back. And I mean it, about helping out with the baby-sitting." He leans over, then, and kisses me. It's not as bad as I feared, those lips. They're soft, maybe a little spongy, but resilient, like ripe honeydew. And he doesn't press his luck by any action with his tongue. He ends with a brisk smack which feels like correct punctuation. And though his lips aren't Louie's lips—and not, as in the Cole Porter song, such charming lips either—there is something about flesh on flesh, a general warmth, a holistic pleasantness. "See you soon," he says. "And don't forget the stories."

I don't forget the stories. I shut the door and go immediately to my desk. I fish my three best stories from the file drawer and put them into a manila envelope. I scribble Jake's address on the front. I lick a row of James Fenimore Cooper stamps—Louie's stamps—and stick them, lovingly, across the top.

9

Sunday night, and I'm on the way to the airport. Traffic stuffs the tunnel like the filling of a sausage. I should have anticipated it, should have left half an hour earlier. I picture my mother and Arthur standing by the curb in front of the American Airlines terminal, tanned, wrapped in the plumage of their tropical leisure wear, toting their cardboard containers of duty-free rum, luggage piled at their feet, eyes searching the spiraling airport lanes. "Maybe Katinka's been held up," my mother will say. "She's usually on time."

"Zenobia is always punctual," Arthur will state unsyllogistically.

My car idles in place. I roll up the windows to keep out everybody else's fumes. I turn off the radio. What was *All Things Considered* is now a crackle of static with the occasional recognizable word like an unfamiliar language with a familiar Latin root. Driving in on Broadway, I listened to a reporter discussing a starlet's as-told-to autobiography; how she smoked pot, had an affair with Frank Sinatra, tricked a tycoon into marrying her. This last item grabbed me. I turned up the volume. Cheryl never did that, I thought, segueing from the general to the specific. Cheryl had an abortion so Louie wouldn't have to marry her. Or so she wouldn't have to marry Louie. Though why wouldn't she want to marry Louie, I wonder now. These questions are rattling around inside my skull like a tune that won't go away. I would like to know Cheryl's reasons for saying no, what she knew that I don't know. Not that I am considering marrying Louie. Not that he would even ask. Perhaps she just didn't want to have the child. The child that Louie wanted. That Louie insists she wanted. I shake my head. My brain is as clogged as this tunnel. My gray cells have been fried by diesel fumes. There's no clear path for my thoughts to follow. Still, they keep coming, random and disordered. Frank Sinatra. Cheryl. Starlets. Tycoons.

I think of great flirts, their poses of devotion, their shining eyes, their tilting heads, the way they listen. But am I so innocent of such wiles? I ask myself, jarred by a chorus of honking that makes me feel as if I'm trapped inside a teenager's stereo. I remember my own beams of adoration as Seamus' student. He lectured at Sever Hall where I sat in the front row, my hair freshly washed, my thighs Band-Aided by my most tantalizing miniskirt. I groan at this picture of myself.

By the time I reached the entrance to the tunnel, the radio had switched from flights of fancy to the flight of political refugees. Shame set in. I was enjoying the frivolous revelations in a celebrity bio when I should have been agonizing over the serious devastation of the dispossessed. I am a shallow person. One who can put down a fellow woman when I myself have made no case for sisterhood.

If I can just say no to sisterhood, however, I am stuck with daughterhood. I could flee like the outcasts, but still not escape. My mother is not a land from which I can emigrate. Not that I'd really want to. But her absence has somewhat simplified my life. I'm content to be the daughter to a mother in Kingston, Jamaica, or Old Town, Maine. It's resuming the mantle of daughterhood in Cambridge, Mass., that frightens me. No wonder I've put it off.

But not for long since the lanes of cars are beginning to move. Progress is as sluggish as a humid summer's breeze. Still, the speedometer's crawling above zero, and I've already passed two of the yellow lights set a foot apart into the tunnel's white tiled walls. The honking has stopped. Seamus knows a way to the airport that avoids the tunnel altogether. It involves negotiating a maze of gas tanks and produce warehouses. You go past King Arthur's Motel where the outlines of voluptuous topless dancers are painted on its concrete blocks and where a police officer was killed in a notorious brawl. I'm always afraid of getting lost, having to stop there for directions, and being sold into topless dancerdom. "You're not well enough endowed," Seamus once snorted when I confessed my fears.

"You're just too cheap to pay the toll," I accused.

I pay the toll. The barrier goes up. And once released, it's clear sailing to the terminal. I find a parking place my first roll through the lot. There's time left on the meter. Nearly an hour. My luck holds. No sign of my mother and Arthur shivering on the curb. Inside American Airlines I check the timetable on the hanging computer screen. My mother's plane is twenty-five minutes late. I am just in time. As I hurry to arrivals, the first passengers are making their way from the gate.

I see Arthur and Janet before they see me. They are walking arm in arm, a handsome couple, tanned, fit. Arthur wears a blue blazer; my mother a dress printed with coconut palms. Over their shoulders are slung identical turquoise travel bags. Youthful, smiling, they could be an ad for Geritol.

"Katinka!" my mother exclaims. She manages to hook an elbow through mine without releasing her other arm from Arthur's brass-buttoned one. My hair gets caught in her eyeglasses as she kisses me.

When we are disentangled, Arthur pecks each cheek as if he were de Gaulle awarding me the Croix de Guerre. "Ah, Katinka," Arthur croons.

On the way to claim their baggage, Arthur and my mother tell me all about Jamaica, about their condo, the food, the other people they met, the comparative restlessness of the natives and tourists. They interrupt each other the way old married people do, the way my quiet father never did. But when Arthur says, "Katinka, we have something to tell you," my mother turns silent as my father, silent as a stone.

"What?" I ask, searching my mother's sealed lips, which are nevertheless turned up into a smile. I think I have a pretty good idea what I'm about to be told.

Which I never get to hear because a voice calls out "Katinka," and the three of us turn to face Jake Barnes.

"What do you know!" he exclaims. He's holding a briefcase and a leather carry-on and is wearing a Burberry raincoat with its matching plaid scarf. The way the scarf is draped makes him look like he has no neck. I am less sad to see him than I am to see the scarf. I don't like the obvious status symbols, the Gucci G's, the Chanel C's, the polo player embroidered onto Ralph Lauren shirts. My mother doesn't either though she is more willing to flaunt them when they're bargains at half the price. When I steal a glance at her she is looking happily expectant with no judgment on her face.

And though my mind is jumping hoops, my tongue can only stammer stupidly, "What are you doing here?"

"I'm on my way to Chicago. I told you, remember, about my business trip."

"Of course. I forgot."

"It's okay. I'm sure you've got more important things to think about." He looks over my shoulder, he shifts his luggage and holds out his hand. "And you must be Katinka's mother, there's no mistaking the genes. I'm Jacob Barnes."

My mother extends her own tanned hand, which lies in his like a nut brown egg in a pudgy white nest.

"I'm sorry," I say, "I'm such a clod." I make proper introductions. Miss Manners would be proud.

Jake Barnes pumps my mother's hand, then Arthur's. He is smiling broadly. "Professor Haven," he says, "besides your work, which I studied in a philosophy survey course at Penn, we have another connection. Harriman is one of my best friends."

"Jacob Barnes," Arthur muses. He rolls the name on his tongue as if he is tasting something from a new food group. Fortunately, perhaps because he's a philosopher, he doesn't segue to Jake and make the connection we lit majors jump upon.

"Harriman and I went to the Law School together," Jake continues, "and Katinka and I—"

"What a small world," I break in, "just the other day—"

But my mother will have none of it. She's fairly beaming. Her earrings are bobbing with delight; the palm leaves on her dress are rustling with her excited breaths. No diversionary anecdotes about small-world-dom for her. "So," she zooms, "you're the friend Zenobia and Harriman arranged for Katinka to meet."

"The very one. We've already had two dates."

From the way she looks, I know she's about to say something incriminating, something about china patterns, something about how nicely a Burberry can accessorize a wedding dress. "When's your plane, Jake?" I ask. About to take off, I pray.

He checks his watch. "About to take off. I'd better hustle to the gate." He bids a charming good-bye to my mother and Arthur, adding pointedly that he's sure he'll be seeing a lot more of them. Delight cloaks my mother like another layer of tan. Then, in front of them, he kisses me half on my upper lip, half on the tip of my nose. I nearly rattle with the aftershocks of my mother's tremor of glee. I blot my nose with the back of my hand as blatant as a child wiping away a grandparent's sloppy smack. But neither Jake nor my mother seem to notice this. "I'll call you next week," he says, "the minute I get back."

I watch him run to catch his plane. His legs splay out from the sides. His briefcase flaps against his coat. He moves like those boys I knew in Old Town who joined the chess club rather than the baseball team.

"Well," Arthur says.

"So," my mother says.

I don't say anything, just shrug.

"A student of philosophy," Arthur says.

"Economics. Philosophy was probably required for the degree." I am in a deflating mode.

My mother is not to be deflated. "What an attractive man," she sighs.

Little does she realize that what she says is the kiss of death. My mother studied psychology. Shouldn't she know that the more a mother likes someone the less the daughter thinks of him. "Come on," I say, "a hunk he is not."

"Not technically," she grants, "but he's got his charms. In the way of intelligent, well-educated, powerful men."

"Powerful?"

"Like Henry Kissinger. No beauty, and yet he was always surrounded by movie stars."

"Mother!"

But she is dauntless. "Take Woody Allen, for instance. Hardly a heartthrob. But he grows on you. If he came up to me right now in this airport, I'd probably fall at his feet."

"I should certainly hope not, Janet," chuckles Arthur. "Especially after what we've read about him."

"I'm speaking figuratively, of course. Besides, with you, I've got intelligence, education, power, and devastatingly sexy good looks." My mother awards Arthur some rays of adoration.

Perhaps flirting's a genetic defect handed down through my mother's DNA, dooming me to emulate that which I most detest. I resolve to fight in the face of heredity. After all, I did get over my thralldom to Seamus. I'm not about to regress by some theatrical swooning over Jake Barnes. I picture Jake's awkward gaited run, the flapping hem of his Burberry. No Ivy League education, no Henry Kissinger power, real or imagined, will turn him into a gazelle. With him I can resist playing Janet Graham. As for Louie . . .

"As for Jake Barnes?" my mother asks now.

"Yes?"

"Has he been married?"

"Divorced."

"Children?"

"None."

"Does he want them?"

"Yes."

"Remember all the trouble I had having you. A woman's biological clock . . ."

"If he has children, I doubt they'll be mine."

"You never know."

"Mother!"

"They say love is better the second time around."

This is a concept I don't even want to begin to contemplate. Is my mother just spouting the cliché without considering the text? Or does she really believe this. And if so, what does this say about my parents' marriage, about my childhood on a set of *Father Knows Best?* Does it boil down to numbers? Does a second love, and its accompanying switch from twin beds to a king-sized one cause passion to increase exponentially? This is a problem Arthur could probably reduce to its logical components. Draw me a diagram that I could see.

I don't want to see. I choose selective blindness. I select the appropriate cliché—ignorance is bliss, a little knowledge is a dangerous thing, while discarding—in my mother's case—love is better the second time around. I know it's fashionable these days, enlightened even, for mothers and daughters to trade intimacies. But I don't want to know what she and my father did, what she and Arthur do. I don't want to know if she loves Arthur more, loved my father less. When I was little, I balked at mother-daughter dresses. Grown up, I rebel against matching sexual obsessions, too. What am I afraid of? That my mother lusts for Arthur the way I do for Louie? That she holds particular parts of Arthur's body particularly dear?

We take the escalator down to the baggage carousel. The luggage hasn't been unloaded yet so we watch the empty rubber track spin round. A toddler with a head of red curls sticks a green plastic dinosaur onto the carousel and runs furiously to get it before it disappears through the rubber-curtained slot. This he does over and over again, laughing with such delight that all the harried airline passengers are beaming like grandparents. I am standing at the widest curve where the toy finally tumbles off the edge. I pick it up. It's not exactly a dinosaur, I see. I hand it to him. Freckles circle his eyes and nose like goggles. "What is this?" I ask.

He looks at me astonished. His mouth drops open as if I'm an alien from outer space. "Mutant Ninja Turtle, dummy," he says.

I think of children, of my mother's miscarriages, of my biological clock. Of the child Jake wants, of the turkey baster one his wife's got, of the one Louie didn't get, of Max. Suddenly, I realize that more than a book, more than a job, more than a man, I want a child. And the minute I think this, I wonder if it's true.

I am saved from further agonizing by the arrival of the luggage. First comes a guitar in a hard case stickered with decals from Southern land grant colleges. Followed immediately by my mother's and Arthur's suitcases leaning against each other as if one demanded the other to prop it up.

We hurry to the parking lot, into my car, and out of the airport where the traffic lanes seem to part like the Red Sea to ease and hasten my mother's arrival back into my life. The tunnel is nearly empty. We glide through it. And just when the opening comes into view, Arthur clears his throat. He taps me on the shoulder, from the back seat. My mother is sitting up front with me though I suggested they both might like to sit together in the back. "And let you feel like a chauffeur," my mother had protested.

"But you'll be separated."

"Only temporary," she grinned.

"Yes," I say now in answer to Arthur's tap. I adjust my rearview mirror so I can see him. He's leaning forward. His expression is serious, professorial. "Katinka," he begins.

"Yes?" I encourage.

"Before, at the airport, your mother and I said we had something to tell you."

I brace myself against the steering wheel.

"Well, I have asked for your dear mother's hand in marriage. And she has graciously accepted."

"How wonderful," I exclaim. "Though I'm not surprised."

"Then we have your blessing?" Arthur asks.

"Absolutely. I couldn't be happier." And I am. My mother has a lovely man, a man to share her life, her bed, to share, if not cure, her seasonal affective disorder. Age-appropriate, education-appropriate. Geographically inappropriate. But you can't have everything. "When's the wedding?" I ask.

"Not soon enough," Arthur says.

"Arthur's getting tired of living in sin," my mother confesses, giving me a little we-girls-together poke.

"That's not it at all, my dear. I mean to make an honest woman of you." His eyes find mine in the rearview mirror. "We thought in the spring. May."

My mother sighs. "There's so much to do. Buy a dress. Arrange the food. Sell the house."

I start. "Sell the house?"

"Of course, dear. We're certainly not going to live there."

"But don't you want to keep it. For vacations and stuff?"

"Katinka, Old Town's not exactly on the coast."

"I know that. I just thought . . ."

I get through the end of the tunnel, pay the toll, maneuver on and off the Central Artery. When I stop at a traffic light, I turn to look at my mother. She is studying me, her face brimming with such sympathy and understanding that it's a relief to turn back to the disinterested and predictable pattern of green arrows and yellow walk signs. My mother leans over the front seat. "It is her childhood home," she confides to Arthur.

"Totally understandable," he stage-whispers back.

"Even at her age, it's an adjustment. She never did like change."

"Stop it," I nearly yell. "Don't talk about me as if I'm not here. Don't talk about me as if I'm chapter one's test case in Introduction to Psychology."

"It's perfectly natural to feel this way, Katinka," soothes my mother the shrink.

"When Zenobia was four," Arthur adds, "we told her we were moving to a big house with a yard and trees and where she could have a dog and her own enormous room. She refused to budge; she preferred what was a converted pantry with no windows and only room for her bed." He nods at my mother. She nods back. Freud and Jung in consultation, diagnostically in accord.

"That's not the case," I say. But of course it is. I think of my room, its pink-painted walls, the pale blue trim, the sprigged quilt and the matching one my grandmother made for my doll's bed. I think of the posters—horses, kittens, acrobats, ballet dancers, teen heartthrobs, black-clad poets with cigarettes hanging from their scowling lips, politicians who lost—that charted the seven stages of my obsessions. Next to the garage lies buried my first pet, Carlyle the hermit crab. Inside its doors I received my first kiss. There's the scrape on the gate the day I got my driver's license. The porch swing on which I'd daydream about getting out of there.

Right now, of course, all I want is to go back. Back where mothers occupy their rightful place, where there is no seasonal affective disorder, where stories don't get rejected, where the only choices to be made are between strawberry and chocolate chip.

"Katinka," my mother says, now giving me a brimful oh-how-I-understand look, "would you mind terribly?"

"Of course not," I lie.

10

Milly's house sits on a hill of large Victorians two blocks from Mass Ave. In summer, with the windows open, you can make out the stop and start of traffic, hear horns honking, impatient to turn onto Linnaean Street. In February, though, you can feel like you're sheltered in a kind of Kennedy compound smack dab in the middle of the city. In times of crisis it's a refuge.

It's nine in the morning and I need a refuge. I'm sitting at Milly's notorious kitchen table crying into my beer, or rather, my reheated coffee though if I asked for beer Milly would immediately supply it. Milly is my oldest Cambridge friend. We met the first day of freshman week, each lugging a box of dilapidated stuffed animals up the dormitory stairs to our adjoining rooms. As Milly and I talked in the corridor, both our mothers had been dramatically cheerful, snapping our new sheets onto the plastic-encased mattresses, folding precise hospital corners, smoothing our Coop-bought Indian bedspreads. Pretending that going away to college was as ordinary as a Friday night sleepover. Pretending that these beds would be aired and fluffed and made in a daily adherence to their fine example.

Milly's mother had a kind face and no-nonsense hair tucked into a bun. Farmhouse wife, I thought, noting her wide comforting lap. Immediately I colored in kittens chasing the balls of yarn from her knitting basket while fruit boiled away in copper pots for the preserves she put up. I was shocked to learn she was from New York, lived in a stately apartment on the Upper East Side, and owned two neurotic Afghan hounds with rhinestone collars named Nick and Nora.

My own mother at that time had an Upper East Side cap of black curls courtesy of Maine Cut at Old Town's newest mall. Her earrings swept her shoulders. "That's a tough act to follow," Milly had said, nodding at my mother from the doorway. My mother had hitched up her skirt and was daubing at a run in her pantyhose from the bottle of clear nail polish she kept in her purse.

Later someone on our floor said she saw both of our mothers getting smashed at Nick's Beef and Beer after they left us. But Milly and I are sure that's just apocryphal.

"So Janet's getting married," Milly says now. "I'm not surprised. I'm only surprised it took this long."

"Oh God," I groan. I turn my head and look out Milly's window. Though the houses on her street are huge, the lots are small. Milly's kitchen looks into the glass-bricked window of her neighbor's shower stall. This is a recent renovation and Milly has just realized that when his light's on and hers is off, she can see his outline as he takes his nightly shower. When Charlie was on a business trip last week, she invited me over to watch. "It's really neat," she'd said, "like ultrasound."

"I'm not that desperate *yet.*"

Her neighbor's a trim man who teaches at the Business School. "What do you think he'd say if he knew I knew he used soap on a rope?" Milly wondered. Milly was surprised he wasn't more careful in his choice of architect.

"Maybe he did it deliberately to tantalize you," I said.

"Yeah, right," she sighed.

"It'll be all right," she says now.

"I'm happy for her, really, but damn, she gets a second good relationship."

"And you didn't even have a first. That's what's bothering you?" Milly asks.

"Yes. No. I don't know. Between Seamus and Louie, it's not exactly as if I'd been celibate. Remember the computer programmer with bad eyes. That reporter who criticized everything I wrote. The orthopedic surgeon—Dick Breakers—what a name!—who already had a wife."

"The pits. Whenever I get sick of Charlie I say Dick Breakers to myself. It's better than Lourdes."

I look out the window again. A squirrel is crawling on the ledge above the glass bricks. For all that I'm miserable about my mother and Arthur living upstairs, it could be worse. Imagine looking out my window and into their shower. I picture them together inside Arthur's shower curtain—clear, bordered with a Greek key—lovingly soaping each other's back. Better to imagine than to know.

That's true about Louie, too. Better to imagine than to know. I can speculate on his past, his life with Cheryl, his secrets, what he feels for me. I prefer to make up my own stories—they have a plausibility that real life lacks. I like tying up all the ends into a tidy little plot. I think of Louie's own little tidy plot. As a piece of writing not good. Not exactly bad. As a story not interesting. As autobiography, however, utterly fascinating. Louie submitted his story as fiction, I remind myself. Even though I tell my students, as I have been told, write what you know. What do I know about Louie? What does Louie know? What is he telling? If I'd gone to Yale instead of Harvard I might have been better trained to deconstruct the text. But saved by Cambridge's icy sidewalks, I'm not going to have to pull apart Louie's story to figure out the truth, not in class anyway. He's going to be in the hospital another few days, then pretty much immobilized. I called the registrar's office to get him his money back. "Because it's a medical emergency he'll receive a full refund," some functionary informed me in a snitty tone.

"You better notify buildings and grounds," I warned. "If something happens on one of your paths, it won't just be a tuition refund you'll have to worry about."

"How's Louie?" Milly asks me now.

"Surrounded by his loved ones. Which may or may not include me. I'm not sure how it's going to work with my mother and Arthur back and Louie both motion-impaired and not easy to hide. A cast does draw attention to itself."

"Then don't hide him. You're a grown woman, dammit, who's been married and divorced. Who can make her own choices." Milly hits the table for emphasis, causing a wave of coffee to splash over the rim of her mug.

"And you'd tell my mother that?"

"Janet? Not on your life."

The squirrel has moved up under the eaves. On Milly's windowsill, ivy plants fail to thrive. There's a rusty lunchbox on the counter and a wicker laundry basket overflowing with a tangle of darks and lights. There are squirrels in Milly's walls—I can hear them scurrying—carpenter ants in the basement. In the attic silverfish are turning the pages of Milly's and Charlie's old Norton anthologies into lace doilies. And yet I know that up in Milly's study where she does her meticulous illustrations for medical texts, the pencils lie precise and sharpened on her desk, whose surface is as smooth and free of dust as those beds our mothers made for us so many years ago.

Milly shakes her head. "You know how fond I am of Janet. Even though, when I count my blessings, one of them is that she's your mother and not mine. But isn't it high time to stop worrying about her?"

"Of course. If only." I pause. "Milly, do you think Louie is my rebellion? My way of getting back at my mother?"

"Seamus was."

"Seamus was my mother's dream. All those degrees. His reputation, though granted overblown. Still . . ."

"He was so much older."

"We didn't think that then. Distinguished, we thought. Worldly."
Milly laughs. "Experienced. Long-tenured in the art of sex."

"Back then I thought that age equaled experience equaled skill."

"In *teaching?*"

"That, too."

"Seamus was a good teacher," Milly admits. "I was so jealous," she adds. "You had this Joyce professor at your feet. And I had Wallace Ross—remember?— the Alfred E. Neuman look-alike. He used to make these elaborate weekly study plans, and every other week he'd pencil my name in for a twenty-minute coffee date." She sighs. "Remember Irish Poets? A lecture hall of three hundred and Seamus was reciting just to you. Wallace was a chem major. He was always obsessively studying the periodic tables. I'd have to quiz him. Then I'd think of Seamus and all that poetry. I'd be pining for Yeats and getting some dry formula. I was green with envy."

"Seamus was a talker. That Irish gift of gab."

"Is Louie a talker?"

"He talks. He walks. He even sort of writes. He's better quiet, though."

"Charlie's quiet. Quiet is nice."

"I don't know Louie's quiet. What's behind it yet. Whether there's even anything there. He's sensitive. He's earnest. He's wonderful in bed. How did he get so wonderful? Natural talent, like being born with perfect pitch? Or years of practice on all different sorts of instruments? If I start obsessing about that I can make myself crazy. But I like him. Maybe I love him. But why? Because he's so different from Seamus? Because my mother wouldn't approve? And since I fulfilled all her dreams as a teenager, at thirty-one I need to rebel? Because he's a diamond in the rough, because he's a kindred soul, because he's a writer in the making, or just right for making, because he's a projection of my wildest Lady Chatterley fantasies, because I'm blinded by desperation or brilliantly clear-sighted." I shake my head. "Then there's Jake. Jake Barnes, yet!" My own coffee slurps into a puddle across from Milly's, two brown islands on a curled Formica sea.

"You don't have to decide anything, Katinka. Not now," Milly says. "Why not just enjoy being courted by two men?"

"If we were back in college I could. In the good old days we used to see four different men on four different nights. But now, dating's a form of serial monogamy. You live in a mini-marriage with someone until you break up with him. Then you hitch up with someone else. God, I know sixteen-year-olds making supper for their boyfriends every night. These days two dates make you a bigamist."

"You're right," Milly agrees. "My kids tell me that by fourth grade you've got to go steady for the sake of your social life."

I look at the lunch box on Milly's counter. Behind the kitchen door hangs the blue-striped apron Charlie wears for his July Fourth barbecue. The glass on Milly's windows is wavy and bubbled with age. Generations of feet have scooped out the wooden treads on the back hall stairs. Generations of squirrel families have skidded through these walls. Milly's house, her world is something solid, permanent with deep-seated roots. I have no roots. My childhood home is being sold out from under me. My mother, though still my mother, is becoming somebody else's wife. There must be a loss with every gain. When the equation changes, everything changes. There's a difference between somebody's blue apron hanging on the back of your door and somebody's blue uniform tossed at the foot of your bed. "Oh, Milly," I sigh, rubbing an edge of chipped Formica, "it's you I'm jealous of."

I must be looking so miserable that Milly takes my hand. "Let's go to the movies," she insists. "We can hit the early show and get the early bird discount."

"How about *Singing in the Rain*? *Tampopo*? We could rent a video?"

"Come on," Milly commands.

We ride the T from Porter to Harvard Square. We walk over to Church Street where, when I survey the titles of movies on the marquee, I nearly fall into a snowbank out of shock. Three out of the four have *love* in the title and one is *Italian*. I feel so suddenly feeble that I'm convinced that they're giving me the senior citizen discount instead of the early bird one.

"Get ahold of yourself, Katinka," Milly orders in the no-nonsense voice of a mother of two. "Buck up. This will be good for you."

"Like cod liver oil," I whine, slipping from old age back to infancy.

"Nonsense." Milly is dismissive. But she really must be worried since she's buying popcorn and Raisinettes, large Cokes, and—oh dear!—two Milky Ways—and all before lunch.

We see the French movie: a love triangle with English subtitles and tragic overtones. Needless to say I identify. I overidentify. I weep from the first frame to the last. Milly pats my hand obsessively. "There, there," she whispers.

I leave Milly with hugs and protestations of gratitude. "Are you sure you're okay?" she asks.

I nod.

"Just live in the moment, Katinka," Milly says.

"As if we ever could."

The theater is halfway between my apartment and Mt. Auburn. I should go home. One quarter of a new story awaits in my hard disk, students' stories are piled on my desk. Upstairs in Arthur's apartment freshly ground French roast is probably just being spooned into the top of the Melior. "Come up for coffee," my mother had said, "and we'll make wedding plans." That they're her plans and not mine doesn't seem to her the least bit out of the natural order of things. But I guess I'm in a morbid frame of mind. I choose the lame, the halt, the sick over the robust bride and head toward the hospital.

• • •

At the nurses' station there's the usual shelf of African violets in little terra-cotta pots. These look healthy, healthier than many of the patients on the floor. Either they've replaced the old plants or taken on staff with greener thumbs.

"I think he's stepped out," says the nurse, pointing to Louie's room.

"Stepped?" I ask.

She giggles. Her hat, a little white sail secured with one hair clip, billows. "On crutches. The PT's been with him since breakfast. He's about ready for the marathon."

"I'll wait in his room," I say, "if that's all right."

"No problem. Chris Smith was discharged last week. Maybe you already know that. The bed's not been filled yet." She giggles again. "You should have seen him walk out of here. What some people will do for love."

"Ain't that the truth," I say, though I have no idea what the truth is or what I have done for love or what I will do. I do know what I've done for lust, however, and what I am doing right now to avoid other people's love. I go into Louie's room. Chris Smith's side has been stripped of all signs of him. The bed is freshly made, the night table Lysoled. A carafe and cup wear their sanitized paper shields. On the bulletin board opposite his bed, though, a photograph of his fiancée, Judy, is still tacked up. She's smiling through a mouthful of rickrack teeth. So this is the face that launched the circumcision. Why did Chris forget her picture? Perhaps he has so many photographs of Judy there's one to spare, and he's left it to the hospital the way other philanthropists endow a wing.

Puzzling about this, I turn to Louie's bulletin board, which is bannered with get-well cards—my own included—and photographs all overlapping like the squares in a crazy quilt. Except for checking that my own offering was given pride of place, I haven't paid much attention to any of these. Now I study them. There's a huge card, a five dollar one, from the post office, with about twenty signatures inside. A flowered one—for those who care to send the very best—from whom I assume is Cheryl signed love—*love!*—C. Children's drawings both primitively Crayolaed and computer-generated. There are photographs of Sal and Rosalie. Of Diane. Of lots of kids. The seven dwarfs I suppose in all sorts of combinations. Kids on slides, around birthday cakes, at soccer practice, at barbecues, at a battered-looking swing set. Bunches of kids who pretty much look like they're on the track to growing into a Louie or a Louise.

I go out in the hall where the nurse with the bobbing cap is waltzing an IV along the corridor. "I've just spotted Mr. Cappetti," she says to me. "He's having one of his nice little visits with Professor O'Toole."

"Professor O'Toole?"

"They've become the best of friends."

"I see." I really do see. Not that "friends" is quite the word, implying equals, involving give and take. Seamus likes disciples, acolytes, people sitting at his sandaled feet. Look at me, look at Georgette, look at the M&M's. These acolytes tend to be of the female persuasion, but hell, we're all getting older and have to take idolatry from any quarter we can. I think of the front row of rapt undergraduates in Seamus' lectures, I think of my own students not exactly rapt although one or two are coming round, of Louie startled and stunned at our one and only class. I think of Jake Barnes across the table from me, his chipmunk cheeks, his apologetic smile. It's only my mother and Arthur whose admiration society is mutual. Except for well-established couples, everybody else is pretty much mentor and mentee.

A notion I'm not disabused of when I walk clear across the corridor to the other side of the hospital and peek into Seamus' room. Seamus is lying on a bed which has been raised so high that he looks levitated. Louie is sitting literally at his feet, on a small bench at the end of Seamus' bed even though there is a more comfortable empty chair drawn closer to the head. But I decide not to take this as some kind of proof since Louie is resting his cast on one of the bars of the footboard. Maybe this position of nonpower is better for a broken leg. The corner-office top-floor view isn't all it's cracked up to be when you've got a handicap.

Seamus is gesturing in his most professorial manner and Louie is nodding his head like the biggest brownnose in a lecture hall. I tiptoe away and go home.

I've been discharged," Seamus telephones me, jubilant. "Though it will be a couple of weeks before I can put on my dancing shoes. I'm in my own bed even as we speak. You should see the little love nest Georgette has made for me," he crows, "a mountain of pillows for my back, a bed tray of delectables, a carafe for potables, a stack of books to feed the mind, flowers everywhere for the eye, and, of course, Georgette."

Whose job I do not envy. I know what Seamus is like when he's sick—the operatic moaning and groaning, the obsessive taking of his temperature, the demands for plumped pillows and smoothed sheets. Even a Stately Home's worth of servants wouldn't be enough to supply the chicken soup and Kleenex boxes and TLC in dosages adequate for Seamus' needs.

"I'm glad you're home, Seamus," I say. I can afford to be generous. I don't have to nurse him. And I can now visit Louie without fear that Louie is down the hall visiting him.

"I knew you'd be glad for me. The brownies and your note were

167

thoughtful, Katinka, a nice touch. I expected a visit though. Louie told me you'd been to see him. I must say I find it rather odd you'd visit your mailman and not drop in on your ex."

"He's not just my mailman."

"Well! Aren't you full of surprises!"

"Not that, Seamus. You always had a dirty mind. My student. At least he was until he broke his leg and had to drop out."

"Let me remind you he was my student until I hurt my back. It was my class after all in which he'd enrolled." He pauses to let that remark sink in. "Well, I'm sure there's a lot you can teach him, my dear. Too bad you won't get the chance."

I am about to say you only wish but hold my tongue. I am above competing with Seamus for students. The ones who expected Seamus and flaunted their disappointment at me I dismiss as sexist and ignorant. I do realize, though, I am not above competing with Seamus for Louie. For his mind. His body is my undisputed property, his broken bones only temporarily being attended to by Mt. Auburn Hospital. "So why did you call?" I ask.

"Other than to announce the good news of my homecoming? To find out about your class, my class. Am I sorely missed?"

"Sorely. Though I am developing my own following."

"Nature does abhor a vacuum." Seamus coughs. "No other students breaking their bones to get out of class?"

"Seamus!"

"Just kidding. Still, they say there is no such thing as an accident. Nobody else trying to get their money back?"

"No," I lie, "even though you are irreplaceable."

"No one's irreplaceable. Not even me. That's what I told Louie as we were being discharged. He's so worried about his route."

"Louie's been discharged?" Though shock clutches my throat I manage to ask this with the same casualness I'd employ seeking out the price of a can of tunafish.

"We were rolled out in wheelchairs side by side. Two cute little nurse's aides in candy stripes."

168

"How did he get home?"

"A blond with an enormous chest whom he introduced as an old friend. Not bad at all. With a little more attention she could be quite the stunner. Youngish. About the age of Georgette. She was there with a rather depressing-looking minivan. They very kindly offered me a ride but Georgette with her usual foresight had arranged a cab with a Charles Atlas driver to help me in and out. And here she is now, little Florence Nightingale, with the most delicious-looking bowl of chicken soup . . . and, aha, a bottle of my favorite single malt . ."

"I'll say good-bye, Seamus."

"For now, Katinka, but keep in touch."

I hang up the phone, furious. The way I often am after one of these exchanges with Seamus. But it's not Seamus I'm furious at. How come Louie hasn't let me know he's been discharged? I saw him yesterday. A quick grope before his sister arrived. Enough time between "Oh Katinkas" for important information to be relayed. And there's always the telephone. Lately I seem to be talking more with Seamus on the telephone than we ever did in person when we shared a bed. Why didn't Louie call? I could have arranged a taxi and a Charles Atlas driver just as well as Georgette. I picture Georgette and me both standing next to yellow cabs. I picture two candy stripers—as cute as Seamus' M&M's—slide the hospital's double doors open on a pair of wheelchairs that straddle the sidewalk like those strollers you see for twins. It's a classic tableau, two devoted women waiting devotedly for their two wounded men. But of course something is wrong with this picture: Cheryl, the potential stunner, and her minivan.

I am, I must admit, not totally an innocent party. If Louie's off with Cheryl in her minivan, I'll be off with Jake Barnes in his center entrance colonial. He's cooking me dinner tonight. When he called, I didn't hesitate to accept, surprising myself. My instincts must be right because the timing has turned out to be perfect. Two minutes after Jake's invitation my mother dropped down to ask me to dinner.

It was a relief not only to say that I was otherwise engaged but also to tell with whom. "That nice man we met at the airport, the one who went to Penn?" said she, zeroing in with sharpshooter accuracy, "and then to The Law School with Harriman?" Typically she was happier that I was eating out with Jake than eating in with her and Arthur. The pleasure of my company was expendable for her pleasure in my social life. Would I rather be spending the evening with Louie? Probably. But it wasn't an option when he was in the hospital. I'm not sure it's an option now that he's out. Given all the churnings and odd pairings of the people in my life, I'm rather looking forward to driving out to Lexington.

Or am I? Do I have the energy? All at once I'm so tired I wish I could climb into bed. I wish I had someone to plump the pillows and bring me chicken soup. A bottle of Laphroaig on a silver tray. Who? Not Georgette, though Louie and Jake Barnes come to mind. I consider them both, their levels of devotion, their latent nursing skills. Jake would be earnest and a little bumbling, might spill the soup or drop the spoon. Louie would carry it just fine—he's good at carrying—but then he'd get into bed and the soup would get cold. Sex but no sustenance. Still I must admit that for some people, sex can be sustenance. But right now Louie's not available for sex or heavy lifting or the light lifting of a bowl of soup. And at this moment it's not sex that I long for or even men. It's my mother. A primitive need that surprises me since I have just been congratulating myself for avoiding breaking bread with her. I want my mother.

The minute I think this I realize I have totally regressed. It's my old mother I want back. My mother as mother. Not my mother reincarnated as sexpot, my mother as Ivy League coed or co-dependent, my mother as fiancée of Arthur T. Haven. I want my mother in the apron she never wore in the house that's about to be sold out from under me. I think back to my childhood. The time I had chicken pox. The time I had my tonsils out. The TV was moved into my room. And the radio. I had a new deluxe box of crayons and coloring books. Things to read, delicious foods to eat. My mother made me eggnogs and ginger ale floats. Dinner came on a wicker breakfast tray with a place for real flowers in a little vase and a side pocket which would have rolled up in it a usually forbidden comic book.

I remember the sense of having my mother all to myself. Such domestic bliss. The kitchen sounds. The telephone. The vacuum. The cooking smells. The old brass school bell on the night table next to me and the instant gratification of my mother's footsteps on the stairs the moment I picked it up. I want my mother encased for eternity in Old Town like a bug in an amber bead. Not my mother in a love nest three floors above me on Prescott Street. I sigh. It is all I can do not to suck my thumb. Does the threat to sell your childhood home make you a child?

I want a mother. I want to be a mother. I think of Max. Of how well he takes care of Daniella. In three days he's coming to stay with me for the four days his parents are in Amsterdam. I can try out my parenting skills.

But right now I need to try out my editorial skills. I go to the pile of manuscripts on my desk. Russell MacQuillen, Junior's, is on the top. It's a story about a hacker who intends to sabotage the computer system of the CIA. I hack through it with my red pencil slashing at the dense language, planting the margins with my own thicket of red-scrawled criticisms. It's almost lunchtime when I have reached the end if not the point. I'm too dispirited to tackle Rebecca Luscombe's story entitled "She's in Her Heaven" and illuminated with far too many exclamation marks.

I am taking inventory of the disappointing contents of my refrigerator when the telephone rings. "Not Seamus," I say.

"It's Louie," he says when I pick up the phone.

"I understand you've been discharged," I announce in a noncommittal nonjudgmental voice.

"How did you find out?"

"Seamus."

"I meant to tell you myself. But then everybody was here. There wasn't a chance. I miss you, Katinka. How soon can I see you?"

There's an urgency in his voice that melts my semihardened heart. When Louie whispers "Tonight?" I whisper "Yes!" completely forgetting that I cannot.

Which turns out not to be a problem because the minute Louie dangles the carrot, he snatches it away. "Gosh, I don't know what came over me—I do know what came over me—but I can't, Katinka, not tonight."

I'm about to ask why not but catch myself. I've got my suspicions having to do with a minivan probably right now parked outside his house in Somerville.

I let it drop. "No matter," I say to Louie. "I've got my own plans."

Which he is diplomatic enough—or uninterested enough—not to ask about.

We discuss how to get our plans to coincide. Louie is after all on crutches and in a cast. Pretty much smuggleproof. What's more, he's off his route. He's out of class. His accident has made it impossible for us to meet by accident. Louie's got two flights of stairs and a smothering family. I've got no stairs but family problems of my own. Also there's Jake tonight, tomorrow school; on Friday Max will come. "We'll work something out," Louie says.

I make a sandwich of wilted lettuce and Feta cheese stuffed into pita bread. I take it to my desk. When I push Rebecca Luscombe's manuscript to the side there is Jake Barnes' *Tenancy by the Entirety* staring me in the face. I pick it up. I always do my homework for any class. I always do the groundwork for any date.

By the end of the first page, however, I decide there are exceptions to any rule. It starts out promising: *A tenancy by the entirety requires five unities*, he writes, *of time, possession, title, interest, coverture.* Except for *coverture*, which I will look up later, this sentence is intelligible, almost comforting, full even, with its talk of unities, of Aristotelian possibility. *In the event of divorce a tenancy by the entirety becomes a tenancy in common.* A few more sentences and I have no idea what Jake is talking about. It reminds me of those tests we used to have in Latin Three. Mr. Kellogg would write a paragraph on the blackboard with all the words mixed up, and we would have to unscramble them, finding the subject, the predicate, the modifying clause according to their endings. I was a whiz at them.

I am not a whiz at this. Halfway down page two I get stuck on the word *moiety*, which makes me think of sperm, which in turn takes me entirely away from tenancy by the entirety. I look again at moiety and realize I am seeing motility. I put Jake aside and pick up "She's in Her Heaven," which I read in penance straight through to its exclamation-pointed end.

My own car having been diagnosed as terminal, I borrow Milly's extra car, the Dumpmobile, which is made available to close friends and visiting relatives. At six-thirty I set out for Lexington. *Take Route 2 and at Lexington Center turn right at the post office* are Jake's instructions. You can't miss the post office, he added pointedly. Winding through the back streets of north Cambridge, I see blue boxes set against the curbs and paired in places with the army brown containers where the mail is stored. It is snowing lightly.

At the rotary, traffic looks like a game of bumper cars. A UPS truck blocks the outside lane and lets me through. There's another jam at the entrance to the Fresh Pond shopping mall. Traffic thins and I barrel along Route 2 doing the maximum, all the while feeling I am just spinning my wheels. Those in the helping professions would tell me I need to work on my self-esteem. I will try to be my own cheering section, a support group of one. I think of Sheila Graham educated by F. Scott Fitzgerald in what the two of them called a college of one. She became a writer. So am I, I remind myself. And when I turn right at the post office, I'm in writers' territory—Hawthorne Street, Emerson Avenue, Alcott Road. It makes sense, the post office at the hub of its greatest appreciators—these writers probably more mail-obsessed than I given the nineteenth century's lack of faxes, FedEx, and a worldwide web.

Still, as I toodle along Walt Whitman Drive, I am more than relieved that Jake lives on a street innocuously posted Betsy Lane, named not for Betsy Ross he has told me but the developer's first-born child. The developer, whose wife is Elaine, pushed for Elaine Lane until some buyers threatened to back out.

Jake's development is fairly flat with streets laid out in a grid and bearing first names in a three-to-one ratio of women to men, the same ratio as current statistics of eligibility. I have reversed this trend if you add Seamus to Louie and Jake and eliminate Cheryl and Georgette. Though this is not quite playing fair. Maybe after Betsy, the developer went on to have two more daughters and just one son. I cross Jennifer Road to Elissa Street to Aaron Avenue. I turn the corner onto Betsy Lane. The houses are fake colonial with brick facades. They boast columns the size of Scarlett's Tara, fronting what would be, stripped down, a modest-sized ranch. There aren't trees yet but fragile-looking saplings dividing the plots.

Jake's front door is painted forest green and opens the minute I turn off the ignition key. Jake hurries down the front walk in khakis and a sweater—no overcoat—and suede desert boots—his feet are tiny—and wrenches open the driver's-side door for me. "Let me help you out," he says. "I mean, is it okay if I help you out?"

He helps me out with the delicacy you would use to deliver a particularly fragile piece of mail. "Katinka," he says. He smiles a Howdy Doody smile, broad with delight, so contagious I catch it and grin goofily back.

Though once inside the hall of his center entrance colonial, my comedy mask turns to tragedy as I survey the familiar terrain of divorce. There are dents in the carpeting where furniture used to stand, blank spaces on the wall where pictures used to hang. In the living room I see a lamp table with no lamp, one sofa beside the fireplace which had clearly been flanked with two. Across the hall in the dining room two folding chairs sit alone at the end of a table for eight stranded like unwanted relatives.

Jake shakes his head. His eyes are sad. He points to a blank space of wall. "The ravages of divorce. You would have thought that Laura, who practically lived in her white lab coat and was always carrying on about natural this and natural that, would have sworn off the material things of this world."

I shake my head. "Seamus and I split everything right down to the last roll of toilet paper. It certainly ripped the scales from my eyes to discover the life of the mind could be cluttered with more objects than ideas."

"People surprise you."

"Amen."

He helps me off with my coat. He hangs it in a hall closet where one yellow slicker sags from its hook and a bicycle pump and a tennis racket lie tangled on the floor. He's about to add my pocket-book, which is a huge brown sack almost mailbag size, when I remember and snatch it back.

"I've got your article on 'Tenancy by the Entirety.' " I take it out of my bag half rolled up, its corners bent. When I shake it open crumbs fall out, shopping lists, receipts, a price tag with its plastic tail. "I'm afraid it's a bit of a mess."

"I'm not surprised."

"Not the writing," I hasten to add, "just the manuscript. I really shouldn't keep good papers in here. My pocketbook's the main trash barrel in my life." I smooth out the cover and see that a ballpoint pen has leaked onto the title page so it reads *Tenancy splat tirety.* "But the writing is clean. Really crisp."

"You've read it?" he asks, his eyebrows raised in incredulous arcs.

"Some," I say.

He grins with such delight I feel ashamed.

"Not much," I admit.

"And no wonder," he says. "Whatever possessed me to give you such dry and deadly prose when your own stories are so . . ." He picks up a folder from the hall desk (minus its chair). The folder is blue and shiny and new with the scales of justice and the name of a law firm embossed on it. Inside lie my three Xeroxed stories as pristine as if they'd been handled with the white gloves you use for valuable antique manuscripts. ". . . when your stories are so wonderful!"

"They are?" I gasp, overdoing the surprise.

"Oh, yes. Now take for instance the baby, a character with no dialogue except a few coos, and he fairly leaps from the page."

"He does?" This time I'm not acting.

"And this diaper delivery man. He's no rocket scientist, no Harvard professor . . ." He looks at me intently, implying that rocket scientists and Harvard professors are my natural habitat. ". . . but you make him real and sympathetic. Not a stereotype but true to his kind. His plans for community college—a lesser writer would have stuck him in the Ivy League and changed his blue collar to white."

And a lesser person like me would stick Louie in a Harvard writing class and change his blue uniform to tweed, but I don't have time for self-flagellation because I need to pay attention to Jake's rave reviews, which are as long and detailed as those articles about Salman Rushdie I have never quite finished in the *New York Review of Books*.

By the time Jake has finished with paeans to my humor, my dialogue, my original use of metaphor, I am consumed with guilt over the short shrift I have given "Tenancy by the Entirety." But if I am not taken by his writing, I am starting to be more taken by Jake. His acute intelligence. His sensitivity. His interest in others—especially me. It's a long time since someone sung my praises about a quality unrelated to my looks, my body, or where I went to school. Of course Louie likes my stories, too, I remind myself, and my body, and me. "I can't get over this, a mailman in bed with a college girl," Louie has said many times. "A college professor's ex-wife!" When I accuse him of being too concerned with the trimmings, he takes offense. "Those are just extras. It's you I want."

And though I know it's the extras that can tip the balance, I decide to believe him. Given the circumstances, what choice do I have?

And now, given the way Jake has studied my stories as if he's cramming for the bar, I choose to believe him. I'd much rather have someone value me because of my writing than for the name written on my divorce decree or the *veritas* stamped on my diploma. Besides, let's face it, Louie's leg has put him on the bench.

Now Jake winds down in a final hosanna to my narrative voice. "You're terrific, Katinka," he sums up.

I nod. I lower my eyes. I try to exhibit becoming modesty, impartiality, even though I'm the kind of juror who'd award him everything plus triple damages. "Let me take your article back," I say. "I hardly did it justice."

We eat in the kitchen where Jake stir-fries shrimp and lemongrass in a new-looking wok. It's a nice kitchen, cozy with gingham curtains at the windows and blue and white Mexican tiles behind the sink. The table is set with a white cloth, chopsticks, wineglasses, and the small handleless cups that the Chinese serve tea in. Two saucepans hang from a near-empty pegboard on which the outlines of several different-sized pots and utensils are carefully sketched. I once saw photographs of Julia Child's kitchen. She had an enormous pegboard on which her husband, Paul, had diagrammed every conceivable cooking implement, each of which hung in its designated place. I look at Jake's pegboard, at the drawing of a skillet without the skillet. Never mind. My grandmother had no batterie de cuisine and still cooked up a storm. As Jake does now.

Jake serves dinner on the kind of thick white dishes you'd find in college dining halls. "Laura's," he explains. "Slowly but surely I'm filling in."

I wonder if the gingham curtains and Mexican tiles are part of his filling in. I wonder what Laura's kitchen looked like before she flew the coop. I picture something cold and white and clinical, more like a lab. This is confirmed when I notice the flowers are not in a vase but in a beaker. When Jake opens the refrigerator door, I see another beaker, which holds the orange juice.

177

Jake tells me about Laura. She was a solid cook if unimaginative. She followed recipes the way literalists follow the letter of the law. Spices were measured out as exactly as if she were handling dosages of toxic pharmaceuticals. She insists she has not sold out by leaving microbiology for massage, which is a valid science, too. She plays Mozart while constructing mathematical puzzles for her unborn child. When selecting a movie, she draws the line at PG13 even while the baby's still *in utero*. She and Harriet will use feminist theory and massage therapy in equal measure in raising this child.

I tell Jake about my mother and Arthur, their wedding plans, the loss of my house. I tell him about my quiet, sweet father who used to send me letters from the office—on insurance company stationery—the summers I was at camp. "I'm hiding out at my desk," he'd write, "because your dazzling mother is having the ladies in for bridge." Or "Greetings from the office. Your clever and enchanting mother has taken up stenciling and the fumes are something terrible. But I love my two girls."

Jake understands my feelings about my mother, about my house. How I am happy for my mother and sad for my father's sake although my father would have wished my mother and Arthur every happiness.

"Your parents were happy together?"

"Absolutely," I say. Jake's eyes brim with sympathy. They are the pale blue of airmail envelopes.

We have coffee in the living room. We sit in the bay window, which though crowned by rods and hooks has no draperies. And thus we see right away that it has been snowing all through dinner. At the curb, Milly's car is blanketed with more than a foot of snow. Jake puts his hand on mine. "The driving will be terrible. I think you should stay the night."

And because the driving will be terrible, and because the dinner is wonderful, and because Jake is missing pans and draperies, and because he's read three of my stories and I've read hardly anything of his article, and because Louie's got a broken leg, and Seamus has

Georgette, and my mother has Arthur, and Laura has Harriet, and because I write for *Playgirl* and am thus a slut, I agree.

We go to bed. It doesn't work. "I'm afraid this Hemingway stuff is a self-fulfilling prophecy," Jake whispers, his voice muffled by the pillow he's burying his face into.

"These things happen," I say. I proceed gently, careful of his self-esteem, sensitive to how the body can let you down. Call Katinka O'Toole at 1-800-SUPPORT. "We've had a lot to eat and drink. We're in your and Laura's house, in your and Laura's bed."

"Actually not. Laura took the bed. This is the first thing I bought the day she moved out." He holds my hands. His fingers are squishy mounds of flesh divided by knuckles and descending slightly in size like the three balls of a snowman. He gives a laugh. "A king-sized bed for a pint-sized guy."

"Nonsense," I say. Though he is small, but proportionate. When we lie side by side, our feet and chins are at roughly the same places. I'm pretty sure my feet are longer than his. The lights are off. There are shades at the window so I couldn't see his face even if he weren't hiding it in the pillow. But from his voice I can imagine it—shy, rueful, embarrassed.

"I'm glad the lights are off," he says, "so you can't see how embarrassed I am. I do wish they were on, however, so I can see exactly how beautiful you are." He touches my cheek, my hair, rolls onto his side and cups my chin. "You are, you know."

"I bet you say that to all the girls."

"Not in the least. Would you believe me if I told you this hasn't happened before? Or hardly ever," he amends.

"Of course," I say. "It's my fault for having introduced the whole topic of Jake Barnes. You're the ideal reader." I tease him, try to make a little joke. "Someone who studies *The Sun Also Rises* for a first date. You've overidentified with one of the characters is all."

"So, Teach, what's the solution?"

"Maybe a different book."

He laughs. "Something like *Lady Chatterley?*"

"Perhaps," I say. Uncanny, I think. In all of literature, these are the two characters we have picked. Though I myself am partially to blame for introducing Hemingway. These are the two characters that we, each in our own way, fear most. And though I'm not sure what character Louie himself would select, at some level I've already placed him in *An American Tragedy*. Perhaps overidentifying with a character *is* a self-fulfilling prophecy. If I'd chosen Anna Karenina, would it follow that I'd be dating an aristocrat and contemplating throwing myself under a train? And what if he'd been named Heathcliff or Stephen Dedalus or—oh dear!—Alexander Portnoy?

But I am stopped from exploring such possibilities and their terrible repercussions by Jake's tremulous sigh. "I so want this to work," he says.

I say nothing. I wonder however what he means by this—the problem at hand—getting it up? Or the wider implications of a relationship? I think of Louie, of his totally responsive body. I have no doubt that Louie's body has never failed to accommodate its desires. At least that part of his body below the waist and above the injured leg. I put my hand on Jake's sloping, narrow shoulder and feel an enormous wave of tenderness. It's a powerful feeling, one I'm at a loss to identify. Is it, I wonder, simply my instinctive need always to cheer for the underdog.

We fall asleep side by side in the middle of Jake's vast bed like two cartoon characters stranded together on a deserted island.

I awake suddenly, not sure what time it is but sure not much time has passed. My mother! I think in the kind of panic I used to feel when I was a teenager out parking on the old Kennebec Road well after curfew. What if she wakes up in the middle of the night in the middle of Arthur's bed and sees the snow. She knows where I am having dinner. But at three in the morning she won't know where I am. She'll call downstairs and get the machine. She'll run downstairs and knock and knock. Perhaps drag out the superintendent with his ring of keys. And then what? Police? Hospitals? When she was in

Maine and I was here, she never knew if there was a storm, how late I stayed out, whether I wore my boots and my gloves, took my vitamins.

But maybe she won't wake up. Or if she does I hope she'll reach for Arthur and think Katinka's grown up and can take care of herself. Maybe she'll think, gleefully, Katinka's spending the night with a graduate of Penn and Harvard Law. No harm could come with someone so prestigiously educated. Or maybe—and this gives me a start—she'll reach for Arthur and not think of me at all.

I must be literally twisting with these thoughts because Jake wakes up. "Katinka!" he exclaims as if he's surprised to find me here. "How lovely," he adds with undisguised delight. He reaches for me.

This time everything works. The blight of Hemingway lifts. And if Jake is not quite Louie—but who is? And if I'm not Lady Chatterley—who I never wished to be—together we are still something rather nice.

12

It's Friday morning and I am in a fury of cleaning. Harriman and Zenobia are bringing Max over on their way to the airport tonight. This is crazy, I tell myself as I scrub out the medicine cabinet and test the childproof caps on bottles of aspirin and antihistamine. I polish the hot and cold water taps on the tub and sink. I burnish the chrome rail which holds the shower curtain. In the kitchen I have to stand on the counter to scour the refrigerator top whose grungy surface only a giant could gaze upon. It's not as if a social worker is about to call to inspect the premises, to declare my apartment suitable for a child, to declare *me* suitable for a child. But if it's crazy and if I'm crazy, I still clean and sweep and vacuum and mop until I am almost beginning to like it.

In my study I make up the folding cot I have borrowed from Arthur with the Red Sox sheets I have borrowed from Milly. I meant to do most of this preparation last night, saving me some morning hours to write. But after last night's class—which went rather well, I must admit; Russell MacQuillen, Junior, took furious notes and Rebecca Luscombe admitted some of my criticism was "interesting"—my students invited me to join them for a drink at the Casablanca bar. How could I refuse this testament to my new-found popularity. I remember when Seamus used to go out drinking with his favorite students, me included, how heady it felt, how he was in his element. I had a good time surrounded by upturned faces seeking the hidden meaning of agents, copyright laws, the perfectly prepared manuscript. And even though I have learned the painful lesson of how little the width of margins counts along the road to publication, I still relished being the fount from which all this crucial knowledge spilled. I confess I did overdo it on a topic on which I'm hardly the expert. After all it's my students who read *Publishers Weekly* and have practically memorized the *Literary Market Place.* Nevertheless, while I did go on a bit about contracts and percentages, I managed to remind them that the actual writing had to take place before negotiating the paperback.

I floated home on my charm, my authority, and the three beers I was forced to drink to show I was both one of the boys and a lubricated literary animal. There were two messages on the machine, both from men. Look Ma, I'm popular, I wanted to sing. One was from Jake saying what a good time we'd had together. Another from Louie asking when we could make a time to get together. It was too late to call either of them back. It was too late to clean, to read Dr. Spock, or *One Hundred Ways to Amuse an Eight Year Old.* I fell into bed and slept the sleep of the Popular.

And woke to the panic of the unprepared. Now I look into my refrigerator and throw out everything that smells or wilts. Which leaves it almost entirely bare. I make a list. I need to go to the grocery store. I plan to go to the toy store. Maybe I'll go to Hollywood Express and pick up some children's videos. *Mary Poppins. The Secret Garden,* I think, or *The Wizard of Oz.* Immediately I segue to *The Postman Always Rings Twice, Il Postino, Pony Express,* and *Deliverance.* I fold my list and stuff it into the recesses of my pocketbook. Jake's article is still there, a reminder that one can live other than a mail-centric life. I have lugged it around all yesterday, even to my class and to the Casablanca afterward. Spying its corner, my students would have assumed the great-American-novel-in-progress—in such a state of progress I'd need to keep it next to me. When I take out "Tenancy by the Entirety," my pocketbook feels significantly lighter. Just as I put it down on the kitchen table my buzzer rings. "Brattle Florist. Delivery," comes the voice over the intercom.

I go out into the vestibule where a delivery man places a cellophane-wrapped bouquet of long-stemmed roses into my arms as if I've just been anointed Miss America. "And it's not even Valentine's," he says. He shakes his head. He leaves and I stand against the mailboxes wishing my mother could see me now. Or some of those cheerleaders I went to high school with. As I am thinking this, the front door opens and in comes another delivery man—this time Federal Express. He is holding a large folder and a small clipboard. "Excuse me, miss," he says, "can you tell me the apartment number for," he checks his board, "Miss Christina O'Toole?"

"Katinka," I say. "It's Katinka O'Toole. It's me. I mean I."

"That's a funny name," he says. "Though hardly the oddest of the ones I've had to deliver packages to."

"I imagine not." I refrain from the delivery of my own prepackaged explanation of my name. I sign on the line marked with an X and accept the package, which is heavier than it looks.

Inside my apartment, I lay my booty on the table. I pull out the card which is attached with a silky pink bow. *For Katinka with thanks for a lovely night from Jake Barnes who is, thank God, no longer the Jake Barnes prototype.* I laugh. I go to the kitchen and find a vase in the newly cleaned and impeccably ordered cabinet under the sink. I arrange the roses, which is not easy since they are, however beautiful, covered with thorns. I prick my fingers. Blood bubbles up. I suck it off.

I put the vase on the mantel where it looks magnificent. I prop the card next to it. Once Seamus brought me an enormous bouquet of pink lilies bigger than a medium-sized child. There wasn't a container large enough; we had to siphon water into a wastebasket. Then I found the card—*Darling, Break a leg, from the Shubert Theatre Management.* Seamus had been called to the Ritz to coach some actress in Molly Bloom's soliloquy. She was leaving for New York in an hour, so had passed the flowers on to Seamus' "little wife." It turned out that the yellow centers of the lilies permanently stained my best white blouse.

Now I sit back and admire Jacob's flowers intended only for me. They must have cost a fortune, my mother will exclaim, with both admiration and shock at the extravagance. But as soon as I think this, I picture Louie's gift, the roll of James Fenimore Cooper stamps, and my heart melts. No one on a mailman's salary could afford the fortune these cost. Besides, compared to flowers, a roll of stamps is the more original gift. I remember the presents I used to make my father for his birthday: a lopsided ashtray out of clay, a tie pin out of old buttons messily glued. "I'd rather have this than anything from Tiffany's," he'd croon. I take Louie's side, feel protective of him, almost motherly. Maybe these feelings come from the child-care books I've been memorizing to prepare for Max. Whole chapters are devoted to being fair and prizing each child for his own particular attributes.

I get up from the sofa and go back to the table. With all this flower excitement I've forgotten about the second delivery. I rip open the FedEx package. I pull out four copies of *Playgirl* magazine. "Yippee," I yell. "Hip hip hooray!" My apartment is so clean and uncluttered my shouts echo off the walls. I clutch the magazines to my chest and do a little jig. A piece of paper floats out. I reach down to pick it up. It's a letter from Betty Jean Williamson, the editor, *my* editor. "Hot off the press," she writes. "Congratulations from me and the rest of the playmates."

My first instinct is to call my mother. My second instinct—the correct one it turns out—is to examine the evidence. Richard Gere's on the cover. Fully clothed and adorable. I breathe a sigh of relief.

I find my story immediately without having to examine the Table of Contents. It's on paper, finished like the inserts that advertise expensive cars. I run my finger over my name, which is printed in large capitals. I read my story straight through twice. I can't find even a comma out of place. I'm amazed at how professional a story can sound once printed professionally. The illustration is tasteful. A couple kissing in front of a computer screen. A line drawing which if you omit the computer could be a Matisse. My head swells.

Then deflates when I notice the glossy left-hand page next to the matte right-hand page where my story begins. It's a full-page ad promoting an elixir to increase your penis size. There's some quasi-medical text that surrounds an enormous and graphic chart of penises in various stages of treatment. There are seven penises in graduated size drawn not with the economical line of Matisse but the overly anatomical pen of a pornographer. The seventh penis, made elephantine by two weeks' worth of elixir, reminds me of the giant phallus of Winston Churchill carted around the Agassiz stage in a Harvard production of *What the Butler Saw.*

I shake my head. Why aren't pleasures ever pure? Roses have thorns to cut your fingers. Lilies have stamens to stain your clothes. Great lovers lack college degrees. Ivy League lovers lack Ivy League penises.

I turn to the Table of Contents, which is ringed with ads for dildoes and edible underpants. My story is the only entry under *Fiction* though the lists that snake down from *Features* and *Warm Bodies* are several inches long. My eyes fix on *Warm Bodies* and move down to "Lawyers of Chicago: Debriefcased and in the Nude," page seventy-five. Though I am tempted, I do not rush to page seventy-five. I shut the magazine. I congratulate myself on my superior restraint. What will be next, I wonder, local pharmacists? I will not take this as any kind of sign. And I'm not going to check out those lawyers for either curiosity's or comparison's sake. No naked lawyers, no tacky ads are going to blunt my pleasure in being published in a magazine with a circulation far exceeding my family and two best friends. I will feel no shame.

Thus feeling no shame, I call my mother before I feel the shame.

"Guess what?" I say.

"You're getting married," she says.

Which takes me so completely off guard that I sit there holding the receiver and sputtering.

"Just kidding," she says.

"Not funny," I say.

"Oh, Katinka. Where's your sense of humor, dear. I assume you spent Wednesday night at that nice lawyer's. I called and called. Quite sensible, too, in light of the storm."

"The weather was awful," I say. My mother and I discuss precipitation, snow emergencies, how preferable apartment living is when it comes to shoveling, how she and Arthur spent a cozy evening at home, the storm making them miss the dinner at the Faculty Club.

I deflect all discussion of my own cozy storm-tossed night and the dinner it would have been a great loss to miss. I know what these discussions with my mother can lead to. You start with men, their degrees, and pretty soon you're graphing degrees of intimacy. "Guess what?" I start again.

"What?" my mother says this time.

"My story. It's out."

"I'll be right down."

I open the magazine to my story. I fold and flatten it until the elixir ad is underneath. It looks good like that, a clean page of prose topped by the title and my name.

My mother knocks with a series of excited little taps. When I open the door she is holding a bottle of champagne and two fluted glasses that I recognize from a shelf of them collected by Arthur's first wife.

"Katinka, I am so pleased." She hands me the glasses and starts to untwist the wire of the cork before she's even crossed the threshold. "We must celebrate."

"It *is* before noon," I point out.

My mother's eyebrows arc over her glasses in surprise. When have you ever refused a chance to celebrate, her glance seems to say, to have a champagne toast?

I don't tell her about my new sobriety in preparation for my four days' trial run at motherhood. My awesome sense of responsibility. It's bad enough Max has to experience single parenthood. Does he need alcoholism, too? Not to mention the traumatic effects on poor Daniella, who's had a hard enough if limited life. But I've got four hours till Max comes. And a full bottle of Listerine. One glass of champagne does not a drunkard make.

"Darling, one glass of champagne does not a drunkard make," my mother says, now underscoring our close relationship. My God, I think, will we soon start dressing alike, too? Sweaters and jeans bought in duplicate?

"Well? Where is it? I can hardly wait!"

I hold it up, the folded part against my chest.

My mother grabs it, opens it to its full lurid breadth.

Which she doesn't seem to notice. She sits down and starts reading, pausing only briefly to pop the cork. While she reads, I have two glasses of champagne. I am just pouring my third when she finishes.

"Darling, it's simply wonderful," she says. Her eyes brim with tears. She cried over my acceptance at Radcliffe, too, blurring the signature of the admissions officer.

Now she discusses my brilliant style, my brilliant use of character, my brilliant dialogue. Praise bubbles up like the bubbles in my glass. She turns to the contributors' page where it says that I was born in Old Town, Maine, and live in Cambridge, Mass. She is slightly disappointed the note does not contain the fact that I graduated from Radcliffe College or teach at a building in Harvard Yard. But this regret does not diminish her pride in me, which is now soaring to such an inflated level I feel the need to puncture it.

"But look at this," I say. I point preemptively at the seven penises.

My mother looks. She smiles. "So?" she says.

"So!" I exclaim.

"So what," my mother says. She shrugs her shoulders.

I am astonished. My mother is shrugging her shoulders as if this were the most normal thing in the world—to have your story surrounded with penises. I remember the set of instructions my mother gave me before I went off for college, about being a good girl and all the things a good girl wouldn't even try. About what you see in a big city, about what you have to close your eyes to. "As if these things don't happen in Old Town," I'd said, "another Peyton Place."

"Katinka, you always try to shock me," my mother said. "Why dwell on the seedy side of life."

"Katinka, nothing shocks me," my mother says now. She slides her hand over the penises. "It's all a part of life."

I show her the letter from Betty Jean Williamson. "Congratulations from me and the rest of the playmates," she reads out loud. She picks up the magazine again. It falls open to one of the lawyers, fortunately not the debriefed centerfold, but a lawyer whose briefcase covers crucial parts of his anatomy. He's sitting on his desk with a brass scales of justice next to a rather fetching dimpled knee. "I wonder who *the rest of the playmates* are?" my mother speculates.

I grab the magazine from her. "The other editors, layout people, printers, the publishers . . ." I compile a list of the kind of support staff that would work at a university press.

My mother doesn't seem to hear. "Speaking of lawyers," she says.

"We weren't," I say.

"Lately they seem to be getting such a bum rap. As if people have forgotten the nobility of the law. Of justice. Of truth."

"Of tax loopholes and multimillion-dollar real estate syndications," I add though my heart isn't in it.

"Your father always wanted to go to The Law School," she says dreamily, ignoring me.

"He did?"

"He said he couldn't afford to. But I think secretly he was scared."

"Daddy. Scared?" I picture my father, cautious and self-effacing. But he championed the cause of the Penobscot Indians. And had faced down some ruthless developers. Quietness doesn't have to mean timidity.

"Remember Frenchy Levesque, a childhood friend of your father's. He was Phi Bete at the U of M?" She sighs. "He had other offers but like me had to attend college locally." She sighs harder. "He managed to get himself into Harvard Law and off to Cambridge. He didn't last more than three weeks."

"What happened?" I spin stories of foul play in Austin Hall or poisoned mystery meat in The Law School cafeteria.

"Utter humiliation. The first day he was told to look to the right of him, look to the left of him—those students would soon flunk out. A few days later he was called on in class. They use the Socratic method, dear. Arthur can explain."

"No need. I saw *The Paper Chase* on video."

"I guess Frenchy was so nervous he stammered. Even though he was prepared, his mind went blank. Then the professor asked him where he'd done his undergraduate work. When Frenchy replied the University of Maine, he was told to go back to that cow college and study agriculture."

"The arrogance," I exclaim.

"The waste. Frenchy joined the family contracting business and went around in overalls."

"Which maybe he preferred to a three-piece suit."

"A trade over a profession?" my mother asks, incredulous. "Sadly, for your father this was a cautionary tale."

I commiserate. I try to remember Frenchy. Back in Old Town I knew three Frenchys. Frenchy the janitor at the Community Center who had guarded his closetful of sour-smelling mops like a bank vault, Frenchy the plumber who dropped a wrench into our soil pipe. Perhaps Frenchy Levesque was the one who had painted our house.

"Imagine," my mother says now, "a Phi Beta Kappa painting our house."

She smoothes her skirt, which I notice for the first time sports a design of little Parthenons. "Given Frenchy's experience, your father was somewhat concerned about how you'd fare at Radcliffe coming right out of Old Town High."

"But Daddy did that himself."

"Things were different then. Admissions committees paid more attention to merit, less to extracurriculars and geographical distribution."

"Are you telling me I wasn't qualified?"

"Of course not, darling. Just that we had our worries. You know, small-town girl in the big city, inadequate preparation compared to students from exclusive boarding schools. That was why we were so pleased about your taking up with Seamus. We figured he'd help you."

"A giant misconception."

"So we learned."

"Seamus was less interested in helping me make the grade than in making me."

"I gather, though there's no need to be crude."

"Frankly, Mother, have ye such little faith in my abilities to think I'd need a man to get me through?"

"What a question, Katinka. We all need a man to get us through."

I am preparing an insightful feminist argument which she deftly sidesteps before I can squeeze the first sentence out. She skips into the living room and lets out a hoot. "Look at these roses!" she exclaims. She cranes her neck to take a sniff. But even in high heels and on tiptoe, she is too short. Luckily, she doesn't seem to notice the card.

I lower my eyes modestly. "From Jake," I admit.

My mother claps her hands. "Such extravagance!" She is as clearly delighted as if she herself is the recipient of this floral tribute to womanhood and the benefits of having a man in a woman's life. "Make some coffee, Katinka, we have a lot to talk about."

We go into the kitchen. My mother seats herself at the kitchen table. This is dangerous territory, moving from the specific of my story to the general of a chat. I put the water on to boil. I have delaying tactics. A bag of whole French roast beans in the freezer. A coffee grinder that sounds like a jackhammer and is excruciatingly slow. "Don't bother with that," my mother says as I unroll the Coffee Connection's insulated bag. "The instant will do perfectly."

I stir the instant into two unmatched mugs. The unwatched pot has boiled instantly. I add water. Offer sugar. Take out the milk. I sit across from my mother. With two hands, I grip my mug, an anchor in this shifting world. "Shoot," I tell my mother, readying myself for the firing squad.

She tells me about her plans to sell the house. How she's arranged to have the trim painted. "Frenchy's son," she confides in a tone that suggests that the father's failure at the law school has condemned the son to a life of ladders and gallons of Benjamin Moore.

"Not exactly the House of Atreus."

"True," she concedes, "but still sad."

No sadness, however, shows when she talks about unloading the house she was brought to as a bride.

"Widows aren't supposed to make sudden decisions," I say. I have read this somewhere. In Ann Landers? A dentist's waiting room?

"New widows," she corrects. "I've been a widow for years."

And high time I'm over it she implies. As if it's a cold or a little patch of depression you need to get through. She goes on about the wedding plans. What date to set. What hall to hire. "Of course I'll want you as my maid of honor."

"I'd be honored." I sip my coffee. I wish we hadn't finished the bottle of champagne.

"And Zenobia. Wouldn't it be nice if she were my attendant, too?"

I mime enthusiasm, a nod, a too bright smile. We only children, solitary and old before our time, can claim the sole privilege of not having to share. No longer, now that I've been afflicted with a sibling like a sudden not quite benign growth. Co-maids of honor, I suppose, in matching taffeta. Or rather—and worse—a matron and a maid. Perhaps in fact there are a few drops of champagne left. I consider going to check when my mother and I hear the clatter of letterbox flaps from the vestibule. My mother's head tilts, ears perk as alert as a Doberman's.

I dump sugar from the bowl directly into my coffee with no civilized temporizing of spoon. Although I usually drink my coffee black, today I yearn for sweetener. I take a sip, add more.

"That's interesting," my mother says.

"I don't *always* drink it black."

"Not that. The mail."

"What do you mean?"

"Katinka, never have I known you not to run out into the hall at the first sound of the post." My mother's got her gotcha voice coming out of her who-knows-the-troubles-I've-seen face.

I am speechless. "I am speechless," I manage to emit.

A problem not shared by my mother, who rushes forward like a tide that can't be stopped. "And I know about your mailman!" This last statement crashes with the hurricane intensity of a wave against a rock.

"What do you mean?" I ask, all innocence. "How do you know?" I ask, all guilt.

My mother shakes her head sadly. She sighs profoundly. Once again I have disappointed her. "The man, let me amend, the *mail*man you kissed at that Christmas party. The mailman whom Arthur saw leaving your apartment at an inappropriate hour!"

I am tempted to ask my mother what Arthur was doing at that inappropriate hour, but I am not an eye-for-an-eye kind of person. Unlike my mother. "Louie said Arthur didn't recognize him without his uniform."

"It's Louie, is it?" My mother rolls the word on her tongue as if it's one of the moldy unidentifiable items of food I have earlier thrown out. "I guess I did know this," she adds with a lack of conviction. His name might as well be one of the Frenchys, she implies, interchangeable people in overalls who provide services. "Of course Arthur recognized him. There's not a sharper eye in all of Cambridge."

"But Arthur didn't say a word."

"Arthur," *this* name she tastes like caviar, "is nothing if not discreet."

I slump against my chair, limp as Raggedy Ann.

My mother is merciless. *She* should have gone to The Law School from the University of Maine. *She* could have stood up to Frenchy's professor. Socrates would have discarded his method on meeting her.

My mother stands up and paces my kitchen linoleum as if she's Clarence Darrow summing up. "Not that I would convict you on just those two pieces of evidence," she continues.

"Phew. That's a relief."

"There have been other clues, other sightings."

Like sightings of Elvis? Of UFO's? "Spare me the details," I plead.

"I guess I will," my mother says not unkindly. She examines last week's to-do list taped to the refrigerator, four of the five items not done. "It's not as if he's unattractive," she ruminates, surprising me. "What happened? Did you break up?" Her voice is hopeful. Give the right answer, it warns, and the quality of mercy will not be strained.

"Not break up. Broke a leg. He did. A mailman's lot." I pause. I brighten. "Aha! You didn't know! Evidence overlooked by your spies!"

"Katinka! What an accusation. I am your mother. I have your best interests at heart." She stops and sponges a counter I have sponged five times. "Believe me, I understand. I understand those Latin looks."

"Latin *looks* but no Latin. In a nutshell, that's the problem, isn't it?"

She shrugs. "Talk of misconception! Still, I of all people understand. I sympathize. But a mailman?"

"What if I told you he was a Harvard student?" I ask, hating myself.

She brightens. "Like that old beau of yours who grilled Big Macs to put himself through Yale?"

I shake my head.

She shakes her head. "I didn't think so," is what she says.

The phone rings. I consider letting the machine answer, then change my mind. God knows what message will roll toward her pricked-up ears. I have made the right decision, I realize, when I grab the receiver just as my mother is reaching for it. "I called you earlier, Katinka," Louie begins.

"Can't talk now."

"Your mother?"

"You got it."

"The mailman?" my mother asks as I replace the phone.

"A student. From my Harvard class."

"I don't want to get in the way of your *work*."

"It's okay. I'll call *her* back."

We sit silently sipping our inferior instant coffee in companionable but sad mother-daughter silence. My mother sighs. I sigh. The kitchen clock ticks. From the hall I can hear the substitute mailman put the last letter in the last box and then thump out the door with a heavy foot, not Louie's foot. My mother removes her glasses. Her eyes are watering. From disappointment. Empathy. Or merely the harsh chemicals I used to scour the kitchen. I start to worry about Max. Max in relation to dirt, then in relation to my arsenal of weapons—Lysol, Top Job, Ajax, Clorox, Mr. Clean—against that dirt. What if Max has one of those environmental allergies? Stop, Katinka, I tell myself, you have enough problems without making them up.

Good advice. My mother, my immediate problem, sniffles and daubs her eyes, which are less the eyes of someone attacked by

Liquid Pledge and more of someone touched by nostalgia. Her eyes have a faraway look, a term I would have once dismissed as belonging to a writer of genre fiction if not for this evidence before me. "It takes me back," she sighs.

"What does?" I ask in the gentle voice the experts recommend for eliciting information from a troubled child.

"Your unsuitable romance. Before your father, I had someone rather like your mailman."

"You did?" My voice is harsh, astonished, almost shouting.

My mother doesn't seem to notice. Her voice is dreamy. "He brought me flowers, too—huge bouquets of wildflowers. Queen Anne's lace, daisies, buttercups—he picked himself from a field he found on Indian Island." She pauses. "Not like your roses, of course."

The way she says this implies that roses are just hothouse consumer goods you put on your MasterCard while wildflowers are nature's blessings you have to wrestle acts of nature for. But maybe I'm misinterpreting her. I know my mother. I know her taste. Maybe this is just an aberration. The misweave in the kilim which placates Allah.

"Any more of that champagne left?" my mother asks now, narrowing her point of view to a focus I completely understand.

"Not a drop. But I do have beer. And wine in a half-gallon jug."

"Better not," my mother says.

I'm not sure whether her declining my offer is a dismissal of a wildflower in a bouquet of cultivated vintages because of rising social status or her realization that the sun is still very far from passing over the yardarm. It's one thing to celebrate my story. Another to hoist one over . . . Over what? An unsuitable romance?

Obviously probing cross-examination is called for. I am just about to ask when my mother interrupts me. "Your kitchen is so clean, Katinka. Whatever did you use to get these cabinet knobs to shine?"

"Half-Clorox, half . . ." I stop. I sound like my mother's housewifely co-conspirator in a commercial break. How can I sidestep this news she's dropped into my Cloroxed kitchen, into my messy life? "Who was this man?" I ask.

"What man?" my mother tries, but it's a halfhearted attempt.

"Tell!" I command. The milkman, no doubt. In Old Town, when I was a child, the milk was still delivered to our door. I remember the cool white bottles with their frilled paper caps, the smaller ones of cream, left in the crate set at the corner of the porch. I can picture the milk truck, milky white with one painted cow and "Footman's Dairy" printed underneath. The milkman wore a uniform and a billed cap. But between the cap and the stiff collar I can't fill in a face. The milkman? I laugh. Impossible. Too trite.

"Don't laugh, Katinka," my mother says in an offended tone. "I know it sounds trite. But at the time . . ." The faraway glance comes again, passing through me, through the cabinet, through the wall. "He was a lovely man, boy, really. He worked at the Sears in Bangor. In Auto Parts. He wore this uniform."

"I know about uniforms."

"I'm sure you do. Afraid you do. But the point is it didn't work out. And then I met your father."

"You loved him?"

"Of course I loved your father."

"I don't mean Daddy."

My mother's voice is soft. "There are different kinds of love," she says nearly whispering.

"What happened?"

My mother straightens. Her voice gets brusque. It's her moral-lesson voice, the one that warned me to stand straight, brush my teeth, be kind to those less fortunate, act like a lady so boys will respect me as one. "It was totally inappropriate."

"*Why* was it totally inappropriate? *Tell* me!"

"That's a question you already know the answer to. *You* tell me."

"*Mother!*" I yell.

That I am shouting doesn't faze her, so secure is she in her sense of rightness. "The answer is obvious, Katinka, as you well know. Because it was like you and your mailman." She pauses. Her eyes fix on my half-Cloroxed half-Ajaxed cabinet knob. "I . . ." Her throat catches. "I broke it off."

What's the lesson here? I wonder. Mother-daughter apartments. Mother-daughter romances. Mother-daughter breakups. As an adolescent, the minute I was told to do one thing I would do the other. I ate everything bad for my skin. Let boys' hands roam over strictly no-trespassing areas. That my mother broke off her mailman-equivalent romance makes me instinctively want to go for broke with my own. But I am, despite my rarefied education, too confused to make an educated choice. "Did you sleep with him?" I ask, astonished to hear these words fly out of my mouth.

"Katinka!" my mother exclaims.

"Well?"

"Well, some things between mother and daughter should be left unsaid."

From which remarks I immediately assume the worst (or best, depending on your point of view). Knowing my mother, if she hadn't slept with the dashing auto parts man from Sears, she would have smugly announced this, trumpeting her virginity and moral rectitude. And now I have to reevaluate her. A process akin to throwing out a novel I have been working at all my life and starting from scratch. I go back to Old Town to my parents' bedroom which even as we speak Frenchy's son is renovating for somebody else. I picture the twin beds with their sprigged spreads made by my grandmother just like my own. But instead of the night table and the slip of rug, what divides them rises up like a Sears knockoff of Banquo's ghost.

Meanwhile, as my thoughts spin off, my mother is maintaining such eye contact that to look away would warrant twenty years to life.

"It's okay, Mum," I say. "I refuse to pry. Unlike other people I could name."

My mother stands up and smoothes the Parthenons over her knees. "I've got to be going," she says. "I'm meeting Arthur in the Square for lunch."

I see her to the door. "I'm so happy about your *story*," she says.

And so unhappy about Louie is the silent but clear subtext. "I know," I say.

She kisses me. Her cheek is damp. I smell Arpège. "Remember what I told you," she says.

"How could I forget."

"Not *that*," she exclaims. "About appropriate choices."

Like Jake. Picking between Jake and Louie is not exactly like picking between Harvard and Yale is what she's telling me. I say nothing. I know nothing, only that at this moment I am incapable of choice—at least of the male kind.

The toy kind is a different story. I drive to Fresh Pond Mall and walk the aisles among Mutant Ninja Turtles and Power Rangers, superheroes and cowboy hats. I pick up a small metal blue and white truck on which is written "U.S. Mail." It's in the shape of a jeep, one of those suburban mail trucks you're always getting stuck behind on country roads. Its doors open onto a sexually indeterminate figure behind the steering wheel. Though you can remove the figure, it's bent into sitting position. No bad back or worn-out shoes for this mailman. This is drive-through delivery, fast-food mail. I myself prefer the personal touch.

I return it to the shelf. I buy crayons, coloring books, games, joke books, a set of cowboys and Indians with a plastic fort. For Daniella I buy a silver cardboard crown just slightly creased in a bin marked "75% Reduced." Next, I go to Bread and Circus where my cart runneth over with organic fruits and vegetables and two loaves of seven-grain no-additives Russian pumpernickel.

There's another message from Louie on the machine when I get home. His mother's inviting me for Sunday dinner he says. From the way his voice rises on the word *mother*, I can pretty much tell the invitation's not his idea. Then, again, maybe it's just the quality of my machine which distorts a string of perfectly uninflected sentences.

I call him back. Get his machine. Where can he be? I wonder, a man on crutches, in a cast. After the beep, I explain I'm taking care of Max, will have to take a raincheck on Rosalie's feast. "But I'm dying to see you," I whisper. I put the toys in the closet, the produce in the crisper, the fruit in a basket. I lie down on the sofa and wait for Max.

Zenobia arrives with Max, who is so wrapped up in a down jacket, earmuffs, and hat and scarf that I wouldn't be able to recognize him if he weren't carrying Daniella. On the other hand, Daniella must be shivering in her skimpy floursack though Max holds her close to his heart. Zenobia is wearing a coat with a Persian lamb collar over a classic suit. On her feet are leather boots with heels. A Hermés scarf floats over a string of pearls. The way my mother used to dress for a trip. The way she still does. Today, successful Zenobia's dressed for success. She's probably going first-class. A privilege which my Yankee soul dismisses and my hedonist self desires.

Seamus never made such distinctions. Soon after we were married, the Joyce Society brought Seamus to London to give a speech. He was sent a first-class ticket, me a coach. Blinded by love and the prospect of clutching hands as we flew up through the clouds, I assumed Seamus would take the empty seat next to me in the center lane of five across. "You do jest, my dear," Seamus had exclaimed. Halfway into the flight he ventured to steerage to praise the beef Wellington and French vintages while I struggled to cut a rubbery, gray-gravied chicken breast with a plastic fork and knife. He then beat a hasty retreat back to the lap of luxury.

"Harriman is double-parked," Zenobia explains now, "and in a terrible rush. He insists on arriving hours early. Traffic and crowds are so unpredictable."

She hands me Max's suitcase, as large for a four-day stay as one I would take on a three-week trip. She puts his backpack on the floor. She pulls a notebook from her own pocketbook—burnished leather trimmed in brass. Hermés, too, I suppose, made from the same leather that crafts those saddles that sheiks and princes order for riding their Arabian steeds. The notebook is more my type, curled vinyl ends and a ring binder, but thicker than the notebook I carry around to note my novel ideas for novels in.

"This contains all the information about Max," Zenobia instructs. I leaf through the notebook; both sides of its pages are covered with dense scrawl. Gee, if Richard Ellmann or Leon Edel had as much information about the early years of Joyce or James respectively their biographies would have filled twice as many volumes. The pages are headed like chapters: doctors, neighbors, emergency numbers, bedtimes, schools and teachers (which chapter I can skip since it's vacation time), dental hygiene, vitamin supplements, likes and dislikes, TV rules, table rules.

I put the notebook on the hall table. "This will be really helpful," I say. "I'll be sure to study it."

"*You're* being incredibly helpful, Katinka. Harriman and I are so grateful." She unwinds Max's scarf, takes off his cap. His cowlicks spring up. His cheeks are round and red, apple cheeks, like the illustrations of Dutch children skating on a canal in a book I once had of boys and girls from around the world. "I worried about a little h-o-m-e-s-i-c-k-n-e-s-s," she spells out, "but Max is actually looking forward to this." She takes off the rest of his winterwear, which is not easy since sleeves and mittens have to be twisted out from under Daniella's sizable girth. She points to the hall closet. "Shall I hang them up?" she asks.

I grab them out of her hands and put them on a chair. "I'll do it later," I say. The hall closet is of course the only thing I haven't cleaned. It is in fact the place where I've stuffed everything I've cleaned out of everywhere else. Zenobia has the unerring eye of a social worker, an investigator from the DSS. I imagine police lines around my closet, stickers affixed which read this place is condemned, search warrants issued by the cleanliness patrol.

But I must have a more extreme imagination than Zenobia, mine fueled by the knowledge of the inside of my closet. None of which seems to interest her. Her unerring eye is now filling with a tear. "I have to go, Max," she says now. "We'll call from Amsterdam. Katinka will take good care of you. And Grandpa is right upstairs."

"I know," says Max.

"So good-bye, my big boy." She bends over and kisses him. "My little man."

"What about Daniella?" he asks.

She kisses Daniella with only a slight diminution of enthusiasm.

"Mummy?"

"Yes?"

"Daddy forgot to say good-bye to Daniella." His smile is mischievous.

"I'll make sure Daddy blows Daniella a kiss from the car."

After Zenobia leaves, I expect Max to run to the window and hold Daniella up for Harriman's kiss. Instead, he stands looking at me expectantly. I have a moment of panic. What am I doing? What do I do?

These questions don't seem to bother Max. He dumps Daniella in a corner and is wandering around my apartment, which he seems to be inspecting with what I fear is his mother's unerring eye.

Though not a judgmental one. "I like this," he says. "It's like Grandpa's but better for kids."

"In what way?" I ask, thrilled that he has noticed this practically germ-free environment I have toiled toward. I, who crave credit for good works, am not an anonymous giver to charity.

"Not so many things to break and spill stuff on."

I look at the clock. He's been here ten minutes and so far everything is going well. I've been prepared for the worst. When I went to borrow the sheets from Milly, she handed them over with a warning. "Don't get your hopes up," she said. She told me about the overnight guests her two boys host. How these visitors might call their parents at three A.M. to fetch them immediately. Some friends demanded to go home in the middle of dinner if they didn't like the way the broccoli touched the rice. And many was the time Charlie himself would throw a raincoat over his pajamas and set out on a rescue mission to the outer suburbs. "We finally set a limit," Milly said. "The kids couldn't sleep over beyond a ten-mile radius of our house."

"A good idea. Max's parents, though, will be in Amsterdam."

"You have my sympathy. Be prepared, Katinka. You've only met Max once. Unlike my kids, he's not going to have the comfort of a brother or a friend along."

"Max has Daniella."

"Well, then," Milly said. But I could tell from her tone her opinion of Daniella pretty much echoed Harriman Slade's.

"Besides, his grandfather's upstairs."

Milly patted the batch of sheets, traced the border of batters with big grins on their brown and white multicultural faces. "Maybe you'll be lucky," she responded, her voice bright, her expression unconvinced. "It'll be just fine."

Now I feel lucky. Max looks just fine, not about to call the airport and get his parents off the plane. He likes his makeshift room. He adores his Red Sox bed. He examines the pillowcases with as much care as you'd check out some valuable baseball cards. "These are the real Red Sox colors," he notes. "In my house we have only white sheets. My father says dyes aren't good for you." He exclaims over the TV, which I gather at home is kept in a vault. He can't believe his luck in having it in his room. "Can I watch cartoons?" he asks.

"Of course," I say.

"Awesome," he exclaims. He claps his hands. He jumps. His cowlick waves like a palm tree in a tropical hurricane.

His enthusiasm puzzles me. Cartoons are for children, right? I tell myself. When I was a kid, I spent my Saturdays watching them from the balcony of the Bijou Theatre where bubble gum was stuck to the underside of the seats and we spent more time throwing popcorn than eating it. Harmless childhood amusements, right? I console myself. Since I don't have cable, I don't have to worry that Max will be surfing through Adults Only channels or learning bad values and bad words from Beavis and Butt-head. I'm sure children's entertainment is not as innocent as when I was a child, but neither is the world. And the sixties were hardly a repressive age.

I bring out the cache of toys from the laundry basket where I have been stockpiling them. Max's joy knows no bounds. He falls into the basket with the same bliss that people who have taken the Lord fall into the baptismal stream. "Power Rangers!" he shouts. "Cowboys and Indians!" he sings. "My parents don't allow me to have these at home," he whispers.

I freeze. How many commandments in the tablet of parenting have I broken already? Colored sheets, TV, war-mongering toys. If (A) he's not allowed these at home, and (B) he's not at home, then . . . "Then, since you're not at home, you can play with them here," I brilliantly deduce. Though my brilliant reasoning is irrelevant, since Max is now fiercely sampling the forbidden fruit.

He is setting up battle lines when I leave him to go into the living room. His parents will hate me, I think. I nearly trip over Daniella, a discarded lump in the corner of the hall. His parents will love me, I think. I have weaned him of an old habit. I start to congratulate myself. And introduced him to a new probably even worse one, I realize before I get carried away.

I fetch the bargain silver crown and stick it on a place approximate to Daniella's head. It makes her look more pathetic. Like a courtesan in the last throes who has wound a velvet bow around her throat. Mutton dressed as lamb, my mother would point out. I remove the crown. I adjust it on my own head where it slides down to my nose. No wonder it was so cheap. I throw it into the trash.

I sink onto the sofa. Being a parent is exhausting. I wouldn't mind a drink. Not champagne but a beer, a glass of jug wine. But in parenting begin responsibilities. I have been irresponsible enough. From my study I can hear Max's voice erupting in "Pows!" "Take that!" "Got ya!" "Bang Bang!" like the words in cartoon clouds. Be prepared for homesickness, Milly warned, for sadness. Max sounds happy. How cheaply I have bought the happiness of a child.

I leaf through some manuscripts, make desultory notes with my pen. What's Louie doing? I wonder. Eating the dinner that I was invited to? Did he find a substitute for me, a second-choice date? Cheryl? Or maybe—this gives me pause—I am the second choice after Cheryl refused. I know what Jake's doing. A partners' meeting. A seminar on real estate. He's got clients from out of town. "My meatpackers from Chicago, you wouldn't like them," he's explained, "but it puts money in the bank. And pays the alimony that provides the money to help Laura make sperm withdrawals from the donor bank." This last was said with more humor than bitterness. Maybe my presence in his life has leavened the usual recipe. At any rate, Jake will be spending Sunday with me and Max. We will play at being a couple, being parents just the way Max is playing now. "Arrrrgh, you're dead," I hear Max yell. Does playing war turn you into a warrior? Does playing house lead to joint purchase of real estate?

I go to the phone to give my mother a progress report. Nobody answers. Arthur is too much of a classicist to own a modern answering machine. And since my mother has Arthur, she no longer has to wait for that certain somebody or anybody to call. They're out yet another night in their wild social whirl. My mother is more popular than I ever was. I do have two men in my life, I remind myself. My mother has one. But I am too old and too liberated to count suitors like notches in a belt. Besides, for my mother, one of my suitors wouldn't even count. Then I think of her Sears man: am I being fair?

At dinnertime I rouse Max from his game to check the menu with him. "I have chicken breasts," I offer, "green beans, broccoli, cauliflower. Lamb chops. Turkey burgers, salad, potatoes baked or mashed. Seven-grain bread. Your choice."

"Pizza," he requests.

I order pizza from the Harvard House of Pizza. Two large pizzas with the works although there are only two of us, both rather small.

"Anchovies?" asks the man who takes our order.

"Anchovies?" I ask Max.

"Please, yes."

We eat the pizza straight out of the box sitting cross-legged on Max's bed and watching *The Simpsons*. A pepperoni falls onto the sheets and looks, Max and I agree, just like a baseball. When cheese dribbles next to it we are amazed at how you can't even tell. "At home my sheets show everything," Max says. "Even the fuzz from my stuffed animals."

"This bed is going to smell like pizza," I warn.

"Great," Max exclaims.

At bedtime, Max takes a bath. I brush pizza crumbs from the bed. Smooth the sheets. I daub at the cheese and pepperoni stains, I scoop away an anchovy that has fallen between the folds of the pillowcase. The bed smells like pizza. Max comes out of the bathtub rosy, smelling of the lilac bath salts I have poured into it. His pajama top is buttoned wrong. His hair is plastered to his forehead. I can see soap bubbles that he hasn't rinsed out. I want to take him in my arms. Put my nose against his hair, hold this delicious flannel-wrapped child in my lap. I restrain myself. Do you hug and slobber over eight-year-old boys? Do they settle happily against you or thrash around in the maternal overflow? Perhaps there'll be hints in

Zenobia's notebook as to what's acceptable in mothering. Perhaps Max will let me know what he wants. Or will tolerate.

I tuck Max in bed. I lie down beside him. Is it my imagination or does he move closer to me and snuggle against my hip. "Do you want a story?" I ask.

"Jokes," he says.

I sigh with relief. I've done my homework. Only this morning I stood in line at the checkout counter reading supermarket joke books for kids instead of the usual *National Enquirer.* The joke books are better value. Even if you don't buy either—which I don't—at least you learn a few jokes to liven up social situations or enhance your baby-sitting skills. Liz Taylor's love life, on the other hand, is not something easily put to use.

I put the jokes to use. "Did you hear about the guy who walked into the bar?" I ask. "It hurt."

Max laughs. I am relieved. I figured it was sensible to choose a book with jokes for kids over ten even though Max is only eight. It stands to reason that the child of Zenobia and Harriman Slade, the grandchild of Arthur T. Haven, would be precocious if not yet Harvard bound. Max and I, in fact, are probably the same age humor-wise.

Proven by the nearly identical hilarity with which we both offer and receive the following jokes:

Max: "Knock knock."

Me: "Who's there?"

Max: "Annie."

Me: "Annie who?"

Max: "Anybody there." Pause. "Get it?" he asks.

I nod. Then . . .

Me: "Knock knock."

Max: "Who's there?"

Me: "Duane."

Max: "Duane who?"

Me: "Duane the tub, I'm drowning."

"That's a good one," he concedes.

"You're telling me?"

"You're funny, Katinka," Max says. "Where do French fries come from?" he adds.

I could pretend not to know the answer. A common flirting maneuver to flatter a date. But for Max—my nephew-to-be by marriage—I choose honesty. "Grease," I say. "You told me that one the first time we met. It's my favorite joke."

"I know," Max says. "Mine, too. I made it up."

"Here's one not quite so good I read in a book." I poke his pajama top, which soft, plaid, flannel, and misbuttoned really touches me. "What did the policeman's pants say to the policeman's shirt?"

Max is already laughing before the punch line. "What?" he giggles.

"I've got you under a vest!"

We go on like this for ten more minutes until I run out of jokes and both Max's laughs and hiccups are running out of steam. "Bedtime," I declare with a sudden leap to maturity.

"Can I read for a while?" he asks. He points to his backpack. "I brought my books."

"Okay," I say. "But only for a while," I add parentally.

I kiss him good night. If he doesn't quite kiss me back, he still flings his arms around my neck and allows me to.

In the kitchen I put away the leftover pizza. I fold the pizza boxes by standing on them until they are small enough to fit into the trash. So far so good, I congratulate myself. The telephone rings. I lunge for it before the sound can disturb Max's reading or his sleep.

"Katinka, is everything all right?" my mother asks. "We wanted to be here when Zenobia brought Max but we had yet another Harvard function we couldn't miss." This last she says in her world-weary tone which does nothing to disguise her delight in an endless round of Harvard functions none of which she'd want to miss.

"Everything's fine," I say. I enumerate my triumphs with Max, our instant rapport, how latent skills have suddenly bloomed.

She and Arthur sign up Max for tomorrow night. "To give you a break," she says.

"I don't want a break. Don't need one."

"Nonsense. Just you wait." She pauses. "Next thing you know you'll have one of your own," she says in her Mother Knows Best voice.

"Right now I've got Max. For now that's all I want." I hang up the phone. If I've got Max I think I better figure out what to do with him. Even with my great instinctive skills, I can't trust that winging it will continue to work.

I go to the hall and get Zenobia's vinyl notebook. I'm struck again by its size. It's heavier than the later Dr. Spock, who covers all of childhood and society. You have to admire Zenobia, her attention to detail. I, too, know how prolific you can get moving from the general to the specific, from childhood to your own child. My obsessions with Louie would fill pages more than a more philosophical discussion of men. His toes alone would merit paragraphs. But I can't think of his toes now, one foot's worth so adorably peeking out of his cast. A foot for playing footsie with under Rosalie's dining table. Just thinking of Louie makes me feel guilty, like one of those untrustworthy girls who sneak her boyfriend in after she's been hired to baby-sit.

I open Zenobia's notebook. Under *Meals* it says, avoid fast food. Dinners should include two green vegetables and fresh fruit. Under *Toys*, it says, avoid action figures, anything that depicts violence or war. Legos and anything from Learningsmith is best. Under *TV*, NO CARTOONS in capitals. Under *Bedtime*, avoid jokes and other kinds of overstimulation. Once tucked in bed, no reading and lights out.

I wish the no-reading rule applied to me. If I hadn't read this, I could still be patting myself smugly on the back. Chastised, I pore through all the chapters, all the lists, all the instructions with an increasingly heavy heart until I get to the end. On the last page— about bathing with instructions that Max's hair get thoroughly rinsed—sticks a square yellow Post-it note. These are the rules for our own home, it reads, we can hardly and do not expect others to maintain such high standards but trust that they will use it as a guideline if they can. This should make me feel better. It doesn't. Perhaps with some syllogistic twisting, however, I can manage to make the case that these rules are too rigid for safe passage through a community. That I am doing Max a favor by exposing him to mass culture, letting him travel in coach with me. But have I exposed him to mass culture—the way you expose a child to bits of a toxin to make an antidote—or drenched him in it? My once proud shoulders sag. I return Zenobia's notebook to the hall table. I notice Daniella swept in her corner like an unloved mound of trash. I pick her up. What if Max should reach for her in the night? I pat her. Dust rises from her in little clouds. What if Max should get h-o-m-e-s-i-c-k and need something familiar? With Daniella against my hip, I tiptoe down the hall. Gently I nudge open the door, expecting to see a sleeping angel bathed in moonlight. Instead Max is sitting up in bed reading by Luxor lamp. I move closer. Propped against his knees is *Playgirl* magazine.

I drop Daniella, who lands with the thud of a half-filled mail bag and a bigger cloud of dust.

Max looks up. "Oh, hi, Katinka," he says casually, then lowers his eyes to the magazine.

"What are you reading!" I exclaim. A stupid question since I know exactly what he's reading. My head spins. I have to hold the door jamb to keep myself from joining Daniella in a lump on the floor. For the first time in my life I find myself considering the value of censorship.

"I found these on your desk," he says. "There's a bunch of them, all the same."

I look over at my desk where the magazines are piled under a couple of flimsy folders of my students' manuscripts, little more cover-up than a peekaboo bra I once bought at Freese's and which my father made me take back. The store gave me a refund even though there were signs all over saying underwear was not returnable. My mind races. When I think of all the dirt I scrubbed getting ready for Max, and then to leave this dirt. I catch myself. Calling a magazine dirt which publishes your story reveals a self-deprecation women need to stand guard against. But what about guarding a child from one particular woman's stupidity? I consider how to proceed. Do I snatch this magazine out of Max's hands as if it's in flames? Or do I approach him carefully, obliquely, with a calm voice, deliberate gestures as if it's an unexploded grenade propped against his knees?

None of my tumult communicates itself to Max. He's turning pages desultorily with a pleasant and measured look on his face that by no jump of imagination could be translated into a leer. His face is a mask of innocence. Innocence I've done my best to destroy. "This has cartoons and jokes," he says, "not as funny as the ones we know."

"Oh," is about all I can manage to get out.

"Some I don't understand," he continues, "and ads with stuff I've never seen before."

"Ohhhh," I say, this time stretching it into two syllables.

"The weirdest is men without any clothes on in their offices." He knits his brows, perplexed. "My dad always wears a suit and tie to work." He considers. "Do you suppose this is in Florida?"

I nod mutely. I'm not going to tell him that these are members of the Windy City bar, that Chicago winters make Maine blizzards seem like slight turbulence.

"In Amsterdam, it's very cold. You even need an overcoat."

"I suppose that's so." I reach for the magazine, grab it, roll it up behind my back, placing myself between Max and it. Too late.

Max giggles. "My friend Joel's dad has a bunch of magazines with naked women in his desk. Joel knows where he keeps the key." He pauses. I can practically see the cartoon lightbulb spark above his head. "Katinka, is this a dirty magazine?"

I know it when I see it, is what Potter Stewart said. Nothing human is alien to me stated Voltaire. "It all depends on your point of view," I equivocate.

Max rubs his eyes. Slips down under the covers. Talk about over-stimulation, I think, pizza, cartoons, war toys, pornography! I wait for him to say don't tell my mother. He doesn't. I am tempted to say let this be a secret between the two of us. That I don't indicates that I have at least a thread left of moral fiber or a well-developed sense of shame. I will have to tell his mother. Who will no doubt tell my mother. Who will . . . what? My imagination fails to conceive of the horrors in store. The repercussions. I study Max. He looks so innocent. Perhaps he is innocent. Sees the photographs as simply men in tropical climates who go to the office in their birthday suits.

I pick up Daniella and place her next to Max. I turn off the light. "Sweet dreams, pumpkin," I whisper. Max curls his body around Daniella the way Louie—back when Louie was a body in my bed—used to curl his around mine. I scoop the pile of magazines off my desk and take them out to the hall closet. When I open the closet door, a broom and an ironing board fall out. I put them back. I hang Max's jacket up. Then I lock the magazines in a suitcase I keep on the upper shelf. In the kitchen I drop the key into the sugar canister.

I sit down and think about Louie. A form of displacement my mother is better at. "Think sun and sand," she'll say, shivering in the middle of a storm. "Think happy thoughts," she'll say through a curtain of tears. I think Louie. I think Max. I think Louie. I think Cheryl. I think Jake, who floats up clearly defined without any kind of emotional excess baggage I have projected onto him. I haven't known Jake long enough to have acted badly. Yet. With Louie I've already two-timed him with Jake. But Louie's got Cheryl. I groan. This displacement stuff can work, though, unlike my mother's experience, it doesn't always make you feel better about yourself. It depends on what you displace to. I displace to Louie again. I call Louie. He answers on the fifth ring just as I am about to hang up. He's out of breath. "I've just got in," he explains. "Going downstairs on crutches is murder."

"Why don't you try it on your rear end."

"Not that I haven't. Tonight I'm wearing a good suit."

This information I tuck away for future obsession. Louie wearing a suit to have dinner with his mother is a subject I can work over and over like a chain of worry beads. But right now I have other worries. I tell him about finding Max in bed reading *Playgirl* magazine.

Louie laughs.

I am indignant. "It's not funny," I say.

"It's great," he says.

"Great?" I am starting to get mad.

"Great your story has come out. Gee, if I wasn't on crutches I'd run to the store and get a copy." He pauses. "Maybe if I change, so I can go down on my butt . . ." he considers.

"I've got a copy for you," I say, "but right now I'm more concerned with Max."

"You're *worried?*" Louie asks, incredulous.

"Yes, I'm worried. It's not actually reading material rated PG."

Louie laughs again. "Kids do this, Katinka. I was checking out skin magazines when I was younger than Max."

Which probably accounts for your getting Cheryl pregnant I think but do not say. "These are naked men," I explain, hating myself for making the distinction since I try to believe in an ideal world where sexual preferences mean as much as whether you take *Newsweek* or *Time.*

"Role models," Louie says.

"Not funny."

"Katinka, don't make a mountain out of a molehill," Louie says.

Don't be stupid, I'm about to say. I catch myself. "Don't be stupid" is what I used to say to Seamus all the time when he was being stupid. Which was a lot. But Seamus had a Ph.D. All of a sudden I feel as if I'm talking to someone whose fly is open or who has peanut butter stuck to his teeth and I'm too polite and embarrassed to point it out.

216

Louie goes on to tell me how much he misses me, my body in bed, my face when he delivered me the mail. He feels terrible about having to drop out of my class, which he was really beginning to like since I am such a gifted teacher. His sweet talk displaces my sour fears about Max. At least temporarily. He'll see me soon he promises. He'll find a way. In fact he's got an idea. Maybe he can arrange a sleepover tomorrow night with me. Sal and Rosalie have a golden anniversary party to attend. He can take a cab to Cambridge after they leave and make it back the next morning before they get up. It's not that he doesn't come and go as he pleases, he explains, it's not as if he doesn't have independence. But with his broken leg and all, well, his mother makes such a fuss.

For a moment my hope soars. Why not? It seems forever since I've been able to make a fuss over Louie up close and personal. I think of his body, imagine myself in his arms. But old desires make way for new maternal instincts. "Not with Max here," I explain.

"Why not?"

"Why not?" I repeat. "Isn't it obvious?"

"Sometimes, Katinka, I don't understand you at all," Louie sighs.

I get off the phone, shaking my head at the limits of Louie's child-rearing philosophy. He has no sense, I decide, because unlike me he has no child to be sensible about. Unlike me he has no child to practice on. Then I remember his hospital bulletin board papered with dozens of photos of his young cousins. There are children in his life. Perhaps what divides us is not class but how we'd raise a child. Are those things linked, I wonder? Do working-class parents have a more casual attitude to kids than working middle-class parents? I reach for literary examples: Dickens, Sue Miller, Rosellen Brown. A worm of anxiety starts to twist. I am relieved when the phone rings. It's Jake calling between meatpackers and developers. I tell him about *Playgirl*'s finally coming out. "That's wonderful," he says. I tell him about Max reading *Playgirl*. "That's terrible," he exclaims, "you must be sick with worry."

I allow that I am. Though I am getting over it. That's a sign of mental health, he says, that I don't dwell on my mistakes. Still he says he'll give this problem some thought. He agrees Zenobia will have to know. He hopes the damage won't be permanent. He'll check with someone in his office whose husband is a child psychiatrist. He can't wait to see us, he says. He's going to take Max and me to brunch on Sunday. We set up the time. "Oh boy, what I would really like is to spend the night," he says, "but with Max there it would of course be inappropriate."

It's Sunday morning and Max and I and Jake are driving along Soldier's Field Road. "It's your pick," I told Max earlier. "We'll eat wherever you say." His pick turns out to be the International House of Pancakes because they offer something called a Rooty Tooty Fresh n' Fruity special he has seen advertised on the TV that has been running almost nonstop in the room where he sleeps. Though Jake kindly invited Daniella, Max had declined on her behalf. She wouldn't be able to appreciate a Rooty Tooty special, he explained. I didn't remind him that when I first met Daniella she was lapping up my mother's consommé and leg of lamb. Poor Daniella. I know how the varying degrees of being loved can affect your appetite.

Max *sans* Daniella is belted into the back. Jake and I sit in the front. Across the frozen river a steady line of cars twists along Memorial Drive. On summer Sundays the street is blocked off and turned into a paradise of skaters, walkers, runners, bicyclers, dogs, and baby carriages. Maybe I can take Max here when the weather gets good. Maybe Zenobia will win another prize and ask me to baby-sit. Or more likely when she discovers what I've done or didn't do, she'll keep Max outside a ten-mile radius of me. I won't think of such things now I tell myself. If they awarded medals for avoidance, I'd be on that plane to Amsterdam.

The heater in the car has finally warmed up and is toasting my feet. Max and Jake are giggling over the same silly jokes Max and I have already giggled over. I lean back against the seat and feel enormously contented, the way I felt as a child on Sunday car trips with my parents when we would sing camp songs and spot out-of-state license plates and stop at roadside stands for lobster rolls.

I must say that despite a few false starts I am really settling into parenthood. Last night my mother and Arthur invited Max upstairs for dinner and a video of *The Lion King*. To give me a break. To give me time to read manuscripts. To write. To wash my hair. They understand what it's like to have a youngster underfoot. The demands. The exhaustion. This from parents of only daughters who, they both acknowledged, were dreams until puberty.

I had a quiet and lonely dinner. The healthy chicken breasts and cauliflower that I had intended for Max topped off by reheated pizza. Max is no fool. Even reheated, the pizza won the taste test. I critiqued some manuscripts. I turned on my computer. I turned it off. I washed my hair, which I had planned to give a deep body cream rinse treatment but didn't feel energetic enough. I read a chapter in a child-care book about separation anxiety. Then went upstairs to watch the end of the movie with Max. "What are you doing here?" my mother asked. She studied my face. My symptoms must have been pretty obvious because she nodded. "I understand," she said.

I wish I understood, I think now. What I do understand, however, is that separation anxiety applies not to Max but to me. Except for my age, I am a textbook case. I want to cling to Max, to pull at his parka the way an about-to-be-separated child might hang on to his mother's skirt. I reach over the front seat and touch Max's sleeve. Jake explains to Max about playing licenses and they find Illinois, New York, Connecticut, New Hampshire, and Vermont by the time we pull into the IHOP parking lot.

Inside, the waiting room is packed. The restaurant is packed. Everywhere is the smell of eggs cooking, of bacon sizzling, of maple syrup and melted butter. Why is it that food smells so good in inverse proportion to how good it is for you? My mouth waters, an automatic reaction that no amount of cholesterol consciousness can blunt. We leave our name with a waitress in a short-skirted teal uniform displaying an IHOP badge over the left chest pocket. She has a saintly pink-glossed smile despite the hordes of children and their families clamoring around us. "It won't be long. Our dining room is huge," she comforts. And I can see beyond her table and around the corner that she is right, that in addition to the cozy booths off the waiting area there's a larger space crowded with tables and chairs the size of a banqueting hall.

Max is jumping up and down with excitement. He pulls off his parka and hat and stuffs them into my arms. "Can I play video games?" he asks. The games, housed in what look like juke boxes with flashing lights and neon colors, ring the wall. "If it's okay with Katinka," says Jake.

"Sure," I say. After three days of permissive child raising now's not the time to disagree. Be consistent the experts advise. I'm not sure Berry Brazelton had in mind my version of consistency. It's the letter of the law not the spirit I am quoting from. Jake fishes in his pockets and comes up with five quarters. I dig in my pocketbook and find three more.

"All right," Max exclaims. His face turns hangdog. "My father says these are a waste of money and never lets me play," he confesses and runs off before we can make a moral stand.

"I figured Max would say that," Jake laughs. Once I confessed to Jake about *Playgirl*, I couldn't wait to unscroll my catalogue of lesser sins. Jake found the pizza mild, the colored sheets hilarious. We squeeze onto a vinyl-clad circular bench with a mountain-shaped backrest which looks like a larger version of a sofa for Victorian wallflowers. As soon as Max's back is turned toward the video screen, Jake takes my hand. "Harriman can be so pigheaded. Some of his restrictions I agree with—violence and . . ." The *and* trails off and I know he is diplomatically avoiding the word *pornography*. That he is sensitive to my feeling touches me. I squeeze his hand. He squeezes back. ". . . but hell, what kind of harm can an occasional video game and pancake do?"

Not much. Games and pancakes are neutral. Naked men in

Playgirl less so. First, do no harm is one of the first lessons med students learn. Something that should be taught to all students, especially those of us learning how to bring up a child. I watch Max. His hair at the back of his head looks electrified. His shoulders are hunched over his game. I play my own game. The murmur of the pancake eaters, the pressure of Jake's hand form a backdrop against which I can project the people in my life. I move them around as if I am trying out furniture in a model room: two men and a woman. Louie, Jake, and me. Two women and one man. Cheryl, me, and Louie. How about two men and a baby, a variation on the name of a movie I meant to see. I know from my writing and from my own life that these arrangements of characters, these configurations of men, women, and children are infinite. They're scenes in a kaleidoscope constantly shifting until finally there's a pattern you can settle upon. As a writer I can set up my cast of characters and push them around. In my story, I know more about them than they know about each other or themselves. In real life, I have knowledge that is always incomplete. Who knows what about whom? Jake knows about Louie, not Louie specifically, but the fact that there might be someone else. Louie doesn't know about Jake. Both Louie and Jake know my feelings about Max. I know the secrets about Louie's aborted baby. About Jake's ex-wife's baby-to-be. In my story I know the end before I start. In my life the outcome is a mystery.

A waiter approaches the bench. He unfurls a paper on which is penciled an endless list. "The Barnes party," he announces. "The Barnes party," he repeats.

We are seated at a table in the large dining room. Our table's in a corner in front of the window that overlooks the parking lot. "We could wait for a booth," Jake suggests.

"This is fine."

We study our menus, which tower over our heads. Though they state *Nobody Does Breakfast Like IHOP Does Breakfast*, they display more photographs of steaks and club sandwiches, pickles and fries than of pancakes or sausages. I check out the tables nearest us, which are reassuringly plattered with bacon and eggs, waffles, and pancakes oversized like the menu. Our order is taken by Mitzi, who has a dollop of whipped cream on her teal collar and whose eyeshadow is aggressively aquamarine. She winks at Max, obviously warming up her kid-friendly act. "What does your cute little boy want?" she asks. Max is too busy trying to figure out his choice of fruit-topped buttermilk pancakes in the Rooty Tooty special to notice this. A look that passeth understanding passes between me and Jake. We don't correct her. We're thrilled that she thinks Max is our kid, that we're a normal family out on a normal Sunday outing having break-fast at this shrine of normality. We play house so well it's taken for the real thing. Another look passes between us, two people burned by alternative lifestyles who yearn for conventionality.

Jake puts down the menu. "Why don't we all have," he lowers his voice, "what our little boy is having." It's worth two more Rooty Tooty specials, his voice implies, just to be able to say that.

When Mitzi takes our menu away with more winks and promises that the food will be "out in a sec even though the kitchen's kinda frantic," we sit back content.

"I knew this would be a nice place," Max says.

"You're right," Jake agrees with a conviction surprising in one who eats at Biba, agonizes over wine, cooks from Julia Child, and subscribes to *Gourmet*.

I sit back and enjoy the din, the smells, waitresses running back and forth, and babies throwing their spoons from their highchairs, grandparents doting and mothers rubbing sticky cheeks with Wash 'n Dris they've stashed in floral-covered diaper bags. Jake is asking questions about Max's school. About how math is taught, about starting oral French in the third grade. He's good at interrogation, at eliciting a telling response. I wonder if he ever considered trial law over real estate. The literature's got to be better—"Murderers I've Known" over "Tenancy by the Entirety," which, alas, I still haven't read.

Max is telling Jake how his class is going to be putting on a pro-

222

duction of *Hamlet* in the spring. There will be five Hamlets and five Ophelias so everyone will get a turn to be a star. They'll divide up the lines. With the same costumes and makeup the audience will never be able to tell the difference, except for the Hamlets and Ophelias who are taller and fatter than the other ones.

Jake laughs. "I'd like to see that!"

"The tickets will be free," Max says. "So you can come."

"Then I will."

Max is going to be one of the Hamlets, he explains, though for a while he was seriously considering the Ghost. He's not sure yet what he'll have for lines. Since all the Hamlets want to do *To be or not to be*, they'll probably have to draw straws.

"I'll keep my fingers crossed," says Jake.

"And bring Katinka," adds Max.

"A good idea."

"My grandpa is going to marry Katinka's mother," Max continues, maintaining such an air of studied casualness I'm not surprised he's been picked for one of the Hamlets, "but they're too old to have a baby."

"They already have children," I point out, "not to mention the world's best grandchild."

"I know," Max says with becoming immodesty. He pats his hair down, which as soon as he removes his hands springs back up. "Maybe you and Jake will get married and have a baby, too."

"Max!" I exclaim.

Jake laughs. "You have pretty good ideas, Max. No wonder you're one of the five Hamlets. You're pretty smart."

"My grandfather says if I stay smart I can go to Harvard."

"Without a doubt," I say. Something your step-grandmother-to-be will love, I think.

Our food comes and we fall on it like starving lumberjacks. "It's just like what I thought," Max says, awarding five forks and four stars.

In between bites Jake regales us with a bunch of food jokes in descending order of corniness. I wonder what book he picked up in the supermarket checkout line. We all finish everything on our plate. This surprises me since love is supposed to make you lose your appetite; maybe parental love increases it. For a while, I ponder this. Now that I think of it, I've also been doing a lot of eating with both Louie and Jake. Not that I'm ready to declare love for either of them. My feelings aren't that clear. Except with Max.

I study this object of my love. Max's lips are ringed with a clown mouth of maple syrup. His cheeks look rounder, redder, more fully fleshed. Not that we aren't all more fully fleshed after a breakfast like this. I push my chair away from the table. I slip my hand up my sweater and unbutton my jeans. Jake leans back in his own seat and sighs contentedly. His cheeks which I admit I first found squirrelly are now looking almost as cute as those of Max. "I knew this would be really good," Max says. "I just knew it. Sometimes when you see an ad on TV, you can't believe it, everything looks fake, but this . . ." He gestures at the remains of his Rooty Tooty special which consists of a few crumbs in a puddle of sauce and the hull of a strawberry.

"Isn't it great," I say, "when something billed as wonderful turns out to be just that?"

"Hear hear," says Jake. Under the table he touches my ankle with the tip of his shoe. This makes me nervous given my intimate congress with Louie's toes.

Jake and I manage to come up with three more quarters. Max runs off to play more video games. We order coffee which Mitzi pours from what she calls "the never empty coffee pot." She nods in the direction of Max. "Your kid's adorable," she says. "He's got a little bit of both of you."

"You think so?" Jake says. "I hope he's got more of his mother and less of me."

"You men," Mitzi says.

"You men," I say after she goes to refill her empty "never empty coffee pot."

I sip my coffee. I look around the dining room, which is beginning to thin out. My eye stops at a table at the opposite corner of the room. A man and boy sit there. Their hands are swooping up and down like gulls. A pair of crutches leans against an empty chair. Even from this distance I can see that the child has light hair and a tilted nose. Even from this distance I could identify this back anywhere. My heart stops.

"Katinka!" Jake asks. "Are you all right? You look like you've just seen a ghost."

Banquo's ghost, Hamlet's ghost, the ghost of Christmas past, the ghost of Christmas *parties* past. "One pancake too many," I explain. I look back at the table where a very unghostly Louie sits with a very real child. Their hands are spinning and weaving over the tabletop. They are talking sign language, I realize all at once. Their hands stop. Louie reaches for his crutches and gets out of his seat. I grab a menu from the table next to us and start studying it.

"You want something else?" Jake asks, incredulous.

"Just looking," I say, looking at Louie, watching him and this child make their way through the dining room—a real obstacle course for someone on crutches though of course Louie does it gracefully. I don't have to worry, however, that he's about to spot me and go for the world's record in awkward moments; his eyes are fixed on the child's flying fingers and he keeps nodding while negotiating a path to the exit.

And when I turn my head to the window which overlooks the parking lot, the first thing I see is a dilapidated minivan pulling up to the door.

The next morning I call Louie. "There's something we need to talk about."

"Shoot," Louie says.

"Not here. Not on the phone."

"Hey, Katinka. I thought you were baby-sitting for Max and didn't want any boyfriends around." This he says with a skim of false cheer over an undercoat of worry.

"Max's parents are coming to get him in a couple of hours."

"Well, then what about tonight? I could probably sneak away. It's been so long . . ."

For a minute I'm tempted. I picture Louie's body, imagine the touch of his fingers. *Playgirl* overload has tipped the balance in favor of the pleasures of the flesh when it's the problems of the relationship that need dealing with. I steel myself. "Tonight's no good. Later this afternoon."

"I'll take a cab over."

"Not my apartment," I say. "Someplace neutral."

"That bad?" he asks.

"That bad."

We arrange to meet at the Pamplona at four. It's a coffeehouse between Bow and Arrow streets I tell him. It's dark and quiet. Though it's in the basement, there aren't too many stairs.

"No problem," Louie says. "You should see me on these crutches, I can really get around."

"So I've noticed." I hang up fast.

I force myself not to think about the scene at IHOP. I'm going to put all my questions on hold until the hour of four. Meanwhile I plan to cherish my few remaining hours with Max. I'm already starting to miss him even though he's sitting right next to me drawing in the sketchbook with the crayons that, in addition to the Power Rangers and cowboys and Indians, I was astute enough to provide. Over the last few days I have honed my maternal instincts to a diamond clarity. This despite the fact that no sooner have I become the good mother than I have to relinquish a motherly claim. Now I am trying to work on my separation anxiety. Max is going home and I'm already feeling homesick for him, hoping, selfishly, he'll feel homesick for me. When I was in summer camp, I hurled myself into the middle of every Sunday night lineup of sobbing girls who were allowed to call home, they missed their mothers so much. Did my mother yearn for the sound of my voice the way I yearned for the sound of hers? Unlike Milly and Charlie, though, my parents didn't grab their coats and drive two towns over to rescue me.

Milly thinks she's such an expert on homesickness but she doesn't know the half of it. I know she doesn't miss her kids when they're off on their overnights. I know the best summers she's had are when the kids are away at summer camp. Maybe that they're your kids is enough for you to let them go. Unlike mere parental affection, my passion for Max has the intensity of first love. "What are you drawing?" I ask Max.

He pulls up the flap of the sketchbook to make a shield. "It's a surprise," he says.

It's no surprise that I'll miss Max. I'm an expert misser, practice having perfected the art. I miss Louie, the pre-IHOP Louie. I miss my father; some days I even miss Seamus' familiar arrogance. I miss my own home which, my mother told me yesterday, may be sold to yet another Frenchy. This one hopes to raise the roof, add a heated swimming pool and state-of-the-art gym, and turn it around for double the price. My mother thinks it's doomed to failure, that Mainers prefer local watering holes and to get their exercise lobstering and splitting wood.

I've probably lived in Cambridge too long to claim a Maine soul. I never split a log or trapped a lobster. I've eaten plenty of lobsters, though, and clams, and bushels of wild blueberries. And no doubt an equal number of Harvard Square's Bartley's burgers and Elsie's roast beef specials before Elsie's closed. When I was a kid I'd pose for photographs at the boot of Paul Bunyan, the gigantic statue dwarfing Bangor's civic auditorium. At Radcliffe I'd perch on John Harvard's lap in front of University Hall. I'm someone whose allegiances are easily switched. As demonstrated by the example of Louie and Jake. I need to let go of the Old Town house. I need to let go of Max.

And because I need to let him go, I pull Max close. Carefully he puts his drawing to one side. Graciously he doesn't protest. How time passes when you're having fun, I think. How time passes when you don't want it to.

And no time at all seems to have passed before Zenobia is ringing my bell.

"Max!" Zenobia cries.

"Mummy!" Max flings himself at her. I have to look away. I have to go away. I go into the kitchen. I put the kettle on. The mother-child reunion does not need a mother wannabe watching jealously. When the kettle whistles I figure time's up. I put two mugs of tea on a tray and a glass of milk for Max (the empty Coke cans are safely stashed in the basement recycling bin) and repossess my living room.

"Tea! How lovely," Zenobia exclaims. She is sitting on my sofa looking immaculate as always, not like someone who has just spent eight hours on a plane and for whom it is already after eight. Max is on the floor, his feet stretched under the coffee table playing with a toy windmill and some wooden figures of children on silver skates. "I'm so sorry about the delay."

If only there were a delay. "What delay?" I ask.

"Well, Harriman absolutely had to go to the office and check his mail. I finally left him there. The whole trip back was a nightmare. We almost didn't make the plane."

If only you didn't, I think. "What happened?" I ask.

"My medal set off the security alarms."

"It was that big?"

"Presumably. Harriman and I were taken to a side room and practically strip-searched. It was inconvenient and unpleasant. But Harriman was incensed. He's probably researching right this minute the channels whereby an American citizen can sue the Dutch."

"Holland must have been nice."

"Cold and gray."

"What about the ceremony? The award dinner. The honor? It must have been wonderful."

Zenobia gives a dismissive wave. She balloons her cheeks, "Pffft" escapes from between her lips. It's a gesture I've seen French actresses make in black and white films shown in art theaters with espresso makers instead of popcorn machines. "Boring. After a while they're all the same."

I nod but feel no sympathy. Zenobia reminds me of successful writers who complain about book parties and editors, talk shows and cross-country reading tours. We on the outside looking in would kill to have such things to complain about.

"And I missed my little guy," she adds now.

"I'm not surprised," I say. Here's something I can identify with.

Zenobia sends Max into my study to gather all his stuff. I hear the TV go on, the raced-up music of kids' cartoons. I hope Zenobia is ignorant enough to think it's some background music to a *Nova* special on endangered species. Maybe she is, because she doesn't rush over to investigate. Instead, she leans closer to me. She lowers her voice. "So how did it really go?" she asks.

"Great," I say. "I've fallen totally in love with your son."

She smiles. "I'm not surprised."

"We've had a marvelous time." I pause. "Though there are a couple of things I need to tell you."

"Max misbehaved?"

"*I* misbehaved. We had pizza, Big Macs, pancakes. From soup to nuts the whole way paved by fast food."

"Is that all?" Zenobia sighs with what sounds like relief. "I left a note to you that I wasn't expecting you to follow my nutrition plan. It's probably good for Max to be introduced to mass culture. In small and limited amounts."

How small? How limited? I wonder. The size of a deck of cards? The size of a Rooty Tooty Fresh n' Fruity IHOP special? Maybe the cure for mass culture is the homeopathic introduction of bad foods to build up immunities. "That's not all," I continue. I hope that once you begin to confess it gets easier. Velocity propelling what starts out in spurts to end in a flood. But confessing to Zenobia isn't exactly like telling a priest behind a curtained grille you stole your little brother's candy bar. "Wait." A picture is worth a thousand words I tell myself, choking on the words I can't quite form. I go to the kitchen and fish the suitcase key from the sugar canister. Zenobia watches the moving picture I make with a puzzled look on her face. I move to the hall closet, take down my suitcase, which I bring to the coffee table and place in front of her. I twist the key in the lock, pop up the top. Inside are dry cleaner's bags, the cardboard from two packages of pantyhose, and five copies of *Playgirl* magazine.

"What have we here?" Zenobia picks up a magazine. "Katinka! Your story's been published."

Not just my story is the problem. "I feel so terrible . . ." I start.

"Did they mess up the proofs? I certainly understand. The fights I've had with editors. Why, I—"

"Not that. But I stupidly left the magazine in my study—Max's room. And he—quite naturally—started reading it."

Zenobia doesn't say anything. I don't know what's on her face since I refuse to look at it. Her silence stretches.

Stretching my own fear along with it.

Finally she responds. "It's your study, Katinka. And Max—well, you can't protect a child from everything."

With this I dare to move my eyes to her face. Her brows are knit. Her hand cups her chin. Her face isn't mad, just concerned. She looks like she's mulling something over. She leans forward like *The Thinker* of Rodin. "This may in fact be a good thing. For the same reason that Max's school assigned Daniella—to show the underside of life, to give these overprivileged kids a reality check. Naked bodies, pornography—they're all a part of our society. Besides," she takes away her hand and thrusts her chin, "I don't believe in censorship."

"Me neither," I state emphatically. After all, in our good old American society *Ulysses* was banned. Bibliophiles bought copies from Sylvia Beach under the shadow of Notre Dame and smuggled them through customs. But there's no disputing *Ulysses* is great literature. I gulp. So my story's in a magazine devoted to the underside of life, in the Daniella floursack equivalent of the literary marketplace.

"So," Zenobia rubs her hands together, "let's take a look."

Side by side on the sofa we each hold a side of the magazine. First we move to my story. Zenobia admires the illustration, the typeface, the size of my name. She can't wait to read my work, she exclaims. I take another magazine from the suitcase and hand it to her. She slips it into her Hermés pocketbook where it fits with the precision of Cinderella's shoe. I show her the ad for the penis-enhancing elixir. She starts to hoot, then covers her mouth. I show her the naked lawyers. Tears stream down her cheeks; she is shaking with the laughter we are both trying to muzzle for the sake of Max. "Look at that! Look at that!" she whispers.

I remember many years ago going with Milly and her two boys to one of the bookstores in Harvard Square. There was a window seat for children then with a stuffed Curious George and a bookshelf of *Tintins* and *Babars* and a rack of magazines. We settled them in. Five minutes later giggles sailed out across the aisles of customers followed by a stentorian "Look at them boobs." When Milly reached them they were convulsed with laughter, two blond brotherly heads bent over *National Lampoon*.

Now as Zenobia and I bend our heads over naked lawyers, I feel we have formed a bond. We could be friends, roommates, sisters. Our shoulders touch companionably. We are two sisters under the skin. Two sisters staring at skin.

Two sisters who stop staring at the sound of Max coming down the hall. We put the magazines back, zip and lock the suitcase. "Are you going on a trip, Katinka?" Max asks.

"You never know. I like to be prepared," I reply.

Our good-byes are rushed in a flurry of overcoats and mittens and suitcases. I hug Max. I hug Zenobia, this natural extension of Max. "I left you a present on your desk," Max says. In a flash, they are gone.

I hang my head. Out of the corner of my eye I notice Daniella slung into a corner of the hall. I run into the vestibule where I catch them just in front of—oh misery! oh symbolism!—the glittering row of polished mailboxes. "You've forgotten Daniella," I pant, out of breath.

"Oh, darling," Zenobia says to Max.

"Keep her, Katinka," Max says to me. "You can throw her away. Or maybe make pancakes out of her. You know she was never really a person," he instructs, "just a bag of flour."

With a heavy heart, I drag myself back to my apartment, the rejected Daniella propped on my hip. I feel so sorry for her, this prince turned back into a frog, this adored child abandoned to a bag of flour. I feel abandoned myself. By my borrowed child, my borrowed sister. And I feel something else—the stirrings of pride. I have weaned Max from Daniella, a feat Zenobia and Harriman couldn't accomplish with all their enlightenment. Still, I can't bear to dump Daniella or sift her into batter. After mothering Max, I'm not too excited about mothering her. I settle her back into her corner in the hall. I go into my study where on my desk is the drawing Max has made for me.

I pick it up. "To Katinka With Love From Max" is printed across the top. I think of the Salinger story, "For Esmé—With Love and Squalor"—another precocious enchanting child. I've always loved Salinger the way some people adore Elvis—with a mixture of identification and hero worship. I had a friend whose daughter attended the same prep school as Salinger's son. Once when this daughter was registering parents for parents' weekend, she watched a slight nondescript man write J.D. Salinger across a stick-on name tag and fainted dead away. That J.D. Salinger broke his seclusion for the sake of his son still touches my heart.

I study the drawing of my own son-for-four-days. It's a group portrait: a little boy with sticking-up hair standing between what I assume are his parents. The mother with a briefcase and a bun. The father with a briefcase and a tie. Over to the side, smaller, more indistinct is another figure, a woman, holding something in her arms. The woman is wearing a red plaid shirt like the one I am right now wearing over my jeans. The blob in her arms could be a baby, Daniella, a magazine, or, even, a pizza-sized bribe. There are trees all around, and flower-strewn paths. In the distance towers the spire of Memorial Church. In the foreground tiny cowboys and Indians are half hidden by the grass.

What can I say? Only that Max is a genius and in a few more years will be hanging in the Fogg. I'm going to have it matted on archival acid-free paper and put into a gold leaf frame. I'm going to center it on the wall across from my bed where I can see it when I first awake and just before I go to sleep. That Max has chosen to include me in a family portrait however remote I am from its nuclear core moves me profoundly and shores up my confidence.

Confidence I'll need to confront Louie. Family pictures slide across my eyeballs. My parents. Arthur and my mother. Zenobia and me. Max and me. The drawing Max made of me. These make way for a picture I have so far held in reserve. It's the kind of picture set up in a small room off the main gallery. On view by invitation only for privileged clientele. Out of view unless you stumble across it on your way to the ladies' room. It's Louie and a child at a table in a restaurant. In the space between their heads two pairs of hands fly up.

I arrive at the Pamplona on the dot of four. I've changed my red plaid shirt and jeans for a neutral gray sweater and skirt. I'm not dressed to kill or dressed for success but cloaked like a nun. This implies serious conversation with no sexual overtones. Louie's already there. I can see his crutches through the basement window as I go down the stairs. My tone must have been enough for him to know to choose a table near the back.

I open the door. Nobody looks up except Louie. Only two other tables are occupied. A woman along the side under the window is stirring espresso and writing in a notebook. A large black-bearded man is slurping gazpacho and reading a newspaper propped up against the sugar shaker. The newspaper is printed in Arabic. Next to the gleaming coffee machines a handful of waiters are murmuring in Spanish or maybe Catalan. They're an interchangeable group, dark-haired, slim-hipped, in black trousers and white shirts. They're too young to be the same waiters who served me iced tea and ginger parfaits back when I was an undergrad. Yet they look exactly the same.

As, dammit, does Louie. Handsome and adorable with his wide-eyed startled innocence. This is not the face of a liar and a cheat you wouldn't buy a used car from. His appeal isn't even watered down by the fact of Jake. Leg trouble and parent trouble, Cheryl trouble, and impending trouble with me have left no lines on his velvet brow. He's not grown fat being waited upon by his mother, missing the exercise he gets along his route, missing the calisthenics in my bed. Why am I recording this lack of change now, I wonder, since I saw him only two days ago. But then it was the child who grabbed my attention, and the movement of Louie's hands graceful as Javanese shadow puppets as they signed to this child became the hypnotist's ball I needed to focus on.

"Katinka," Louie says, and the delight on his face is something Laurence Olivier might have found hard to approximate. He starts to get up.

"Don't get up," I say. I pull out the chair opposite him. I plunk myself down.

He leans forward, his lips beginning to form one of his earth-moving kisses.

I avert my face.

"Uh oh," Louie says.

One of the slim-hipped waiters glides over to take our order. Up close I notice that he is not that young. Though who is anymore, except for Louie's knee-weakening boyishness. I harden my heart.

While we wait for our coffee, I think how to proceed. How do I lead up to this? Now Louie is studying the menu with the kind of intensity I've only seen on Jake. But it's pretty clear Louie's is a delaying tactic since we've already put our orders in. It's pretty clear Louie needs something to hide behind.

He pokes out from behind his menu, which nevertheless is still covering his mouth. "Remember Chris Smith?" he asks. "The guy who shared my hospital room?"

I nod.

"The one who was circumcised?"

"Of course I remember," I say. "It was only a couple of weeks ago. Besides," I add pointedly, "I never forget a name or a *face.*"

Does his own face which I have committed to my fabulous memory (along with selected body parts) look a little stunned? Or am I imagining this?

"At any rate," he goes on, "he's getting married in a month. He sent an invitation, addressed to me and guest. How about it Katinka?"

"You're inviting me as the guest?"

He nods.

"You want me to go with you?"

"Of course."

"As your *date?*"

"Of course, as my date." He's getting exasperated, explaining to someone with a learning disability what is obvious. "You're my girl, you know."

This touches me more than I care to admit, so much in fact that I don't even bother to amend "girl" to woman. I feel my resolve starting to melt. Am I your girl? I want to ask. And if so, what are the components of that possessive pronoun? The standard-issue forsaking all others, the mutual revelations of past and (in comparison to the present) failed loves, the vows of monogamy, the pledges of honesty? I'm afraid of what I might say, so I don't say anything. The silence stretches to such a level of discomfort that Louie adds, "Who else would I take?"

A tactical error. Who else, indeed. With that question I am set back on course.

"Please go with me," he implores.

"It depends."

Before he can ask on what, our cappuccinos arrive. I lick off a clot of steamed milk. I spoon up the rest until all that is left is a surface of black coffee dotted with a few drifts of foam like floating islands. Louie, on the other hand, seems to be saving his froth for last. In Maine we used to have philosophical arguments over whether to crack open the lobster tail first or hold off till the end.

You can tell a lot about a person by the order in which he eats. For instance, do you start at the widest arc of a pie or its narrowest point? Studies have probably been made of this.

Now Louie seems to be making a study of me. Never mind the mechanics of coffee and my own reluctance to get to the point, Louie can hold on to a thread. "Depends on what?" he asks.

It depends on the right answer, I want to coach, though given the facts—the minivan, the kid—the odds aren't good. Less good even than for the lottery and its windfall of megabucks. Still, hit the jackpot and you win the refrigerator, the trip to Hawaii, and the grand prize of Katinka O'Toole. Answer wrong . . . I plunge right in. "I saw you Saturday, at the International House of Pancakes."

"You did?" he asks. He picks up the menu again and keeps staring at the list of coffees as if they're troops he can summon to surround the enemy.

"You were with a little boy."

"I was?" he says.

"I think he was deaf. Or at least," I search my internal dictionary of politically correct terminology and come up with: "hearing impaired."

"He *was* deaf. He *is* deaf." His voice is flat. The voice of someone surrendering to defeat. His body crumples in on itself like buildings that have been wired to implode.

"Who *is* he?" I persist.

"Tony . . ."

"Tony who?" I ask. I feel as if I've been stranded in the middle of one of Max's knock-knock jokes.

"Tony . . ." Louie's voice trails off. He spins his fingers in the air. Is he signing a name?

"What's that supposed to mean?" I point to his hands. "A bird, a plane. It's superman?"

"Not funny, Katinka."

"You think I don't know that? Oh, brother . . ."

He sits up, although his eyes are now riveted on a little basket of Sweet 'n Low. "Actually, he's my brother . . ."

Sure, as in "He ain't heavy, Father." I may come from Maine, not exactly the show-me state, but I'm no bumpkin. "Don't insult my intelligence. Rosalie's well beyond the age for a ten-year-old. You don't have a little brother, Louie." Did Louie hit his head when he fell on the ice and broke his leg in three places? Did some part of his brain disconnect and float away?

"Not that, Katinka. The Big Brother program. You know the one they're always promoting on TV."

I am incredulous. Many's the time we've watched those public service announcements tangled postcoitally in one or another set of my carefully selected sheets. It's a pretty easy transition from TV to *speaking of big brothers* . . . "You mean this is something you've never bothered to tell me. That you're a big brother to a little brother who's deaf? Who you learned sign language for? Who you spend a lot of time with?"

Louie is now looking as if he's just confessed to a crime rather than a generous act of public service. He straightens all the packets of Sweet 'n Low so their corners line up. He shifts the salt and pepper shakers and the little bottle of Tabasco so they form a triangle. He folds his napkin into a precise square and wedges it under the wobbly table leg. Order in the face of chaos.

Which is something I understand though a compulsion for geometry does little to neaten your basic messy world, a world now spiraling out of control. "Louie," I say, and my voice, surprising me, is not unkind.

"So much is at stake," he says.

"I agree," I say.

"I feel like such a jerk," he says.

"I won't disagree, Louie. Just tell me," I urge.

"To think," he goes on, "I made up such a stupid story for someone who's so smart. For someone I care so much about. For you who . . ."

"Who what?"

He shrugs. His shoulders go limp. He's collapsed so far down in his seat he could be Daniella or, more appropriate, a half-empty sack of mail.

"Go on," I say.

The words come out in a rush: "I didn't tell you because I was so ashamed. Because once we started, from that first kiss, I felt like there was no stopping us as long as I didn't rock the boat. With you everything was so exciting, so much fun. I felt interesting, free, not just a mailman with a lot of—well—responsibilities. Not just someone whose life was set, whose future was predictable. Remember those flowers that were served at Gregory's party? I never knew such things existed. You ate one. I didn't, but then I thought that next time I would. That I could. That eating a flower would be something I could do. That with you I could have adventures." He pauses. Takes a ragged breath. "I was afraid to tell you in the beginning because I figured you wouldn't even consider seeing me. And then later—I wanted to. I knew I had to. But I was afraid of losing you . . ."

"Louie," I say. "Tell me what?" I must be nearly yelling because the man looks up from his Arabic newspaper and the woman freezes her coffee cup in midair. Who is this crazy woman making a scene in such a sanctuary? they seem to say. I lower my voice. "Please, Louie."

"Okay, okay. Tony . . . he's my son."

"Your son?" I gasp. The appropriately hammy response to a soap opera or some romance novel I'm in the middle of. I picture the photograph in Louie's hospital room, the child on the other side of the restaurant. This is something that underneath the layers of denial, the fairy tales of my own making, I have perhaps always suspected. You jerk, I think. You jerk, I want to say. And yet my development is arrested somewhere along the path from girlfriend to antagonist because what comes out is, "He's beautiful."

"Which doesn't make it easier."

"*It?*"

"Everything. Having Tony. The guilt. His handicap. Every time I look at him—it's so painful."

"You should have told me."

"Don't you think I know that?"

"Not telling me spoils everything between us."

"No need to rub it in. The story of my life." Louis groans. "I just wanted to keep things the way they were. I was ashamed. Afraid you'd change your mind about me."

"Because of your lie or because of your son?"

"Both." He nods. "I was—I *am*—afraid that you'd look down at me. That I wouldn't have a chance."

"A chance at what?"

"At you. A classy college girl like you."

"Class!" I spit out the word. "Oh, Louie, I hate when you do that," I say. "It's not class. It's the lies. The lack of trust." I go on. "But you must realize that it's the *secret* about your son that hurts the most. The simple fact of having a son is not necessarily the end of a relationship. You know how I feel about Max."

"But Max is different. He's perfect."

Max *is* perfect, I think. "No one is perfect," I say.

"Tony is deaf."

"That's not the issue. It's not telling the truth."

"I know that, Katinka. I went to a parochial school. I was taught lying is a sin. Believe me, I don't make a habit of it. When I wrote that story for you in class? Well, I guess I kind of tricked myself into thinking the story was really my life. Was not a lie, but—well—fiction. For a while, I even started to believe it. In class. With you. I guess that's why I liked writing so much. You can mess with the facts, put yourself in a better light. The real story, Tony's deafness, is so bad I wanted to change it. It's changed my whole life." He pauses. "My mother says it's a sign. A punishment."

"A punishment for what?"

"For being young and stupid. For not being a good Catholic. For

241

wanting an abortion. For not doing the right thing by Cheryl. For not being ready to settle down. For thinking that, for imagining that you . . ." He hits his fist against the table. "My mother says I've got just what I deserve."

"And what do you think?" I ask, recoiling from a vocabulary belonging less to a writer, more to a therapist.

"That she's right. That I'm being punished. Still am being punished. Look at you and me. It was silly to hope. I should have figured it wouldn't work out. The differences between us. Plus the way I lied. About the abortion. About everything. We did intend to have the abortion. We were in the doctor's waiting room when Cheryl changed her mind. I tried to convince her to go through with it. She wouldn't listen . . ."

I stare at Louie. He is a study in misery. His hands grasp his cup so tightly, it looks like it might break.

"I baby-sit Tony every Wednesday. Cheryl's taking classes at night to get her RN. We both went to school to learn sign language. You wouldn't believe the expenses for Tony, special classes, tutors. One of the reasons why I am still living at home."

"In addition to your mother's manicotti." It's a pathetic stab at levity.

Which he ignores. "At first Cheryl wanted us to get married— before we knew about Tony's deafness. Our parents agreed. But there was so much I wanted to do. I even thought maybe I could go to college. Meet a different sort of girl. After Tony was diagnosed, I ended up having to quit school anyway. To go to work. After a while I figured maybe Cheryl and I might as well marry. Then it was she who didn't want to. Don't do me any favors, she said. Don't feel you have to do your duty by me. I was like a robot going through my life. Until I met you, Katinka."

The waiter brings the check. He tucks it under the salt shaker, ruining Louie's triangle. Louie doesn't notice. Straightening bottles of condiments will not straighten Louie's tangled web. "Now I've lost you, Katinka."

About that, I'm not yet sure. We've probably lost each other, though I'm not ready to take any bets. But if he's lost me, maybe Cheryl will be the consolation prize. Sometimes you can't use the refrigerator. Or the trip to Hawaii is scheduled wrong. Sometimes you're happier with the toaster oven or the microwave.

Louie reaches over and touches my hand. He gives a little squeeze. "You know Katinka, I really like your stories. If I was a college kid, I would have loved to be in your class."

I pull my hand out from under his and give his a quick pat, a motherly pat, a teacherly pat, devoid, I hope, of sexual content. I busy myself blotting puddles of coffee on the black marble tabletop. Louie's hand lies pale and forlorn like the cheese that stood alone. Is it my imagination or are his fingers trembling slightly?

Louie takes his hand from the table and reaches inside his pocket. He brings out his wallet and a roll of stamps.

"Hey, I've got a present for you," he says.

"I can't be bought."

"That's pretty clear," he says. "But from the tone of your voice on the phone when you set up this meeting . . . I guess I was desperate." He opens his fist and holds out the roll which, when I take them, I realize are Love stamps.

"I gather these didn't just happen to be at the top of the box?"

"You gather right. I nixed the Stars and Stripes, the sheets of Marilyn Monroe, tons of Nixon stamps that nobody in Cambridge would touch with a ten-foot pole."

"Under the circumstances, I better give these back."

"Oh, don't Katinka," Louie implores, and his voice cracks.

My fingers fold over the stamps. An involuntary motion since I know they're a hot potato I need to unload.

"What about Chris Smith's invitation?" Louie asks, pressing his luck.

I shake my head. "Are you sleeping with Cheryl?" I ask.

"No," he says.

"Really?"

"I did," he admits. "We'd be feeling kind of lonely, sad. Worried about our kid. It wasn't like with you. No stars or anything. And since I've been with you, I've been—what's the word?—monogamous."

Which is more than I've been since I've been with you, I think. I feel a twinge of guilt. I do have my secrets, I remind myself, though secrets are not lies. Not until Louie asks me who I'm sleeping with. Why doesn't he ask me? I wonder. Is he too egotistical to entertain the possibility of someone else. Or too modest to presume? I am so confused. Can I even believe Louie when he tells me he's not sleeping with Cheryl?

"What about us?" he asks now.

"I don't know. I am so confused."

"I don't blame you, Katinka, if you never wanted to see me again. If you went so far as to move away to avoid me even bringing you your mail. You don't need to tell me I'm in the market for a heavy dose of reality. Why, I'm so crazy that Chris Smith's invitation got me to thinking . . ."

This is a sentence Louie has the sense not to finish. "You couldn't possibly imagine," I begin, then stop. But of course this, along with the Nobel in literature and Teacher of the Year, is something I have been imagining. I've made a logical leap from two bodies naked in bed to a bride and groom on top of a wedding cake. Ignoring the fact that the groom is wearing a mailman's uniform and is lying through his pearly teeth. Ignoring the fact that the groom prizes the bride for her differences from him—not a foundation to build a marriage on. Ignoring the fact that the bride prizes the groom for the fleshly incarnation of something you can see in certain magazines. Ignoring the fact that all these unsuitable alliances can end in tragedy, *An American Tragedy*. Or if not tragedy mere unhappiness, which is bad enough. I shudder. I look at Louie. What to do? For a writer who is supposed to be a keen observer of human nature, I'm pretty much at a loss. All I know is—as one of Max's classmates will soon say—there's something rotten in the state of Denmark. "I'm not sure what to do or what I believe," I admit, "only that there's something rotten in the state of Denmark."

"Don't think I don't know that's from *Hamlet*, Katinka."

"I wouldn't have had a doubt," I say though I am not exactly telling the truth. I am glad he knows *Hamlet*. It lifts my heart the way finding out he was a library user once did. I signal the waiter, who starts to detach himself from his cluster of clones.

"I'm so sorry, Katinka, I've screwed up royally. Is there any chance we could just keep things as they are? As they were?"

I shake my head.

We fight over the bill. Louie insists on paying. It's my treat, I demand, since I set the meeting up. Louie argues chivalry. I champion independence. We finally split it down to the last nickel of the tip. The coins, slightly tarnished, make a sad pile, a reminder of Seamus, of how dissolutions bring out pettiness.

The waiter sweeps our money up with the check just as tears start to spill from Louie's eyes. He smears them away with the flat of his hand. The waiter averts his head. It's unseemly for a man to cry in a coffeehouse while sharing cappuccino with a woman, his posture seems to say. But of course the waiter's Spanish, the land of macho men, and Louie's Italian—or Italian-American—a heredity from which feeling soars as flagrantly as Pavarotti's handkerchief. "So it's over?" he asks with the wrenching cadences you might hear in a rendition of " 'O Sole Mio."

"Probably," I say.

"I'm not ready to give up yet."

"Dragging things out is no solution."

"It's all my fault. Please let me make it up to you."

"Perhaps we need some time," I stall, though I suspect that Louie and I as an item is getting as stale as day-old bread. But he looks so crushed. And I feel so before-the-fact bereft. "Let's have a moratorium for now." I open my hand on the roll of Love stamps. I flick them over to the side of Louie's table. "Good-bye, Louie," I say.

"Keep them," Louie says. "You can always use the stamps."

On the way home I shed a few tears. Once inside my front hall they really gush. It wasn't all sex and lies and, well, letters instead of videotape. There was sweetness. We shared a bond. Poor Louie, I think, who at least has, if not a consolation prize, the consolation of a son. Perhaps if I'm out of the picture, he'll start to view Tony not as a punishment but as a gift. My mother might say things happen for a reason. That the reason Louie was given such beautiful hands was for talking with his son. I pick up Daniella. I cry into her lumps, which my tears will soon dilute into paste. How the mighty have fallen. Once Daniella dined at Arthur T. Haven's table. Now she'll be good for smearing onto construction paper. In my childhood books, bad guys were always turning horses into glue. In grown-up real life princes turn out to have secret children and insufficient consciences.

The phone rings. "Katinka," my mother says, "you sound terrible."

"I may have broken up with Louie."

"The mailman?"

"What other Louie is there?" I sob.

"I'll be right down."

"I prefer to be alone."

"Nonsense. For a broken heart only a mother's love will suffice."

When I let her in she's doing a good job keeping the glee from her face even if the corners of her lips are pulled down somewhat theatrically.

"I said good-bye," I explain.

She puts her arms around me. "You did the right thing."

I snuffle. "You only say that because he's the mailman."

"Not so."

"Is so. I know you disapproved because of his job. Because he didn't have a suitable degree."

"How can you accuse me of such a thing. After what I told you of my Sears man."

"Whom you gave the old heave-ho."

My mother releases me. Looks me in the eye. One brow slightly raised. Her chin determined, teeth clenched. It's her I've-got-something-to-tell-you look.

"I've got something to tell you," she says now. "I didn't dump him. I was too embarrassed to admit this, but the fact is . . ." Her voice rises to a pitch of incredulity. "He dumped *me!*"

"No!"

She nods. She sighs. Her eyes are sad. She shakes her head. "Among other things, he called me a snob. Can you believe it?"

I can believe it. But this is not the time to say so. I need her motherly bosom too much, her motherly sympathy. "Oh, Mom," I say.

She puts her arms around me. "So now you've got nothing to rebel against."

We have gin and tonics. Summer drinks in February. My mother after all has just come back from Jamaica, and I have a seasonal affective disorder that only the symbols of summer will cure even without the promise of white sand sliding between Louie's tanned toes.

My mother leaves. I assure her that I feel better. "Gin helps," she says. "So will Jake."

Now that I know she was dumped by somebody with no degrees, a man who snubbed her for being a snob, who wore a uniform with his name embroidered on the pocket flap, a Sears man she would—might—have taken if he had wanted her, I don't feel so bad that she's cheering for Jake.

Whom I call as soon as she is out the door.

"What's the matter, Katinka? You sound terrible."

"You know that other relationship I told you about? The other so-called contender in the great battle for my affections?"

"I'm on my way," says Jake. "Put the wine on ice."

15

The weather suits my mood. Outside my window the sky weeps. I weep. I'm three weeks into my moratorium with Louie. Three weeks into my exclusive relationship with Jake. Jake's happy. My mother's happy. Louie's miserable. He leaves plaintive messages of love and longing on my machine. I've taken to monitoring my calls. "Are you there, Katinka?" he'll plead. "Just let me hear the sound of your voice." I don't trust the sound of my voice in response to the sound of his. Sometimes, when I am feeling especially melancholy, I'll fill a glass with brandy, rewind the tape, and play "Katinka, are you there?" over and over as if it's my favorite concerto.

Still, for the most part I am doing better than I would have thought. Most evenings my dance card's penciled in with Jake. Some nights I sleep over at his house in Lexington. The sex is better if not yet stars. Though Jake's not a natural like Louie, he's a good student and a hard worker. Right now we're more like proto-stars—those masses of gas heading toward fusion and, then, ultimate stardom.

What's really nice about Jake is he's not a tit-for-tat kind of guy. He understands that I've declared my own apartment a sex-free zone. Not just for you, I explain, but all members of the male persuasion with the exception of Max. Why does my one bedroom with great location and wood-burning fireplace feel less like home and more like an encampment surrounded by enemy territory? I ask him. He surveys his own center entrance colonial, its plundered remains of matrimonial battles. Funny, he agrees, how fast a castle can become a dungeon. With my mother upstairs, Jake can appreciate the stress-relieving properties of geographical celibacy.

When everything gets to me, I throw myself into my work. Mornings, I slave over my prose. Afternoons, I study my students' manuscripts and devise writing exercises to shake them up. "Two pages of a doomed romance," I assigned last week. India Germaine wrote a piece about a tubercular violinist and the man who launders her bloodstained handkerchiefs that had Eddie, the cab driver, shedding tears on his tattoos.

The truth is I've become a good teacher. After a rocky start—due to standing in for Seamus and my new-at-the-job nervousness—it's been smooth sailing, to use one of Muriel Kingsworthy's navigational metaphors. But what's really amazing is that I've developed a spine.

Maybe the suffering over Louie acts as a kind of calcium for assertiveness.

It was last week when I put my new resolve to the test. I was in the middle of critiquing one of Muriel Kingsworthy's novel sections. The phone rang at eleven at night, not Louie's time to call. I still considered letting the machine pick up. I was afraid of losing the thread. But the problem was there was no thread, I realized, and lifted the receiver. A mistake. "Katinka," Seamus bellowed, "I want my class back."

I had a sudden picture of a cartoon child banging a spoon and demanding his strained applesauce. Boy, was Seamus, gray-bearded and professorial-browed, an illustration of how looks deceive. "What do you mean?" I asked.

"Exactly what I said. I'm a new man and raring to go. I'm off my bed. Fit and ready for work. I've neglected my students long enough."

"Too bad," I snapped. "No! No! No!" I shouted. And surprised myself.

And Seamus, too. "Am I hearing you right?" he asked.

"You gave the class to me."

"And you had the privilege and fun of teaching it, not to mention the enhancement to your résumé. I didn't realize my rallying powers. Georgette's introduced me to Chinese herbs and acupuncture. And over in Watertown, there's this extraordinary Swedish masseuse . . ."

Watch out, Georgette, I wanted to warn. But if Seamus is a good rallyer, so am I. "No Way, José," I emphasized.

"Be reasonable, Katinka."

"I am."

"Then you are seriously misguided." He paused, and I could practically hear him put on his thinking cap. "Well, perhaps at your next meeting you might summon a vote."

"I just might. And I wouldn't be so sure of the outcome if I were you. Indian giver!" I yelled and hung up the phone.

I passed a few hours in misery. But if Seamus wanted a popularity contest, I was ready to fight. I considered my troops. Who I'd need to marshal for my support. My ranks have already been decimated by the desertion of Cindi and Louie. Rebecca Luscombe's dropped out, too, for reasons other than my inadequate attitude toward sisterhood. She's been appointed the editor of a new feminist magazine and has switched to premed. My other students are making good progress. Except for Muriel Kingsworthy, who writes the most high-blown prose larded with a thesaurus' worth of adjectives though I keep admonishing her to simplify. And Russell MacQuillen, whose capacity for being boring deserves the Guinness record book. Since I wasn't pasting silver stars onto their manuscripts, these two were the obvious Benedict Arnold candidates.

When I presented the problem to the class, about Seamus' desire to come back, Muriel Kingsworthy was the first to jump to my defense. "But you're a great teacher," she exclaimed, "the best." (Which resulted, I must admit, in my unusually warm praise over her latest offering.) "Certainly more pleasing to the eye," Eddie Horgan added. "I've learned a lot," Jonathan Marshall said. The vote was almost unanimous, the lone dissenter being Russell MacQuillen, who felt he'd be better understood by Professor *Seamus O'Toole*.

I savored my victory for a long time. You're a great teacher, I told myself, even "the best." But despite my class-confirmed abilities, lately I've come to realize I prefer to write rather than to teach writing. The truth is I've started a novel. It takes place in Cambridge. It's about a romance between an artist and a policeman. The artist's father, who lives around the corner from her studio, is having an affair with the widow of a Harvard archaeologist. And there's a child confined to a wheelchair whom I might change to being visually impaired. I've checked out three library books on Braille. Central to my novel is a CPA with a big heart and red socks. If you're supposed to write what you know then I certainly know what I'm writing about. And I'd rather be writing my own pages than writing criticism on somebody else's. I wake up in the morning panting to get to my desk.

Which, in addition to providing a surface to write on, is taking the place of the analyst's couch. Writing about what's happened between me and Louie has given me distance. Transforming Louie from real life to fiction is a form of therapy. The faster I write the faster I am recovering. Still, I must admit that when I hear the clatter of mailboxes I have a little pang.

Even though I know it's not Louie. He's graduated to a walking cast and has been given a temporary desk job at the Central Square post office. This suits me just fine since I buy my stamps and send my packages at the Harvard Square branch. I figure that between writing about Louie and putting actual space between Louie and me, I'm making real progress in getting over the relationship. Not to mention the fact that because of my suffering, I may end up with a book. Still, it's amazing how the symptoms linger after the disease is gone. Jogging by the library yesterday, I spotted a mailman who was short and balding and still nearly tripped off the curb.

We've got a substitute mailman in the building who is a mail-woman. She wears her hat at a rakish angle and her standard-issue blue hems folded under to the length of a miniskirt. Her skills aren't Louie's either since she keeps mixing up my mail with Mr. O'Riley's on the third floor, as if O'Riley and O'Toole were interchangeable. Some nights I can keep myself awake worrying that a *New Yorker* acceptance might turn up lost in the pages of one of Mr. O'Riley's *History Today*'s. Unlike Louie, she doesn't seem to value her work.

The young men in my building, however, seem to value both her work and her miniskirt. Two of them, grad students with odd hours, do a lot of hanging around the vestibule from noon to one. I must say it doesn't add to the tone of the building to see people leering in the lobby in the middle of the day.

Nevertheless, despite my problems dealing with various aspects of the mail, I had no problems dealing with Seamus. After my vote of confidence, I called Seamus to tell him the results of the ballot. He wasn't home. I didn't announce my victory on the machine. I needed to crow in front of a live audience.

The next morning, Seamus called me back. He apologized for not being reachable. He's been spending a lot of time on the table of the Swedish masseuse.

"The *table?*"

He let that pass. "And in the library whipping my lesson plan into shape."

"Which you don't need," I explained. "They took a vote."

"And?"

"And elected to stay with *Katinka* O'Toole."

There was a long, sputtering pause. "They say a good deed never goes unpunished. Lord knows what wiles you've used."

"You're a poor loser, Seamus. You don't play fair."

"And you do? You've certainly made the most of *my* name!"

He hung up the phone in a fury a second before I could hang up the phone in a fury. *His* name! Katinka O'Toole, Katinka O'Toole, I said, and it tasted like food gone rancid.

Katinka O'Toole, I say to myself this morning. It's a cracked record that for the last few nights has been playing on repeat. My next step is becoming clearer. Still, Katinka O'Toole is the name on my stories—my professional name. Katinka O'Toole is the name on my mailbox—my domestic name. I picture Seamus' syllabus with Georgette's notes scrawled over it. On the back of the last page she had written Georgette Elizabeth O'Toole, Georgette Elizabeth Edmunds O'Toole, Georgette E.E. O'Toole, G.E. O'Toole until the ballpoint pen ran out of ink. We women can be so pitiful. I think of my own scribblings in the margins of elementary school books, attaching my name to the sixth-grade flavor of the week: Katinka DuBois, Katinka Goldberg, K.G. MacFadden, Katinka G. Quince. Even if as a writer I am known as Katinka O'Toole, I can't exactly say I've made my reputation with that name. My public can adapt. Look at the rock star Prince whom all the newspapers now refer to as "the rock star formerly known as Prince."

I call Jake at the office.

"What a pleasant surprise," he says.

"I need to find out about legally changing my name."

"By marriage?" he asks.

"From marriage," I exclaim.

"That was an unenlightened question," he retreats. "I do apologize."

"Accepted. I want to take back my maiden name."

"I see. I'll connect you to our family law department," he says. "Just hold."

I hold for less than a second when a voice announces "Evelyn Atamian" into my ear.

I explain what I want.

Couldn't be simpler, says Evelyn Atamian as if mine is the easiest problem she's ever had to deal with in a month of overlong and overscheduled days. I can file a petition for a change of name in the Middlesex County Probate Court. And I need to publish a legal notice of the citation at least seven days before the return date in *The Cambridge Chronicle*.

"Publish a legal notice?" I ask.

"A technicality," she says. "Ostensibly to give anybody who wants to a chance to object."

"Like in a wedding, like in 'if any person present can find just cause why these people should not be joined in holy matrimony . . .'?"

I must sound a little hysterical because her voice slips into professional tones of reassurance. "Objections rarely occur. Besides the print is so fine in those legal notices hardly anyone looks at them."

"That's a relief," I say.

I am about to hang up when she adds, "Of course you'll need your birth certificate. A certified copy with a raised seal. You can try to get it through the mail, but I always advise clients, if they don't come from too far, to get it in person. That way you can make sure it's exactly what you need."

I know exactly what I need. I call Milly and arrange to borrow the Dumpmobile for the weekend. I explain why. "Go, Katinka, Go," she cheers. "Finally you are taking control of your life."

I take control of my laundry. Between declaring my apartment sex free and declaring my life Louie free and thus freeing myself up for work and misery and taking control of my life, I have let my housework slide. My sheets haven't been changed for weeks. When I toss my jeans onto the floor they practically stand upright.

I grab a basket of laundry. Next to it is another basket equally stuffed to the brim. In addition, there's a tangle of kneesocks and tights I have raked into a neat pile behind the bedroom door. But you have to start somewhere. I wedge the basket against my hip and chug down to the basement laundry room where—guess who?—is folding undershorts on top of a sawhorse-propped plank.

"Katinka!" my mother exclaims. "Fancy meeting you here."

Is this a standard greeting or a comment on my personal hygiene? I decide not to follow this train of thought since my mother is managing to look both delighted to see me and concerned about the degree of brokenness of my heart. I study Arthur's undershorts, which are stacked across the table like the higher-end magazines in upmarket bookstores. They're a colorful bunch: stripes, polka dots, rows of sitting ducks. I notice one with a border of hearts, another an overall pattern of miniature *veritas*es on their crimson shields. Gifts, no doubt, from my mother. I'd know her mark anywhere.

"Those look crisp," I point out.

"It's a combination of bleach and detergent. And grabbing them from the dryer before the wrinkles can set." She stops. "So how are you?" she asks. She's not about to discuss undershorts with somebody who might be sensitive about not having her own basket's worth of hundred percent cotton, colorfast men's mediums.

"Managing."

"Jake must help."

"Yes. And no. It's not quite the same as substituting mustard for mayonnaise and being equally content."

"If that's your analogy. But I might pick something else. More like champagne and beer."

"I could have guessed."

"I can't say I like your tone," she objects, then catches herself. I watch her smooth out her features, make allowances for the suffering of her child. "No word from the mailman?" She is trying not to look hopeful.

"Words, yes, on the machine, but no sighting."

"That's a start," she says in her you-can't-expect-everything voice which nevertheless expects everything. "Though I always believe absolute cold turkey is the way to go in affairs of the heart."

"Is that what happened to you. With the Sears man?"

"Yes. I think it was much too painful for him to see me ever again. I was grateful in the end. If he hadn't broken it off, and so cleanly, I wouldn't have become a Graham." She snaps the elastic on a pair of blue Oxford cloth shorts for emphasis. She brightens. "And I wouldn't be becoming a Haven."

The way she says it, it sounds as if Graham is one of the lower stations of the cross on the way to Haven.

In a fury I empty my basket into the nearest machine, stuffing together my black socks with my white bras, my navy turtlenecks with my khaki pants.

"Katinka," my mother points out, "you are mixing up your blacks and whites!"

I ignore her. So what if everything turns gray. It will suit my mood plus save time trying to coordinate.

My mother sighs. "Your underwear will turn gray," she states. Her voice sounds resigned to the fact that her daughter's limp dingy bras will never induce pheromones in a gentleman's crisp red-striped undershorts.

"So, you're changing your name? You're becoming a Haven?" I accuse.

"Naturally."

"Well, isn't that funny because I'm changing my name, too."

My mother claps her hands. She executes a pirouette on the cement floor. I know she's thinking *to Barnes* just as I say, "Back to Graham."

"Graham?" she ponders as if it's a word she's never heard before.

"It is my name. It is *your* name," I point out.

"But what about O'Toole?" she asks. "Seamus is so well known." This from the mother of a daughter whom Seamus left for the M&M's, whom he humiliated, condescended to, from whom he tried to steal back his class. Talk about Benedict Arnolds! Talk about motherly love and loyalty!

I empty half a box of Tide into the machine and slam down the lid. I press a bunch of buttons, not paying any attention to which one is what. I can't look at my mother. My so-called mother. I turn my attention to the bulletin board across the room: A marmalade

257

kitten has run away. The couple in 7C have a StairMaster to sell. There are instructions about recycling. About storing bicycles. "Warning," one notice proclaims in black letters outlined in red: "All tenants should take extreme caution against allowing access to unwanted visitors." I should have read this earlier. In comes my mother and there goes my neighborhood.

My mother continues as if my back isn't turned, as if my back isn't rigid with anger. "O'Toole's been your name for so long."

"I could say the same about you and Graham."

"I know, dear. But I'm making changes, being open to new things."

"So am I."

"But you're going back to the old." She pauses. "Of course, it is a problem in Boston, in Cambridge, always having to make the distinction between the Boston O'Tooles and the Dublin O'Tooles."

I press my lips together. Maybe I'll buy the StairMaster for my mother so she can get in shape for climbing the stairway to Haven.

"*Graham* is better than some," she sighs. It's a bigger-than-a-breadbox kind of statement—not better than Barnes or O'Toole, but better than . . .

"Better than what?" I ask. I turn around to face her.

"Than . . . What was that mailman's name?"

"That mailman's name, as you well know, is Cappetti. Louie Cappetti."

"Thank God for small favors," my mother says.

"Snob," I yell. "No wonder the Sears man dumped you. You are a terrible snob. Snob. Snob. Snob!" The words bubble out of me like the rabid froth of a raging maniac. To the accompaniment, I soon discover, of clouds of soap bubbles which are oozing up from under the lid of the washing machine. The bubbles pour over the side to frost a landscape of hills and dales across the floor. Within seconds, the washing machine starts to shake, rattle, and roll. None of these amazing phenomena distract my mother, who stands frozen to the floor, her mouth open, her eyes bright with tears. Then she turns on her heels and stomps upstairs, abandoning me, the belching, dancing washing machine, and three neat rows of Professor Arthur T. Haven's underpants.

The next morning, I go to Milly's and get the Dumpmobile. I pack my bag. I write a note for the super's box. *I broke the machine,* I confess, *please send me the bill for repairs.* I scribble a curt message for my mother: *Am going to Maine. Will call when I get back.* I should add a post-script of apology. I don't. The Maytag man can fix the broken washing machine. I can try to fix my broken romance with Louis. But who in hell can repair this mother-daughter relationship?

I ride the Dumpmobile like a cowboy on a rodeo bull, I race out of Boston and across the New Hampshire turnpike. I am so far over the speed limit that the dials for the radio fall out. I'm fed up, fed up with my mother, with Seamus, with Cambridge, with Harvard and all it implies, with Boston and its distinctions between the Boston and Dublin O'Tooles, with an apartment building where you can run into just anybody in the basement laundry room. The faster I drive the faster I am putting all this behind me. A car coming in the opposite direction beams its lights. A speed trap? This doesn't slow me down. What's a mere ticket when I'm already resigned to being wrapped around a tree. I imagine my funeral. My mother, the newly minted Mrs. Haven, will have a hard time deciding what to wear. Seamus will toot his act of generosity: he gave me his class, thus initiating in me a final flame of self-esteem before its all too early extinguishing. Daniella will talk (okay—so it's fantasy) about how well I mothered her. Barney Souza will say what a faithful customer I was, how I never tried to chisel into line or seek out the discount chains. Max will say I told good jokes. Betty Jean Williamson, my editor, will mourn a great writer cut down in her semi-youth. My tires spin. My thoughts fly. How did Lady Chatterley end up? I wonder. In *An American Tragedy*, Roberta was pushed out of a boat. I am being pushed to the edge. At my funeral, Louie will be sad. And Jake. Milly will really sob. I start to sob. Then catch myself. If I slow down maybe I won't be measured for a coffin just yet. I lift my foot from the gas pedal. My spirits lift. And by the time I am halfway across the Portsmouth bridge and see the sign: *Welcome to Maine, Vacationland,* I am heading for home.

I arrive at Old Town in the early afternoon. I am ravenous. I'd like to say it's because of Maine's pure air, the scent of pines, cleansing breezes coming off the sea. But the truth is, Old Town and what surrounds it—Bangor, Brewer, Veazie, Orono (which at least has the university), Stillwater—are the camping grounds of paper mills and shoe factories, grim towns with boarded-up centers, more gas stations than comfort stations, and, circling their outskirts, rings of going-out-of-business malls. "Oh, you come from Maine!" my college friends would clap their hands, and extol the glories of rocky coast, of surf, of idyllic weeks at summer camp, of forests not yet deforested. "Maine is lovely this time of year," my mother might say though lovely is not the adjective she'd pick for Old Town, for her town.

But it's the one I pick for *my* town—if lovely is an adjective used freely for what is loved and not what is beautiful. I drive down Main Street, past the Old Town Canoe Factory, past shabby buildings and deserted stores. Clumps of snow are banked against the curbs. A man in a cap and the plaid coat of a lumberjack gets out of a pickup truck. *This Maine-iac climbed Mount Katahdin* is stuck on the bumper. Old Town is a lovely city, I decide, a city without pretense, without snobbery.

I go down Water Street. At the crossing there's a handmade notice broadcasting bingo on Monday nights, another promoting a church supper featuring Mabel Corcoran's homemade pies. Two feet from these, there's a more official sign, hexagonal, announcing Deaf Child. I slow down. I study it. I make a right onto Chester, drive past the McClellens, the Boudreaus, the Richardsons, and pull up in front of number 58. I look at my house. My heart gives a thump. I recognize that thump, it's a close relative to the one I had when I first saw Louie over the tops of trays with flowered food and across a crowded room.

The house is small, clapboard, painted white with green shutters and red trim. There's a wide front porch and a narrow garden in the back. From the dormer window you can see a slice of the Penobscot River. It's modest, sweet, not a house you'd think of as having the potential to be part of a hotshot renewal scheme. But it's not a house that looks deserted either, abandoned by my mother, left to my father's ghost. When I get out of the car, I see a ladder propped at the side and hear someone hammering on the roof. "Hello! I lello!" I yell.

The hammering stops. A face peers out just where the roof peaks.

"It's Katinka. Katinka," I hesitate. "Graham," I add.

"Well, I'll be," somebody yells. "Hold your horses."

A man skips down the ladder lithe as a monkey even though he's wearing a heavy coat, boots, cap, and, I notice as he comes nearer, thick gloves.

One of which he removes. He holds out his hand. "Frenchy Levesque. Why the last time I saw you was at your high school graduation. You were valedictorian."

"Salutatorian, really. Jesse Cornman, the first in our class, had a speech impediment."

He laughs. His lips are chapped. His face is weatherbeaten, with a natty gray mustache, and eyes bright as black jet beads. "I still remember that speech. About the importance of roots."

I am amazed. Until this minute I had forgotten it. Had I chosen that topic or had the drama teacher, whose polished product— me—was going to be credited to her manufacture, suggested it? I cast my mind back. It was a generic speech. I remember the end: "In conclusion, faculty, parents, friends, fellow students, even though after commencement we will all be branching out in separate ways, blossoming and ripening on individual and often distant vines, we have in common our roots, sunk deep and strong into this soil we call home." I cringe.

"So how long are you planning to be here?" Frenchy asks now.

"Just a night."

"Too bad," he says. "I suppose you'll be wanting to stay in the house?"

To stay in the house never occurred to me. "I thought a motel."

"And pay those prices? For that cardboard construction?"

"Well . . ."

"The house is fine. With spring coming, the melting snow, I'm making sure the roof is watertight. I've got the key."

And I've got a key, too, I realize all at once. It's on my key chain among the keys to my apartment, the basement door, the storage bin, the mailbox, and a molted rabbit's foot. "I'd love that," I say. "But I thought the house was about to be sold, or already has been, to a developer."

Frenchy grins. "That was no developer. That was my son." His face turns serious. "A fool-brained scheme. Naturally fell through. The kid's always looking for something better, never content with what he has. Now he's got some ridiculous idea about making his fortune down in Florida. Damn silly state if you ask me. Anyway. Kids have to go. Branch out. Make their mistakes. He'll soon be home."

"So the house is still for sale?"

He nods. "And your mother's lowered the price. She seems awfully eager to get rid of it." He pauses. "You've got your mother in you. And a bit of your dad. How are things up in Cambridge?"

"Fine," I say. "The usual."

"I spent some time there myself," he says. "Didn't like it much."

I tell Frenchy I'll return later. I have things to do. He gives me the name of the real estate agent. I ask what's the best bank in town for mortgages. He checks his watch. The bank's closed, he explains, but I can call Tubby Burnside at home. Everybody does. He hands me his key just in case mine's rusted out and doesn't work. He'll get the roof finished before night. It'll all come back to me, he says, how cozy it is, what a nice house.

I call Tubby Burnside at home. "Katinka, old buddy!" he exclaims. He was a year behind me in school. A fat kid who wore his jeans pulled too high and was the president and only member of the Old Town High investment club. I explain my plan. "Have you eaten yet?" Tubby Burnside asks.

"No, and I'm starved."

"Me, too," says Tubby with enormous sympathy. "Let me get hold of Marge Gilmore—was Marge Goodreau—the real estate agent, and we'll meet you at Auntie Vi's in half an hour."

Tubby and Marge are already sitting in a booth at Auntie Vi's Family Restaurant when I arrive. In front of Tubby quivers a tower of ruby Jell-O studded with marshmallows on a leaf of iceberg lettuce. Marge is dipping a spoon into a fruit cocktail piled onto a scoop of lime green sherbet. I slide in next to Marge since there's more room on her side. They beam at me. Tubby's in a plaid flannel shirt and jeans which, these days, are slung low enough for his belly to hang over. Marge, who was head cheerleader and known as Goody-Goody Goodreau, is in jeans and an Irish sweater. Her hair's pulled back in a ponytail. She looks just the way she did when we made a pineapple upside-down cake together in home ec. I think of city real estate agents in their padded-shoulder power suits. And of bankers, for that matter, in their pinstripes. Of course it's Saturday. Still, Marge and Tubby could be anyone: rich man, poor man, beggerman, mailman. I remember my mother told me that Tubby had gone on to Wharton after the U of M. That he had been a prodigy. In Old Town, people surprise you.

Which holds for our waitress, who turns out to be Pollyanne Mulligan, my best friend from the neighborhood. "I'd know you anywhere," Pollyanne says.

"You, too," I lie.

The truth is she has the severe face and no-nonsense mousy

brown braid of a professor of women's studies whose class I once audited. At the end of eighth grade she went on to John Bapst in Bangor, and we lost touch. Who knows how parochial school changed her. I'd have never recognized this serious person as my devilish friend. Except maybe for the cross dangling over the top of her striped apron. "She once was a nun," Marge whispers, implying that in Old Town waitress can be substituted for nun as easily as green beans for broccoli.

Over submarine sandwiches layered with sweet pickles, I explain to Marge and Tubby that I want to buy my house. I pull out the small looseleaf notebook I always cart around for jotting story ideas in. I've filled one section with all the necessary information. The money my father left me, my stocks, my savings. Marge and Tubby take out their own notebooks, their own pens. They do their own arithmetic. For a moment the only sound is the crunch of pickles and the scratching of writing implements. "We can just about do it," Tubby says.

"I second that," Marge agrees.

"I'll send you a mortgage application," Tubby says.

"I'll get to work on the Purchase and Sale Agreement," Marge adds.

Tubby nods. "Things move fast in Old Town. We can probably have you in your old front yard for the Memorial Day parade."

Tubby orders another submarine sandwich. He offers me half. I'm tempted, but I have to go, I say. We shake hands all around. Pollyanne Mulligan refills Marge's coffee cup. "Katinka's moving back," Marge tells her.

Pollyanne Mulligan smiles, it's a beatific smile, but then she was once married to God, and now lives with Jesus. She fingers her cross. "Alone?" she asks.

"We'll see," I say.

There's no line at the Town Hall even though all the notices make a point of their Saturday hours to accommodate working parents and busy citizens. My birth certificate with raised seal is produced with high-tech efficiency without high tech by a clerk named—I see from her tag—Glory who had been doing geometry problems in a composition book. I write out my check. At ten dollars, it's a bargain. But then my lunch was only $3.29.

As I am leaving I notice a table under an *Information* sign. I pick up a sheaf of brochures. One section is labeled "Our Public Schools." I study a leaflet called "Mainstreaming," subtitled "Special Education for Children with Disabilities." *Paid for by Your Tax Dollars* is written in bold letters at the end.

I drive around for the rest of the afternoon. I drive down old familiar streets. I drive to Orono, and across the campus of the university. Students stroll the paths or stand in clusters under trees. The campus is large, open, with rolling grounds and vast distances between buildings. I cross the bridge to Indian Island and explore the reservation. In Big Chief Thunder's Trading Post, I purchase a feathered headdress and a peace pipe for Max from a woman with lots of turquoise jewelry and few teeth. I could teach writing here, I think. There would be a need. And at the university.

On the way home, I buy a steamed lobster from a shack which advertises they sell them "live and kicking all year long." I stop at the liquor store for a six-pack of beer. I make a wrong turn. A one-way has been reversed. What used to be a shortcut to Birch Avenue is now a dead end. Another street has been paved over for a skating rink. When I see the Deaf Child sign, however, I know exactly where I am.

My key sticks a little in the front door but opens it. In the kitchen three chairs are arranged around the maple table in their usual place. It's the house that time forgot, that I never have. Automatically I pull out my own chair from the side between the head and the foot. I change my mind. I feel strange, like a character in a feminist retelling of *Goldilocks and the Three Bears*, but, still, I take my mother's seat. I eat my lobster. I drink my beer. I wander the rooms figuring out which will be my study, where I'll put a guest. By nine o'clock, I'm in my own room fast asleep in my own bed.

16

There's a Post-it stuck to my apartment door when I return to Cambridge. "Truce," my mother has written beside the outline of a dove.

What can I say? Only that she is my mother. That she has her good points, too, though none at the moment spring immediately to mind. I dig for compliments on her behalf. She's funny, generous, a Democrat (in party if not philosophy). She's a good cook. She loves me. And come Memorial Day when my absence from Cambridge will make the heart grow fonder, I'll be able to love her back.

But before I accept her olive branch there's something I need to do. I take pencil, pen, scissors and go out into the vestibule. I measure. I cut. I write *Katinka Graham* on the piece of paper and slip it into the slot on my mailbox eclipsing the *Katinka O'Toole*. I admire the new me even though it's not a legal new me yet. Just as I start to turn back I begin to worry: can I count on the substitute mail deliverer to recognize my substitution and thus parcel out the mail accordingly? Under the *Katinka Graham* there's just room for me to write in parentheses: *formerly O'Toole.*

I am proud of myself. I feel strong. Once inside my apartment, I tap Max's peace pipe for good luck. Then I phone my mother.

"Thank God," she says.

"I left a note."

"For which I'm grateful. Though part of me was afraid you'd gone to Maine for good."

I bite the bullet and tell her. That I'm buying my old house and moving home.

This is greeted by an astonished silence followed by a series of gasps.

"I'm filling out the papers now. I'm about to notify the landlord not to renew my lease."

"I don't believe it."

"Believe it. Goody-Goody Goodreau is drawing up the Purchase and Sale even as we speak."

My mother groans. "How can I *sell* my own child her childhood home? Let me call the bank and see what can be arranged."

"And deny me my rediscovered Maine-born gene for self-sufficiency? I insist on buying it. Besides, it's a bargain."

"That's true," my mother agrees, "but only because it's in Old Town. Only a fool would actually choose—"

"Mother . . ." I warn.

"It's my fault," my mother says, her voice contrite, "because of what happened in the laundry room."

"You *were* impossible," I admit. No absolution. Not so soon. "It's something I've wanted for a while, just hadn't realized yet."

"Do you know that I was so upset I forgot all about Arthur's shorts and a repairman left a dirty wrench on them."

"Try a little bleach . . ."

"Oh, Katinka! You're moving back and all my life I couldn't wait to get out of there."

"The ironic twist in our mutual biography."

"I feel as if I'm leading the life I wanted for you."

"You can't want a life for somebody else."

"Then we've switched places. I'm taking Arthur's name and moving to Cambridge. You're taking mine . . ."

"And my father's."

"And your father's and moving back to Old Town." My mother sighs. Her voice is sad, segueing into hopeful. "They say you can't go home again."

"That's fiction. The name of a novel a novelist wrote."

"I guess you'd know," my mother concedes. "What about Jake?"

"Jake's not relevant."

"Then, the mailman. He's—"

"Mother!" I yell.

She pauses. Harrumps. "Don't think I haven't learned my lesson, Katinka. His name will never pass my lips."

I am about to ask, Promise? Cross your heart? "I'm glad you've learned your lesson," I tell her instead. "I'll talk to you later. Give Arthur a kiss." It's amazing, now that I'm on my way out of here, how easy it is to forgive.

And because to forgive is not only easy but also divine, I call Louie while the receiver is still warm with the milk of my human kindness. "I forgive you," I announce.

"This is my lucky day. This makes me so happy." He proceeds to list his varying states of joy until he runs out of superlatives. "Do you mean now we can go back to the way things used to be?" he asks.

"Not exactly. But I've got a plan."

"Change the sheets," says Louie. "I'll be there faster than superman."

I don't change the sheets. After all, I washed them the day before I left for Maine. Besides it's not sex I have in mind. Sex is only a minor element of the master plot. I set the scene. I take out a map of Old Town, the brochures on public schools and children with disabilities. I bring out a copy of the change-of-name petition I will file in Middlesex Probate Court and the form for the legal notice which I will take tomorrow to *The Cambridge Chronicle*. I add the mortgage application, and three photographs of the Old Town house, an exterior shot, and two inside. I pile on a catalogue from the University of Maine and a leaflet listing their extension services. I prop up a postcard of downtown which shows the post office figured prominently. There's also a pamphlet on taking courses toward your high school equivalency degree. All these I arrange on the coffee table of my living room.

Louie arrives by taxi. This I know since I am sitting at the window peering down the street. A walking cast thickens one leg of his pants. He carries a cane. He hobbles adorably. I refrain from running to the front door. Minutes pass before he rings. What's he doing? I wonder. Maybe touching base with the rows of mailboxes he's been homesick for.

I know what that feels like, being homesick. I'm homesick for home, homesick for him. I buzz him in.

When he limps across my front hall, his face is lit up like a kid's. He opens his arms.

"First things first," I say.

He tilts his head in the direction of the bedroom.

"Not that," I say. I take his elbow and lead him into the living room. His cast makes loud thumps. I am relieved I live on the first floor. Soon enough I won't have to worry about disturbing the neighbors, I remind myself.

He sits down on the sofa. "What's this?" he asks pointing to my arrangement of literature spread out on the coffee table like a tray of hors d'oeuvres.

I feed him brochures. He looks at each in turn and puts it down like the last person in a chain of lumberjacks passing logs.

"Frankly I'd rather spend my vacations in Florida."

"Florida's a silly state," I say, echoing Frenchy Levesque.

"But it's got sun and Disney World. Space Mountain is an incredible roller-coaster ride."

My life is an incredible roller-coaster ride, I think. "I prefer Mount Katahdin, its authenticity," say I who have never climbed any mountain, real or fake.

He lets that pass. "Why are you showing me this?" he asks. "I know it's where you're from and all . . ."

I hand him back the leaflet on students with disabilities. "Look. Look at the programs they have for the deaf."

He gives it a cursory glance. "That's nice," he says, "but not much to do with Tony and me."

"It could," I say.

"What do you mean?" He puts his arm around my shoulder and I feel swaddled in the warmth of fur or at least multi-ply cashmere. I nestle against him. He squeezes, "What say we do this chamber of commerce stuff later," he whispers.

I shake my head. "I'm moving home," I say. "I've bought back my childhood house."

"No kidding." He studies me. "You *are* kidding, right?"

"I'm completely serious."

He sits up. "You mean you're moving away, voluntarily, from the 02138 zip code?"

I nod. "And not soon enough," I emphasize.

"Moving from the city of Harvard? The city of Seamus?"

"My very point. The city of Seamus. The city of shame."

"I'm shocked, Katinka. You fit in here. How can you turn your back on Cambridge?"

"Easy."

"Easy for you. Me, I've always been so proud to be delivering mail to 02138. To Nobel Prize winners. And college types. Proud to be living only one zip code away in Somerville."

"That's pathetic, Louie," I say. Shades of my mother. I wince. Maybe the wounds from my encounter with my mother are so fresh

271

they're bleeding all over everything and thus distorting what I hear.

Though there's no distorting what Louis says next. "But you're an *O'Toole*," he pleads.

"A Graham. I've taken back my name."

"So that explains the mailbox. I kept staring and staring at it."

"Oh, Louie," I sigh, "it's time to get you out of here."

I explain about my trip to Maine, the house, the procedure for changing my name. I describe Old Town, its salt-of-the-earth people, its down-to-earth life. How everybody pretty much wears the same clothes, how people who attended Harvard repair roofs and people who used to be nuns serve submarine sandwiches. How where you went to school is less important than where you're going to go on Saturday night. "And so," I finish up, "I want you and Tony to come and live in my house with me."

Louie must have perfected his staring while eyeballing my mailbox because he stares at me with pupils wider than I would have thought was humanly possible. Even in the insect species such eyes would have been an anomaly. He takes my hand in his. "Is this a proposal?" he asks.

"Sort of. Do you want me to get down on my knees?"

His human *slash* insect eyes fill with tears. "Katinka, this is the most amazing compliment I have ever received."

"I should have brought a ring."

"Now you're teasing me."

"Come to think of it I've got a roll of Love stamps somewhere. We could put them around your finger and pretend . . ."

"I don't need any stamps to remind me I love you," Louie says.

He loves me! My heart soars.

"But can't we keep things just the way they are?" he asks.

The catch. I shake my head.

"Even for me? Why can't it be Louie Cappetti and Katinka O'Toole right here like it always was?"

My heart sinks. "Katinka *Graham*." I shake my head again.

"They say if it's not broken don't fix it," he pleads.

I knock my knuckles against the cast on his leg.

"I wouldn't want to go someplace I didn't know," he adds.

"Even for me?" I use his own words.

He doesn't exactly say no but he hangs his head. "I'm not big for change. I mean, I've got my routine. By the end of May I'll be back on my route. Then there's my parents and my sister. All in the same house . . . I know I complain, but I've gotten kind of used to it. And there's Tony. How can I take him from Cheryl. How can I take care of him by myself."

"You won't be by yourself."

"But Tony's not yours," he exclaims. I must look as hurt as I feel because he hurries to add, "I don't mean it how it sounds." He rushes on. "Why would you want to live in Maine by yourself anyway?" he asks.

"By myself wasn't my plan," I say.

"It doesn't make sense that you're leaving just when your mother's moving here, when you're going to have Arthur's family, all those people right next to you . . ."

"*One* of the reasons that I'm getting out."

"My parents said when I got married they'd move downstairs and let me have the top floor."

"I could never move into your parents' house with you, Louie." I pause. "Not that you're asking."

"I would ask if I thought there was any chance you would."

"Then you know me better than you think you do."

And maybe that's how he likes me, safe outside his own safety zone.

All at once, it comes to me in the pure and startling light that sad truths force on you: Louis won't leave home. Won't change his route or his routine. He's his parents' little boy. He's a Hamlet who can't commit. A mailman stuck between deliveries. He might prefer Cappetti-O'Toole (the Dublin O'Tooles) to Cappetti-Corelli. But not on a permanent basis; he only wants visiting rights. For him it's the best of both worlds: guest privileges in the 02138 zip code and his meals at his mother's table in Somerville. Why blend into the citizenry of Old Town when you can stand out in Cambridge as the mailman who delivers more than the mail to the ex-wife of Professor O'Toole? "I guess I don't know you as well as I thought I did," I say. "I gather your answer is no?" I ask.

He wipes his eyes. "I'm sure I'll live to regret it."

We kiss good-bye. His body—a body I have loved and lost, or rather, pushed away—folds around me, then steps aside. "Well, no regrets," he says.

"No regrets," I echo. I attempt a brave smile.

His smile is wistful. "By the time I'm back on the route, you'll probably be all moved out. Gee, I can't imagine the mailbox without your name."

The instant he leaves, I cry. Maybe tears are simply the Pavlovian response to saying good-bye. But it's not the great weeping which followed the Pamplona debacle. This is our second parting and I'm more used to it. I've seen Louie's clay feet. I think of his broken leg. It's a metaphor for how he can't stand on his own two feet. But if Louie's lame, I've been blind. So blinded by Louie I've overlooked the Jakes of this world. Like my mother, I've been dazzled by surfaces. Unlike my mother, I can dig deeper. Louis and I are not compatible. Not for reasons of class, my mother's reasons, but because he's as bad a snob as my mother, is as resistant to change as Seamus, and unlike me, hasn't grown up.

These multiple epiphanies do little to vanquish my misery. For several minutes, I sag in my hallway wrenched and tragic. I hear a door slam. Somewhere outside on the street, a car pulls up. Then, a burden lifts and I feel a lightening.

Spring comes late to Cambridge. By mid-April, the igloos of snow which border the streets like an abandoned Eskimo encampment have thawed to puddles. When I walk home from Sever Hall these days, it's nearly light even though some of the trees are still bare. Now I look out my window and see a few early crocuses shooting up. I have passed through the most amazing winter of my life. I feel caught between seasons, caught between chapters in a book.

Though one chapter is about to close. I'm in the process of packing for the move. I fill milk crates with novels and biographies. I make three piles of clothes, one for summer, one for winter, one for Goodwill. I place my stack of *Playgirls* into a metal file box that has a lock. In the apartment upstairs somebody is dragging furniture across the floor. I look around my own soon-to-be-vacated apartment. The packing is leaving these rooms as decimated as Jake's.

Jake's been especially attentive lately. I haven't told him any of the Louie story, but some of it he may have guessed. He's asked a lot about the house in Old Town, about the Indian reservation, the library. When I describe the people, Tubby Burnside and Goody-Goody Goodreau, Frenchy Levesque, Pollyanne Mulligan, he sighs with envy of their Down East qualities. "Sure beats the meat-packers," he says. "And Laura's crowd."

I tell him he can visit often, that there's a guest room.

"Not as a *guest*," he objects.

The room's for Max, I explain. Zenobia and Harriman will drive him up for a week in August. I've promised to take him to Indian Island, to the Old Town Canoe Factory, to the drugstore for cherry Cokes. "Or we can just hang out," I said to Max.

"Awesome." He'd waved his peace pipe, which seems to be filling the vacuum Daniella left; he takes it everywhere.

For Jake and me, there's a double-canopied bed. He is relieved. He was afraid, he jokes, that Old Town still had bundling boards.

You'll see for yourself, I say, how great it is.

I take down some posters and study the white spaces in their wake. Funny, but I'm not feeling at all nostalgic about this apartment, about these walls, and stove, and mantel, and door. Even about the bed-room, the site of so much ecstasy. The apartment's already been rented, to a retired Harvard couple. My mother's sent them a note to come up for drinks the day they move in. The wife, Mrs. Lowell, has shown up twice to measure for curtains. Around her neck she wears a discreet Phi Beta Kappa key. I am delighted. They will be fine com-panions for the Havens and no enticement for Louie. Frankly, I'm not ready to turn my mailbox over to some young, available female without the buffer of an elderly couple's one-year lease.

I go to my study. There's no sense clearing my desk until my class ends. I sit down and pick up India Germaine's manuscript. Her story is called "Leaving Home." I put it down and look at Russell MacQuillen, Junior's, which is titled "Software: A Computer Story in Three Parts." I open to Part One. I brace myself.

I am saved by the phone. It's Seamus and he's mad as hell.

He gets right to the point. "Katinka," he shouts, "I've just seen your legal notice in *The Cambridge Chronicle.*"

"You read legal notices?" I ask.

"I read everything, as you should recall. I was in the bathroom. I finished with the news articles. I went on to the toothpaste bottle and the box the soap comes in. Then I started with the legal notices. The print's so small, I was lucky I had my spectacles. To my horror, I saw that you'd petitioned for a change of name."

"And . . . ?"

"*And* I was shocked. You've had O'Toole for years. It's my name. A distinguished name that you were once more than eager to acquire. And, let me remind you, it's your *professional name!*"

This gives me great pause. Seamus wants me to keep his name professionally? He has faith in me professionally. He thinks that the stories and the novels to come under the name Katinka O'Toole will reflect on him. That they'll be a light worth basking in. Oh glory be! Once you start taking steps to stand on your own two feet you can climb to the height of Mount Katahdin. "I'm flattered, Seamus," I say.

"As well you should be, my dear." Seamus' voice turns sly. "It is, of course, entirely within my legal right to object."

"On what grounds?"

"Several. I can figure out the specifics later. As for now. Well, just take this as a warning. If you don't give me back your class, I'll object to your name."

I look at the first sentence of "Software: A Computer Story in Three Parts." "It's yours," I say.

Seamus is flabbergasted. He backtracks. His voice is gentle. Then expands with generosity. "Of course you can finish out the last few weeks of the term."

I thank him. I don't tell him that at the end of the term I'm moving to another state. I don't tell him that I didn't want his dumb old class anyway. I am beyond childish *take thats* and *so theres.*

And for once so is Seamus. "You know," he says, "it makes me kind of sad. About the O'Toole. I was always proud of you."

Yesterday Gregory the Florist put a note in all our boxes. This was done by hand so I didn't have to worry that Mr. O'Riley got mine or the other way around. *Our former and loyal mailman, Louie Cappetti, is getting married,* it read. *Could all residents of the building please contribute five dollars toward an electric pasta maker and a congratulatory floral arrangement.* I stuffed five dollars in the box provided. I sat in front of my desk for half an hour trying to decide whether to call or write a note. If Ann Landers had had an 800 number I would have cleared this point of etiquette with her. Finally I called him at the post office, neutral territory I brilliantly deduced. Besides it was Wednesday. I didn't want to reach him later at Cheryl's and cause problems so that the pasta maker might have to be sent back.

"Hey, Cappetti, some dame's on the phone," the man who answered yelled.

"I hear congratulations are in order," I said. My voice sounded so happy for him I had the fleeting thought that if the novel didn't work out I could try the stage.

"I planned to send you a note, Katinka. I didn't want you to find out through the building grapevine. Cheryl decided she'd have me after all," he said, sounding not unpleased. "She and Tony have already moved into my parents' place. I took her to Chris Smith's wedding where we got the idea."

"It must have been quite a wedding."

"Not exactly. Not the way that you mean. They were supposed to get married at eleven-thirty with the hands of the clock going up—for good luck—but nobody had figured out the Hebrew name for Christopher. I guess you need it on the wedding certificate. The rabbi and the families had to have a conference. We could all hear them arguing in a side room off the aisle. By the time they were married, the hands of the clock were heading down past twelve." He paused to let this ominous information sink in. "Chris called me when they got back from their honeymoon. They found out they had nothing in common but, well, sex. And since the circumcision, Chris has been a little . . ."

"Circumspect?"

"Something, anyway. They're getting divorced."

"And that was your inspiration?"

"Sort of. We figured we had more in common. And real problems to worry about."

I pictured the Deaf Child sign two blocks from my soon-to-be home. I would have taken Tony to Indian Island and bought him a feathered headdress and a peace pipe. I would have plied him with cherry Cokes. I would have done up his room in bright colors—visual stimulation to compensate for auditory loss. I would have studied how to speak his name on my fingertips. I would have probably learned to love him. I would have certainly worried about him. A privilege and a responsibility. A responsibility from which I wouldn't have shirked and from which I've now been spared. "Well, good luck," I said.

"That means a lot, Katinka, coming from you."

Jake has donated a Sunday to help me pack. I told him it wasn't necessary. I'd book him up for moving day to load the U-Haul I've already left a deposit on.

"That, too," he said, "but I do insist."

He arrives wearing blue jeans and a plaid shirt layered under a green poplin vest. "L.L. Bean catalogue," he explains. "I'm ready—among other things—to change my look."

"It suits you," I say, "though it comes as a shock. I think I've hardly seen you out of a gray or navy pinstriped worsted wool."

"The city lawyer's uniform," he admits, lacing the words with disgust.

I look down at my own jeans and T-shirt. We all have our uniforms, I think, though some are more quickly identified. My T-shirt says "Save the Square." I bought it during the campaign to save the

Blue Parrot Café which was torn down after months of protest to make way for a concrete and steel office tower. The Harvard Square I'm leaving is unrecognizable as the Harvard Square I saw when I first arrived for freshman week.

Jake hands me two bottles of wine. I read the labels. "Chardonnay," I say. "My favorite, thanks to you."

"Let's stick them in the fridge," Jake says.

I take the bottles into the kitchen. "Do they need to be stored on their side?" I ask him.

"Oh, Katinka, stick them in any which way. I should apologize for all the fuss I usually make about the wine. I can be insufferably pompous when I'm insecure."

I put the wine on its side in the refrigerator just in case. "Are you feeling insecure these days?" I ask Jake.

He takes my hand. "Less and less," he says, "now that I'm making changes in my life." He folds his fingers over mine and clasps them tight. "Especially now that you gave that other guy the boot."

"I didn't exactly give him the boot. In fact, he refused me."

"Impossible!"

"But true," I confess. As soon as I say it I'm amazed: I didn't even attempt a white lie to make myself look good. "Though now I realize it was inevitable. We weren't compatible. It was an alliance bound for failure," I add.

For a long time Jake doesn't say anything. Instead he takes my wineglasses down from a kitchen shelf and starts wrapping them with the old *Boston Globe*s I have piled up. He is doing such a good job, wadding *Business* into their bowls, winding *Metro* around their stems I don't have the heart to tell him they're cheap glass, probably relics from Sears before it became a Gap. That I planned to throw them out and start again. When he lovingly swathes the last one, I realize we'll have to sip the Chardonnay from coffee mugs. More suitable, perhaps, to my back-to-basics lifestyle.

Jake arranges the glasses in a box and places *Real Estate* on the top.

"Cambridge Rents Skyrocketing" a headline proclaims. Jake clears his throat. "If you don't mind my asking," he begins.

"Not at all," I say. "In fact I want to tell you."

We pour the wine into the mugs although it isn't even noon and the wine isn't chilled. We take the mugs into the living room and wedge ourselves onto the sofa next to a stack of stereo components sandwiched between old towels. Jake puts a plaid Pendleton arm behind my neck.

I take a gulp of wine. And then a second one. I am drinking it like medicine. Not doing justice to what I'm sure is a special pressing if not an outright glorious vintage. Jake doesn't seem to notice. Like me he's letting old habits die. "He was my mailman!" I confess.

"So," Jake says.

"So!" I exclaim.

"So what? I'm sure if you loved him, Katinka, he had special qualities."

I tell him the whole story from the moment I saw Louie in my vestibule to the electric pasta maker I contributed five dollars for. I tell him about the party where he bid on my story, about his connection to Seamus, about our playing house with Daniella, my class, his broken leg, Cheryl, and Tony, Sal and Rosalie, about our sad scene at the Pamplona, our last good-byes. I even confess my obsession about Louie's body parts.

Jake listens with such attention I can practically reach out and touch his waves of empathy. He's open, impartial, fair—everything you'd want in a juror or a judge not to mention the significant other in your life. "Aren't you shocked he's my mailman?" I ask after I have done my summing up.

"Why?" he asks. "Let's face it. Some people think lawyers are pretty close to the bottom rung."

"Not you," I say. And it comforts me that another word for lawyer is counselor.

• • •

We go to bed. It's the best yet. Almost stars. Maybe because Jake is less insecure and I am more secure. Maybe because now that I've told him about Louie it's removed the last barrier. Maybe because along with our clothes we've stripped away all pretense and are down to bone. Afterward, lying there amid my boxes and crates and piles of mismatched socks we could be lovers sprinkled with gold dust in a flower-strewn glen.

18

It's the middle of May. My last class. My students sit around the table in Sever Hall like children forced to eat their spinach before they're allowed to go out and play. On New England college campuses, spring fever arrives with a vengeance. This evening all the windows are open. Even India Germaine, queen of the drafts, doesn't protest. Outdoors, undergrads walk through the yard resolutely wearing shorts above goosebumped knees. Somebody is tossing a Frisbee. A dog barks. A drama student announces Gilbert and Sullivan tickets on sale.

Indoors, I am trying to discuss Muriel Kingsworthy's chapter but even she doesn't seem interested. They're moving on. I understand. I was a student once. *Summer vacation* were two of the most beautiful words in the English language. Next to first love. In the fall, they'll be on their way to other classes, other teachers. Some of them, even, to Professor Seamus O'Toole. My eyes drift from one to another of their faces. I stop at Russell MacQuillen, Junior's. I look down. In his lap is an enormous bouquet of flowers peeking over the tabletop from their paper cone. My heart melts. I have vastly underestimated him. But he, on the other hand, has not underestimated me. Under his nerd pack beats the heart of an appreciator. For this last class he has brought me a token of his esteem. Maybe it's not just his personal contribution. Maybe the class took up a joint collection and he gets to hold it. Like the loving cup our Latin club won once in the inter-city Latin Club Olympics. We each got to keep it for a week. It ended up in the school trophy case where it tarnished to such a state of unpolishable green as to be mistaken for a Roman artifact.

I smile tenderly at Russell MacQuillen, Junior. He doesn't notice me. Perhaps his glasses are too thick. It's all been worthwhile, I suddenly realize, my anxiety over my wardrobe, my hours deciphering Seamus' syllabus, the humiliation of being fourth choice. My teaching is so great that even the lone voice in the wilderness has come around. I award the table at large my benevolent smile.

Which they quickly take advantage of. Let's forget everybody's stories, they implore, and talk about how to get an agent, And, hey, what about the size of the advance?

"First you have to do the writing itself," I explain for the zillionth time, "and make it as good as you can. Publishing is a whole separate issue."

And the only issue they want to talk about. For the last half hour, I improvise a riff about agents. I had one once, who has now switched to telemarketing. Does this make me an expert? I try to remember articles I have read in *Publishers Weekly*. The experience of my more successful friends. Half this stuff I must have already told them the night we had a drink at the Casablanca after class. But if they don't mind the repetitions neither do I. Like Max they probably like to hear the same stories over and over again. I must be doing a good enough job because they sit rapt, more attentive than in any class since February when I started teaching them. I wind down five minutes before the hour. "I've enjoyed teaching you," I say. "And wish you good luck."

There is a polite murmur of thank-yous. And a lot of shuffling of backpacks and books. I sit back and wait for Russell MacQuillen, Junior, to stand up. Perhaps the whole class has joined together to write a speech to accompany the bouquet. I feel like an Oscar nominee with her eye on the envelope.

Russell MacQuillen, Junior, stands up. With his books in one hand, the flowers in the other, he leaves the room.

I don't exactly sail back to my apartment. I trudge there like a thousand-year-old creature fighting through a blinding storm. By the time I make it to my front door I am shivering. Last night I packed my woolens away in mothballs and stored them under the boxes of books waiting for the U-Haul. A terrible mistake, I think tonight. I am feeling grumpy. I am feeling even grumpier when Mr. O'Riley corners me in the corridor just as I am putting my key into the lock. "Miss O'Toole," he says.

I don't bother to correct him.

"This is getting entirely out of hand, Miss O'Toole," he goes on. He has the nose of a drinker and a miser's mouth.

"I entirely agree," I say. "What is getting out of hand?" I ask.

"The mail, of course."

"Of course. The mail."

He hands me a thick white envelope. "This came today," he says. "Yesterday I received Professor Arthur T. Haven's *American Scholar!*"

I shake my head.

"Dealing with such an incompetent makes one really appreciate what a gem our old mailman was."

Suddenly I feel incredibly warm. Mr. O'Riley shuffles off mumbling about tax dollars. I promise to check for his mail among my sheaf of Citibank Visa promotions and invitations to join a health club. After tonight, my class, my hallucinatory false expectations, my megalomania, I should be joining a mental health club.

And I'm even more convinced of it when I open the envelope

Mr. O'Riley has handed me. It's an invitation to Seamus and Georgette's wedding. There's a Claddagh ring engraved on the top. Presumably the same Claddagh ring that graced the announcement of our own mis-nuptials. Only Seamus would have saved the plate and recycled it. I call Seamus immediately.

"How was the last class?" he asks before I can vent my astonishment.

"Fine. They brought flowers," I say, neglecting to add: then took them away.

"I'm not surprised," he says generously.

"But I am. Not over the flowers, naturally. Over your wedding invitation. That you're getting married!"

"They say practice makes perfect, after all."

"And that you're inviting me!" I exclaim.

"But of course. The tie that binds weakens but never really breaks."

I think of this. It's true of course. Here I am talking to Seamus. I've just talked to Louie. Who, in turn and when we were most passionately linked, never broke his connection with Cheryl. Jake still talks to Laura. Over the phone she demonstrates in short little pants the breathing she and Harriet are learning in Lamaze. Jake's been shopping for the baby gift trying to decide between a car seat or a silver porringer. "Laura's so practical," he explains.

"Then the porringer," I advise. God, it occurs to me now, I'll have to get Seamus and Georgette a gift. Electric pasta maker? Electric chair?

"Will Georgette be taking your name?" I ask now.

"Indeed. And with such enthusiasm it warms my cockles. The wedding will be grand," Seamus adds. "Feel free to bring a guest."

I will, I say. I don't say to make sure that the wedding's on time so the hands of the clock won't be heading down. I try to remember what direction those hands were heading when Seamus and I were wed, but that day, the honeymoon, the whole marriage is a blur—

which is just as well since not remembering allows me to wish Seamus the best with absolute sincerity.

I put the envelope facedown on the table and stagger to the refrigerator where there's an inch of wine left in a bottle whose cork has fallen into a bowl of leftover applesauce. I drink the wine from the bottle. I better watch it.

There is a knock on my door. I dispose of the evidence under the sink and go to answer it. Not Mr. O'Riley again, I hope, with yet another example of the diminished quality of our mail delivery.

It's my mother, standing at my threshold with an enormous bouquet of roses which are wrapped in cellophane and tied with red ribbon from which dangles a tiny envelope. My mother's had her hair done, sculpted into a shining but stiff helmet of curls. "You look like Miss America," I say.

She pats her head. "It's the hair."

"No, actually it's the bouquet."

"Oh, right," she says. She thrusts the flowers into my arms. "It's your bouquet."

"You shouldn't have . . ."

"I didn't," she explains. "I was just coming in from the store and the florist was ringing your bell. I explained you were teaching—at Harvard. I promised I'd deliver them to you myself."

I open the florist's envelope. *Congratulations on your last class, love Jake.*

"They're from Jake," I tell my mother.

"I thought as much."

I find a vase. I arrange the flowers carefully. Jake has sent me my second glorious bouquet. The roses fill my whole kitchen with their sweet smell. I think of Jake. How sweet he is. When I told him about giving Seamus his class back, his eyes turned into little pools of sympathy. "Now you can go to Old Town and have more time for what really counts," he'd consoled.

I admire the flowers.

"They are lovely," my mother agrees. "Naturally I've already put Jake down on my invitation list."

We discuss my mother and Arthur's wedding, which will take place on May 21, my mother's birthday and the day Arthur passed his orals for his doctorate forty-two years before. The flowers have been chosen. The caterer's all signed up. Together Arthur and mother picked the music for the string quartet. Last month Zenobia and I and my mother went shopping for her bridal dress. We didn't even descend into Filene's Basement, though in anticipation I wore my most comfortable shoes. We went upstairs, straight to the designers' section where my mother paid full price for a gossamer confection in lilac silk. She tried to talk Zenobia and me into matching blue taffeta. She was a good sport, however, when we chose complementary linen suits in pale coral (me) and aquamarine (Zenobia). Afterward we had a lady's lunch in the Ritz café for which my mother grabbed the check. Zenobia ordered champagne. She made a moving toast about gaining a mother and a sister. My mother beamed. I was touched. Ever since Max and *Playgirl* my fondness for Zenobia has increased exponentially. Then we all flirted with the adorable waiter who had the kind of eyelashes mothers always say are wasted on a boy.

Now my mother sits across from me at my kitchen table. I offer tea, wine. I even have a quarter of a wheel of Brie, I inform her. She shakes her head. "I can just stay a minute," she says. "I have something for you." She reaches into her pocket and brings out a square of folded tissue the size of a quarter. "Here," she says. One tear spills out of her eye, reminding me of those Christmas cookies with their raisin tears we made so many months ago.

I open the tissue to reveal my mother's wedding ring. I am speechless.

As is my mother. She kisses me. She squeezes my hand. She waves her own hand. And then she leaves.

What the hell. I open a new bottle of wine. I pour myself a glass and take it, with the ring, to my bed. I study the ring, this band of platinum thin as a wire. Once my father's initials chased my mother's on the inside of its circle like the lovers on Keats' Grecian Urn. Now I can just make out faint scratchings. Old hieroglyphs. The tops of the letters have worn away. I slide my mother's ring onto my finger where it fits perfectly. On the wall hangs the drawing Max made for me. It's framed like a Rembrandt. It's my Rembrandt. I lie back against the pillows and sip my drink. I think of Shakespearean comedies. Their final scenes in which all the couples are sorted out. Twins are reunited. Men passing as women and vice versa reveal their real genders. The false combinations are switched to the true. Feuding suitors make peace. The star-crossed lovers are uncrossed. Then follows this gala spate of weddings. Equaled by Louie and Cheryl, Seamus and Georgette, my mother and Arthur T. Haven . . .

And I lie on my single-occupancy bed wearing my mother's wedding ring.

On May 19, we are assembled in the auditorium of Max's school for the third-grade production of *Hamlet*. We're all here, the whole extended family, the whole, until the wedding, family-to-be. Plus Jake, who wouldn't miss it for the world, whom Max invited personally and who is treating us all to a post-performance celebration of cholesterol overload at the International House of Pancakes.

Harriman has arrived early and saved us a whole row, middle and center right behind the seats of the first- and second-graders. Harriman's on the aisle with his camcorder at the ready and enough tape to document the Hundred Years War. Next to him is Zenobia, then Jake, me, my mother, and Arthur.

The program—color-Xeroxed and illustrated with a castle complete with drawbridge and moat—lists five Hamlets—one Asian and two girls if you can deduce that Tina Chung is Asian and Rainbow Gonzales is female—including Max and someone with the surprisingly plain name of Tom Thomas. There are five Ophelias, too, though a careful study of the program shows that no young man has agreed to don Ophelia's robes to strew Ophelia's violets. An assortment of Ghosts and Gertrudes, and even two Bernardos though I can't remember who Bernardo is.

Every one of them is adorable however. And once the play gets underway there's a constant murmur of doting parents and significant others tsk-tsking over each actor's adorableness. It takes a little getting used to, though, with the shifting of players sometimes in mid-line and the mishmash of costumes recycled, Zenobia has explained, from past productions of Robin Hood and Euripides. The Euripides was staged last year, Arthur adds, and was a revelation.

When Max finally appears—Hamlet number three—in a green Sherwood Forest costume to which is pinned a rudimentary Danish flag, he is a revelation. He's been awarded the *to be or not to be* lines. It's no surprise he was picked for them since he articulates exquisitely with a huge grin and a lot of lashing of sword. He's a natural. And I, I suddenly discover, am a natural stage mother. Mouthing the lines along with him, my eyes focused on every gesture, my ears alert to the rest of the audience's exclamations of how cute! how darling! His struts and frets upon the stage are far too brief but signify incredible talent (I know I am taking enormous liberties). When Tina Chung glides in on her cue: *perchance to dream,* Max exits the stage to volcanic applause whose gale-force center erupts from our row.

At intermission, my mother, Arthur, Zenobia, and Harriman join the lemonade line. Jake takes my hand. "What's this?" he asks. He rubs his thumb along my mother's wedding band.

I explain.

"Hmmm," he says. "Interesting," he adds.

I don't ask him what "interesting" means. I have no need to know. Instead, I look at him. At his red bow tie. His lopsided grin. His intelligent eyes. His kind eyes. I try to concentrate on the red whorls of hair tufting his knuckles as he holds my hand. I try to picture his feet. I think of Seamus, who was a mistake. And Louie, who feels less like a mistake than an auxiliary road which ended in a cul-de-sac. I force myself to picture Louie, beautiful Louie, but his edges are blurred, his face an out-of-focus photograph. He's fading into the distance like one of Shakespeare's ghosts, like something mailed but never delivered, left unclaimed in the dead-letter repository.

Jake squeezes my fingers. "You know," he says, "Maine used to be part of Massachusetts. I just found out."

"It was one of my first lessons in grammar school."

"I've been studying up." He pauses. "While looking into reciprocity between the states in regard to the bar exam."

"Jake!"

"The meatpackers are getting me down. I've done city life, suburban life. They've lost their appeal. Don't worry, Katinka, this is all just a possibility."

I'm not worried. I figure Old Town is the glass slipper. The test for which man will come to me. I put my arm through Jake's.

I settle back against my chair. It's a folding one, metal with a crossbar that jabs into my spine. Still, I feel oddly comfortable in this grade-school auditorium surrounded by chatting families and kids running up and down the aisles. If I were writing this story, this might not be the ending I'd pick: Katinka Graham, formerly O'Toole, at a third-grade production of *Hamlet* wearing her mother's hand-me-down wedding ring and sitting next to someone—more character actor than leading man—with the improbable name of Jake Barnes. Yet it feels like a happy ending. Or happy start. "Here come Arthur and your mother with our lemonade," Jake says.